Allan Massie was born in Singapore in 1938 and was educated at Glenalmond and Trinity College Cambridge. He is the editor of the *New Edinburgh Review*, is married with three children and lives in the Scottish borders. *The Death of Men* is his third novel and won a Scottish Arts Council Award.

THE
DEATH OF MEN

Allan Massie

"Man at present is a predatory animal . . . the
sacredness of human life is a purely municipal
ideal of no validity outside the jurisdiction . . .
between two groups that want to make inconsistent
kinds of world I see no remedy except force. I may
add what I have no doubt said often enough, that
it seems to me that every society rests on the death
of men."

Oliver Wendell Holmes

ROBIN CLARK

Published by Robin Clark Limited 1982
A member of the Namara Group
27 Goodge Street, London W1

First published in hardcover in Great Britain by
The Bodley Head Ltd, 1981

ISBN 0 86072 060 8

Printed in Great Britain
by Mackays of Chatham Limited

First, for Alison,
then for friends of Roman days:
Caitlin Thomas, Colm Thomas, Ses Hine,
and in memory of Al Hine, writer and good friend,
who died Autumn 1974

ACKNOWLEDGEMENT

Part of this book was written at Butterstone House School, Dunkeld. I should like to thank the Headmistress, Mrs Elizabeth Langlands, and Lt-Col A M Lyle, Chairman of the Governors, for their kindness in giving me the use of a room on my visits to Perthshire.

AUTHOR'S NOTE

It will be apparent to most readers that the central events of this novel imitate the abduction and murder of Aldo Moro, and that the main character resembles Moro, and occupies a similar position in Italian politics. Beyond this, however, characters, relationships and events are purely imaginary. In particular I should like to stress that the Dusa family in no way resembles the Moro family, and that I have used only such aspects of the case as are public property. This is a work of fiction, with all the aspirations of a novel, and not a work of history or reportage. It would be improper were it to be treated otherwise, and it would distress me also if it were regarded as a *roman à clef*, which it, most emphatically, is not.

THE DEATH OF MEN

I

RAIMUNDO

May 3 I am a dandy who can no longer be troubled to dress.

Once I had my suits made in London, my shirts in Paris, and my shoes in Florence. It seems a long time ago, though it is in fact only a few years since I retired, early, from the Ministero dell' Estero, and until then I always made a point of visiting London in September to call on my tailor. Now I slop about the apartment in flannels and a sweater, with casuals on my feet. At six o'clock when I go down to the *osteria* or to one of the *caffès* in Piazza Navona if the weather is fine, I sometimes put on an old suit, but I shall never have another made. They greet me with respect in the *osteria*, but the younger waiters in Navona are beginning to judge me by my clothes. They can tell last year's suit at a glance, and as for one three or four years old . . . So they no longer hurry to serve me. It doesn't matter. I have after all nothing to do but wait. For the rest of my life.

Remarkable how things have, quite simply, gone. I'm left with just my books and my cat and, of course, what no Italian can entirely escape, the Family. I have no children of my own; my brothers' fully compensate.

My marriage finished long ago, when I was at the Washington Embassy for the first time. I always recommend an American trip to friends who wish to achieve that consummation. There is, for Italians, something liberating in a land where divorce is the norm. It is like being an adolescent all over again.

Not that my adolescence was anything like my nephews' now. We studied hard, kept close to the family bosom. The utmost dissipation was an August flirtation when we went to the seaside; oh those beach umbrellas and white flannels and girls

7

with parasols. The nice girls we knew tried to cultivate an English pallor. Quite in vain of course.

It accorded however with their fathers' political stance at the time.

I remember my own father in furious argument with a cousin who supported the *Fascisti*—this must have been in 1923 or 4, soon after Mussolini had come to power. He accused him of betraying our class; the *Fascisti* were nothing but shopkeepers and bully boys. That was the general attitude among people we knew. Mussolini's supporters were frightful people from out of town.

Of course we came from out of town ourselves. There are practically no true Romans. How could there be? I still think of myself as a Calabrian, though I haven't seen my miserable native province in twenty years. My brother tells me it is less wretched now. I doubt it. Merely a different style of misery in my opinion. But he has to go back; it is after all his political base.

The attitude to the *Fascisti* changed of course. They became the Establishment, as my brother Corrado is in his turn. And they made the Concordat; the nice people queued up to join them. Their adulation of Mussolini became so extreme and so abject that you might easily have foretold the contempt to which he would eventually be exposed. This eagerness to rush to extremes exhibits the despicable side of our national character. I wonder if Corrado ever reflects on this.

It's curious how little I exchange thoughts with him. Of course he knows that I have that certain scorn that elder brothers so often have for their juniors who have met with success. In our eyes it is a little vulgar. We regard them as deluded beings, who have failed to recognize the vanity of existence. It is a comfortable sentiment.

Actually I have always stood at an oblique angle to things. Perhaps I am still a dandy after all, like Sasha who has just jumped on to my writing table and is rubbing his face in mine while he holds his plumy tail aloft. He's never been neutered, but he can't now be bothered to go out on the tiles at night.

May 4 My nephew Sandro telephoned this morning and said he would like to see me. I didn't, to my credit, try to put him off. He suggested that he come to the apartment, but I said no to that. It wasn't just the natural instinct to turn down any proposal (though I recognized that the feeling was there); it was rather that I don't like anyone to come here. Is it perhaps that I'm ashamed of how I live? I don't think so. Anyway I said that I would meet him at the Caffè Greco.

Afterwards I couldn't imagine why. The Greco was sure to be full of people I used to know. I thought of telephoning to change the meeting-place, but it seemed too much trouble. Besides it occurred to me that Elena might take the call and I would have to make some excuse. I supposed the boy wanted to borrow money, and his mother would certainly suppose that too; why else, she would think, could he want to see me?

I walked down from my broker's in Parioli, not once solicited on the Via Veneto. I rarely am nowadays. Do I wear my dead heart so obviously on my sleeve? (But it is not hearts they buy and sell on the street, after all.)

Sandro, to my amazement, was already in the *caffè*. He had taken what he knows used to be my favourite table, just below the portrait of Major Alfred Burke and opposite Colonel Cody. He was very elegantly dressed in a white linen suit. It's perhaps for his taste in clothes that he is my favourite nephew. But there is a softness, an amiability about him too that is attractive; and he is very decorative. Certainly an English pederast at the next table couldn't take his eyes off him.

He stood up when I arrived and leant over to embrace me.

'It's very good of you to come, Uncle.'

'My dear boy, I'm always delighted to see you. Out of the family circle at any rate. What's the matter?'

'Let's have some chocolate, shall we? Or do you prefer coffee?'

'No, chocolate will be admirable.'

When I used to bring my nephews and nieces here for rare treats, we always had chocolate, as well as ice creams. Old habits die hard. Perhaps Sandro merely wanted to recall these afternoons to me. On the other hand I wouldn't be surprised if he still has a taste for chocolate. And I've recently re-acquired mine, lost for many years.

What's the matter, I nearly said again, but I decided he could

9

approach it himself, in his own way.

'How's your father?' I said instead.

He shrugged his shoulders.

'I suppose he's all right. We don't as you know see very much of him. I'm sure he's overworking, but there's no alternative. They still say he's the key to the crisis. Do you think that's true?'

What answer could I give? I saw no way out of my poor country's political inferno, certainly not by my younger brother's agency. (And why do I write that carping 'certainly'? There is after all no politician who merits the same respect as Corrado does.) But how can you tell a boy of eighteen that his world is crumbling? That the barbarians are mining the citadel and he'd better start preparing for a Brave New World, where, as it happens, his particular qualities are not going to be much in demand.

I said therefore, 'It won't be resolved without him.'

'I'm sure that's true.' Sandro gave me a quick, warm, grateful smile. 'That's why it seems to me so terrible that he shouldn't be getting every assistance within his own family.'

'What do you mean?'

'It's Bernardo,' he said.

I didn't care for Bernardo, a humourless, earnest child.

'Bernardo's joined the PRR.'

'I'm sorry,' I said, 'these initials, they proliferate so.'

'Popolo Romano Rosso.'

'And who are they?'

'You mean you haven't heard of them?'

I smiled. 'You're forgetting, my dear, I seldom read the newspapers, and never watch television. I'm out of touch—an old fogey. But I take it they're a group of extremists. On the Left obviously. In favour of extra-Parliamentary protest et cetera. Yes? How boring.'

'More than boring for Papa. They're committed to violence, you see. And there he is in charge of the Ministry that has to deal . . . you see how difficult . . .'

Indeed I did, but I couldn't imagine what Sandro thought I could do about it. . . . I gave a little shrug and spread my hands.

'I thought perhaps you could talk to Bernardo.'

I raised an eyebrow.

'I've tried,' he said mournfully.

The last time I had had serious conversation with Bernardo had been sometime the previous year. Then he had talked to me. He had, with outrageous impertinence, told me to leave Sandro alone. 'We all know why you had to leave the Service,' he had erroneously asserted. I told him he was talking nonsense, on both counts.

Now I said, 'If Bernardo wants to make a fool of himself . . . have you considered that he may be deliberately embarrassing your father?'

'Oh yes. It's terrible,' he said. 'I don't know if Papa has paid much attention to it yet, you know how calm and self-controlled Papa always is, but it's making Mamma very unhappy. You see, apart from anything else, he consorts with such awful types.'

As he said this, his high, fine, unfashionable cheek-bones took on a dewiness, as if lit up from behind, and his voice quivered. I felt very sorry for him; to be so out of tune with his generation must be painful. There could be no doubt that Bernardo would be happier, for all that he opposed a savage misanthropy to Sandro's natural blitheness. Doubtless he would have put it differently, claiming that he set social conscience or social justice at a higher premium than bourgeois selfishness; that was the sort of language he would be talking, and it's true of course that every action, every attitude, can be read in a variety of ways.

'I don't know what to do about it at all,' Sandro said. 'It's making me edgy. My tennis game's gone to pieces and I'd hoped to play in senior tournaments this year, but I simply can't concentrate. Look, Uncle, can't you perhaps come to lunch on Sunday—yes, I'll tell Mamma you're coming—and see things for yourself? We're all at odds and ends with each other. There are terrible strains.'

He gave me a winning smile—I was aware of the English pederast freeze in the action of raising his coffee cup. I weakly assented.

I suppose a sense of family duty survives even curiosity; and it would be a pity if Sandro were not able to play in his senior tournaments. He is a very elegant player. Though I don't suppose he will ever go beyond the point which you can reach on natural ability alone—a lack of killer instinct—that is no reason why he should be denied the chance of disporting himself, and others the pleasure of seeing him do so. . . .

May 5 It is extraordinary that one continues to accept obligations.

May 6 I approached Corrado's with misgivings, deliberately travelling out on the Cassia by bus; a mute protest. I dislike presenting my credentials to the guards at the lodge of the villa, and having to wait while they are checked not only on a list of expected callers, but with the house, by telephone. It is not how one ought to visit one's younger brother.

But it is a sign of the times. We have passed the nineteenth-century afternoon of our civilization. The sun is extinguished; we relive the experience of the Dark Ages. So our leaders, like the robber barons of the tenth century, have retreated within their *castelli* and pulled up the drawbridges. They exist there, protected by armed retainers, who are at present paid for by the State or the Party. How long, I wonder, before they are simply personally recruited, personally maintained? How long before rival gangs club each other to death in the streets? Or doesn't it, in some degree, happen already? Last month three policemen were shot, and four terrorists. It's become fashionable, in perfectly respectable circles, to equate the deaths. And, reluctantly, one sees why.

The oleanders were in flower in the garden. Three or four Doberman Pinschers lay chained beneath them.

A Filipino servant showed me into the saloon. Except for Maria, who was our nurse and comes from our family village of Cropolati, all Corrado's house staff are now Filipinos. But the Roman Emperors found foreign slaves ultimately no more reliable than Italian domestics; gold knows no frontiers, no other loyalties. And the same goes for ideology.

Elena's saloon always takes me back in time. With its purple hangings, ormolu, and heavy black carved furniture, it reminds me of my grandmother's apartment in the Via Giulia. Elena has always declined to be up to date. When Corrado dies she will certainly wear black for the rest of her life, which is now done by nobody but peasants. She advanced towards me heavy and big-bosomed and stately, and extended a cheek yellow with disapproval.

'A long time,' she said.

She would dislike me no less if I came every Sunday, but she would prefer it if I did. After all, that would be the right thing. . . .

'How's Mamma?' I said.

'She is very well. She has wonderful vitality.'

The words were correct and quite without expression.

'Will she lunch downstairs?'

'She always does on Sundays.'

I nodded.

'We all appreciate how well you care for her,' I said.

She inclined her head in turn.

'And the children?' I said.

She gestured towards the group giggling in the window. 'They are all well. As you see.'

'You are fortunate in your children,' I said. 'And I in my nephews and nieces.'

We have talked like this for over thirty years. The first time I saw Elena, Corrado didn't introduce us. Indeed he cut me. I was with my mistress, a dancer of mixed origin, partly and stridently Hungarian; her name was Mishka and she was a tempestuous but obvious creature. Corrado explained later that it would have embarrassed Elena to meet Mishka, so he had pretended not to see me. I could understand that, but I thought it rather shabby that he hadn't replied to my raised eyebrow, even by a wink. Surely, I thought, he could have risked a wink.

Actually of course Corrado has never hazarded such a thing. You never know who might be watching.

We were interrupted, Elena and I, in our animated colloquy by the surging arrival of my youngest brother, Ettore, his wife Anna-Maria, and their daughter, Bella. Ettore planted two smacking kisses on Elena's chaste cheeks, and began pumping my hand.

'Ah-hah, ah-hah, and how goes it? How goes Augustus?'

I am engaged in writing a study of the Emperor Augustus,

13

sanest of our race. I have been so engaged for a long time, and have no intention of disengaging myself. There is no alibi like history.

Ettore put his arm round my shoulders and led me to the far corner of the room, full of brotherly solicitation, about my health, my happiness and so on. Why did I never come to see them? There was always a place for me at their board. Besides, he wanted to help me, there were all sorts of good things he could put me on to . . .

'Only, you never come to see us and when I try to speak to you on the telephone, whew! you are so cold I think I have maybe somehow offended you. I haven't offended you, have I, Raimundo?'

'No, Ettore, of course not. How could you have offended me?'

He began to tell me of some complicated deal in which he was involved. I didn't listen. Ettore is a financier, a contractor, I don't know exactly what. Like many stupid people, without much sensibility, he has a feeling for money. There, where that is concerned, he is as sensitive as a truffle hound. Of course, it helps to have a brother who is a minister. People think that obliging Ettore will stand them good with Corrado. Ettore naturally doesn't disillusion them. It occurs to me that he may even share the illusion himself. How odd if he did. Surely not? After all, he and Corrado frequently don't see eye to eye. And never have.

Now I didn't listen to what he was saying, but gave only the occasional encouraging murmur. Instead I watched Sandro approach his cousin Bella, and saw her face momentarily alight. Bella is all her name suggests, so simply suggests, a creature so entirely captivating that I can never quite believe she is the product of the union of Ettore and Anna-Maria. She has a mouth made for kissing and pouting, and when she moves I have a hollow feeling in the pit of my stomach. Sandro is too lightweight for her; too lightweight, as the English say, by half.

I looked round the room and couldn't see Bernardo. He would certainly despise a family Sunday lunch. I didn't doubt though that he would appear. Our revolutionaries have their respectable domestic side. Few of them quite escape from

14

Mamma. Prince Radziwill, whom I meet regularly in the wine-shop, tells me of his doctor's grandson, who has served a short prison sentence for crimes against the State; the boy always lunches at home on the day his mother makes her *tortellini*. And to think it's over sixty years since Marinetti denounced *pasta*.

The door opened and Corrado came in, greeting even his family with the certain arrogant embarrassment of a lecturer who has kept the class waiting. He slipped in, grey-faced and grey-suited, as if perversely hoping we would think he had been there all the time; suggesting we should have spotted him previously.

'Is lunch ready, my dear?'

'We are waiting for your mother.'

'Mamma says she will come down for coffee. Maria will feed her upstairs.'

'Then we may go in.'

But first, as if correcting the implied impression that he had been there all the time, Corrado had to go round the circle, greeting us all individually. It occurs to me that it may be the only time in the week he sees some of the children.

As we went through to the cavernous dining-room Bernardo joined us. He was asserting his ideology by a polo-neck jersey made of some synthetic material. He had grown a beard too since I last saw him. It didn't, even with the help of an enveloping moustache, disguise the greedy and pudgy mouth. Bernardo has always been inclined to cover you with spittle as he speaks. One of the children—I forget which, Nico the ironist probably—used to say that Bernardo shouldn't be allowed to travel on buses, since he could neither keep silent nor avoid contravening the injunction not to spit. A childish gibe, but the kind that fixes character in the mind.

A momentary silence while we were served with a glistening golden-topped *maccheroni* pie, all except Corrado, who, ever ascetic, ate only a slice of York ham and some *mozzarella*.

'I detect Maria's hand in the pie still,' I said.

'Yes indeed,' said Elena, 'in fact she still does it all by herself. She insists on doing it once a fortnight. It upsets the Filipinos having her in the kitchen, otherwise she would do it every week.

A fortnight seems a reasonable compromise. Besides we don't want to eat something as rich as this every week.'

'Me,' said Ettore, forking it in, 'I could eat this every day. Do you know, Bella darling,' he shouted down the table, 'the angels in heaven eat Maria's pie. The Virgin herself cooks it for them. It is the Holy Madonna's own recipe. Maria told me that years ago.'

He crossed himself, with the hand that wasn't waving a forkful of *maccheroni* and chicken livers. I glanced at Bella. She was eating with gusto. Who wouldn't want to make love to a beautiful girl who can eat *maccheroni* like that?

Ettore drank some of the dark wine Corrado has sent from Longobucco. Even though he only drinks mineral water himself that doesn't mean that he would like to see a table without wine. I understand this; in the same way I respond in sympathy, feel more alive, when I see Sandro lean over to Bella and whisper something, and her dark ringlets brush against his honey cheek.

Ettore put down his fork and wiped his brow with a red bandana.

'My word,' he said, 'that pie. What a pie! Fifty years I've been eating it, and it's still supreme and I haven't worked out just how she does it. When Maria dies a miracle will vanish. Lost to mankind. Bella, my angel, you must learn how to do it. It's the proportion of truffles to chicken livers that makes it perfect. I know that, but just what is the proportion?'

'It's the little touch of saffron, I think,' said one of the children.

'My word,' said Ettore, 'it does you good. A real Sunday blow-out. And what do you think, Corrado old boy, of the May Day riots? Pretty rum, eh? Are you maybe backing the wrong horse?'

'Oh come,' said Elena, 'no politics at table. No politics on Sunday.'

A grey, quasi-moribund shadow snaked across her face. I doubt if she was really hoping to be able to head off discussion and dissension. Her expression however spoke eloquently of her deep distaste for politics. She would have liked Corrado to remain a Professor of Jurisprudence, and she had always interpreted the motive of his political involvement as disinterested duty, not seeing or refusing to recognize that it was his metier; in the political world he was a fish in water from the start.

'Yes, but', cried Ettore, 'we live in exceptional times you know. And you don't appreciate, my dear sister-in-law, just what my position is. Here am I, with my brother the Minister, the only man, everyone says, who can get us out of the crisis, and when do I see him? Only on Sundays. So take pity on me, don't put me in the ridiculous position of having to reply to anyone who asks me what my brother thinks, that I don't know, that he never talks politics when I'm about because I only see him on family occasions, on Sundays. I tell you, people would take me for a real zany, a dolt, what the English call a ned—isn't that right, Raimundo?'

'That's right,' I said, 'people might easily think you a ned.'

'You see,' Ettore spread his hands wide in emphasis. 'That's how it is.'

Corrado made a gesture with his hand in turn, a sort of fanning motion. It moved across his face, the palm open to us and the fingers spread, and came to rest on the table before him. The long arthritic fingers wrapped themselves round a piece of bread, and began to crumble it. He closed his eyes.

'It's of course a complicated question,' he said, speaking very slowly. Corrado's great quality, invaluable in our political world, has always been his ability to lower the temperature. 'There are too many sides, dark aspects of the question, which are usually ignored,' he said. 'In the first place we must ask ourselves whether there were in fact any riots on May Day. What, ultimately, is a riot?'

He dropped his words among us like pebbles falling singly from a bridge into a pond. The room darkened as he spoke.

'But when I say backing the wrong side,' Ettore protested after allowing the ripples to exhaust themselves, 'you must see what I mean. What do we gain by playing along with the Communists if all that happens is that they can't any longer control their natural supporters?'

'Natural supporters?' asked Corrado. He opened his eyes for a moment. 'Would you agree with that, Bernardo?'

Bernardo's mouth was full of *maccheroni*, but he spoke

17

through it. 'As far as I'm concerned the PCI are just another bourgeois party, nothing more or less, committed like them all to the perpetuation of the system and the exploitation of labour's surplus value.'

'You see, Ettore,' Corrado said.

'But when you say, what is a riot, well then I don't understand you. I mean'—Ettore sweated with intellectual effort—'we all know what a riot is. How many people were killed and wounded and how many arrested on May Day? That's all. I tell you, I told Bella to keep at home when I heard the first rumours on the radio.'

Corrado's hand on the bread opened and closed again.

'There's the question of spontaneity,' he said.

Corrado's method has always been to introduce philosophical speculations into practical discussions and vice versa. It's a way, I suppose, of retaining the initiative. Now there was a pause, a silence. He could keep his eyes open. I made some remark, banal enough, to Elena about the weather or plans for the summer. She smiled at me, gratefully I'm sure. My effort, certainly tiny, was in vain. 'What I don't understand', it was Bella's voice now, and her words seemed immediately disingenuous, for I couldn't imagine that there was anything that concerned her that she didn't in fact understand exactly, on her own terms, 'is what Bernardo has against what he calls the bourgeois parties. I mean, I can't think of anyone more bourgeois than you, Bernardo.'

Bernardo glowered, especially when his brother Nico smiled and said, 'Oh Bella it's refreshing and delightful to find a girl like you still existing. I bet you're saving up to be married, and visit the department stores to select furniture. I mean, you're talking like a little secretary with no understanding of praxis and the historical process. Or put it another way, you have a totally inadequate perception of reality. You think that because Bernardo keeps his comfortable room here, and eats family lunch on Sunday and allows Papa to pay for his clothes and Mamma to have them laundered and hasn't got a job because he's still after seven years studying political science at the University, you think because of all this, he's still really bourgeois. Not at all. He's a true revolutionary, Bernardo. He's undermining the system, that's what he's doing. Anyway, he has a grasp of intellectual reality and the praxis of history, which you've never heard of, and wouldn't understand darling if you had, and that's the important thing. Bernardo is a red mole.'

'Nico,' said Elena, 'finish your pie. We are all ready for the salad.'

May 7 I woke up in the night which is unusual, with Corrado's question drumming in my head. What, after all, is a riot?

The pity is that I have no very clear conception of what happened on May Day. I think a Communist meeting was broken up. The original impression, I'm almost sure, was that the Neo-Fascists were responsible. What, after all, would we do without them? Like Cavafy's Barbarians, they're a sort of solution. Later there was a bomb at the PCI headquarters, planted in spite of the closed-circuit television that covers all approaches to the building. All this of course at a time when the Historic Compromise seems just round the corner, thanks to Corrado and the 'good sense' of the Communist leaders. All the extremists naturally hope that this attempt to give formal recognition to the new respectability of the PCI and the fact that henceforth it will be part of the Establishment will somehow or other be thwarted. All see it as betrayal.

Corrado is sixty and he still concerns himself with the good of the country.

I got up and opened a bottle of mineral water, and sat in my pyjamas reading Stendhal. Just what did he mean by that energy he so admired? Was it simply violence?

I like being awake in the middle of the night, with the city sleeping. After a little I went out on to my terrace and gazed over the courtyard at the silent shuttered windows. What dreams are pursued behind them, what adulteries committed, in fact and in imagination?

The light began to flicker on the leaves of the oleander bushes, first casting a filmy veil over them, faintly opalescent. I picked up Stendhal again, but there comes a time when even the literature one has deeply loved fails to hold the mind. If literature is, as they sometimes say, a mirror to life, well eventually one has no desire to confront oneself in the glass.

I found for the moment at least I couldn't care what he had to say.

Mamma yesterday looked at me sadly. She said, 'You are the eldest, Raimundo, but I find myself wondering what would become of us all if something happened to Corrado.'

'Oh come, Mamma, you're just quoting the newspapers,' I replied.

She made a gesture of irritation and turned her face away from me.

I looked at the clock. It was only half-past seven. The day had scarcely begun. I strolled back on to my little terrace. Across the courtyard I could see movement in one of the hotel bedrooms. A man stirring—he must be English or American for he had been sleeping with windows and shutters open. He was naked to the waist, below a head of shaggy dark hair. I saw him sit on the bed and stretch his hand out. The next gesture I recognized from the cinema. He was pumping the shells out of a revolver. He got up and walked across the room with a long lurching stride. He turned and crossed to the window opposite me, and leant on the sill, not apparently aware of me watching; he held a glass between his hands. I couldn't help thinking that the revolver had been left loaded overnight in case he decided, suddenly, to make an end of things. I suppose he was about forty-five, the second age of suicide.

Seven forty-two.

I would take a little walk, among the thousands going to work. Often as I watched them surging along the narrow streets, edging their little cars against each other, testing the other's nerve, I was aware of a twinge of envy. To be going to work: I remembered how as a schoolboy, and then as a student, I had longed for the day when I would go to work; would be free of this world of affairs; no more dependent.

Our lift shuddered to a halt. Maria, the *portiera*, nodded to me. For many of the other residents she comes chittering-chattering out of her lodge. I can't decide whether her reticence towards me indicates respect or distaste. Curiously enough, I find this worrying. I have myself after all a considerable respect for Maria. She is a virtuous woman, but not a prig.

My walk took me through the old ghetto, the walls ochrous

and bedecked with fading and tattered posters. '*La Lotta Continua*' scrawled in large literate hand in several places. Light motor-bikes and scooters surged around me, nipping at my heels like terriers. There was no malice in it. They were young men and girls, clerks and shop assistants, hurrying to work, their minds on the shirts and gramophone records and jeans they were planning to buy later in the day.

In Campo dei Fiori I stopped for a coffee. The market outside the bar was busy of course, thronged with housewives who were buying their fruit and vegetables, many of them before setting off for work. But so many others, here, in this old part of the city, had no jobs—their husbands were still artisans or often unemployed—and they would go home to tend house; some of the older ones would even take the bowl of vegetables down to the door of their tenement to peel and prepare.

At this hour Campo dei Fiori was still an Italian market; the foreigners who lived around, students, teachers, writers, painters, journalists, girls of less than a fixed occupation, layabouts and remittance men, were still in bed. But the local unemployed youth were already gathering round the *caffè* doors and already, as the sun climbed higher into the azure bowl that pressed down on the jagged roofs of the piazza, there was a murmur of simmering discontent in the air. It is not sweet to do nothing in Campo dei Fiori. The mood is too sultry for that. One day, two or three weeks back, sitting with Prince Radziwill outside the little wine-shop two doors along, we saw a young man, a boy, in a striped towelled shirt and white jeans sprint, wild-eyed, round the corner. 'A thief,' said the Prince, unconcerned, as the crowd opened an avenue for him. A fusillade rang out, in little thuds, not rings at all. He was thrown heavily forward, belly-flopping to the cobbles. His left leg kicked two or three times. That was all. His face was turned to the side and rested on a cabbage leaf, a note of surprise caught in the open calf-like eye. A *carabinieri* squad car screamed into the piazza, and various officers quickly debouched and began drawing chalk-lines and driving the crowd back. We sat there quite half-an-hour, and then a *carabinieri* ambulance took the boy's body away. 'The times we live in,' said the Prince. 'Well, he'd have had to endure three or four years in prison before his

21

trial, I suppose. Better possibly just to get rid of him like that. No loss, but . . .'

'Where will it end?' said Fr Ambrose, the English Augustine, who had joined us. His red squirarchical face ran sweat as usual.

As for me, I remarked that the boy's shirt had been striped like a brand of candy I used to buy on Coney Island.

I had my second cup of coffee in the Corso, at Bernardo's in the Galleria Colonna; and here, the mood was different again— it was just a city, almost any city, going to work. Only there was a difference. You could imagine the work done by the artisans and shopkeepers in the ghetto and towards the Tiber. Here, under the marble pillars, which supported office blocks, reality had become purely surreal. (Oddly enough, I was talking about Surrealism just yesterday afternoon with Nico at Corrado's, immediately before leaving. How we had got on to the subject I can't recall, but he said to me: 'but Nuncle, don't you see, it's your generation that's surreal, not mine. After all, you're a product of the twenties, aren't you?' I had no answer for the boy, though I told him I would introduce him to Di Chirico himself if he cared to come to the Greco about noon. He could discuss it with the maestro in person. For my part, I said, and then found myself shrugging my shoulders unable to recall what I had been planning to say.)

The words of the English poet, Eliot, came to me: 'I had not thought death had undone so many.'

I sipped my *cappuccino*, thinking that thought now.

'What a strange place to see you, Uncle.'

It was Bella, looking like a nectarine.

'If it comes to that,' I said, 'what are you doing here?'

'I'm here every morning. I work in one of the offices above.'

'What do you do there?'

'I import and export. It's one of Daddy's subsidiaries. How little you know of us, don't you?'

She sat beside me and laid her long pale fingers lightly on my wrist. I was distressed to see how freckled and worn it looked; a blotchy old man's wrist.

'Extraordinary,' I said, 'you have a job then?'

'But of course.'

22

'And do you do it brilliantly?'

'What do you think?'

'I can imagine . . . will you have some coffee with me?'

'Yes, please, and a doughnut. No, two doughnuts. Usually I can only afford one, but since my wicked uncle's paying . . . you looked, Uncle, as if you were thinking very mournful thoughts . . . so mournful I almost didn't stop.'

'I'm glad you did.'

'What were you thinking though?'

'You were quite right. They were mournful, my thoughts.'

'On such a beautiful day? How could you? Tell me what they were then.'

She bit into the softness of her doughnut. Her teeth were beautifully white. A little spurt of the confectioner's cream the doughnut contained escaped from the corner of her mouth. A quick snake's flick of the pink tip of her tongue retrieved it.

'I was thinking of a poet. An English poet. Well, he was American really.'

'Oh poets,' she said. 'They used to make us read poets at school. I don't read them now. What had he to say, this poet?'

'He said, "I had not thought death had undone so many".'

'Oh,' she said. She gave me a long candid, deeply brown-eyed look. 'Nico writes poetry,' she said, 'did you know that?'

'Nico?'

'Yes, very restrained, very ironic, very dry, he says. You see, you don't know anything about us.'

'Yes, that's obvious. I'll have to cultivate you all. I had chocolate with Sandro the other day.'

She smiled. 'It is exactly like Sandro still to drink chocolate. You know he still sleeps with his Teddy-bear? Sandro's very sweet, but so young. And therefore confused. I could easily worry about Sandro if I chose to worry about people. Of course, it's all terribly difficult for them. I mean, I do think Aunt Elena's weird, and as for Uncle Corrado, well it may be true what the papers say, that he's the only man who can save the country and so on, but that's not very real, is it? I mean, as a father, he's a bit of a wash-out. What I don't understand is how Papa is so comparatively sane. Of course, I know he's only a half-brother though you always call him brother, but I mean there's Uncle Guido too isn't there?'

'There is indeed.'

'I've never seen him of course, but from what I hear . . . will you take me to see him some day.'

'You wouldn't like it. Ask your father.'

'I wouldn't expect to like it. Papa can't bear to go any more. It's years since he's been.'

'I know.'

'You wouldn't think Papa was so sensitive. He says he can't bear it.'

I shrugged.

'Think about it,' she said, 'won't you? I must go. I'm late.'

'Why don't we have lunch together some day? Let me get to know you.'

'Love to.'

'Today then?'

'No. Tomorrow.'

She spoke without a note of interrogation, certain that my life was without engagements.

'Splendid,' I said, 'I'll meet you here. I'll be here when you finish work. One o'clock? Right. We'll go somewhere where they have good *maccheroni*.'

She made a little moue.

'It pleases me to watch you eat *maccheroni*,' I said.

She smiled again. 'In that case,' she said, 'certainly.'

I watched her go, swinging the shoulder-bag she still defiantly carried, daring the motor-bike thieves. A game she would enjoy. I watched the long swing of her legs, the free movement of her chestnut hair. The crowd closed behind her.

In the afternoon, guilty, I took a taxi to Monte Mario to visit Guido in his asylum. The nurse said, 'You had better not enter today. He's been having a bad turn. I'm afraid it was necessary to strait-jacket him. He's weak now but the sight of you might excite him again.'

He had a big strong face, the nurse, and a Sicilian accent.

'All we can do for him really is keep him from hurting himself and others,' he said. 'If the doctors tell you differently it's a pack of lies.'

24

I looked through the spy-hole at Guido who had been my favourite brother. He was curled up, foetus-like, in the strait-jacket, which came half-way down his thighs. He was wearing no other garment and had fouled himself. I could hear a sort of whimpering. An eye glared redly in a yellow-mottled and dirt-streaked face. His mouth, half-pressed against the floor, was open, the lips very red as if he had been biting them so that the blood surged back.

'They'd like to take his teeth out,' said the nurse. 'They irritate him and pain him and we think make him even worse. He'll have them out next week, when he's calmed down. There'll be something for you to sign, sir.'

The body on the floor began to heave, the movement coming first in sharp little spasms. Then it stumbled to a position half-erect and, with short nervous paces, keeping its thighs together, began to scurry across the room, then round the far side. The head darted right and left and the feet scurried, hardly leaving the ground. It was a sort of insect shuffle.

'He'll do that for hours sometimes,' said the nurse. 'Like something in the zoo, isn't it, sir? You know, he occasionally seems to be laughing.'

I nodded. Nausea kept me from speaking. Maybe I should bring Bernardo, not Bella, to see this. Maybe it should be Corrado came once a fortnight.

'Your brother, the Minister, was here yesterday,' said the nurse. 'He doesn't often come, but when he does, you know, I think the lunatic knows him. He senses his power maybe. I'm not of your brother's way of thinking. I have'—he lowered his voice—'older allegiances. Like yourself I think sir. Indeed I regard your brother as a traitor, but there's no doubt, sir, the lunatic responds to him. Only it's a false response, sir, because he's always worse afterwards. He has a reaction to the experi-ence, as you might say. It's a different sort of experience,'—the nurse licked his lips quickly and rubbed his hands energetically together—'a different sort of experience he really understands.'

We had reached the end of the long stone corridor, the nurse's keys jangling against the wall on his side, as every now and then he swayed against it. He knocked on the heavy deal door.

I didn't know the man behind the desk. He was new here,

though the ash pallor of his face suggested years of half-life in the half-light of this half-world of the asylum system.

'I am honoured to meet you,' he said, 'only the day after your so distinguished brother. It is, *dottore*, encouraging to think that even so hopeless a case as your unfortunate brother can still attract the attention of two such distinguished and busy men.'

'Busy?' I said, 'I'm in no way busy.'

'Your historical researches,' he said. 'I'm sorry', he said, 'that you've found poor Guido in such a low state. He's had one of his bad turns.'

'Couldn't he even be cleaned up?' I asked, but I was aware of the naivety of the question and didn't require his deprecating administrator's smile.

'We do try,' he said, 'but of course he doesn't co-operate. As soon as we have him clean he fouls himself again.'

'The smell,' I said, 'really a stench . . .'

'It doesn't worry him, you may be sure of that. When he's round the corner, it'll be different of course. You know how he usually is. I assure you, *dottore*, he'll be nicely cosmeticized in a day or two.'

I sighed and, ignoring his expression of distaste, lit a cigarette.

'You don't mind, do you?' I said.

'Not at all,' he replied, and made great play of searching for an ash-tray.

'That nurse,' I said.

'Devoted.'

'I'm not making a complaint,' I said.

There was a silence.

'He doesn't perhaps have a certain relish for physical treatment?' I asked. 'He doesn't beat him, does he?'

'*Dottore*,' he said, 'you've been more affected by the sight than I thought you were. I apologize. Sit down. You must sit down. And perhaps a restorative. A glass of cognac perhaps.'

I allowed myself to be persuaded; weak and foolish of me. Yet to stir up trouble and such-like could hardly do Guido any good. And where else, except the State asylum along the road, could we take him? Mamma would never hear of that.

But why should that nurse—that gaoler—have concluded that I was a Fascist too?

And he did it with approval. Not like our committed young who apply the opprobrious term to anything they may chance to disapprove of. I don't really mind being called a Fascist by them, since it's practically impossible to avoid it and I have never been one for spitting against the wind, but I'm hanged if I'll submit to being claimed by the tawdry crew themselves.

I took a little nap after I had written up this diary that I don't know why I keep, and woke, after a bad dream, with Sasha lying on my chest purring. I was tempted to stay in bed fondling the cat, and, if I didn't, it was only because I felt that succumbing to this I would always succumb. I have after all little enough cause to rise at any time. So, like a moralist, I pushed Sasha aside, my hand deep in the softness of his fur; and ignored his little protest. I showered and looked over the violet-lit emptiness of the courtyard, scent of magnolia rising towards me. I could see the not-quite-suicide of the morning, or rather I could see the top of his head, a grey streak showing. He was sitting at a table, doubtless one of those gimcrack little tables, inadequate for any purpose, which are made specially for the bedrooms of second-rate *pensioni*. The sound of typewriter keys, uncertainly and irregularly struck, came to me. I pictured him hammering out a dime novel in despair, trying to re-animate an old dream of genius with the aid of bourbon. 'If I were kind,' I said to myself, 'I would go and greet him and say, Brother.'

Instead, I went down to the *osteria*, where I had no need to call for a *quartino* of white wine to be set on the table before me. It was cool and damp out of the evening sunshine. My stomach tightened at the sour smell of stale wine and sawdust. Fr Ambrose smiled at me.

'I was beginning to think our little club would be thin tonight,' he said. 'The Prince has gone to the country, I'm told.'

I sipped my wine.

'They still haven't made any arrests in connection with the May Day riots,' he said, 'other than those who were picked off the street at the time, that is. But I understand they've decided they weren't spontaneous, and that they were indeed instigated by the Left.'

'I wouldn't know,' I said, 'Left, Right, does it matter? I never read the papers, of course.'

'You can't need to,' said Dr Eustachio, a pert young lawyer who has taken to dropping in on the sessions of our wholly informal club, 'with your connections, that is.'

'When I see my brother,' I said, 'we talk about family affairs. Or literature.'

'Oh certainly,' he said.

'Well,' said a young man in a dark suit I didn't know, 'I should think he might be happy to. He's certainly, as they say, the key to the situation, and he must be grateful for any respite. But if you ask me, the key won't turn. There's no way out of the crisis by Parliamentary means. We're heading, within months not years, for a dictatorship, whether of the right or left depends of course on the development of the next weeks. It depends possibly on just what precipitates the more intensive crisis that is bound to arrive in one form or another.'

'And it follows that that must be done deliberately. By a single positive act. An act perhaps shocking in itself but yet made in accordance with the truly perceived demands of historical necessity. An act therefore entirely autonomous, containing its own justification in its own being.'

The speaker was a pale young man I hadn't seen there before. I divined at once that he had come with the man in the dark suit, though he wore, a little uneasily, the conventional uniform of blue denim; he sipped a lemonade. I had seen his face before, but not in the flesh. He was without doubt a Caravaggio Christ.

'That sort of language worries me,' said Fr Ambrose. 'I don't want to seem to be taking advantage of my cloth, but it smacks of Jesuitry; and I think the Jesuits have a lot to answer for. I speak as an Englishman of course.'

The Caravaggio Christ was unmoved. His face had the immobility of a wax creation.

'The Jesuits were Spanish in origin,' he said, 'but it's true they accommodated themselves to the Italian genius. And in turn moulded it. Bourgeois morality is alien to the intellectual structures within which they operate. As did Machiavelli. As must we today, transcending such. How can it be otherwise?

28

Bourgeois morality is a papier-mâché structure.'

'This means then that you would condone violence,' said Dr Eustachio. He pulled at his moustache, drawing attention to his superiority.

'Condone is a term wholly without significance,' said Caravaggio. 'Say rather we recognize and consequently accept its inevitability. Consider, if you like, the new *autostrada* that by-passes Padua. Some big politician wanted that highway built and it cost one and a half trillion *lire*. Right; money for his friends. That could have been spent on cardiac or dialysis centres, which naturally we still don't have, but the *autostrada* was worth more votes than the hospital. So someone whose life could have been saved is dead because of this cynicism, and others are dying because that road has been built. So who is the worse killer? That politician or the boy—maybe me—with a machine-gun?'

I looked at Fr Ambrose. His rosy English face had lost all rigidity, his cheeks sagged in pendulous bags of inertia. And yet the argument lay in his territory, I felt. As for me, I recognized the language, the diseased poetry of Romanticism that could scrawl the words, 'the machine-gun is beautiful', on the walls of university buildings.

'What we have to say is this,' said Caravaggio. 'In our circumstances violence has to be a central ingredient of a true communist programme. The fact is inescapable since violence already thwarts the programme. The State cannot arrogate to itself the legitimate use of violence. Remember that. Come,' he said to Black Suit, 'we must be about our further business.'

Fr Ambrose drew back the skirts of his habit as they passed. I watched them out. The beaded curtain trailed across Caravaggio's shoulder, and the strands fell separately back. He was the real thing, Caravaggio; no doubt about it. Black Suit by contrast was the opportunist every movement attracts, but Caravaggio was the sort you would find on a cross or before a firing-squad. Yet it was Black Suit was the worrying portent; when men of that stamp joined a movement . . .

Dr Eustachio said, 'We ought to report to the police, don't you think . . .?'

'My poor *dottore*,' I said, 'what would you have us report?

29

That we have heard some foolishness? Some talk, even advocacy, of violence. You can hear the same in any Roman *caffè*.'

'That chap,' he persisted, 'he meant it, you know. It's no laughing matter.'

'But that doesn't mean there's anything we can do about it.'

I sipped the harsh thin Marino wine. 'Nothing at all,' I repeated. 'Unless you really wish to make yourself an object of interest to the authorities.'

'That story of his, example or what have you,' Fr Ambrose said. 'Not as quick on the uptake as I might be, y' know, but it shows their lack of logic. After all, what did he admit? That there were more votes in the highway than in the hospital? So it was more democratic, would you say? Yes, the present system, on their own admission, don't y' know, gives people what they want. That makes it undoubtedly more democratic. In my book or any other I can read.'

'Oh,' I said, 'he would have an answer to that. He would say, wouldn't he, that the people have been deceived; conditioned to want things they wouldn't want if their judgement had been left free. It's a matter of induced desires. Propaganda. Written into the capitalist system. Imprinted. So it's got to be got rid of. People have to be freed from this sort of thing. Accordingly it's no good just continuing to demand reform of the State. That just means more of the same, even if in a slightly different form. No, no, the State must be abolished. The argument, you know, hangs together . . .'

Fr Ambrose clapped his hands, great hams of hand coming heavily together.

'Bravo,' he cried, 'I must say you do it jolly well, Raimundo. You have the patter absolutely. More wine, *signora*. The abolition of the State, yes well, what they're really asking for is the abolition of human nature as it's always been, don't y' know.'

'You could put it like that,' I said. 'Of course it's what the Church has always asked for too. In its more enthusiastic moments at least.'

Fr Ambrose wiped his big fleshy hands on his skirts. He picked up the wine-jug and poured two glasses. He eyed his wine and sipped it, then took a deeper swallow.

'Of course,' he said, 'that's true, but at the same time we have to accept things as they are.'

'Oh,' I said, 'so do these types. Up to a point, I think, anyway.'

There was a moon over the Colosseum as I walked home, and I asked myself: 'What made me respond to Caravaggio as I did? There was a note there struck home.'

The fat whore at the corner of the street beckoned towards me as she always did, and I touched my hat, courteously, as I always do. She comes from San Giovanni dei Fiori in Calabria, and has worked in Rome twelve years. She takes a bus out to the suburbs every dawn and is home in time to see her ten-year-old son off to school. Her name is Margherita. Good-night, good-night, good-night.

May 8 I woke thinking of Bella, and thinking I had dreamt of making love with her. And had I dreamt this, or had I not?

My hand was hot on the bed-cover, sun-streaked through the slatted shutter. I must therefore have slept better than usual, where better means longer. Depth of sleep is something I no more look to have. I pictured Bella, in a way uncles should not picture nieces, on my bed, lying back, not teasing, but open and generous. That afternoon, after lunch and sun and wine in a restaurant, I pictured my hand, my blotchy sexagenarian hand, not being resisted.

Groaning, I eased myself to my feet. The tiles were warm to the touch. It was eight o'clock.

I threw open the shutters and leant on the wall of the terrace smoking a cigarette. Spring was over; there was no freshness even in this morning air. Summer was upon us, the all-devouring Roman summer.

I could hear movement from the kitchen. It must be one of Katrina's days. I called out to her, requesting coffee. In a few minutes she padded through, grumbling at me beneath her breath.

'What is it?' I said, but she didn't reply. Katrina is no old family servant. Her husband used to have a shop, but for some reason he didn't make a success of it, and fell into debt. Now he sits at home reading the papers, while Katrina, who must be almost seventy, goes out cleaning. It's no wonder she doesn't care for me.

And what she does to the coffee I can never understand. As usual I poured it away, and dressed myself in a thin jersey, an American sweatshirt in fact, and slacks, and, muttering about cigarettes, went down to the bar for an *espresso*. It was already hot; time to move slowly, in the shade of the wall.

The barman who knows my connection with Corrado tried, as he often does, to engage me in a political discussion.

'I'm a socialist,' he said, 'and I say it must come, this historic compromise which brings the Communists into the fold, but the time isn't ripe yet. Of course your brother's a clever man. He doesn't really want an alliance with the Communists. He just knows that the talk about it will eventually weaken them. After all there's no point in being a Communist if they are in fact coming into the Government, no point at all. You might as well join one of the Centre Parties and so make a proper arrangement. Conversely, it will dilute the attraction the PCI still holds for the really enthusiastic Red, who doesn't want to have to make the compromises and temporization the system demands. Undeniably therefore, what's proposed is subtle. Still you can't deny its dangers either. There can be no doubt, that in the interim, before it bears fruits, the situation will exacerbate itself. What will the CIA have to say, for instance? If you ask me, things will have to get worse before they can improve. That's clear enough . . .'

I reflected, as I occasionally acknowledged his remarks with a little grunt or a nod of the head, that conversations, identical to this in opinion, if not in exact expression, are going on all over the city.

On an impulse I asked for a *gettone* and went to the telephone and called Corrado at Party Headquarters. I knew he should have arrived there; for years his routine has been inflexible. It took some time to be transferred to him—I wondered if they imagined that I had discovered some means of exploding telephonic bombs. At last, when I had convinced them of my identity, I was put through. The note of caution in his voice meant nothing; I have never known it absent.

'This is unusual, Raimundo,' he said.

'Yes, unusual and uncharacteristic. You were in my mind.'

'Ah.'

'This line?'

'Obviously not. You must know that; on the telephone, it is impossible to protect anything on the telephone. That is why I am always so reluctant to use the instrument. If you wish to talk to me—it's family, I take it?'

'Yes.'

'We had better arrange to meet. Family matters should remain as they should remain.'

'Yes.'

'Would you like to come over late tonight? There is a dinner I have to attend. For some African president. But after that. You know I never stay at these things, and this one is of no importance.'

I hesitated. I didn't want to go out on the Cassia at night; and anyway I have never felt comfortable in Corrado's house, which is not really his, but Elena's.

'Why not come to me?' I said. 'It would be a change . . .'

He hesitated. The pause was long, perceptibly longer even than Corrado's manner has accustomed me to. Perhaps he was taking advice.

'No,' he said. 'There might be difficulties. I have to remain . . . in touch. You will understand, Raimundo, how it is. So if you don't mind . . . we can give you a bed for the night if you like.'

I didn't of course accept that offer, but Corrado's position occupied my mind, off and on, for the rest of the morning. I was convinced he had turned to some security adviser and said, 'Will it be all right if I go to my brother's apartment?' and received the reply, 'We can't guarantee your safety if you do that.' Perhaps I was accounted a security risk; more probably, my quarter and my apartment were simply deemed too great a danger, hard to protect.

There are those who consider Corrado the most powerful man in Italy; but keys of course have no autonomous power.

I didn't tell Bella what was on my mind when we met. Instead, in a resurrected grey pin-striped suit, with a dark red carnation in my button-hole, I tried to look debonaire, if

33

dated—the wicked uncle she had mentioned. She advanced towards me with her floating liquidity of motion, and we kissed.

'I have a fancy', I said, 'for being seen with you,' and took her arm; we went to the Bolognese restaurant where Via Ripetta runs into Piazza del Popolo.

How to describe what I felt? I am anyway out of practice in feeling. I took her elbow again as the waiter guided us to our table. She removed her dark glasses to look more closely at the American film stars two tables away. They were rather passé film stars and their laughter rang a little hollow. We ordered *tortellini*, and then some veal. The sunlight made her hair shine and then the sun ducked behind a fleecy little cloud, the only one in the May sky, and a shadow moved across her cheek like youth vanishing. I poured her a glass of white wine. She touched its rim and sat, elbows firmly on the table, glass held in both hands, looking at me. She began to talk very quickly, telling me about things I had no wish to know of—her work, her mother, her little brother, Ettore himself, my dear clumsy stupid rich and successful brother, a father whose love for his daughter was, in her words, 'ridiculous and totally excessive'.

'You know,' she said, 'Papa is so jealous of any boy who looks at me.'

She smiled, putting on the thought like a fur coat. Ettore's possessive love made her feel warm and safe.

'He might like me to marry Sandro of course, if I marry anyone, because, well, Sandro is sweet. There would be no trouble with a dispensation, there never is, is there? I'm very fond of Sandro of course, but you know, he's very pretty, but the sort of appeal he has is for men or other boys and maybe married ladies of forty—there have been two of them trying to fix their claws in him in the last year—not for me or for any of my girl-friends. He's too nice really, Sandro.'

I watched her talking with this empty and decisive vivacity; and it was all I could do to keep my hands from straying from my control. Of course it was youth and energy I was responding to; an attempt to deny my present condition flickered into life.

She wanted, it was clear, to talk of Guido. He was after all the family skeleton. She had only recently realized that he was still alive. I was surprised by her curiosity, not immediately

34

recognizing it as a form of egoism, an expression of the egoist's need to know everything about whatever seems even vestigially to belong to his or her life.

'I want to see him,' she said. 'You will take me, won't you?'

'But why?'

'I just do. It seems so terrible to know nothing about him.'

'To know about him? Well, I can help you there.' I placed my blotchy hand on her wrist. 'You know,' I said, 'Guido was the most talented of us. When he was very young he published a book of poems—*The Shades of Things*—I thought it wonderful and it still seems to have had a rare quality. But,' I sighed, 'Guido felt the need for a faith. He rejected the Church, he believed passionately in Science you see; and they seemed to conflict. Perhaps that was already a little old-fashioned. Then, as a young man, a very young man, you must understand, because (I don't know of course) this may shock you, he believed equally passionately in the Regime. But then, there were incidents that shattered both his faiths . . .'

'Yes?' she said, 'I do want to know . . .'

'Oh I've no doubt they would seem very trivial. He had a job in the Department of Statistics and he discovered that the figures there were being cooked, figures which purported to give scientific justification for certain practices of the Regime, and there was simply no such justification. It was a political ramp. So he resigned, not in hatred, simply indifference. That was the terrible thing,'—I gazed into my glass fearful of reflection—'his indifference. What he had believed in was shown to be false and tawdry, and so he found there was nothing left to care for. That was, you see, all no good. On his good days, or rather one should say in his good periods, for his condition goes in cycles of weeks, even months sometimes, that's still his state, indifference. He just found there was nothing to care about. Do you know, he was married, to a very lovely girl? One day he came home and found her in bed with the chauffeur, and what do you think he did?'

Bella's eyes opened wide in expectation.

'He sat down on the edge of the bed and chatted. Then he began to ask the chauffeur when a car that was being repaired would be ready. That was shortly before they took him away.'

35

She turned her hand round in mine and scratched my palm gently.

'But even in Italy surely,' she said, 'it's not a sign of insanity is it to decline to commit a *crime passionel?*'

'But understand,' I said, 'he truly didn't care.'

'What did he look like? You know I don't think I've ever seen a photograph of him.'

'He looked very like your Uncle Corrado. They were sometimes taken for twins though actually Guido is five years older.'

'He sounds like Sandro,' she said. 'Something like that happened with him and me. I don't mean I was in bed with a chauffeur or anything like that. Not my style.' She held her face up to the sun. 'But simply there was an occasion when Sandro should have been jealous and instead he started talking about tennis. Not to cover-up how he felt but rather because he couldn't feel what I thought he ought to be feeling. Does that sound awful?'

I said, 'There are always things we ought to feel, but you can't will feeling. You can't force it. Perhaps you can educate it, but at the critical moment, it's either there or it isn't. We've all had experiences—I'm speaking of us as a nation and a civilization, as well as individuals—that make it difficult, often, to have the fresh natural feelings we think we ought to. You're lucky in your father, you know. He's still spontaneous, and not given to this sort of gloomy reflection.'

For a moment there was something blank, warm and blank as a young heifer, in the beauty that confronted me; she lacked the imaginative reach that would allow her to understand what others felt. For her, Sandro's action had been quite incomprehensible; and she shied away from anything like that. She had instead to be able to take things in both hands, as she held her wine-glass, elbows firmly planted. She put on her dark glasses.

'Oh,' she said, 'I know I'm lucky in Papa really. When I think of the difficulties my cousins have, it's clear enough how fortunate I am. All the same . . .' she tilted her chin, 'Uncle Corrado makes me curious, you know. You never know what he's really thinking about things. And all this politics, everyone says it's so important, but I don't know, Uncle, I live my life happily without politics.'

'That's the ideal condition,' I said.

'Anyway, they're so boring.'

And it is indeed the ideal condition, I thought, as, having watched her swing off down Via Ripetta a little later, I moved to Rosati's and ordered more coffee. But it is a condition which can only be attained by those who are happy enough to benefit from others' achievement, others' struggle; and that achievement, that struggle, can only take the form of successful political action. The poor are always oppressed by politics, even where they themselves employ no political vocabulary. All this is true, but yet, when I hear a politician say, 'this Italy of ours', I shudder . . .

I sat two hours at Rosati's watching the ebb and flow in the piazza. Towards four o'clock crowds began to surge back through the Gate, coming from the bus station beyond, on their way back to the shops and offices where they worked. The girls looked younger as well as smarter than the girls of my youth. Most of them wore trousers. They chattered like confident starlings. They were the fruits of Corrado's Italy; thirty years in which we have built a society to satisfy needs in as short a time as possible. But of course needs spawn needs. Expectations rise.

The American film stars—perhaps only she was a star, he her agent or lover or ex-husband—had finished their lunch also and came and sat at the next table.

'O.K?' he said.

'Scotch,' she said.

'It's a bit early,' he said.

'It's the way I feel.'

'If it's the way you feel, I guess it's the way I'd better treat you.'

He slapped his thigh, a big tawny man with bloodshot eyes and a too ready laugh. She snapped at her cigarette-lighter as the shop-girls scurried past, chattering still.

Corrado was waiting for me at the villa. I had paid off my taxi, identified myself at the gate, waited while they telephoned, and then finally approached the house in the glare of a searchlight. Probably there was a gun trained on me, in case I suddenly tore off the mask I was wearing and revealed myself as a terrorist, no brother at all. (But there is always the dire moment when the terrorist is discovered to be indeed your brother.)

Corrado sat in his library. A Filipino ushered me in. The room was draped in brown velvet. Behind the drapes the walls were cork. My brother suffered from noise, though he lived so much of his life surrounded by it. He was wearing a dinner-jacket with an air of embarrassment. Despite years of official dinners he still wore it as though it was fancy dress, something they'd compelled him to put on for sport. I glanced at his hands; they were less blotched than mine, but the long fingers of his Chopin-playing youth were curled by arthritis.

He said to the Filipino, 'Bring some tea, will you, please.' He moved his head infinitesimally in my direction, 'Perhaps you would prefer something else, Raimundo? I forget about these things. Tea is all I take nowadays. It's not too much to say that I depend on it. I'm rather ashamed of that . . .'

I told him tea would be admirable.

'We never seem to find the opportunity to talk,' I said.

There was a chess board on the desk in front of him. Perhaps he had been playing over a game, following the thinking, the intuitive flashes and nervous schemes of the Grand Masters.

'Do you still play?' he said.

'Chess was never my game. I played bridge when I was young and again when I was posted in Washington. Now, nothing, I'm afraid.'

'Not even *scopa*? In the *osteria* you frequent?'

'Not even *scopa*. Not even there.'

'I am sorry to have had to drag you out here, and so late. But you will understand, the way things are, whatever my nominal position, I have in certain ways to do as I'm told. Nothing, Raimundo, is so easily exaggerated as the power of a politician.'

'You don't have to tell me that. You forget I was in Washington—for my second term there—during the Vietnam years. I saw the last year of Johnson in '68 and Nixon's first two. You don't have to remind me of the impotence of politicians.'

'Yet impotence isn't the right word. Not impotence. You

know what we are? People think we're technicians or, more grandiosely, executives—they have this image of the executive, who says do and it is done, and so forth—and we've inherited of course the idea of leadership, though for fairly obvious reasons the word itself is suspect, nowhere more so than here in our Italy. But none of that meets the case. Viewed candidly, we are mages.'

His face abruptly twisted itself into a sort of mask, like a primitive idol. 'We are witch-doctors,' he said, 'our task is to bring on the rain. That's all. It's an uncomfortable role because it so easily infringes the legitimate one of the priest's. But that's what we are: Fisher-Kings, symbolic victims too. I don't usually talk like this, you understand.' The corner of his mouth moved. The Filipino entered and placed the tray on the desk and poured us two cups of tea, pale straw-coloured, with lemon in it. He went out without a word.

'But then speaking to a brother is a rare luxury,' Corrado said. 'Do you know the only other person I have spoken to in this manner? The Holy Father, no less. So you are privileged. And do you know what he replied? He put his hand on my brow and said, "My poor son".'

I thought: at the age of sixty Corrado is learning to laugh at himself. I sipped my tea.

'I went to see Guido yesterday,' I said.

The only light in the room shone down on the desk, directly on the chessmen; it was a lowered and shaded lamp such as you find in billiards-saloons. Corrado's face lay just in shadow, now that, with his tea-cup in his hand, he was leaning back in his chair. He took another little sip of tea.

'But you go every fortnight,' he said.

And of course we never discuss it.

'The nurse told me you'd been there the day before.'

'Yes.'

'I'm not happy about the situation. I feel guilty.'

Corrado said, 'What Guido is, what has become of him'—did we both have the same instantaneous vision of the young Guido in a pageant, laughing, on horseback, standing in his stirrups dressed as Guiscard conquering Calabria?—'is beyond us. The Guido we knew and loved is buried. His personality is

39

extinct. All we can do now is care for the body which houses the immortal soul and its condition, the soul's that is, may, for all we know, be immaculate.'

'I know nothing about Guido's soul,' I said.

'No.'

'I think the nurse beats him and the new director is no good at all, he's one of those people corrupted by the atmosphere in which he has lived. The nurse is a neo-Fascist, did you know?'

Corrado closed his eyes and made a bridge of his fingers.

'He's not now a Party member,' he said. 'It's not, you know, Raimundo, a job likely to attract a good class of recruit, not at all . . .'

'Naturally,' I said, 'I understand that. But one looks for a little sympathy, a little tenderness. I have the impression that all he is interested in, is simply control.'

'There are times however, in any government of any sort, when that is all one may hope to be able to achieve.'

I sighed.

'Do you mind if I light a cigar?' I said.

Corrado made a vague fanning gesture.

'Toscani,' he said. 'Whenever I have thought, as I have often found myself thinking in the past, that we were losing you, that you were becoming that dead thing, the cosmopolitan, I have been happy to remember that you have always smoked Toscani. Of course, do smoke one now. You can have no idea how much I am depressed by the cosmopolitan. Even in our Party, you understand, which is an historically authentically Italian Party, we have these Euro-types, or even worse, the half-Yankee businessmen. They understand nothing, nothing but making money.'

We both found ourselves smiling.

'No,' he said, 'our dear Ettore doesn't really, despite appearances, belong in that category. He is something different, an older model as they say.'

He picked up a pawn and moved it across the board.

'What fatigues me is that I see our problem so differently from the way they see it; and they will make no effort to see it my way. They are blind to the sort of reality that most of our countrymen in fact experience. But you haven't come here to talk politics, and yet in the end I often find myself wondering whether there is indeed anything else. You've come to talk about Guido. Yet, you know, even there, well . . . political analogies abound. Where he is, Guido is in safe hands. That's all. There is nothing else we can do for him, except pray, except pray. We have there reached the limits of action. The limit of action, you can come up against that more abruptly than most people think.'

As I looked at my brother, and heard these words, 'the limit of action', I had a picture of an old peasant on a hillside in Calabria ploughing a field cut out from the *macchia*, a field which required that each year its boundaries be defended and redefined; and I saw the old peasant every day mounting his donkey to ride out from his village and renew the struggle. That was the sort of struggle which, in reality rather than in rhetoric, in fact continued. There was no ultimate point to it, except the experienced necessity of survival.

'All the same,' I said, 'when I think of Guido, as he was . . . well, I suppose one of the characteristics of being Italian, something that has formed our sensibility and outlook for centuries, is that we have never been able to avoid the consciousness of ruins. We've always had very directly before our eyes these reminders of the instability of fortune, these images of the vanity of human aspirations. Guido is our family temple of Antiquity.'

Corrado was long silent. The dark-blue-grey smoke of my cigar drifted between us.

'Yes,' he said at last, 'but there is a sort of hopeless self-admiration about that, a Narcissus who has no desire to do anything but continue to gaze at the pool which reflects his folly. I distrust it. All the same to be quite frank I find it hard to determine my position. It sometimes seems to me, Raimundo, that all I am really trying to do is shield our people from any true knowledge of things as they are. What after all have we achieved since the war, in the more than thirty years of Christian Democracy? We have given the people, or made it possible for them to seize for themselves, everything they wanted. Everything they have asked for. And are they

41

happier? Do they understand their own natures better? Or the world's? Aren't they—forgive me, Raimundo, because I know that you too no longer believe—but aren't they further from God? Sometimes, in hours when the traffic is silent, I find myself saying of them:

Questi non hanno speranza di morte
e la lor cieca vita è tanto bassa
che invidiosi son d'ogni altra sorte.

It is not a comfortable thought to bear . . .'

'I shall match it,' I found myself replying, 'with a thought that we are in the western world in danger of forgetting; denying perhaps by the way we live now. Do you know the American liberal, Oliver Wendell Holmes? He became a Supreme Court Judge under Roosevelt. Well, this is what he said: "Every society is founded on the death of men". You won't find the sentiment remarkable, you must often have thought it yourself. Still, from an American liberal . . . of course Holmes belonged to the Civil War generation, he lived to be very old . . .'

'It's what many of our young are of course coming to decide for themselves again.'

'And yet, in one sense, that decision is itself profoundly depressing, isn't it?'

Something hung between us. We were talking more like the brothers we might have been than we had done in years; possibly ever. One comes up, now and then, against these moments, few and fugitive admittedly, when what might have been momentarily crystallizes into what almost is. It is like taking an ice-tray out of the refrigerator at the very moment when the thinnest coat is forming on the water. Of course, almost at once, you put it down on a table in a warm room, and in instants it is as if it had never been.

'Sandro', I said, 'asked me to speak to you the other day.'

'Sandro?' A line carved in his cheek displaced itself an instant.

'Yes. He had asked me to meet him. He is perturbed. It's a question of Bernardo's political affiliations apparently. I hadn't thought I would ever mention it.'

42

And that was true; it had seemed futile. The sight of Bernardo on the Sunday in his absurd synthetic polo-neck had rendered Sandro's alarm ridiculous.

'Poor Sandro,' Corrado said. 'He understands very little. He is, I think, entirely a creature of sensation, of reflex. Impossible to imagine him otherwise. He would do better to go on amusing himself on the tennis-court. He is skilful and graceful there. That ought to content him.'

The brown velvet softness hanging all round us swathed our words. Once the telephone rang and Corrado answered it, speaking with remote caution, polysyllabically negative. He put it down and sipped tea, and smoothed his hand over the leather surface of his desk, the palm flat, the fingers bent.

'You may think I don't really know my children. Certainly I see less of them than many fathers, less, clearly, than I would like; but yet I do know them, I see where they are tending. Sandro's vacant romanticism which is really nothing more than an indolent sensuality. You see that reflected all over our poor country. Drive round the Ligurian coast, so beautiful in our youth, and it is full of Sandros. They are the Italy we have been making. Nico now, Nico is of the past. The Italy where sharpness worked itself out in hopeless irony. Only Bernardo suggests a possible future, by which I mean a desirable future. I expect that seems silly to you, but Bernardo is serious. He has ideals.'

On an impulse I told him about the Caravaggio Christ I had met in the *osteria*. He nodded, slowly, deliberately.

'And yet they see destruction as the only way forward,' he said. 'I am sure they are wrong. I hope they may change. As for Bernardo, well, there is of course, another aspect. Let's be frank. For us Italians the State has still only a dubious validity. Even I in my position can recognize that. So, we are thrown back on the family. If we can hold things steady then Nico can take on the responsibility as head of the family. He will grow into an admirable Governor of the Bank, cynical and shrewd. But if everything turns out differently, then the family will need Bernardo. They will need him in the position he seeks. So I am comparatively happy to see him where he is. And anyway I respect his convictions.'

43

May 9 This journal I am keeping continues to surprise me. I have just read over what I wrote yesterday about my strange day ending in my inconclusive visit to Corrado, and apart from the fact that I surprise myself by the act of doing what I do—bothering to record it at all, that is—I have a suspicion that I am always just missing the point. It never is exactly as I have put it down.

All my life I have resembled a man caught in a game of blind man's buff, permanently masked.

Sandro telephoned in great agitation. Bernardo has disappeared. He didn't dare tell his father, and as for the Security men, there was such a mixture of violence and untrustworthiness . . . he just didn't know whether he dare commit himself to mentioning it to them . . . no, he was telephoning from a *caffè* of course . . . the thing was, could he and Nico come round to see me?

I consented; how I am being drawn into things.

Afterwards I sat on my little terrace and watched the windows across the courtyard. My American suicidal writer lay on his bed—I could see a foot pointing to the ceiling. The strains of jazz drifted from his open window; an old music, the plangent wail of Bix Beiderbecke's trumpet, striking a note of curiously innocent, because entirely personal and unsocial, despair. But from another window I saw the flash of binoculars, and knew I was their target, which was absurd of course.

I let my nephews in, Sandro in soft high-necked lambswool jersey and linen trousers, both the colour of a pale canary, and Nico in dark suit and spotted business tie. Sandro was nervous. He moved about touching things, his hands unable to rest; and he talked in a quick gentle voice about my possessions.

'It's worse than I told you on the telephone,' he said. 'I've got in the habit of not talking on the telephone. Because at the villa they're all bugged you know. It's making me neurotic. I'm even wondering if my bedroom is bugged too.'

I didn't tell him his ridiculous idea was ridiculous. On the contrary it seemed only too likely. Naturally the security people want to know everything that is said in the household of a leading politician; they never know what might not be useful. Besides, there were men of influence, in his own Party and elsewhere, who didn't like the direction in which Corrado was moving. They would be happy to find any means of thwarting him. Of course the villa would be bugged and its telephones tapped. That is the world we live in.

Nico sat in a cane chair and crossed his legs. He said to Sandro, 'Stop it. Control yourself. We haven't yet told Uncle what it is. Uncle, Bernardo has indeed disappeared, but the day before yesterday, security men came to the villa looking for him. They would like to question him about his affiliations, they said. Because of Father they were being very discreet, but still . . . There are aspects of the PRR which are "disturbing"—their word. Bernardo was out at the time. So I asked if Father knew of their interest. They said, no, it was a different department, though actually he has overall responsibility in that area as I understand it. But it was clear that they didn't awfully care if he knew. Otherwise of course they wouldn't have come to the villa. That suggests . . .'

'Have you spoken of this to your father?'

Nico looked at me sharply.

'That's the curious thing. I tried to. I admit I approached it obliquely, but you know that's normal in conversation with him. He pretended not to understand. Well, you know Father—he just doesn't fail to understand. Anything. Words, implications, hidden significance—he has the most sensitive antennae. So, if he didn't understand, it was because he chose not to. And then, this is the other thing, Giovanni, his driver, who has been with Father for years, ten at least, is worried. He's seen too many unaccounted for faces, which he nevertheless recognizes now, on their route every morning. He says Father won't listen to him either. He says he's becoming a fatalist.'

'But why have you come to me?'

'Talk to Father. That's what we'd like you to do. We're aware of things moving under a dark surface, and we're frightened . . .'

Nico gave me a quick smile of excuse; the language was as hard for him to pardon as the emotion.

'I saw your father last night,' I said. 'I came out to the villa and spoke to him about Bernardo, as you asked me to, Sandro. He is comparatively happy, he said, about the boy. What more can I do?'

45

'But that was before all this.' Sandro's voice trembled; he was an actor lost behind a vast proscenium arch, remote from the audience, cast in the wrong play; hired for drawing-room comedy, thrown down on the Theban plain.

We went on talking a long time, though there was really nothing we could say that was of any purpose. To bend the metaphor we were all spectators of a drama we couldn't understand. Bernardo and Corrado were fish viewed in an aquarium; the fact that we had them under our eye, could track their movements, didn't help us to comprehend them, since their element was different. And it was probable they couldn't have explained themselves. I asked the boys if they had talked to their mother.

'She makes a virtue of not questioning Father,' Nico said. 'I don't know,' he said, turning the slim gold band of his wristwatch so that it caught the light, flashing messages of agitation, 'I have the terrible feeling some disaster is impending.'

'I had a terrible dream last night,' said Sandro. 'I was lying in bed, or rather on my bed, sweating and there was a great thud, a sickening weight on my chest and a bird sitting there. A great big bird, some kind of buzzard or kite, perhaps a vulture. It pressed hard on my chest and dragged its beak across my belly and then put its tail in my mouth so that I couldn't scream. I woke up shivering and the sweat running off me, and I was sick. Terribly sick, the way I sometimes was as a little boy. Do you think dreams have any meaning, Uncle?'

I knew they did but I could only give Sandro an empty gesture, spreading my hands wide. I got up and opened a window. A different, keener music was wafted to us.

May 10 Hot this morning with the promise of a grilling day. I was reluctant to get up, though I know of course that as the summer advances, the early morning and occasionally the late evening will become the only tolerable hours of the day. Now, I sit at my desk, doodling with this journal. There is no reason to go out, I could make coffee here, and yet I shall because suddenly, looking round the flat, I feel a yellow emptiness such as Guido once described to me in a lucid moment, early in his

46

confinement. I can hear the American's typewriter, already moving fast.

4 p.m. I didn't answer the telephone I heard ringing as I left the apartment in the morning.

It wouldn't have made any difference if I had; except to my day.

At 8.33, as he was driving from Mass to his office, Corrado's car was ambushed. Five members of his bodyguard were shot. Automatic rifle fire. He himself was abducted.

I haven't known how to record this. I don't know why I am doing so, except that there is nothing else I can do. It is almost as if I commenced this journal eight days ago in preparation for this moment.

The telephone must have been alerting me to what had happened.

By chance I went for breakfast to a bar where I am not known. I remember that I sat there reading the paper, the *Corriere*, with a sort of abstracted attention. It was an article about the Historic Compromise and of course any of us could have written it in identical language; the language of meaningless authority.

A young American, in jeans and a torn shirt, came and sat at the next table, and began reading Henry James. *The Bostonians*. Occasionally he nodded his head as though James had got it right. He didn't look like the Bostonian friends I used to have.

My article said: '. . . in any case it is necessary to consider whether the realignment proposed by the Honourable Dusa is on the one hand dictated by parliamentary or electoral strategical requirements or represents on the other a veritable intellectual realization of new structures and the obligations these impose on ideology'.

(I record this, like this, which is how my mind's camera took it, simply because I am waiting; and if I do not sit and force myself to write, I find I walk about the apartment, which feels emptier and more frightening every minute, and more distorted, so that the only object that can retain actuality is the telephone.)

The American was joined by a girl. She had big dark eyes and dark hair and was very thin. I thought she was perhaps a dancer. She kept pulling at strands of her hair with vague

47

fingers. He looked at her for a minute and said, 'All right then, why don't you sit down? You're late, I was thinking you weren't coming.'

'You are silly,' she said—they spoke in English; she had a very soft voice—'why shouldn't I?'

He shrugged his shoulders. 'I could think of reasons,' he said.

'It was the police. They stopped the bus three times and turned it out. Three different sets of police of course.'

'What the hell,' he said. 'I mean, Christ, what the hell.'

'Apparently some politician's been kidnapped. I don't know. They take more notice when it's a politician.'

'Who cares, but you know, Judy, this country's crazy. It doesn't make sense like. The things that go on happening. Maybe we should think of getting out.'

'You can then. How the hell can I? I couldn't take Toots,' she said. 'She counts as an Italian citizen, remember. Her father would never let her—I'm stuck here, Ted. Things have to get much worse before he'd . . .'

I went on listening to their conversation, storing up their artless revelation of their private problems. No doubt they spoke frankly, not thinking that they might be understood, but perhaps not caring whether they were or not; they were clearly absorbed in each other. At one point, contradicting the vigour of her words, she extended long thin fingers and drew them lightly down his cheek that looked as if it had never felt a razor. I went on listening, storing it up, my memory on automatic pilot, occupying myself with what they said, to dull the awareness of the fish that had begun to swim deep down in my belly.

I told myself there were countless politicians. It couldn't be Corrado. There was no reason why it should be.

Only.

I knew it was.

And yet I continued to sit there and listen to them, and they were now talking about Henry James.

'You don't get the sense of evil in this one,' the boy said. 'It's a comedy of course, and yet you know it's potentially there. That's the marvellous thing about James. He knows where you find corruption, and he knows what it can do. He just knows. I tell you, it's kind of frightening.'

I said to myself, 'You ought to go and find out. You ought to telephone Elena.'

I did nothing of the kind. Instead I found that my hands were shaking and my legs felt watery. I called to the bar-boy and asked him to bring me a cognac. As I drank it, taking it down in two gulps—it wasn't very good brandy and it burnt my throat as it descended—I found myself wondering where my brother was, what he was feeling. I shuddered again.

Somehow I got home. I expected to find—I don't know what—some evidence of what had happened I suppose. But Maria was out of her lodge and there were no police. I took the lift up to my apartment, and again there was nobody waiting for me. I let myself in; the sun still streamed through the open window. Someone had put a parrot in its cage out on a balcony opposite.

The exact sameness of the apartment was terrifying.

I wished I had spoken to the young Americans. Or to somebody.

I turned on the wireless. Within minutes there was a newsflash which confirmed everything I had shrunk from knowing. It said too that the police were certain Corrado must still be hidden in the city.

That was it. Of course I telephoned the villa at once. A voice interrupted my call to say no calls were being received. I explained who I was.

'I'm sorry, *dottore*. It's in the hands of Security. Instructions are the lines are to be kept clear for information. I take it you don't have any to offer?'

I protested. In vain. Should I go out to the villa?

May 11   I was still wondering about that when the doorbell rang. To my astonishment it was Bella.

'You don't mind?' she said, 'that I've come here, I mean?'

I spread my hands wide.

'Father told me to—he's coming round himself.'

'Ettore? But why?'

49

'I'm shattered by it. They're so vile, these people. Will they kill him?'

I had been shrinking from the question which she brought out, after a pause, staccato. Her young directness brought me up against it. She threw herself down on a couch, her hair tumbling over the arm which supported her head. She was actually anxious to consider the question on its merits.

'We don't yet know who has him. Which group it is,' I said, 'Nobody's claimed credit yet, have they?'

'Credit?'

I had left the wireless on; waiting. It was playing Rossini. I wondered at the programme that had continued unchanged.

'You should see the police and army activity,' she said. 'There are road-blocks everywhere already. Have you managed to speak to my aunt or to any of my cousins?'

'No, it's impossible to put a call through.'

She lay back. Now this is what seems extremely odd to me, though perhaps simply the product of unusually heightened emotional receptivity—yet if I were the sort of person to be disgusted by myself, I would be disgusted—now, at this moment, in these circumstances, with my poor brother in the hands of people I knew would kill him, I was standing in the middle of a mottled marble floor, with a bearskin rug at my feet, and my beautiful tawny niece, aged twenty-two, stretched out on a divan and wearing a black shirt and cream coloured jeans, and I was lusting after her, wishing the clothes off and her naked on the rug. Her lips were slightly open.

Of course I in fact did nothing and we would anyway have been interrupted by her father, but that wasn't, I'm sure, the reason why I turned away, and went through to the kitchen for a bottle of brandy and some mineral water. I put them on a tray. The glasses clinked together as I added them to the load. Bella was now leaning forward. The moment had passed. Ettore arrived red-faced, sweating and puffing.

'We've got to do something,' he exclaimed, waving aside my offer of brandy. 'Let me tell you how I see things. There can be no doubt that very soon we shall receive a ransom demand.'

I nodded. 'The liberation of comrades either awaiting trial or

50

already convicted. Other things too doubtless, but that certainly.'

'And there is equally no doubt that the offer will be refused.'

Bella sat up straight.

'They couldn't. They couldn't possibly.'

She looked at me, candid eyes searching: 'They couldn't, could they?'

'Your father's right, they almost certainly will.'

And that was of course the case. There was doubtless an official policy, a decision long taken, in the abstract. Probably Corrado had approved it himself, though it would not have been in his nature to initiate the definitive and categorical negative. But the line would be: 'In no circumstances will we submit to blackmail. We shall not parley under duress.' How often had I heard the big words. Naturally there was reason behind them, naturally, the reason of logic and gesture. Othello's reason: 'Yet I must kill, else she'll deceive more men.' Not that the cases were strictly analogous. Desdemona after all was innocent, even though the play might have a sharper point were she to be played as one guilty. Yet it was the same specious logic.

To it one could oppose another reason: the reason of the feeling heart. They would be deaf to that; oh, deaf.

Later in the evening I was at last able to make contact with the villa. To my relief it was Nico I spoke to. Elena had gone to bed. 'She's distraught,' he said, 'desolate. Mind you she's been expecting it. Or something like it. She's been living on her nerves.'

'And your grandmother?' I said.

'All she did was nod when she was told. She hasn't spoken a word about it. She's years away. Look, Uncle, I can't now ask you about the hundred things we ought to discuss—I'm not of course going into the Bank tomorrow. But the complications . . . may Sandro and I come to see you in the morning, at eleven?'

I agreed of course and am waiting for them now. And sitting at my typewriter while I wait because, quite simply, what else is there to do?

Stacked against my desk, between the desk and the wall, are my notes and reference books for Augustus. Katrina is an inexpert duster. My indolence is all too clearly revealed. Only,

51

indolence is the effect, not the cause, of lack of belief, of the inability which has governed my life, ever to commit myself wholeheartedly to any course of action; except, some might say, a new style of dress.

Last night I sat alone after Ettore and Bella had gone, she kissing me as she left with what might have been impulsive desperation; who can tell? I held her body hard against mine a living instant. I don't think Ettore noticed anything.

I expect they have drugged Corrado. If he is still in Rome they must have drugged him.

The police will want to interview even me, which is absurd; I am a person of no significance. I listened to the American's typewriter, to the wireless, to an unending series of concerts, to moments of silence. Finally that was all that was left to me, an ever deepening and extending pool, the dark waters of which were rising with inexorable motion.

I went to bed and did not sleep, but lay in the dark. Corrado suffered from nightmares as a child. We shared a room and I have often been woken by his screams. He would find himself in an empty ruined temple in the half-death of summer noon, in a colonnade untrodden by sandalled feet; but somewhere in a place he could not identify, he would hear a shuffling. And the shuffling would creep round him, louder and closer.

The sea stretched away, boatless, in the distance.

May 14 I haven't written in my diary in three days. Three days of activity and hopelessness. There is still no news.

Sandro and Nico came round. Nico was holding himself in control, his *quattrocento* face frozen. Poor Sandro couldn't stop trembling. There had been no sign of Bernardo, nor word from him.

'We must be worried,' Nico said. 'It's unthinkable that he could have anything to do with the kidnapping. It must be sheer coincidence, because anything else is unthinkable. Only . . . I can't help thinking it.'

Sandro shook his head.

'As for mother,' Nico said, 'the doctor wanted to give her a sedative, but she refused. She's determined to be fully aware when anything happens. But nothing will happen just yet, will it? They'll stretch our nerves a bit first.'

'Yes,' I said, 'delay plays on the nerves.'

They asked me if I would go to Party Headquarters with them. They feared that if they went by themselves they would be brushed aside. I would know the ropes. I had a certain *gravitas*. Moreover, my experience meant that . . . and so on. They flattered me. What they said wasn't true. And Nico probably knew this. Still, how could I oppose them? Certainly if they went by themselves they would be received with sympathy but little more; they would be shunted off to a ward of consolation. They would see nobody who mattered; nobody like Schicchi or Donati.

At first it seemed as if I would have no more success. My telephone calls were vain. I met with wooden clerkly insolence. Corrado's case was, they said, reserved. That was that. Besides, identification would be necessary before there could be any discussion even on the telephone; I had no idea how many cranks telephoned every half-hour. I repeated that all I sought was the making of an appointment with Signor Schicchi. The Honourable Schicchi was giving no interviews.

'This is not an interview, you dolt,' I said. 'I am Dr Raimundo Dusa, brother to Corrado and formerly First Secretary in the Washington Embassy . . .'

'One moment I will transfer you . . .'

But not of course to the top . . . oh no, that came later, after long silences, silences as profound as that of the morgue, three transfers to dusty offices and the eventual mediation of Carlo Poggi, old friend of the family and protégé of Corrado, to whom I had been denied access half an hour previously . . .

'It will be difficult, *dottore*,' he said. 'You can hardly imagine how little weight I carry here today, with Corrado gone. My consequence has shrunk. I have already lost one secretary. I tell you, it is macabre. Even I who know the intimacies of the maze, am astonished at how quickly I am made to feel my altered position, my impotence. Nevertheless . . .'

At last our combined persistence achieved the promise of ten minutes with Gianni Schicchi at half-past four.

Before then, however, we had a visit from the Security

Branch. The officer was suave, affecting surprise at finding Nico and Sandro there. He commiserated first about Corrado. That wasn't the purpose of his visit. He realized that in the circumstances it was assuredly embarrassing and painful; nevertheless duty was duty. He was conducting enquiries into Bernardo's disappearance. Naturally he realized that Bernardo had friends who were more likely than I . . . nevertheless there was always the possibility, besides which of course there were those among his friends whom they would be anxious to lay hands on also; I would understand that, and also the intricacies and delicacies of such an inquiry . . .

As he spoke, one of his men examined my bookshelves, while the other, a Sardinian, and probably illiterate, picked his nose.

'No,' I said, 'Bernardo has never confided in me. It is in the highest degree unlikely that I should be able to assist you.'

'Quite so. Still you must agree the coincidence is alarming.'

'Coincidence is merely coincidence, nothing more unless you can provide connection.'

'Quite so. He's a silly young man. But we find unfortunately that so many, often of good backgrounds, are in the same condition. You may not be aware of it, but one of those we arrested after the May Day riots was a close confederate of your nephew's.'

Friends become confederates when they enter official records.

The officer moved fat well-manicured hands softly about as he spoke. He sat down in a Directoire chair and folded them on his soft lap. There was a long noon-time silence. Sasha came and jumped on my knees and I ran my finger under the line of his jaw.

'Confederates,' the officer purred. 'In the end, you understand, police work—and I'm not ashamed to confess that my work is essentially police work—police work is really a matter of establishing connections'—the Bari accent gave a softening lisp to his sibilants—'just that. For example, *dottore*, you are accustomed to drink in the Osteria del Lupo, isn't that true?'

'Yes.'

'Well then, would you be so kind as to take a look at these photographs? Tell me if you recognize any of them . . .'

I felt myself standing on the edge of a marsh, with a keen breeze blowing the methanic vapours towards me. All my life I have preferred to remain on the sidelines, the detached observer, resistant to any commitment; an attitude long expressed in my clothes. But I glanced down at the grey cardigan I was wearing, with a cigarette burn in the right-hand pocket, and at the flannel trousers baggy at the knee. I was still in carpet slippers. I said to Sandro, 'Be a dear boy, go to my desk and bring me a cigar.'

The third photograph showed me the Caravaggio Christ.

I shuffled through them.

'I've never had a memory for faces,' I said. 'I recognize no one. It's unfortunate, but that's how it is. Actually, I've often been accused even of cutting old friends if I should meet them unexpectedly in the street.' I don't understand why I replied in that way. Eventually, whether persuaded or not, they departed. I couldn't feel happy about the interview. I couldn't feel happy. We sat down to wait. The telephone remained silent.

I have known Gianni Schicchi since we were students. He was then a slight and fiery boy, with deep brown eyes, big eyes of a visionary, and a lock of hair that fell over the side of his face. He was full of passion, the only son of a mother who adored him. What had happened to the father? I don't remember but I have a faint iridescent impression, like one of those English water-colours of the Norwich School, indeterminate but evocative, persistent in the memory like the fusty smell of an attic explored in childhood, that he had been in some way disreputable. Certainly Gianni never spoke of him. Gianni's mother had hoped the boy would become a priest and for a long time he had thought of himself as having a vocation. He had been disappointed of that, but had later associated himself with an order of lay brothers, concerned with what would now be called social work. When he first entered politics many distrusted him because of this; he was regarded as a crypto-socialist. That was never the case; his devotion to his mother, which was, I'm sure, genuine, made such a development impossible. And in those days socialism was still generally atheistic, while Gianni's religious devotion amounted to zeal.

55

He came from Florence; I have never been easy with Florentines.

Corrado once called Gianni the evil genius of the Party. Of course that was in a private conversation, he knew I wouldn't repeat it, and indeed this is the first time I have done so. Gianni had moved a long way to the Right over the years. He is a Cold War man. Yet I've never heard it suggested that he takes money from the CIA like so many of our politicians. Something harder even than money has corrupted Gianni. He has lost faith in humanity, and with this, his ideal of service has rotted. Gianni likes the feel of power. I remember in Washington once, when he was Foreign Secretary, seeing him stamp on a wasp. I remember the upward tilt of the corners of his mouth as the insect squelched under his heel.

He received us in the office of the Party Secretary, though he has never held that position.

'I am desolate, Raimundo,' he said.

Something had happened to his voice. Gianni had made his name first as an orator, a little man with a baritone voice of liquid purity. It had been an astonishing voice, but what came across the Louis Seize desk to me, isolated in a carved chair on an ocean of marble, some five feet back from the desk, was a cancerous rasp. Yet Gianni had put on flesh and colour. It was a comedy, his proclamation of desolation.

'I will serve you however I can. I have already conveyed my commiserations, sentiments that spring from the heart, I need hardly say, to your revered mother.' He widened his hawk's eye in Nico's direction.

'All we can do is wait.' His hand folded on a lump of carved marble that rested on the top of some files of papers. 'And', he gave a little cough, 'pray. Pray fervently. His Holiness', he crossed himself, 'has intimated that he will celebrate a special Mass of Intercession.'

In the prolonged silence only a twitch in his left cheek disturbed the holy effulgence of his expression.

'What we would like', I said, 'to be assured of is that no definite decisions have yet been taken. In particular we are anxious that any existent policy, such for example as one which might be held to preclude parley with terrorists or the discussion

56

in the fullest and frankest terms of any ransom demands, be at the very least held in abeyance and considered open to revision.'

I had summoned up official memories, striving to attain the bland tone which was necessary, I felt certain, if our request was to be taken seriously. I had explained this to Nico and Sandro. There was no hope of success if we could not discuss matters in that dead tone which would permit further discussion.

'One breath of human sympathy,' I said, 'and they will take fright.'

If I could have appealed to the spirit of the Resistance! But Gianni had spent the war years working in the Vatican Library and, as for me, from 1943–5 I had written a novel. It was set in Naples in the 1790s and told of the coming of the French and the Bourbon reaction. It constituted my personal elaboration of liberal values and provided no basis of shared experience from which I might appeal to Gianni's sentiment.

The room was too hot. The electric fan had broken down. Some Party Secretary had installed it perhaps as an illustration of modernity. Certainly it hung oddly amidst the Baroque splendours, though itself outmoded of course when compared to air conditioning. Gianni passed a dark-blue handkerchief across his brow. He had always sweated freely, unlike Corrado and myself, accustomed in boyhood to the grilling heat of the Mezzogiorno.

So, having no other choice, I spoke in official accents.

Gianni smiled, a pike's grin. I was aware of Sandro tensing himself, horrified by the realization that Gianni could still smile. But why not? Others' problems offer us opportunities.

Gianni said, 'Raimundo, you must not think I do not feel for you and for the family. And, even more, I know what Corrado has meant for the Party. Three men made this great Party of ours: de Gasperi,' (he crossed himself) 'Corrado,' (was he on the point of repeating the action?) 'and myself. Do you think I don't at this moment feel my isolation, and feel that it is awful? But it is nevertheless our duty to appraise the situation.'

'I would be grateful if you could let me have any information which has not been released. Do you, for example, yet know just who is responsible?'

'There can be no doubt. It is the PRR.'

He smiled again; the smile of a pastrycook who takes his tarts from the oven and sees that they have risen to exactly the right degree.

'I do not', he said, 'have to elaborate to you the complications and embarrassments that may ensue from that fact. Do you know, six months ago, I advised your brother to send the young man to New York. There was an opening there, a delegation to which he could have been quite harmlessly attached. And who knows, the experience might have had a beneficial effect in itself. If only he had taken my advice. But of course this knowledge only discloses to us a deeper and more pertinent question. Who, ultimately, backs the PRR? Whence do they derive? Are they in reality of the Left or are they rather, as some would have us believe, of the extreme Right? Are they self-conscious or deluded? Myself, I have my opinions. But we must wait. We must temporize, since the correct answer to the query is of an importance quite incalculable.'

'And the ransom demand? When it comes? What response will be offered?'

'When it comes, we must consider it in all its implications, with sympathy and resolution, and then act with the dignity that is in accordance with the necessity imposed by the correct political strategy.'

He rose and walked—fat-bottomed these days—to the window. He stood a moment with his back to us, looking on the *piazza*. Over his shoulder I could see a bus-load of tourists debouch and troop, with their aquarium look, into the Jesuit Church.

'God does not grant us all the opportunity of martyrdom,' said Gianni Schicchi.

Sandro leapt to his feet. 'But we are not', he cried, 'talking of martyrdom, we are talking of humanity.'

Gianni turned. His tongue flickered like a serpent's fork.

'It is good to be reminded that the young can be generous,' he said. 'Pray, dear boy, that the same spirit animates your contemporaries who hold your father.'

Carlo Poggi was waiting for us in an antechamber.

'Let us have some coffee,' he said. 'I can now at last tell you

58

how the position truly is.'

There was, he explained, a document. It recorded the decision of the Grand Committee of the Party. In the event of the kidnapping of one of their members, the others undertook in no circumstances to negotiate with the putative kidnappers. On the contrary, these were to be pursued merely as common criminals. Any appeals, purporting to come from the prisoner, were to be discredited. They would be denounced as drug-induced, the result of brain-washing.

The document was signed, in holograph, by all the members of the Committee, including of course Corrado.

'It reads', said Carlo, 'as though he drew it up.'

'I will be surprised', he said, replacing the coffee-cups on the little tin tray so that they concealed the cross with which it was marked, 'if they don't adhere to it. I'm sorry to have to say this, really sorry, but as your uncle here will recognize, apart from the grand question of Reason of State, there are elements here who are less than heart-broken by what has happened. The policy which your father and I have been driving through does not command universal support. Even many of those who back it do so with resentment, not conviction. Corrado was finding himself lonely, even here.'

As we left the building, Nico put his arm round Sandro's shoulders. I said, 'There's a press photographer there.'

The picture was in next morning's *Messagero*. Nico's face is blurred and in shadow, but Sandro is clearly enough in tears; at the same time he resembles Leonardo's John the Baptist. 'No comfort for Dusa's children' says the caption. Nico telephoned me this morning; it might do some good perhaps.

'If that's the opinion of the Party, the policy, just as that bastard Schicchi indicated, then the only thing that can move them is public opinion. And we need sentiment to move that. Sandro in tears is a beginning.'

There is a hard elegance emerging in Nico.

Meanwhile, there is still nothing; the silence is Acheronic. The newspapers of course are full of speculation. They repeat the suggestion that Corrado is being held in the city. It seems this is the official line, but is it merely maintained to allay opinion? After all, the corollary is that if he is still in the city,

59

then the police and *carabinieri*, 'working with their customary assiduous efficiency', as the journals have it, will eventually hit upon the PRR's Headquarters and place of concealment. I wish I could believe it. But while such a belief is general it is easy for the authorities to refuse to negotiate.

Not that any offer has yet been made by the kidnappers. After their first paean of triumph, the silence is worrying. It is like waiting, beleaguered, for plague to reach the city. Perhaps there are internal dissensions. That is my only hope. And then it frightens me in its turn. If they fall out with each other they will panic. Prisoners are never safe when their guards panic.

I have spent hours walking the streets, not because I hope for anything, but because it is an alternative to sitting at home, a substitute for action and a refuge; at least the telephone will not be so insistently dumb in the streets.

Yesterday in the afternoon I walked through Parioli, absurdly scanning the shuttered villas, as if one of them would suddenly reveal that it held my brother. But the half-doors opened and fat women emerged with poodles. I sat in *caffès* and watched small businessmen, parodies of my dear Ettore, cheat despair by activity, ice-cream and conversation. A woman with an apricot-coloured poodle wearing a ribbon of yellow silk leant over and set it in the chair opposite and fed it walnut cake; her fat lips blubbered endearments. An Englishman with a worn and lined face that remained obstinately young—something about the wide eyes and the too red, fleshy lips, the mouth that was never quite shut—and with the long swept back hair of the Public Schools, came in with a bundle of books and set them down loosely (so that one of them slipped to the floor) and fetched himself three glasses of brandy from the bar, and came back, sat down, and drank them. He pulled a book from the pile and began to read; it was a battered Penguin copy of *Under the Volcano*; a book, as it happened, which I myself read, actually in Mexico City, when I was Second Secretary there, and which then seemed to me surrealistically Anglo-Saxon and self-indulgent. That refrain 'they are losing the Battle of the Ebro'; why not admit that it was a battle not worth fighting in a dishonest war?

When I saw him reading this, I revolted. I asked for a *gettone* and called Elena. I proposed that I come—'as usual', I said—for lunch on Sunday. She thanked me.

I thought to myself as I sat down, 'If we had this Anglo-Saxon obsession with alcohol and self-destruction, which makes of life such a private affair, none of this would have happened.'

The afternoon died on me in that *caffè* in Parioli when a little man came in. He wore a faded grey suit with a faded grey stripe. His shoes were polished but the leather was cracking across the uppers and his tie was a little frayed. A long knife-scar ran down his left cheek. He made no attempt to summon the waiter and, when one came to serve him, didn't look at him as he asked for a glass of mineral water. He glanced at the young Englishman who was drinking more brandy and drumming with long yellowed fingers on the table. The little man's lip twitched and he turned his head towards me.

'Good evening, *dottore*,' he said.

For another moment I still failed to know him; yet he spread disillusion about him like a marsh gas, decay like a Fascist housing scheme; and he had the petulant lips of a spoiled priest.

'I've been saying to myself all day,' he said, 'since I saw the photograph of you with your nephews in the paper, that we would meet again. Then when I was passing and saw you sitting here, not a bit changed, still with that look of a certain superiority, I knew it was time. I've had this sort of coincidence happen to me often.' He picked up his glass and sipped the mineral water; the level in the glass scarcely fell. 'You can imagine,' he said, 'I've got mixed feelings about what's going on. I warned your brother over thirty years ago, remember. Or maybe you preferred not to know. They were about to hang me. That's the sort of thing you've always preferred to be able to ignore, isn't it, *dottore*? As a matter of fact they did hang me; only it didn't take, and I lived. So here I am still.'

It was the lisping Barese accent that brought back the past: Enzo Fuscolo, once my father's clerk and protégé, the brilliant young man from the poor part of town.

'You can't,' I said, 'imagine I want to talk to you. I've been thinking you dead since 1945.'

He tittered; a little sound, light as a feather, airy as a madhouse.

'But I've kept in touch, you know. Eventually Corrado found me useful. Politicians sometimes need unsavoury intermediaries. I don't mind telling you I had a hard time of it in the years just after the war. Do you know, I worked as a dishwasher for a bit? Then I got a job as a clerk with a transport company. I only retired from it last year.'

His treachery had early destroyed my father, nearly involved us all in ruin, and he took another sip, smaller than a finch's sip, from his mineral water.

'And if you ask me,' he said, 'Corrado has been seeking this. One way or another. Either his policy has been, as it certainly has been, wrong in conception and execution, so that it has provoked what has happened; or he has more simply desired martyrdom. They could do with a good martyr.'

The titter again, the little titter of the choir school that had stayed with him through treachery, sentence of death and long neglect. It was the partisans of course had tried to hang him, stringing him up from the lintel of my father's house (which had been my maternal grandfather's before) in a Sabine village.

'A political movement that is the political wing of the Church militant and they don't have a martyr. At least we provided Matteoti for the Socialists.'

He put his hand in his pocket and withdrew a little crumpled brown paper bag and took a currant from it, a single slightly yellowish squidgy currant with the body of a well-fed insect, and popped it in his mouth.

'You realize, don't you, that he's had it?'

'Yes.'

'So?' He held up the copy of the *Messagero*.

(I was finding that though I despised him, and had cause to wish him nothing but ill, he was yet someone I could converse with; we were intimate with the knowledge of shared guilt. The thought bred leeches on my body.)

'Yes,' I said again, hearing my voice sleepy. I lit a cigar, gesture against the imposition of intimacy. 'Of course you are right. He is doomed. But you should also realize that one is compelled to go through the ceremonies, even without hope, because it is only by doing so that one gives hope a chance of birth. By all the rules, by all we have reason to expect, Corrado is a dead man already. Only he still breathes. What did you feel when they put the rope round your neck?'

He smirked. The memory pleased him. It is not after all everyone who merits a hanging. 'I felt important. I had done my duty.'

Had the second life he was vouchsafed been an anti-climax, a long parade of bathos?

'You may be hoping,' he said, 'at this very moment that our encounter is not accidental. After all,' he popped another currant in his mouth and his little tongue flickered again as he glanced at the Englishman who was sinking lower in his chair, his shoulders deep-hunched, 'you may be wondering—and why not?—whether Corrado's captors are really and truly of the Left or whether they are either agents provocateurs, or are being used? Being used. And do you know, you are in good company. Some of them themselves, the more intelligent and thoughtful, must be pondering that question. It keeps them awake at night.'

I was the fish he played and I couldn't tell whether he desired anything more than to tug the hook and twist it in my mouth.

'Every society', he said, 'is built on death. So they could be making a mistake. They might do better to release him. But first, either way, he must be humiliated. That's axiomatic, thoroughly stripped of dignity and made to cry. To cry publicly. He cannot be allowed to emerge as a hero.'

I nodded dumbly. Enzo Fuscolo was shedding years as he spoke; his own humiliations were withering; the years as a humble transport clerk shrivelled before me.

'You say Corrado found you useful?'

A faint pink touched his grey cheek, like the very last touch of a watery November sun on a crumbling and dirty wall.

'There are always times', he said, 'when it is necessary to make secret contact with your enemies. Old friends make the best intermediaries; there is less to be explained between them. I don't claim much for myself. My own career was broken in two. But it was a career.'

He slipped a card from his breast pocket and placed it before me.

'If I can be of service . . .'

He had drunk perhaps an inch of his mineral water.

The Englishman lurched to his feet, again spilling his book. I could hear him at the *cassa*, demanding three Stocks, doubles. I wondered if he would get home. I picked up his book . . . a line of Spanish caught my eye: *los manos de Orlac*, a murderer's hands . . .

Night had fallen by the time I left the bar where I had indeed had nothing but a *cappuccino* and a cheese sandwich. The air was heavy with flowers in the streets, it was an evening for enjoyment, and the pavement *caffès* in the *viale* had no empty tables. Here and there children, still allowed up by indulgent parents, darted to and fro between the tables, calling for ices. Motorbikes roared and left behind faint nostalgic echoes. I walked among the crowds. Would I have halted everything still, or stifled animation, if I had called out who I was? Did they care? They whom, in a sense, Corrado had made possible.

But that was an empty rhetorical way of looking at things.

It yet contained truth.

My apartment resembled a family vault. I laid my clothes across a chair or hung them up with the neatness and care of an old dandy who can no longer afford a valet. But I had always found it distasteful to have male servants. For some years, when I first lived in an apartment of my own, Maria used to come over from my mother's several times a week to tend to my clothes.

I got into bed, hearing little noises of the summer night.

Of course I couldn't sleep. I could not accept. That was what, at last, when I had thought myself wholly acquiescent, I had come up against. Because it wasn't for me, but for my brother. I turned on my face and saw him as a child. I turned on my back and heard Guido's voice from the corner of the room. I sat up, pulling my long, thinned, old man's legs beneath me, hugging my knees and groaning as I have always imagined the old in asylums groan.

A cry of pain or shame disturbed me. Did it come from without or from my own breast?

I rose and padded through the apartment exploring its dim and vacant recesses. Sasha was out; it was hard to be more alone; only elsewhere in the building countless slept. And all over the city.

A solitary light across the courtyard attracted me. The American's.

A figure appeared at the window, a younger figure than the American's and slimmer, with an aureole of curls framing an oval face. I sensed rather than truly saw his nakedness. The American approached from behind, laid an arm around the shoulder and drew the boy away from the window, drew him downwards and out of sight. I could reconstruct all that had gone before, what was to come, the enaction on the cheap divan, the movement from grey to dark purple back to grey.

I went out into the night. In fact it had passed its nadir. The smell of blossom wafting from the Gardens of the Palazzo Colonna now, for a moment, made itself felt in the city, so briefly almost free of traffic. My feet led me, as though I was recovering the American's tracks, to a little bar off the Via del Tritone, where all through the night, the despairing mingled with the curious and the mercenary. Once, years back, for a few months of hollow insomnia, I had found myself there once or twice a week, rarely advancing to the action which simultaneously expressed a wild hope and self-contempt.

There is no more hopeless act than that in which, at the moment of climax, you cannot look into your lover's eyes.

I ordered a glass of beer and leant against the bar. My young Englishman from Parioli had found his way down here to these lower depths, still reading his novel, still drinking brandy, but now wearing an old Army greatcoat. It hung open, the skirts trailing on the floor. He closed the book and lit a cigarette, having to snap the lighter two or three times before succeeding. His blue eyes were blood-flecked. Except for a couple of furtive Arabs there was no one else in the bar.

Corrado could never have come to a place like this. Once, when we were all young, Guido proposed that Corrado should be made to see life, as, somewhat naively perhaps, he called what he might be intending to offer.

'You can't get it all from books,' he said.

'If I want to know something like that—and I can't see why I should—I ask my priest,' Corrado replied. How much of a joke was that?

But a politician couldn't continue to function if he admitted the sharpness of despair; they were wise to deny themselves that. Even the most conservative of them believes that somehow the fabric can hold together; and Corrado, however ultimately sceptical, was committed also to a belief in the possibility of amelioration; and such a belief excludes this sort of bar.

Was . . . was committed . . . was?

Can he still exclude the despair Guido confessed far more fully than I? Compared to Guido's situation this bar is nothing but a border town; a customs post where you are searched and asked to declare whether your luggage contains even the smallest particle of that drug called Hope.

May 15 They have released a photograph of Corrado, posed against a background which features a copy of yesterday's *Messagero*. Proof that he is still alive, which of course one had not yet begun to doubt. They have stripped him down to a singlet, he who has never been seen in public without a tie. His face has twisted itself into a mask of passivity and endurance; but if you did not know his situation you might read irony in the twist of the mouth.

The manner of his dress emphasizes his helplessness; and emphasizes also that he has been reduced to his essence; the trappings stripped off.

What surprises after the initial horror has been absorbed is that his kidnappers are not apparently the PRR, but a group nobody seems to have heard of, calling themselves the 'Partisans of the Proletariat'. Cynically, I don't feel it can make much difference who holds him; they are all the same moral *canaille*. Experts (a concept I profoundly distrust) speaking on the wireless in their most instant capacity, have with their fullest Nescafé sagacity, propounded the theory that the PDP is a splinter group of the PRR, itself of course the offshoot of some acronym I can't recall.

They proclaim that they are proceeding with the trial of Corrado before a 'People's Court'. They are too ignorant of history, even recent history, to know that the term stinks.

He will be charged with crimes against the Italian People, more of whom went away on holiday last year than ever before, fewer of whom die as infants than ever before, fewer of whom are in serious want than ever before.

It is too silly; and I suppose will mean death.

But first of course their comedy, and we on our part can't give up. Nico came to see me. He has organized a rally, without, naturally, any support or assistance from the Party hierarchy. The speakers, who will include Manbola, the dissident Communist, will demand that the Government offers to negotiate with the kidnappers. Nico wanted me to speak. I demurred.

'We can't', I said, 'make it too much a family affair. It has to go beyond the family. One speaker to represent us, and it must be a son. You, my dear Nico, since I can't imagine our dear Sandro could carry it off.'

'I was afraid you would say that. It's a pity I'm no actor. My manner shows—I'm always being told—my social and hence political prejudices only too clearly. A friend once told me I spoke in public with a sneer and a sniff. And I feel it's essential we strike a popular note.'

'Well,' I said, 'an old dandy like me . . .'

I left the sentence finished only by a shrug of the shoulders. The rally is for Sunday morning, ten o'clock in the Piazza dei Santi Apostoli, just down the road.

'I'll sit on the platform,' I said, 'but I won't speak. It would not be beneficial. However, have you got Carlo Poggi?'

'I haven't been able to reach him.'

'Leave him to me. I'll oblige him to speak.'

He nodded and set off for his office. He has decided to resume work as usual. He is of course quite right. What else can he do? And work serves as an anodyne. All the same I wished he could have stayed. The apartment rang with emptiness as the lift descended.

Later in the morning when I was on the point of going out, thinking I might stroll down to Navona for coffee, pretending to myself I might stop in an *antiquaire* on the way, the telephone rang. It was an American journalist, one I had known in Washington. The next phase of the campaign beginning. Could we meet?

'Naturally, but I doubt if I can be of any service. But, as you say, we can meet. Would you like to come round here?'

He was called Ed Mangan, a lean rangy type such as one once thought quintessentially American, now undoubtedly, like myself, a little out of date. He had once had a reputation as a roving correspondent, the man who could bring back the good, odd-angled story. 'No stability though', editors used to say and many of them viewed his reports with almost as much distrust as professional diplomats automatically did. Like so many Americans of his generation and stamp, he ran through wives, jobs and bottles with the certainty born of that American affluence, that there was always a fresh supply available from the same stock. He had none of our European frugality. I used to find that attractive. When I last met him, his fourth wife, an Israeli photographer, had just left him. (Or was she his fifth?) At any rate her complaint that she was tired of his Errol Flynn heroics had curiously hurt him. It is of course depressing for a man in his fifties to discover that a girl half his age regards him as insufficiently adult. But once he would have dismissed her as a prig.

He was uncomfortable in my apartment.

'Let me take you out to lunch. You know I've always been a guy for public places, Ray.'

'You're looking good,' he said, as we settled ourselves at a table in the little restaurant in the Piazza dei Santi Apostoli, outside which, on Sunday, Nico would plead for his father's life. Like so many journalists, Ed has always tended to be unthinking in his observations. He has never really looked at people; close examination discourages articulacy.

'I guess you're not getting far with that skunk Schicchi,' he said.

'What sort of thing are you hoping to write, Ed?'

'I'm not filing anything just now. I'm working for a news magazine these days, not a daily. It's a heavy piece I'll be writing when I write one. That's why I'm digging deep.'

'Ah,' I said, 'the lamb is always very good here.'

He waved aside the bottle of Barolo the white-haired old waiter had brought.

'Should have told you, Ray, I'm on the wagon these days. How do I see it? I'd like to think Schicchi fixed it. You know, my views have veered a bit recent years. Well, you can't stand stuck in the same place. I'm a 'forties man of course, and I started in full reaction to 1930s Ivy League New Deal Socialism and all that shit. I really thought Richard Nixon had it right about Alger Hiss. Matter of fact, I still do. Hiss was a motherfucker if ever there was one. So was Nixon of course. But that's not the point, not any longer. It's not original to say that Vietnam opened my eyes. I came to see what the United States had come to stand for in the world. Not original at all. But who the hell prizes originality these days? We're through with all that shit too. But the way I see it, what we were legitimately trying to defend in the Forties and Fifties just isn't worth defending these days. The Free World's evaporated. I mean if we're engaging in dirty tricks to make the world safe for the Seven Sisters and ITT and John Connally—and there's a jerk if ever I saw one—well then include me out, as Sam said. We've got to move on, loosen up. Now I see this as a matter of principle and expediency. Combined. It's right and it's smart too. And that's unbeatable. And that's where I reckon your brother had got to also. You know, Ray, I used to think of him as just another stooge politician, but he's been covering ground, same as me. So if you ask me who fixed this, assuming for the moment it's a fix, then I'd say Schicchi. He's just the same sort of rat-fink as Hiss or Connally.'

I found I couldn't eat the lamb after the ravioli. My teeth shredded the meat but I couldn't swallow. Ed might have given up drink but when he got excited his eyes were still shot with bloody streaks.

I said, 'That's the sort of theory you journalists love to cook up. Gianni's not unhappy about this, but to think he could devise anything of this nature . . . no, no.'

'Maybe so, maybe so. We'll see. Now tell me, Ray, what about your brother's boy, Bernardo? What's the story there?'

It was foolish of me not to have anticipated this. I fell back on a plea of ignorance.

'Aw, come off it, Ray,' he said. 'You've got me all wrong, you're reading the wrong story. Listen, I'm not primarily interested in getting a story right now. I'm interested in something bigger. A deal. I estimate there's just the basis of a deal. Look, these kids who have your brother, they're

69

approachable. And your nephew's right there, ready to make the first move. Hell, listen, if we can get it over to them that there's the basis of a deal, that'll get them off the hook. You don't think they really want to have to kill Corrado, do you?'

'Yes,' I said, 'I think they do. I think they're crazy enough to like the idea.'

'Shit,' he said, 'straight from the shithouse, that. Whatever else they may be, these kids are idealists.'

'Yes,' I said, pouring myself a glass of wine, 'with all the frightening purity of the idealist.'

'Look,' he said, 'if we could get a message through to your brother, telling him to retract, publicly, make a confession of error, that would put them on the spot, wouldn't it? It would place them on the same side. And boy, these kids needs a leader.'

I was lost. My sort of logic couldn't move, couldn't breathe, in this world.

'Anyway,' I said, 'as far as I know Bernardo has just vanished.'

'Sure, he's gone to ground. What else could the kid do? Boy, that kid's been living impaled. Impaled.'

He forked a mountain of green salad into his mouth. A huge benevolent herbivore.

I said, 'It's been put to me, Ed, that the group who hold Corrado are a front for a right-wing organization. I don't mean your suggestion about Gianni Schicchi, which I take as a joke, however much you'd like to think it true . . . what's your reaction to that?'

'Hell, there's plenty of these goddam Fascists want your brother out of the way. Sure. And they're not crying in the streets now, you can bet on that. All the same, the idea's balls. These kids are smart. They're not going to be fooled by some half-assed guy in a black shirt. No, no, they're what they say they are, pure idealists, and the only hope there is of saving your brother, is to persuade him to join them, to become their leader. Hell, there's good precedent for it.'

'There is?'

'Sure. You ever study any English history?'

'Of course, an Anglophile like me . . .'

'Well, you recall the story of young Richard II and the Peasants' Revolt.'

'Yes, but I'm astonished you do.'

'My day, we learned something at Princeton. I'll be your leader, he said. Remember? That's what we've got to get across. That's the message. It'll defuse the situation.'

I crumbled bread.

'A bit subtle, don't you think? And, as I recall the story, the boy king tricked them.'

'Hell,' said Ed, 'history doesn't have to repeat itself that close.'

The idea was mad. That was certain. Yet, as I said to Nico later in the afternoon when I called on him at his bank, we were in a position where sanity didn't promise to achieve much. I was, though, in the wrong surroundings in which to advocate madness. Nico's office (which he shared with two other young executives whom he had asked to leave us alone together for a moment) was a monument to the bad taste of the first decade of the century. No doubt it all represented money. A Cupid on the cornice had folded his wings over his eyes, as though denying the mercenary nature of whatever was transacted there—an attitude which invaded his world also of course. The furniture was heavy, dark, mahogany, and oppressive; full of sharp edges. You could hear, in a dull rhythm, the traffic from the Corso below.

Nico looked at home there. I could see him growing harder, darker, more stick-like as the years passed; more respectable too, like the furniture. It was difficult to believe what Bella had said, that he wrote poetry.

But then he said, 'Living and working here I am learning the limits of sanity. Some day, Uncle, I should like you to take me to see my Uncle Guido. Or at least his asylum. I confess though I don't entirely follow the mechanics of your American friend's plan.'

'I don't think he has reached that stage. Nothing concrete. He was in a very excited condition. Let me explain. Here's a man who has devoted all his life to spurious action and intense but fabricated emotion. He has been dominated by instant Romance, urgent politics, deadlines and bourbon. Now, in the

71

middle of the way, he has his revelation; his encounter with his own particular leopard. He stops drinking. His political beliefs change direction so abruptly that you might speak in terms of a religious conversion. What's the result? A buoyancy. The sudden conviction that everything is possible. I'm afraid I can't share it. Indeed I don't know why I have troubled you with his speculations.'

Nico shifted pens on his desk; old-fashioned dip-pens with nibs that you replaced from time to time. I wondered where on earth you could still buy such things. Possibly the Bank had a store of them; possibly there was an ageless stationer's shop in the Vatican City that would still supply them.

'But do you think', Nico said slowly, 'that he may have some sort of scheme and that it could possibly have a chance of success?'

'No,' I said.

'And even if the answer was yes, could we possibly adopt such a scheme? Is Father's life worth preserving at that price? For it would be a price, wouldn't it? The price of integrity. His integrity and ours.'

There was an intolerable itching in my right calf. I leant forward and scratched under my trouser-leg. Nico sat and watched me. He frowned.

'He looks so terrible in that photograph, though. I wish to hell I knew. Mother is becoming hysterical. Suppressed hysteria of course. She has telephoned me three times today. She keeps saying we must do something and then crying out that of course she knows there is nothing to do. Do you know what I have found myself thinking? That I wished they would kill him without further delay. I am ashamed to confess such a wicked thought, but there it is. He would never forgive us if we tried to force him to do as your American suggests.'

'You can't', I said, 'be sure about that. You can never be sure of people's reactions. Even if he survives this, he'll emerge a different man. He has now had these days to look into his soul—we'll agree to call it that—he'll come through different. You see, he has been so busy for years, he can't have submitted himself to this sort of examination. And then he's so alone . . . though I imagine they never leave him physically alone . . . by

72

the way, I've got Carlo Poggi for you. He didn't want to speak . . . but he's going to . . .'

'Carlo didn't want to speak? Father made him.'

'And I imagine he's always resented it. You have to be a better man than politicians tend to be not to resent the man who helps you to rise. Besides, Carlo is convinced—though he didn't say so—that Corrado is doomed, that his policy is doomed, that all this will cause the Party to swing back to the Right, and he has remembered that he is almost fifty-five. But I persuaded him that the appearance of loyalty would still be a future service to him. "Assume a virtue if you have it not", I said to him.'

Nico rose and walked to the bookshelves. For a moment he stood there, his elegant back turned towards me, his long manicured fingers playing lightly on the calf-bound volumes of Annual Reports. Shadows fell across his face—several of the bulbs in the electrolier which, hanging from the centre of the ceiling, alone lit the room, had died and had not been replaced. Nico pulled a slim gold cigarette case from his pocket and lit a cigarette with a slim gold Cartier lighter.

'We can't', he said, 'have anything to do with a scheme of the sort that your friend seems to be proposing. I grant it's only embryonic and we don't know its shape, but look around, Uncle. Look at me where I stand. I laugh sometimes at the Bank, of course I do, and at times I resent it. I have my other life. I write poetry, I love my parents. Some day I shall have a wife and children. Meanwhile I have my enjoyments—that's not important. I don't have much respect for Father's Party. And the treatment we received from Schicchi hasn't encouraged respect to develop. All the same, I work here because I believe, among other reasons of course, that work of this sort has to be done and done properly. It's in its way a métier. Money has to be managed, and managed sensibly and honestly. That's all. But, as a corollary, this belief imposes a certain view of society—represents one too, of course, I can't deny that. So, apart from all other considerations, to try to initiate negotiations such as your friend has outlined, or to be party to such plans, would constitute a denial of everything that Father himself brought me up to believe in. I would be cheating him. Besides,' he looked me full in the face and smiled with a release of charm, 'I don't believe it could possibly work. Father would never do it . . .' (Was there a slight hesitation in his voice, or did I imagine it?) 'We should simply look fools.'

May 18 Today might have been written by a humorist. Voltaire perhaps, or more savagely, Swift.

Nico's rally in the morning was well attended but feebly conducted. It wasn't Nico's fault. Nobody on the platform, however, could do anything more than trot out stale rhetoric. I except Nico himself, of course, whose few words were from the heart. But they were drowned in the flood of dirty words the other speakers loosed.

After it, I said to him, 'You're not, I trust, too disappointed. The crowd was gratifying.'

'Oh yes,' he said, 'and a good deal of empty indignation was released, wasn't it? You were right, though, Uncle. They're not going to do anything for him. You know, I despise Carlo Poggi even more than I do Schicchi. Schicchi has at least his own game he's playing, and my father is not a pawn of course, but a piece he's still prepared to sacrifice for strategic advantage. There are after all times when one throws one's Queen, aren't there? Yes, there's a case for Schicchi, who perhaps genuinely believes that Father's policy is disastrous, and who anyway may hope to extract something from his martyrdom. But Poggi is nothing but a rat.'

A Cardinal, whom I didn't know—one of Roncalli's more eccentric appointments I should imagine—approached Nico and congratulated him on 'so fine a display of filial devotion'. I took Nico's arm and guided him out of the piazza, down a narrow lane and across the Corso to where he told me his car was parked.

'Sandro was in the crowd,' he said. 'He'll get home on his own. He'll be able to tell us how things felt down there. You always, I suppose, get a different impression there.'

Arrived at the villa, we found ourselves in a simulated normality. Elena was going through the motions of real life. Sunday lunch would be ready for us in twenty minutes, as though everything beyond the walls of the garden was an hallucination. She extended the same half-dead cheek to me in the same manner that spoke of distaste yielding to duty.

'How's mother?' I said.

'She will come down to lunch today. Maria is with her now. Only,' she said, 'it is ageing her this.'

'I am as ever grateful to you for the care you take of her.'

I went through into the drawing-room and found Ettore already there.

'Raimundo,' he said, 'you're back. How did it go? Myself, I couldn't face it. It will do no good anyway, we know that.'

He walked up and down the room as he spoke, taking quick puffs of his cigarette and stabbing it in my direction to emphasize his meaning. He kicked his legs out.

'Did you see Bella? She insisted on going. Accompanying Sandro. I tried to dissuade her, but no good. Girls nowadays. She's taking the business to heart. I had no idea she was so fond of Corrado. Of course she's an affectionate girl.'

'No,' I said, 'I didn't see her. There was a big crowd.'

'But no trouble, eh? No trouble?'

I shook my head.

'Thank God for that. You never can tell nowadays.'

He stubbed out his cigarette but not before lighting another from the butt.

'You see', he said, 'the state of my nerves. I thought I had stopped smoking. Raimundo, is there any hope? You've seen the politicians, haven't you? They're not going to do anything, are they?'

'No,' I said, 'they're not going to do anything.'

'I thought as much. Bastards, that's what they are, one and all, bastards. There's only one thing left then. And that's money. These people have their price. It's got to be paid.'

'Perhaps it's not monetary.'

'Oh no, Raimundo, if you'll forgive me, it's in matters of this sort that chaps like me have the advantage over you intellectuals. In the end, outside family, it's always a question of money. Finally, you know, that's all there is. It's how things are done. All we've got to do is find the price they can't refuse.'

'Outside the family you said. One thing, my dear Ettore. These people, these young idealists, may be in the habit of thinking of themselves as a family. You remember the appalling Manson case in California. That's just what they called themselves, the family.'

He wasn't to be convinced of course. Nobody ever is by argument or illustration. Silenced perhaps, but not convinced. In the end he said in exasperation, 'Well, what would you suggest?'

I could only spread my hands.

Elena, overhearing us, said, 'We can only pray. His Holiness has agreed to receive me. I shall ask him to bless our prayers.'

'Heaven helps those who help themselves,' said Ettore. 'What will His Holiness do?'

Elena gave him a cold look and left the room.

'I didn't hurt her, did I?' he said. 'But it annoys me to encounter this reliance on prayer. It's true what I said anyway.'

He lit another cigarette.

'It's this waiting I can't stand.'

I knew what he meant. I wished they would get on with it and kill him; only somewhere, refusing to die, was a particle of hope.

It was momentarily freshened when the door was thrown open and Sandro and Bella came in together. She was pulling him by the sleeve and her cheeks were flushed.

'Oh,' she cried, 'you should have come, Daddy. It was wonderful. Nico's a genius. Uncle Raimundo, I wished you had spoken too. You looked so fine up there on the platform.'

'There was such an expression of feeling in the crowd,' Sandro said. 'They can't ignore that. They will have to compromise. You know, I felt really proud of Father. To be the son of a man who can generate such feeling, such sympathy, it's rather wonderful.'

They were both buoyed up. Something, invisible to us on the platform, had warmed the crowd. For a moment I was tempted to believe; only, as we passed out of the drawing-room which received sunlight flooding through leaves and half-closed shutters, into Elena's shrouded dining-room, I realized that it wasn't hope they had truly brought; merely youth. And more determined and desperate youth was to be found on the other side.

Lunch was lugubrious. The children tried hard enough, and

Ettore, though lost for material, spluttered manfully, but I could feel the children's zest evaporate moment by moment. Hope, enthusiasm, even a feeling for life, all seemed in poor taste there; seemed also immature and empty. Elena's eyes spoke eloquently of the vanity of all aspiration that was not directed towards a heavenly crown. My mother, eating nothing, but challenging each countenance in turn, with her half-dead eye of a despairing hawk, chilled the air. We were all relieved when it finished.

I stepped out on to the terrace to smoke a cigar, hoping that Bella would join me. A silly hope, of course—I could hear her laughter, as she played billiards with Sandro. I could understand the laughter—a release from tension.

'How can she, Raimundo?' It was, to my distress, Elena who had come out, looking gaunt in black, with her head covered by a mantilla, as though she were a widow already.

'Oh,' I said, 'she feels it. Too much perhaps. I should say her nerves are over-extended.'

We walked silently up and down the terrace twice. A police car drove up to the gate, two or three men got out and disappeared into the lodge. Almost at once, two or three came out and got into the car which drove away with an unnecessary acceleration. One of the Dobermans lifted his head and barked, two clear staccato barks.

'I can't speak to the children. I have never been able to. I have tried to do my duty, but Corrado is the only person I have . . .' Elena made a vague, uncharacteristic sweeping gesture with her hand. 'I am so afraid,' she said.

What could I say?

'Not, you must understand,' she continued, 'of what will happen. I am resigned to that. Corrado is a dead man. Both your mother and I know that. We have already commended his soul to the Almighty. I am afraid of what has happened. Raimundo, what part did Bernardo play?'

All I could say was that I didn't know, but of course it wasn't enough. It never is. If I had our national passion for ratiocination I could have made much of it, with a 'therefore' here and a 'nevertheless' there. In the end, I said, 'I know what you fear, that in some way Bernardo has brought this on. That his disappearance is connected. I don't know. I can't know. We none of us can. Only, Elena, one thing, this . . . this horror isn't the work of boys. It can't be. If Bernardo has anything to do with it, be sure of one thing. He's a victim himself. I don't, you understand, mean by that that he is dead, not at all, I mean he has been deceived.'

'And dishonoured,' she said.

The sky was a deep azure, the sun grilling. All over Italy families were finishing large luncheons at wayside *trattorie*. They were crouched over transistors listening to the prognostications for the afternoon's football matches, due to begin in half an hour.

Before I left, I spoke briefly to my mother. As always, she dismissed me curtly. Corrado has been all her life for a long time now. But, you know, his death won't kill her. That sort of thing only happens in bad novels. It used to be frequent in real life if one can believe the historians, but it's a long time since any doctor certified a broken heart as the cause of death. As for me, I believe neither historians nor doctors.

I refused the offer of a lift.

'I like travelling by bus,' I said. 'Now more than ever.'

No doubt they all thought the remark meaningless, an inappropriate display of a tiresome affectation. I couldn't be bothered explaining that I meant it. I find the sight of people going about ordinary sensible business comforting. Especially so on Sunday afternoons, when the buses are always full of families going to visit their sick relatives in hospital.

A comedy therefore: so much said, so much felt, so little communicated.

I look up from my typewriter and I see my American novelist . . . if he is a novelist—oh yes, what else could so lost a man be?—a retired diplomat perhaps? He is sitting at his window, a glass in his hand. Involuntarily, I raise a hand towards him. He lifts his glass and then, returning my salute, turns down the thumb of his other hand.

But which of us is in fact Caesar and which the gladiator? We are all of course gladiators, and all our triumphs merely postpone that moment when we salute Caesar as we recognize that we are about to die.

II

TOMASO

The bus moves from the railway station down a pot-holed street criss-crossed by overhead wires, past straggly houses, the yards dotted with rose-bushes, chickens, bare-legged children and thin and tawny dogs, and out across a plain towards the hills. Baked earth gives way to fields of maize and peas and beans, the last filling-stations are left behind. It is evening light, turning to violet, and the cypresses are black. The road runs straight for miles and then makes abrupt changes of direction to fit the configuration of crop lands and irrigation channels. Within, the radio plays loudly, mid-Atlantic pop. No one seems to notice.

The bus is almost full, but coming to a little village, the last before the hills, yet takes on more passengers than descend. The two young American girls make ready to shift their rucksacks which block the rear of the passage, but a peasant insists that they needn't trouble themselves and instead squats on the sacks. He wears blue overalls, open at the neck to reveal wisps of grey curly hair against a chest the colour of rich earth. From time to time he turns round to wink. The girls smile at each other. One of them moves her legs slightly to the side. She is short and fat and wearing blue jeans and a cream coloured shirt, with sweat-stains under the armpits. She says something in bad Italian to the peasant who laughs and turns half-round again so that his shoulder presses against the other girl's long, naked Californian legs. These have for the last twenty miles attracted the disapproving stare of the fat, black-clad peasant woman further along the back seat. She in turn keeps her body pressed well forward, disregarding comfort, so that the young man, on her left, will be spared the sight of these legs. The old woman's lips move all the time, as if in prayer.

Beyónd the other American girl, the one in jeans, is a young priest. The girl has been unhappily conscious of his garlic and winey breath since the journey started; wrinkling her nose in distaste. The priest hasn't spoken to her or to the young man on the window side of him, who for his part has not spoken either, but kept his face averted, his eyes searching the landscape as if for marks of recognition.

He is very pale this young man, and could be compared to a Christ painted by Caravaggio. A tooth pulls back his lower lip, making it deep red. Every now and then the silent American girl, the one in shorts with the long Pacific Ocean legs, sneaks a quick glance along the line at this young man. His name is Tomaso, which is how some of the other young men in the bus greeted him at the bus-stop. Then he nodded politely but distantly, as one who could no longer put a name to his fellows. This is true enough. Once, a lifetime ago when they were all at the village school, he knew them well, but now acquaintance has withered. (They still recognize him, for he is a person of consequence here, being a local landowner, and indeed nobleman.) He has moved on and away. His new associates, his comrades, don't even know him as Tomaso. They call him Vlado, or sometimes Vlad.

The bus leaves the plain and begins to climb into the mountains. They pass an inn, a chapel, and see, down in the valley below, the lights of two or three little towns. At each stop, where tracks from the mountain villages come down to join the road, passengers descend. No one now joins the bus. When there is a motor road to a village, the bus diverges from the main route and climbs tortuously to the little piazza. There is always a church in the piazza and a *caffè-bar*, with three or four men sitting outside in the still-warm evening, not drinking but just sitting. Usually in silence. They are labourers who have ended their day's work or young men who have never held a position. Always, when they see the church, the fat woman crosses herself, and mutters to the young man beside her, who follows suit. His movements are careless, the gestures of an idiot. The Californian girl, at whom, despite his mother, he keeps trying to look, hasn't dared glance in his direction since she took her seat. The sight of his baying mouth with the lolling tongue displayed turns her stomach. She can't bear deformity.

The priest makes no sign that he has noticed the churches. Nor, of course, does Tomaso. Once, at one village, he seems to recognize one of the young men outside the bar, and makes a gesture; the merest gesture, one finger momentarily raised.

The road becomes steeper, and it is now quite dark, the thick warm pall of summer mountain night. At last with a great crashing of gears the bus rounds the last hairpin and passes through a narrow gateway, up a long narrow cobbled street, which it almost fills so that a woman carrying a bucket of water has to press herself against the wall to let it pass, and in to another little piazza, its destination. The dozen or so passengers left, who of course include all those in the back seat, get to their feet, seize their various luggage and prepare to descend.

There are only two lamps in the square which is therefore deep in shadows. The peasant helps the girls with their rucksacks. They thank him, and look for a moment as though they are getting ready to ask a question, but he has vanished.

'Hey,' says the girl in jeans, 'that was quick.'

'I'll say so,' says the other girl, whose name is Kim.

'Well, you wanted to come here. What do we do now?'

'You got to admit it's different, Ruthie.'

'It's certainly different. It feels like the end of the world.'

'It's kind of what I wanted,' says Kim as she swings her rucksack on to her back, 'after all that culture.'

They make to cross the square to the little bar.

'Guess they'll know over there where they live,' Ruthie says; there is a touch of Brooklyn in her voice, the ever-present suggestion of complaint.

Even in the dim light Kim's long legs seem to shine and attract every eye. You could imagine eyes at every crevice, behind every slatted shutter. Only, exceptionally, Tomaso does not follow them with his gaze. But he notices that when their backs are turned the fat woman spits into the gutter.

He lets them go, and himself, in dark denying suit and shirt pale as his cheeks, moves slimly in the opposite direction and up a dark alley, round a corner where two mangy dogs fight over a dirty bone, and up steep worn and slippery steps to a house built seemingly into the hillside. There is a big ancient studded door against which he bangs a heavy iron, dog-headed knocker. Silence extends itself. His fingers clench and unclench. Dogs bark in the valley, a distant radio can be heard playing Puccini, and a cock crows. Tomaso waits. At last he can hear a key being inserted in the lock. It turns grindingly. The door opens, on a chain.

'It's me, Mother,' he says, and the chain is unhooked.'

They don't embrace. They are long past embraces, even as a formality. But she puts her hand on his shoulder for an instant and very lightly, not giving herself time to receive any stiffening or shrinking response. Two spaniels come barking from within the house. She says 'quiet, dogs'. They see Tomaso and something goes out of them, animation and excitement, and they keep close to their mistress's skirts.

'I never know when you're coming,' she says.

'It's impossible that you should.'

She gives a little shrug of her shoulders that says it would be nice to know, but that she has long stopped hoping for consideration.

He follows her across the little courtyard, warm with the scent of oleanders, and under a doorway, over which glows a candle lit to St Veronica, for whom she has a special devotion. The room they enter has a fine mahogany table and a set of dining-chairs which date from the second half of the last century, and a big carved sideboard, which is much older, almost certainly sixteenth century and genuine. Over it hangs a painting of the Madonna and Child from the same period. The walls are yellowed by old candle-smoke.

Tomaso sits down at the table, his ear keen to the silence. His mother moves on slippered feet and places a jug of wine and a bottle of mineral water and two glasses before him. Then she sets out a basket of grey, thick-crusted bread, a bowl of wrinkled black olives, and she retires to the kitchen and comes back with newly sliced rough country ham and black-rinded *pecorino* cheese. She sits down and looks at her son. He pours himself a glass of water and sips with long straight lips, like a serpent.

'Eat something. You are too thin.'

'I've always been so,' he says, 'and survived.'

All the same he tears off a crust of bread, pours a glass of the yellowish wine, dips the bread in it and nibbles. He puts an olive in his mouth; and lets its bitterness refresh him.

'You're well?' he says. 'I hope.'

'Oh yes,' she nods.

'How is he? My friend.'

'He's strange. He seems nervous.'

'I told you he's been overworking. The doctors feared a total nervous collapse. Where is he now?'

'In his room. He spends most of his time there. "Anyone would think you regarded yourself as a prisoner", I said to him. He listens to his radio a lot. News programmes.'

'He hasn't gone out, has he?'

'No, not at all.'

'That's all right. I didn't think he would.'

Tomaso tears off a piece of ham and eats it.

'Good,' he says, 'there's nothing like real country ham.'

'There's been nothing happening here, has there?' he says.

'No,' she says, 'nothing. Nothing happens here. You know that. The cow had a calf, but you're not interested in that sort of little event, are you, son? It would be nice if you were.'

'It will be nice when I can be . . .'

He knows that she would like to take the conversation further, to explore his answer and all that it implies. She would like, or part of her would like, to call for sympathy. He looks for a moment directly at her fine, modulated features, her retired elegance, her goodness, which gives her strength to suffer and yet endure, but not to act, never to act, and for that moment he would like to speak his heart. He would like to put his head again in her lap and say 'Mamma' and not the cold 'Mother' which is all his lips can bring themselves to frame. The desire is vain and fleeting. There is that between them which makes anything of that nature impossible. It is not because of what has happened but of what is missing. A profound gulf separates them; they stand on opposing cliffs; and it is crossed only by a fragile, rickety suspension bridge sustained by duty and a worn love.

83

The moment passes, the silence remains.

'It's so peaceful', he says, 'after Rome. I was thinking that all the way up in the bus. It's good.'

'And poor,' she says. 'The peasants leave the land, more and more every year. Three more holdings abandoned since last summer. Not that they were worth anything to us in rent. But it means the life departing.'

Of course there is one other support for their bridge and that is the trust he unhesitatingly lays in her; that is, after all, why he has sent Bernardo here.

'I'll go up to see him now,' he says, not wanting to talk about the estate and peasants and rent.

'Yes,' says his mother, and sighs. 'You'll want to talk to him.'

No other woman, he thinks, could have said that without irony in such circumstances. He takes an oil lamp and crosses the courtyard again and mounts the staircase that rises above the shed where they used to keep cows in his grandfather's time. At the turn of the staircase he lifts his head to the sky and sees stars twinkling and a young moon rise. He pauses there, looking at the heavens, into a space which makes sense to him, even while that sense, of necessity, includes the mockery of all that he is aiming to achieve; and yet the mockery is not directed at him—indeed in moments he is at one with it—and when he thinks of the frenzied activity that the forces of repression spew out, he relaxes, looking still at the stars and feeling good.

Along the corridor to Bernardo's room, he finds himself shivering. It is always, even in summer, colder here than you remembered. He knocks and enters, not waiting for a reply. It is a knock they agreed on a long time back.

Bernardo is stretched out on the bed, reading. He throws the book aside, leaps to his feet and flings his arms around Tomaso. Tomaso stiffens; he can't help it, ever.

'Vlado,' cries Bernardo, 'at last. I've been on edge. Oh yes, I've been on edge.'

Tomaso holds him at arms' length. Bernardo feels soft and pudgy to him and his fingers shrink from the synthetic material from which his polo-neck jersey is made. Also there are dark patches under Bernardo's armpits, and he smells.

84

Tomaso says, 'No need for that. You'll have heard every-thing from the radio, everything anyone else knows. It couldn't have gone better. It couldn't possibly have gone better.'

All the same something has changed between them, or rather has intervened. Tomaso recognizes the interloper; its name is responsibility. They have passed from the sunlight of the perfect liberty of the abstract. He finds for a moment that he doesn't want to meet the questing gaze of his friend. Instead he picks up the book Bernardo has cast down. A novel by Camus.

'This,' he says, 'in the last resort Fascist, whatever he thought of himself.'

'I know of course, but it is imperative that we acquaint ourselves with all philosophy, all psychology, and come to understand it . . .'

'That is easy. Know yourself, Bernardo. That's enough to know all men, who are never unique as they imagine. In their egoism.'

Bernardo nods; he hasn't thought of it like that before.

'I never thought it wouldn't go to plan,' Bernardo says. 'It was a good plan, and you found my information just right, isn't that so? So how could it fail?'

'Failure is always possible. One should recognize that, even while acting as if . . .' Tomaso pauses, and for the first time that evening, smiles slightly, a broken smile, 'as if we were the Pope. Infallible.'

Bernardo throws back his head and laughs, arrests the sound and says, his voice suddenly a croak, 'How is he? How's he taking it? You know, I've been testing myself to see if I feel any guilt, but,' he wipes his hand backwards across his brow, 'all I experience is curiosity. So how?'

Tomaso smiles again, 'Like a gentleman,' he says. 'No, I'm serious.'

'Does he know about me?'

Tomaso has been given notice of the question; he will certainly want to know that, they had said. And you must tell him the truth. Once he knows the truth, he can never retract.

'Yes, he knows.'

85

'And . . .' Bernardo is panting like a dog interpreting such signs as may suggest his master plans to take him for a walk, 'and . . .?'

'I think it helped,' Tomaso said. 'Psychologically it prepared him to co-operate. It emphasized his loneliness. He's un-educable of course, but still ready to co-operate. His first letter will be in the paper tomorrow. It'll be delivered just before the paper goes to press. You'll see, it'll be sensational. It'll have them re-casting their front pages. That's why I came here today. I've brought you a copy.'

He puts his hand into his inside pocket and withdraws a slim, long brown envelope. 'Here,' he says, 'you'll like this. You'll admire the style.'

The letter hangs a moment between them. Bernardo has gone pale. Far away in the house a telephone rings, the sound reaching them faint and blurred. It rings several times, at least a dozen.

'What a risk,' says Bernardo. 'Suppose you'd been stopped.'

'Why should I be? I've no record.'

'You're very sure of that.'

'I would never use my own house if I had a record. My house where my mother lives. Here, you must remember, I'm still the *marchese*, someone of standing.'

When they had first met five years ago, Tomaso had been very much the *marchese*, the little nobleman; there was after all little else for him to be. It was after a lecture at the University, and Bernardo was standing in the middle of a group, arguing fiercely, disproving everything their lecturer had said about the origin of law, and holding the little group of his fans spell-bound. There were always half a dozen of these, two or three of whom were in fact still excited by Bernardo's status as the son of a prominent politician (Corrado was indeed the Prime Minister of the moment). The excitement was sharpened by Bernardo's defiance of his father's principles. It made them feel wicked and daring. They were all very young, and feeling wicked and daring in this way was new. Suddenly Bernardo noticed a young man on the edge of the group whom he didn't know; but who was paying him close attention, even though he was trying to disguise his interest by leaning, as it were nonchalantly, against a pillar. Bernardo dropped his voice. He didn't yet like to be overheard by people he didn't know—his rebellion was still a young plant. Everything he did and said remained experimental.

The students drifted off to a *trattoria* they frequented where the helpings of spaghetti were huge, the prices low and the clientele reliably radical.

The next day, in the same place, as he lifted a gargantuan forkful of *rigatoni*, Bernardo saw the same young man at a corner table; still watching him. Had he followed them there the previous day? Was he trying to force himself on them? And if so, what were his motives? Was he simply interested? Or perhaps making a report? (Bernardo couldn't doubt that people somewhere would be preparing his dossier.) He seemed an unlikely recruit. He belonged, in Bernardo's opinion, rather with his brother Nico's set. He had the same elegance that Nico's friends displayed—it always made Bernardo feel clumsy, set his teeth on edge and caused his palms to sweat.

'Who's that, in the corner?' he said. 'He was spying on us yesterday too.'

'Oh that; a nobody.'

'Actually he's a *marchese*.'

'Well he's in the wrong place, we've no time for his sort here.'

'I'm told he's a very poor *marchese* though.'

'Poor or not makes no difference. Is he a spy?'

'A spy? Look at him.'

They all did; he was very slim with short dark hair that waved slightly and a pale oval face. His mouth curved and his dark eyes were soft; they shifted under the students' gaze. He wore a dark suit and a white shirt and dark blue tie. A gold signet ring knocked against his plate as he stretched out his hand for his glass.

They began to laugh. A spy? What a joke.

'I don't think Security use such obvious poofs.'

The insult, ridiculous and unfounded as Bernardo realized when he got to know him, was quite understandable. In those days Tomaso had a certain pliable elegance that would undoubtedly attract one type of aristocratic pederast. He was often bothered by such admirers whom he innocently took some time to recognize for what they were. His modesty in this respect surprised Bernardo, all the more so, when Tomaso eventually confessed to him that he hadn't voluntarily attended church since one of the Dominican Brothers at his school had made advances to him in the vestry after he had served Communion.

'I was very devout till that happened.'

He could smile about it. Like most egotists Bernardo wasn't curious about others, and he never wondered whether it was this incident which had broken the sweetness of Tomaso's smile. Of course the break, like most such breaks, was gradual, and some of the sweetness was still there when Bernardo first met him.

'But yes, I assure you,' said the student who claimed to know him, 'he's a very poor *marchese* indeed. He comes from some broken-down place in the Abruzzi. You know the sort of place, where they still share their quarters with the pigs.'

Again everyone laughed loudly, one or two concealing the knowledge that this was just how their own grandfathers had lived.

Tomaso pushed his chair back and crossed the room.

'I think', he said, 'you are laughing at me.'

'It was', as one of Bernardo's friends who was studying literature said later, 'exactly like a nineteenth-century novel. Not Manzoni, of course, but Stendhal.' This confused them since Manzoni was in fact the only nineteenth-century novelist most of them had read.

Still, Tomaso's gesture had its effect. They were all, though callow, decent enough young men, and since he didn't actually do anything so absurd as challenge them to a duel, they admired his nerve in approaching them and felt a certain embarrassment too. So they asked him to sit down, made a good many incoherent but sufficiently sincere apologies and ordered another bottle of wine. Fellowship was established.

Bernardo never analysed his relationship with Tomaso. Because he himself was voluble and, when free of his family, bubbled over with exuberance and argument, he easily passed as the leader. And indeed Tomaso learned much from him.

His upbringing had ensured his complete ignorance, so that Bernardo easily represented a superior culture to him. He came, as has been said, from an old house. Ancestors had been petty lords in the Abruzzi since the thirteenth century. The family had produced a couple of cardinals at the time of the Counter-Reformation, grim loveless men, both Dominicans. Mismanagement, a peculiarly un-Italian lack of vitality, had caused the estates to dwindle. Tomaso's father had lived through the Fascist Era in lethargy. He had served un- enthusiastically in the Army, returned home slightly wounded in the Western Desert, and viewed the Partisans, very active locally, with a *bien-pensant* indifference. They might be right to rid themselves of the Germans and the Fascists; all the same he couldn't be expected to consort with such types. The local leader was a Communist grocer after all. They were sure to want to steal the little land he had left to him. So he remained at home, and, too stupid to read, played endless games of patience and counted his ancestors.

Somehow he had married about that time. His bride was a distant cousin who had almost had a vocation. Her father, a Roman lawyer—the cousinship was on the maternal side— had deplored this, and talked her out of it. It did him little good. Either way he lost his favourite daughter, for, as he was to say mournfully, the difference between a convent and a broken-down castle in the Abruzzi with a half-dead husband wasn't as wide as a needle's eye.

Soon the castle became uninhabitable—there's a limit to the degree of decay that even decayed aristocrats find acceptable— and they moved a few hundred yards down the hill to one of their houses in the village. The shame didn't exactly kill Tomaso's father, but he now found it intolerable to be seen in the piazza. For the last five years of his life he never ventured further than the courtyard, and went that far only when the outer door was closed. He died when Tomaso was eight; perhaps, as his priest said, he had never recovered from his desert wound.

Tomaso was then at the village school, a quiet reserved child, but not unhappy playing with the other children of the village, who, with natural good manners, somehow contrived to treat him as an equal, a good fellow, and someone who deserved a certain respect, all at the same time. Nothing that happened in his life made a more positive impression than this.

Of course he couldn't stay there, and it was impossible he should proceed to the *liceo* (the grammar-school) in the nearby town. Who knew what sort of irreligious ideas he might imbibe there? For one thing was certain: despite all precautions a good many of the teachers were Reds, Socialists, even Communists. His mother, for all her piety, might have allowed herself to be guided by her own father, who advised her to give the boy a good modern education, an ordinary one. 'Let him learn', he said, 'that he's a citizen of a modern democratic republic, a Christian one certainly, and let him forget his ancestry. That sort of consciousness is obsolete, brings no kind of happiness these days. Let him forget all that. He's got no estates worth a penny. After all, I earn more in a week than his patrimony'— he dwelt on the word with a resounding irony—'his patrimony will bring him in in five years. The boy's got some talent for mathematics. Let him set out to become an engineer. That's what Italy needs after all, engineers and technicians.'

However, he didn't have the final word. That lay with the boy's uncle, his father's brother, a man corrupted by bigotry. He insisted that Tomaso follow the family tradition and receive his education from the Dominicans. Accordingly Tomaso was sent to an appropriate Church School. For two years, adoring his mother, he adored her God. Then he noticed the hypocrisy routinely imposed on his fellows. He shrank from it, fastidiously. Then came the incident in the vestry. There was of course no one he could tell—his grandfather had despaired of conversing with him. To tell his mother was patently impossible, and as for his uncle . . . There was nothing to do.

In this atmosphere of frigid piety and coarse hypocrisy, his mathematical talent withered. He fell back on books, especially poetry, and made himself drunk on Leopardi, Ungharetti and Quasimodo.

He would have liked to do his military service. He explained this later to Bernardo who found both desire and explanation incomprehensible. Somehow Tomaso felt there was a stain on him, that he had something to expiate. The truth was that, in his withdrawn condition, he had become infected by Romantic notions. He had concluded that he could only put his life right by service which would rid him of his father's disgrace in North Africa. The idea was absurd. He couldn't imagine that he would see action, and he couldn't have begun to say how eighteen months' clerking in an Army barracks would do anything to salvage honour—he was actually thinking in words like that. His youthful diaries reveal a subtler and deeper explanation; reading between the lines, you sense that he hoped to find in the barrack-room the comradeship and decency he hadn't experienced since he was on close terms with the boys at his elementary school.

But they discovered that he was unfit, a lesion in his lung. That dream of comradeship paled. At last he went to Rome, to the University, to study law. It bored him stiff, till he met Bernardo.

He had first lived with some of his mother's relatives, bright social people who didn't know what to make of the silent boy; soon, they were almost unaware of his presence in the household. Tomaso rarely talked to them but the apartment irked him. He walked much in the older parts of the city—his relatives lived in Monteverde which didn't appeal to him. Soon he moved out, again almost unnoticed, and took a room in what was really a lodging-house in the Via Leonina. The gloomy building in the Suburra might not seem any improvement on his aunt's apartment; it was all heavy, dark smoked-oak furniture and tasselled lampshades and thick velvet curtains hanging in doorways. But there were no obligations. The landlady quickly proved to be a slut, whose cleaning-woman had taken her measure.

She was in fact a White Russian, brought up in Shanghai and briefly married to an Italian engineer who had built bridges for the Kuomintang. He had been killed in an air-crash in 1940, leaving her this large apartment and little else. Soon after the war she had taken her first lodger; now there were eight of them, mostly medical students whom Tomaso found immediately unsympathetic. The landlady, Lenya, would drift through the apartment in unbuttoned kimono, her fat yellowing poodle at her heels, lamenting the changed times. Curiously something in him responded to her; she appealed to the same element that governed his taste in poetry. 'It was better under Mussolini,' she used to say. 'Look at me, I didn't have to live like this then, not at all.' She took a fancy to Tomaso; White Russians and an impoverished *marchese* had a good deal in common. As for him he listened to her in their loneliness, sitting sipping camomile tea while she complained of headaches, poverty, strikes, crime, her liver and the modern world.

One night he found her entertaining another guest in the kitchen. A small man with a scarred face—he was the first non-resident (apart from the cleaning lady and a Jewish girl one of the medical students used to smuggle in on Saturday nights) that Tomaso had ever seen in the apartment. Lenya introduced him merely as 'my friend'. It was Enzo Fuscolo.

Tomaso found the little man's look both insolent and disconcerting.

'Lenya has told me about you,' Fuscolo said.

He didn't go any further, and the next half-hour was devoted to the habitual litany of Lenya's woes. All the time Tomaso was made uneasy by the intimacy with him that Fuscolo's nods, raised eyebrows, and twisted smile seemed to insist on. The little man sat otherwise still in his shabby grey suit, neither eating the *petit-fours* (actually a little stale) nor drinking the tea that Lenya had placed before him, but all the time seeming to involve Tomaso in a conspiracy of complicity.

That was the first time. Thereafter Enzo came often enough, and soon was talking over Lenya's moans in a harsh compelling voice that spoke to Tomaso of desecration, broken honour and a cold piercing nihilism. Tomaso never consciously committed himself to this, but he listened. What he heard, and hearkened to, was despair; there was no meaning to action.

During the long summer vacation that first year he stayed in the Abruzzi village, alternately reading Nietzsche and considering suicide.

Of course most young men of any sensibility consider suicide, many of them no doubt seriously enough. It was only when in the autumn Bernardo, seen by Tomaso for the first time in many months, said over a *cappuccino*, 'But of course,

Tomaso, life is meaningless if there is no social purpose', that the mists began to rise. All the same it was Christmas before he had freed himself from Enzo Fuscolo and moved away from Lenya's apartment to a room near Campo dei Fiori. Still, he noted in his diary at that time:

'Of course there will always be a part of me that recognizes that Enzo's philosophy of existential nakedness contains an ultimate truth; only it is a truth which is quite unacceptable. For it is impossible to confront the void and agree to live. And I have discovered that I desire to live. So there is only one direction in which I can move.'

Later, he had added to this, in red biro, 'more than ever true today, and my steps are on that road. Let us go on.'

Bernardo looks up from the paper, 'I never thought we could get him to write like this; it's marvellous . . . how did you manage it?'

'We talked to him, we talked to him for a very long time, till he saw things from our point of view. We were very convincing and very persistent. But gentle. Your father is a man who can be persuaded by reason and facts. Nothing more was needed. He asked me to assure you of that . . .'

'He asked you that?'

'Yes, he said he was worried about your state of mind . . .'

Bernardo squirms on his bed . . .

'Being here, alone,' Bernardo says, 'I get worried too. I'm sure it's because I'm alone. I'm afraid it's not going to succeed.'

Tomaso does not reply, but looks at Bernardo enquiringly.

'Do you see what I mean? They're taking it too quietly. I had thought there'd be more panic.'

'They're worried enough.' Tomaso keeps his voice low, perhaps in response to the little trill of hysteria Bernardo's registers. 'The bourgeois state is adept at concealing its fears. That is all. Everything is going well. You don't need to brood. The one thing I was afraid of isn't going to happen. I had been terrified they would give way at once and accede to our demands. Fortunately they are even more corrupt than they are feeble, and there are those within the system who are blind enough to believe that they can profit by these events. As of course they may; very briefly.'

Bernardo frowns, 'It's not because it's my father, you understand.'

'Of course.'

'I'm not sure everyone in the group does. There was no need to banish me here. You should know that. I agreed that he should be the one picked. It was a democratic decision.'

'You're nervous,' says Tomaso, 'I can see that.' His voice is completely cool and very quiet. 'But you would inevitably have been interrogated. We are all agreed on that.'

'You can't think I would have given anything away.'

'We have discussed this before. Nobody can be trusted in an interrogation. Everyone has a breaking-point. You remember what the Algerian expert told us. As for me,' Tomaso moves across the room and opens the shutter a few inches, 'as for me, I shall never be interrogated. I'll kill myself first. That's all.' He looks out of the window again. 'I thought I heard the gate open, and voices. I don't understand. Nobody comes here.'

'There was that telephone call. A few minutes ago.'

They look at each other. Fear enters the room like a blind man tapping his white stick round the skirting-board.

Leaving Bernardo in the bedroom, Tomaso moved downstairs on silent feet. He crossed the courtyard, keeping just in the shadows; then straightened. Whatever happened, he was the young *marchese* returned home. That was all. He had no record. He was certain of that. He had never belonged to any Left-wing organization, had never spoken in public, published nothing. Quite early on, the Professor had made his role clear. And he'd stuck to it; even to the extent of joining the Christian Democrat Youth Movement. Therefore what he feared was impossible and absurd.

Absurdity of another sort met his eyes. His mother was in the dining-room, and she looked puzzled and embarrassed. But it wasn't his mother who held his gaze. There, in his dining-room, one of them perched on the table, the other stretched out in a chair that wasn't intended to be occupied in that manner, were the two American girls who had travelled up in the bus with him.

The one in the chair—the one in shorts—cried out when she saw him, 'Oh no,' she said in English, 'isn't it just crazy?'

He stopped short, following her words but not understanding any meaning.

His mother looked at him too and made a sort of helpless gesture with her hand. She made as if to speak, but the girl continued, 'You must be Tomaso. I should have recognized you, but, well, I really did, I guess, only I wasn't sure. I'm your cousin Kim.'

She leapt up and moved towards him, 'Say,' she said, 'what do I do, do I kiss you?'

His mother intervened. 'You should', she said, speaking slow, hesitant, rust; English, 'have told us. You should have written a letter or telephoned. Yes, telephoned. We are not prepared.'

Kim turned to her quickly, cornflower eyes wide and unformed face soft in apology.

'You're right,' she said, 'I'm sorry. I should have known. Mom hates surprises too and maybe you're just like her. I should have thought of that, shouldn't I, Ruthie?'

'Guess so. I did warn you, baby.'

'I'm sorry, Aunt Maria. Gee, I just love saying that, Aunt Maria. Yeah, I'm sorry. But it was so sudden. Course I was always planning to come and see you, I just suddenly felt I couldn't stand another goddam church or art gallery a day more. And I don't like your Italian beaches. Hey, Tomaso, can you follow me? It's terrible, my Italian's so goddam lousy I have to speak to my own family in English. But I'm sorry.'

Tomaso looked at his mother for elucidation.

She gave a surprisingly wide and open smile and threw her arms open too.

'But you're here,' she said. 'That's the main thing. You must not think us inhospitable. It was surprise, surprise, you understand . . .'

She was all at once bustle. A room had to be prepared—the girls could sleep together, yes? Yes? It would be more convenient. 'Yes, of course,' said the Ruthie one and began to speak to his mother in an Italian that was rapid and confident though ungrammatical and hideously pronounced. Kim is so impulsive, she says, making her apology sound like commendation. When she takes an idea into her head, it's immediately like it was riveted there. Just like that. So, all at once tiring of being a tourist, she just had to come and see her aunt and cousin. Why, they hadn't even been to Rome yet. Of course it could wait, they had the notion of spending a year in Rome, there was work they could both get there, and of course, just at the moment, with this kidnapping and the police activity, she had the impression that Rome might not be too pleasant, even for foreigners.

'No,' said his mother, 'not even for foreigners.'

It was terrible, wasn't it, Ruthie continued, and did she know? Kim had a notion her father might be there. So that showed how strong was her sudden desire to see her aunt and cousin that she hadn't bothered to check whether he was really there.

'Her father,' his mother said, 'I never met him. And do you know, it is twenty-five years since I saw my sister. She came back to Italy once, but I didn't see her.'

She began to set the table. They must eat. It was nonsense to say they had had a sandwich in the bar—she could imagine the sort of sandwich it would have been—salame made from donkeys that had died of the plague. So, please . . .

Kim, still leaning on the edge of the table, with her long legs crossed at the ankle so that she stood on her right foot, the left one resting lightly on its toes, which gleamed ruby-red out of the open sandals, stretched into her bag and withdrew a packet of cigarettes.

'Look,' she said, 'isn't it neat, cigarettes with my name.'

She took one and put it between her lips and pushed the pack towards him.

KIM in red letters on the white pack.

She snapped a lighter and lit her cigarette and blew smoke towards him while he still hesitated; her look was insolent and yet innocent; could it be both? He took a cigarette.

When she wasn't smoking she let the cigarette dangle from her hand. Everything she did, every gesture, was ridiculous, phoney, B-feature movie.

He said, speaking with a slow politeness, 'Have you been long in Italy?'

'Three weeks; Florence, Venice, Verona, Parma. Verona and Venice were great, but Florence was a real drag.'

'Sorry?'

'A drag. A bore, you know.'

'Ah yes.'

'You don't live here, do you?'

'It's my house.'

'But you don't live here all the time.'

'No.'

'You live in Rome, don't you? I guess you still do.'

'Most of the time. Or sometimes.'

'Do you have a job there?'

'No, I'm a student.'

'A student. Still?'

'In Italy we stay students a long time often.'

'Oh.'

'There are no jobs, you see. For most of us that is. So, we stay students. It gives us a reason for being.'

'Oh.' She kept her eyes on him and her mouth hung a little open, then she said, 'But our aunts in Rome—it's funny isn't it, Tomaso—hey, I can't manage that word, not all the time, what do your friends call you . . .?'

He swallowed. 'They call me Tomaso, I'm afraid. Italians don't find it difficult to manage.'

'Uh-huh. Mind if I call you Tom then? Or Tommy? What was I saying? Oh yeah, our aunts in Rome, and it's funny to think we share aunts, they told Mom they hadn't seen you for a long time.'

'No, I suppose not.'

She shrugged and smiled at him. 'So what, Tom? I'm glad to meet you.'

They sat down to supper.

'It sure is funny', said Ruthie in her quick, bad Italian, 'how I've picked up the language and Kim who's half-Italian hasn't.'

'Didn't your mother speak to you in Italian?' Tomaso asked Kim.

'No, never. She wasn't exactly popular with her family after her first divorce, and maybe she just decided to let it go. It's only the last few years since her operation she's wanted to repair things. Of course it's maybe been easier since our grandfather's death. I wouldn't know, but Mom says it has.'

'Tomaso,' said his mother, 'maybe your friend would like to join us?'

He gives her a long, dead look and then rises to his feet. Perhaps the girls will be difficult to move. In that case it is better they meet Bernardo now and don't wait till he has become a mystery. They are not after all the sort who will have read the newspapers and anyway the photographs of Bernardo were unrecognizable. No foreigners of course ever watch television, and there isn't one here to alert them. So he rises, and goes to fetch him.

Towards the end of the meal the talk inevitably turned to the kidnapping. Up to that moment they had kept to generalities, empty talk, never easy but at least all on the surface. It was sustained mostly by Ruthie and Bernardo, who gave the impression of experiencing a sense of liberation. He must have been bored. Tomaso was never bored that way. He never felt restless and anxious to be doing things; only empty and numb.

They ate bread, ham, salame, and olives, the *pecorino* cheese and a salad of fennel, his mother apologizing all the time for the inadequate nature of the food. 'Tomorrow', she said, 'it will be different. Tomorrow I will have a lamb killed, but we won't eat that tomorrow. Still I know that Piero shot some partridges and pigeons yesterday. Of course partridges are out of season, but Piero pays no attention to that, and we can always call them all pigeons. Pigeons are never out of season. Do you like pigeons, Kim? What sort of name is that? Haven't you another, a saint's name?'

'Pigeons? I don't know that I've ever eaten pigeons.'

'Maybe you don't get them in California,' said Ruthie. 'We call them squab in Connecticut.'

'No, I guess I never ate them. And Kim's my only name, Aunt Maria. My mom wasn't too keen on the church when I was born.'

'Kim,' said Maria, shaking her head.

All the time Tomaso was aware of Kim. She kept looking at him, not slyly as people had looked at him, nor with the open invitation that he had known whores and some peasant girls give, but in a new way he found disturbing. It seemed as if she was going to make some demand on him. And it would be a demand he would find hard to refuse.

The impression strengthened when his mother left them. They had a quick exchange first in which each urged the other to be the one who would tell Kim she couldn't dress that way in the Abruzzi.

'You tell her it's not safe, Son.'

'Or decent, Mother.'

'That goes without saying, but it is that she might not understand. No doubt over there they have other standards. But here, it's dangerous too. You tell her that.'

'You must try, mother. I can't speak to her about things of that sort.'

It was Ruthie who raised the subject of the kidnapping. Tomaso experienced distaste; he recognized her type so immediately and unmistakably.

She said, 'However desirable reforms are, you corrupt them by means of that sort. I'm prepared to be convinced that this group—what do they call them? The PDP is it?—are idealists, but this sort of thing does no good. It puts them out of court.'

Bernardo laughed; he could deal with liberals any day.

'Absolutely,' he said, 'if you think of reform merely as a desirable correction of the existing state structure. What you don't realize is that reforms of the kind that I imagine you would consider desirable are in themselves utterly and completely unacceptable, inasmuch as anything which serves to ameliorate the existing state of society is in fact worse than leaving it unreformed in its present corruption. Don't you see? Reforms perpetuate injustice.'

'That's just clever talk,' said Ruthie whose brows were wrinkled and whose Italian might also be considered to be under attack.

Tomaso looked at her over the rim of his wine-glass. Americans were not absolutely hopeless. He must guard against that prejudice. Still they were even more deeply stained by the delusory lies of liberalism than any other people. And since she was, he imagined, Jewish, she must be wedded to the imperialist conspiracy.

Bernardo spread his hands wide in pity. 'Clever talk,' he cried. 'Listen. Do you agree that society is organized on a basis of injustice?'

'Sure.' Ruthie blushed. 'I can see that. I'm not dumb, you know.'

'And reforms are intended to ameliorate social conditions without changing social relations.'

'I don't get you.'

'All reforms are intended to keep the present structure operable and prevent revolution.'

'Well, I see where you're heading. Yes, I guess so, ultimately.'

'Good.' Bernardo beamed like a prosecuting attorney who has elicited a damaging admission. 'In that case reforms are counter-revolutionary.'

Kim smiled at Tomaso. 'I don't follow all this, Tom, but that poor man they've captured. He's kind of sweet. You know who he reminds me of? Snoopy.'

'Snoopy?'

'Surely you know about Snoopy. I guess most everyone's heard of Snoopy. Charlie Brown's Snoopy.'

'Oh yes.'

Bernardo laughed. Tomaso looked at him swiftly. There was a quality in the laugh that made him wary. A dangerous note of strain.

'Oh yes,' cried Bernardo, with a great whoop. 'You're absolutely right. Absolutely right. It's no good saying that sort of thing to Tomaso here, he's a sort of saint, you know, a lay saint, and he knows nothing of that sort of culture, but you're absolutely right. Corrado Dusa's a sort of Snoopy. And what's more, he's a good man, the best of the bunch by a long way. That's why he was chosen of course. To take someone like Schicchi for example, Gianni Schicchi, would have been pointless. Not only would nobody care what happened to him, but, more important, he represents the system at its worst.

He is therefore irrelevant. But Dusa's different. He's decent and humane and, so you see, in the last resort, dangerous. He's the sort of man who can even make people believe in the present state of things. So . . .' he spread his hands wide again. 'Alternatively you can say he's the cornerstone. You pull him out and, crash, the whole edifice will begin to crumble. But Gianni Schicchi, he's nothing but an excrescence, a gargoyle. Rip him off the building and its appearance is actually improved. Pointless. Moreover, objectively Schicchi is working for the Revolution. You know the policy Corrado Dusa has been advocating?'

'Not exactly,' said Ruthie.

'He has been advocating what we call the Historic Compromise. In case you don't understand that, let me explain.' Bernardo's voice warmed to the authoritative tone of a university lecturer. 'You know that in Italy we have had this curiosity of thirty years of one party rule, all because the official opposition, the Communists, the PCI, have been unacceptable to our two masters, the Vatican and Washington? Just so. Therefore the corruption of the state has proceeded unchecked to a point where it may be seen, objectively again, to be preparing the way for a real, an effective, revolution in which the working-class and the intellectuals in historic alliance will seize power and dismantle the State apparatus. Now the most intelligent of the establishment, which includes the leaders of the Christian Democracy and the leaders of what we call the lay parties, and of course the leaders of the PCI, have come to see that only one thing can avert this and create conditions in which counter-revolutionary ameliorating reforms are possible. This is naturally the admission of the PCI to the Government, so that all the parties which support the State, as it is presently constituted, will collaborate. Dusa has been the leader of this move. He has possibly won the consent of the Vatican though not yet of the CIA, who are of course historically stupid and slow to appreciate reality.'

'You could say', said Tomaso, 'that objectively the CIA are working for the Revolution.'

'So,' Bernardo said, 'it is evident that Dusa had to be the target of all true revolutionary forces, simply because he is a

101

good and intelligent man. The wrong idealism is the worst corruption.'

His words hung in the night air. Two or three moths hummed flutteringly and demandingly round the light beyond which the room fell away into darkness. Kim yawned. She had found the discourse hard to follow. What she understood made no more sense than what she didn't. She stretched out her long leg so that her toes touched Tomaso's ankle. He moved his foot away. She let her long fingers play with her cigarette lighter, then took a cigarette, lit it and blew smoke in his direction. Nothing in her life had prepared her for being here, for listening to this sort of talk any more than for finding herself in a mountain village where women spat in the street behind her and hens and donkeys wandered in the lanes. She said to Tomaso, 'Why don't we go out for a breath of air; it's kind of stuffy here.'

It was the moral atmosphere she referred to. He could do nothing but accede. Both felt she had gained a point, but Tomaso knew his will was weak only in inessentials.

Outside, 'It's so peaceful,' she said, and leant back against a tree, drawing one of her legs up behind her and keeping face-on to him; she knew she looked her best that way . . . She looked him straight in the eyes. If she couldn't make him sense her body, she didn't know where to begin. She wanted very much to begin.

'He's a funny one, your friend,' she said. 'He's very intense. I could never be that intense about things. In fact, I always reckon intensity's a drag.'

He didn't reply, looked up at the moon.

'You should see the moons we get over the Pacific,' she said.

'I'm thinking of spending next year in Rome, did I tell you? I'm an actress you know. I want to get into films. All I've done so far is some TV work back home and a rep season in San Diego. I'm told Cinecittà's still the best place in Europe to find work. I've a friend who says he can get me some TV commercial work too. Do you know anyone in the film business?'

He made a tired gesture. He would have liked to say it was all meaningless, that sort of thing; but Bernardo had already gone far enough; too far perhaps, even with innocents like this one. Innocent? It wasn't perhaps the right word. It was wrong to confuse ignorance, wilful blind ignorance with innocence. He knew something about innocence. The peasant children he used to play with had been possessed of it. Thinking of them, he could feel no pity for Kim. Bernardo was right; family was the deepest, most corroding corruption of all. If he'd been another sort of man, he might now have raped this American girl, in her insulting shorts, and that would be it.

He said, 'No, I've no friends in that business.'

She said, 'You're shy, aren't you. I hadn't reckoned you would be shy. Do you know, Tom, you're one of the reasons I came to Italy?'

'I don't understand you.'

'No? It's easy. You see, a few years back, when Mom decided she wanted to mend relations with her family and wrote to our aunts in Rome, they sent her some photographs. It must have been about the time you were first a student and staying there. And there was one of you. I kind of took a fancy to it. You won't maybe believe it, but you were one of my pin-ups. Between Bobby Darin and Dustin Hoffman—I still think he's great. Of course my girl-friends thought it was great me having an Italian cousin . . . it was sort of glamorous, you know.'

It was like opening a gate to a garden and finding yourself abroad. He was momentarily lost.

'So, you see,' she said, 'I think I've a right to do this,' and put her arm round him, and kissed him.

'My,' she said again, 'you are shy. It's kind of funny finding an Italian boy who's shy. I hadn't reckoned they existed. The way my ass got pinched black and blue in Florence, I wouldn't have believed it possible.'

She kept her arm there. She smelt all fresh, of deodorants and flowers.

'Are you still awake?'

Ruthie padded about the bedroom that was not quite dark. Moonlight slanted through the shutters that Kim, fearful perhaps of bats, had closed. She tossed her jeans into the

103

corner. There was a heavy clang as the buckle struck the tiles. Ruthie's breathing came hot and urgent to Kim who didn't answer her, but lay in the bed, one leg drawn up, sweating slightly under a heavy bedspread.

'He's kinda funny, your cousin, how did you make out?'

Kim could hear Ruthie scrubbing her teeth vigorously, and then splash some water out of the jug into the basin and rinse her face. When they'd started out as room-mates Ruthie had had no sort of notion of personal hygiene. Kim often wondered how she had been brought up, really . . .

'I can hear you're awake, you know. I can always tell. You know I can.'

She clambered into bed like an urgent little animal. The bed heaved. Kim lay still, still saying nothing.

'Yeah, he's kinda funny. Not really like an Italian, is he? Maybe it's being a marquis, that's what it means, *marchese*, doesn't it? Not that I know just what a marquis is either, honey. Some kinda duke, I reckon.'

She put her hand on Kim. It was always sweaty, her hand, hot Jewish hand, but Kim mustn't think of it that way.

'I guess you struck him dumb, honey.'

Kim turned over on her side, away from her. The hand followed.

'Aw honey.'

'I'm sleepy.'

Silence crept up between them. In the distance sounded the sharp bray of a donkey. Dogs set up a barking. Ruthie's fingers worked restlessly, like a mouse in the wainscot.

'Kinda funny,' she breathed. 'I'd say he wasn't that pleased to see us. Wasn't pleased at all, baby. But it's funny here, it's nice. I like it you know. I've been wondering if it sets up some sort of race memory in me . . . your cheeks are wet . . .'

'It's just my cream, oh well . . .'

'That's better, baby . . . that's better.'

They were alone, yet both, their perceptions heightened and quickened by the experiences of the day, kept a sense of the house brooding above and around them, and of themselves being sojourners in a strange land. It was not a feeling that had come to them elsewhere in Italy.

'I don't know', said Kim finally, 'why I . . .'

'Oh baby, you're so physical, honey. I mean you're a very sensuous girl.'

Kim relaxed, reassured in her nature. 'He's cute, Tom,' she said.

'Kinda funny.'

'I think it's just that he's shy. Anyway,' she said, 'what about you? It's hours since I came to bed. What have you been doing all the time?'

'Oh, just talking. Talking and listening.'

'Christ, what about? More politics? More of that shit?'

'Like I said, he's very extreme, you know, and there were

Kim stretched herself and nestled her head in Ruthie's shoulder.

'Well,' she said, 'rather you than me. He's a real crap-artist, that one.'

'But you know,' Ruthie said at last, 'it's funny him being up here. He doesn't strike me as the country type. He's very extreme, you know. I asked him what he was doing here and he said he'd had some sort of overstrain working for his exams and was taking a rest. I don't know why, I didn't believe him. It's a thing about being Jewish, honey, you get to not believing people's explanations. He talked more about that politician they've kidnapped. It would be really something if they had something to do with that and he was hiding here, wouldn't it?'

'Don't be silly.'

'Like I said, he's very extreme, you know, and there were things he said. He obviously sympathizes with the terrorists.'

'He's just a friend of my cousin's.'

'So?'

'Well then, surely it's obvious.'

'Yeah, I guess so. He's a bit wet, your cousin. Pretty but . . .'

'Oh Ruthie . . . Ruthie . . .'

'You like it baby, don't you? You like your Ruthie . . .'

Tomaso's sleep was troubled by bad dreams and he woke early and unrested. He could rationalize the pursuit dreams; they were an inescapable fact of his chosen life. But dreams where limbs twisted, bodies offered themselves and his tongue swelled and filled his mouth, afflicted him. He would have liked to disembarrass himself of his body, to enter into abstraction. The transformation refused to happen. And tonight, voices had argued with him, songs had sung themselves to reluctant ears, fruit had fallen from the trees into his mouth. He woke shivering.

He rose and dressed himself in the same dark suit he had worn yesterday, and went out into the courtyard. A girl, wearing the local costume of scarlet and black, her head decently scarfed, was drawing water from the well. She filled the two paniers and slung them across the back of the waiting donkey. It flicked its ears as it felt the weight settle. Tomaso waved to her, a half-moon gesture with his right hand, but she lowered her eyes, struck the donkey's hindquarters with a switch of gathered twigs, and, together, girl and ass, they made their way out of the yard. He could hear its hooves clip-clopping up the steps just beyond the wall. Would all that be changed? Or would it be possible somehow to translate that decency, that order, that respect for rhythm, into a new life?

Tomaso went into the great vaulted kitchen where his mother was already at work, kneading the flour and eggs and water for the *fettuccine*. She abandoned her task to give him a cup of coffee.

'Did you speak to your cousin?' she said.

'I told her . . . that's to say, I told her something about how people here lived and dressed. Their standards. I spoke of the differences. I hope I said enough.'

It was tiresome to be reminded of the American girls, so early in a morning that he had felt belonged to him.

'It is curious to have a niece like that,' said his mother.

'I suppose you are certain she is actually my cousin?' The words stumbled from his mouth.

'Of course, yes, it would be ridiculous to suppose otherwise. Anyway, I knew about her, naturally.'

'Well then, yes, but, as you say, it is curious.'

'It is.'

'I have to go out for a little. Being Americans they will probably sleep all the morning. That is what Americans do.'

He went upstairs to check that Bernardo was still asleep also.

The door was locked. No answer to his gentle tap. Bernardo slept heavy. As long as he also slept alone . . . Tomaso hadn't liked those two heads nodding together under the little pool of light over the table. He had almost interrupted, but unable to think of anything convincing, had shrunk from doing so. Downstairs again, he got his Vespa from a shed, unwrapping the tarpaulin in which he had swathed it at the end of his last visit.

The streets were never quite silent or empty in the early morning. He roared past a long line of peasants, mounted on donkeys, going out to tend their fields. His greeting was shy. He had no right to be on a scooter, no right to be their landlord, no right . . . It was good to leave his native village with its accumulated guilt, and free himself for the cleansing savagery of action. The road curved down through the olive groves, the trees as twisted as the civilization that had grown from them. Tomaso let the east wind, blowing up the valleys from the Adriatic, fan his face. He passed a shrine and an old woman kneeling there. He passed a flock of sheep and their black-toothed shepherd, a boy of twelve or thirteen; soon they would be off up to the higher mountain pastures for the summer. The road swung down to the plain. Little Fiat vans and cars now shared it with him, and the occasional big lorry or bus carrying workers to the local factories. Italy was on its way to labour for its masters.

Tomaso stopped his scooter in the main piazza and parked it among a number of others under the statue of Ovid, a native of nearby Sulmona. Well, it was better to offer statues to poets, even dissolute ones, than to generals. He went into the biggest *caffè* and ordered a *cappuccino* and a pile of tokens for the telephone. Two labourers in blue overalls were drinking *grappa* along the bar. A small fat man in a striped suit, who had the air of a local lawyer, a small town man of importance, was eating a pink sticky cake. There was no one else in the bar, apart from the barman, a thin, feverish youth. Tomaso set himself to wait till the lawyer left. He sipped his coffee.

The lawyer finished his cake and took a paper napkin from the stand and wiped his fingers. The labourers watched him. Tomaso read suspicion in their look. The lawyer picked up his newspaper. As he did so, Tomaso caught a glimpse of the headlines. Good; he had of course known that the letter would be there, but it was always possible that something might have gone wrong. He smiled to himself. He hadn't bought a newspaper, because, here in the Abruzzi, he had no interest in public affairs. He waited, looking out on the piazza where life was certainly slow enough this morning.

The lawyer's voice, calling his name, startled him from his reverie.

'Forgive me for addressing you in this way. I was surprised to see you. Ah, I see, you are wondering who I am and why I am taking the liberty of addressing you. Here is my card. I was honoured to do a spot of business on behalf of your lady mother and therefore in fact yourself, *signore*, a few months ago.'

Tomaso found himself turning over the piece of pasteboard the little man had given him. A name, letters, honorifics.

'You are surprised that I recognized you. I make a point of memorizing faces, even of those whom I have not yet met, but with whom I have the honour of being acquainted indirectly or by repute. The camera is a wonderful invention, I always say. I am its most diligent student; indeed it is, *signore*, a great aid to such as I, who have a multitude of diverse business and clients. And how do you find life now in Rome? Fevered? You are better just now back in your native province . . .'

He tapped his newspaper with pale soft fingers.

'I see you have no newspaper. Perhaps then you have not yet heard of this shocking development in the Dusa case?'

Tomaso stared at him, his mouth a little open.

'Allow me then to have the honour of enlightening you. There is a letter published this morning, an appalling letter in which the unfortunate Dr Dusa castigates—there is no other word I can use—castigates,' he dwelt on it lovingly, 'yes, absolutely castigates his colleagues in the DC for their failure to liberate him. Now this is a shocking and disgraceful development, isn't it?'

Tomaso said nothing.

'You understand, it can only either weaken the resolve of the Party hierarchy, than which nothing could be more disastrous, for you will agree with me that it is imperative that they stand firm. Firm and resolute. It is meet that one man be sacrificed for the nation. Meet indeed.' The little lawyer rubbed his stomach and ordered two cognacs. 'Or,' he said, 'alternatively, the accusations that Dusa now casts at his Party, which go far beyond this charge of abandonment, will serve to discredit the Party among the electorate, just at the moment when it is more than ever vital that it retain the support of all the best men. So, *signore*, you appreciate the deplorable nature of this development. Either Dusa has been pusillanimous or these devils have worked appallingly on him. Drugs and torture distort the personality in ways you would hardly believe . . .'

'You have no doubt then as to the genuineness of the letter?'

'None at all. Doubt is untenable. The letter has been accepted as genuine . . . but how it was obtained . . . what dark means were employed . . . there I am in the dark . . . There are naturally various possible means. For instance . . .'

It was perhaps twenty minutes before Tomaso was relieved of his company, the lawyer having meanwhile given him a variety of speculations.

Tomaso went to the telephone and called a Rome number.

'Is that the dry-cleaners?'

'Sorry. Wrong number.'

'My mistake.'

He hung up the receiver but remained by the telephone, looking through a small address book as though seeking another number. In exactly ninety seconds, the telephone rang. He answered it at the first ring, and it was probable that neither the barman nor the two labourers realized that this had happened and that he hadn't placed the call. None of them, certainly, would have been prepared to swear to it one way or the other.

'Vlad?'

'Yes.'

'Good. How does it go?'

'All well, I think, though it's time our friend here had a change of air, the mountains don't suit his condition.'

'I was wondering if that mightn't be the case. We'll see to it.'

'Directly?'

109

'Yes, Carlo will handle it. Understood?'

'Understood. What about yours?'

'OK.'

'Does he need a move?'

'No, he's fine where he is. He's a home bird.'

'I'm relieved. I had a letter from him. It was good.'

'Oh he's writing a lot of letters now.'

'In the same style?'

'Absolutely. You know where to find Carlo?'

'Oh yes, there's a complication by the way.'

'Yes?'

'I've had a visit from an American cousin and her girl-friend.'

'Oh.' There was a long pause. 'Well, be natural. Do whatever is natural.'

'You know what girls are.'

'Indeed I do.'

And, thought Tomaso, indeed Stefano did. But as for himself, he wasn't so sure . . .

There was a change in mood. Ruthie realized this almost at once. The boys had accepted their presence without argument. It had seemed natural that they should accompany them on this little trip. She fancied Tomaso didn't like it; but he didn't argue, and anyway, as she had already decided, he was a funny one. Ruthie had no doubt of her ability to pick funny ones. She had an inherited talent. Kim of course was an innocent—she couldn't help but be fascinated by Kim's inability ever to see anything. She really meant that: to see anything. How you could go through life like that? It was a mystery. The answer of course was that Kim was a swan, a real swan, and swans could afford to know nothing. Or seem to afford it. Seem, that was the operative word. Seem. It made Ruthie feel protective of course. Kim needed to be looked after. That degree of innocence made you vulnerable. Maybe any innocence did.

Bernardo was restless, nibbling his fingernails and glancing out of the car's window, though it didn't seem likely that he was the sort to take pleasure in scenery. To Ruthie it seemed as if he was sulking. When she spoke, trying to revive last night's conversation, he answered in monosyllables; once he even turned the back of his head to her, a rapid movement, a non-verbal snap.

No conversation in the front of the car either; but then Kim didn't need to talk. Though she often did, it wasn't her way. She put her hand on Tomaso's collar; he shifted uneasily.

'It disturbs me,' he said. 'Please, I have to concentrate to drive.'

It was dark when they reached a town. The girls were quite lost; Bernardo too probably, for he kept rubbing the window and trying to read the signs. Neither he nor Tomaso spoke except to answer questions.

They got out of the car and went into a big *caffè*. Bernardo and the girls sat down while Tomaso made a telephone call. Then the waiter came to their table. They ordered beers. Bernardo kept drumming his fingers on the table. He fingered his moustache and ran his hand over his face which was sweating, even though the *caffè* was cool and cavernous.

'It's my head,' he said, and put on a pair of dark glasses.

Tomaso found his fingers tingling. All his life he had been waiting for this sort of action. He recognized this now. Everything else had been simply inadequate. Now he felt good.

He could smile at the memory of Bernardo's nervous reluctance. He hadn't wanted to hear the news, to shift ground. Tomaso explained this to himself; Bernardo was essentially an intellectual, with the intellectual's characteristic hesitation at the point of crisis.

'Don't you feel good now?'

Bernardo gave a small tight shake of his head.

'Act natural.'

Bernardo brushed little beads of sweat away with a dirty brown handkerchief. Tomaso glanced about the bar. It wasn't necessary. Nobody was interested in them and it wasn't their responsibility to make contact. Besides, Kim was a distracting focus. In her tight-bottomed white jeans there was certainly no girl in town as sexily dressed, but at least she wasn't flaunting nakedness. Something, if not much, was left to the imagination. But actually her presence was working to their advantage. It made Bernardo and him invisible.

Time passed. They all drank another bottle of beer and Ruthie had a sandwich. In a bar like this Tomaso knew that everything they were doing, every sacrifice they made, was necessary. These people around them, especially the young men, were deprived of any real life. They were, in the purest sense, victims.

Carlo was late. It might have been better just to have taken Bernardo to the railway station and put him on a train. Only—the Professor had been clear about this—he couldn't now be trusted alone. He was, in every way, too dangerous.

Kim said, 'Maybe we could go to a movie. Your friend's not coming. Or is there any dancing?'

He had only been tempted to disobey the Professor once. He would have liked to tell Bernardo everything that he had spoken to his father about, arguing with him, letting him know of Bernardo's involvement. It was just after he had dictated the letter to him. Corrado Dusa had opened one eye—it was the first day they'd let him have the bandage off, and he'd known of course what that release meant; Tomaso was almost sure he had known it—and when Tomaso spoke of Bernardo, all he'd said was, 'Does that sign both our warrants?'

Tomaso had pretended not to understand, but it was that shaft of penetration made it impossible to tell Bernardo more of the meeting than he had already done.

Kim said, 'That man over there in uniform. He keeps looking at us. Is he a policeman or what?'

'I guess he just fancies you, honey. Most every man in the room does.'

Tomaso looked at the policeman. He saw a big, swarthy, blue-jowled man, wholly unremarkable, except perhaps as being a perfect realization of the type. The man got heavily to his feet and crossed the room to their table, kicking his legs out as he moved. He sat down without waiting for an invitation and picked up Tomaso's beer-glass and swallowed the quarter-litre that remained in it.

'Well, boys,' he said, 'nobody told me you had girls like this in tow.'

112

Tomaso shrugged. 'They're new. My American cousin.'

Kim said, 'You're a policeman, aren't you?'

The big man nodded.

'Wowee.' She gave him a long under-the-lashes look.

His only response was a fat satisfied smile and then he began to talk rapidly to Tomaso in what Ruthie was sure was dialect.

'Least I couldn't make out a word of it,' she said later.

After a little they all got to their feet, Kim and Ruthie not knowing at all what the next move was to be. It proved not in any way dramatic, no further than the restaurant next door, where the big policeman ordered for all of them.

'If I order they know it's got to be good,' he said. He patted his huge belly. 'Food and I are good friends.'

The restaurant was a dull, bleak sort of place with dark varnished wooden panels covering the walls and plain white table-cloths, not too clean. There was only one waiter, an old man, with the flat feet of his trade. He sighed when the policeman tried to be jocular and shook his head. They were the only customers in the place.

Ruthie again tried to engage Bernardo in the sort of political discussion they had had the previous night. But he was unable to respond and she soon desisted. The only conversation was a laboured flirtation between Kim and the policeman, whose approach would have seemed old-fashioned in her grand-father's day. Ruthie sulked. It annoyed her to see Kim letting herself down like this.

Tomaso crumbled his bread and only took a few forkfuls of the macaroni which was all the policeman had promised. He made an equally half-hearted attack on the lamb which followed.

'Do they really kill lambs this young?' said Kim. 'I've never seen lamb like this before.'

'Is a baby,' said the policeman. 'Very succulent. Like you.'

At last the meal was over. Tomaso leant across the table to the girls.

'I'm sorry,' he said, 'we've a little business to do, part of what we came to town for. You girls would be best to wait for us here. We'll order some coffee for you as we go out.'

His tone gave them little choice. Kim half-rose to her feet in

113

protest, but the policeman's heavy hand was on her shoulder.

'No, no, please, I insist,' he said. 'We won't be long and then we'll go dancing.'

'We will?'

'I promise.'

The three went out into the street.

'There's something funny going on,' said Ruthie. 'I don't know what it is, but it's something weird. Don't you sense it?'

'No.'

'Oh Kim, you're hopeless, you're so innocent.'

'She's pretty dumb, your cousin,' said the policeman to Tomaso as they re-emerged in the street from the restaurant's swing doors. 'She's lovely but she's dumb.'

'If she wasn't so dumb she might be dangerous.'

'Lucky for her then she's so dumb.' He put his hand on Bernardo's shoulder and squeezed. 'Hey, Professor,' he said, 'you're pretty low. It's only a little trip you're taking, you know.'

Bernardo nodded. Tomaso thought, he thinks this is the definitive step, that's what it is. Doesn't he realize that we stepped into the cold night air weeks ago? We're a long way on this side of the Rubicon.

They walked out of the piazza and through two or three twisting narrow streets of the old town and into a big avenue lined with chestnut trees behind which stood large and often clumsy concrete buildings, blocks of flats, shops and offices, all built in the 1950s, as evidence of the town's development, all now looking shabby. Cars lined the street which had a dead sort of look. The policeman stopped at the corner just in front of a grocer's shop and held his hand up. A big car parked in the shadow of the side street started its engine and drew up beside them. A young man's curly head was poked out of the driver's window.

'This the boy?' he said. 'Into the back.'

For a moment Bernardo hesitated. Tomaso caught the light from the street-lamp shining greenly on his face, which was sweating. The policeman put his hand on Bernardo's shoulder and pressed hard. 'Think of where you're going,' he said. 'Count your luck, son.' Tomaso held out his hand. 'Good luck,' he said. 'We couldn't have got this far without you. But it's the next stage you've got to concentrate on now. I don't know when we'll meet again. Just remember, the work is more than the individual.'

'Vlad,' Bernardo managed to say, his voice breaking. He climbed into the back of the car, without help.

At once the car drove off, accelerating at the end of the avenue. They could hear it roar for some time in the evening stillness. Then they turned back to the town.

'We say Bernardo met some old friends and decided to spend the night with them. Then tomorrow he telephones to say he's going on a trip with them. That'll do for the American bints.'

'Yes,' Tomaso said. 'I suppose we have to make some explanation. Do we really have to go dancing?'

'It's the natural thing to do.'

'I suppose you know best, Carlo. I wish we didn't. I hate dancing.'

III

CHRISTOPHER

'I shouldn't have, Christopher,' she said, 'not now. I can't think how I came to . . .'

I rolled over on my back, thinking 'Why do they go on like this?', and reached out to the bedside table for a cigarette. My hand was still shaking; nausea tightened in my belly. I didn't light the cigarette.

'I'm going to take a shower,' she said.

The room was warm with the heat of afternoon shading into evening. I could hear the traffic and the shouting, all the horns, from Campo dei Fiori just down the alley. And shuddered, needing a drink. I'd got up—making my journey off a rajah bat—and been on my way to the office of the news magazine where I work, and turned back, not feeling up to it, intending to spend the afternoon asleep. But I'd met Bella across in the Corso, and so . . . Now I just lay there, happily laid, but fragile. Spiritually, or whatever, I felt fine.

She called out from the shower. 'Haven't you got a decent towel?'

It had taken me all my time to get the shower fixed.

She came back wrapped in a towel that was certainly a bit lacking, and dirty as well, and sat beside me and lit two cigarettes, one from the other, and put one of them between my lips.

'It was silly what I said. There's no reason why I shouldn't. I always have. In fact there's more reason than ever to do it. If you look at it one way, Chris.'

Bella glows after sex. She just glows. I've never known anyone give off a glow like it. And yet she's thoroughly bourgeois and groomed, and the sort of girl, if she'd been

English, that you'd have found at Lady Margaret Hall. I put my hand on her thigh, just under the ragged fringe of the towel.

'No,' she said pushing it away, 'I've no time for another shower, and if I'm late Daddy will go through the roof. He's terrified of what might happen to me just now. You can't blame him. We're all under siege . . .'

I pushed my hand back and let it rest moving ever so gently on the warm moist flesh. 'Help me break through the defences then,' I said. 'Fix me an interview with your cousins. The one, Nico, especially.'

'I don't know,' she said. It was unlike her to be indefinite, I'd never found her indefinite.

'Go on,' I said. 'Build me up. Remind them of the piece I did on the van Meer case.'

'Van Meer,' she said, 'I don't remember . . .'

'The Dutch industrialist they held in Genoa. I did a long investigation piece on him for *Domani Politica*. I'm an expert on terrorism.'

'But you're of the Left, Chris. They won't like that. They'll distrust it.'

'OK but I know, I can help, I can advise. Give me a build-up.' I didn't say I needed to write a big piece.'

'I'll see what I can do,' she said. 'Stay in circulation though.'

'OK I will. You fix it.'

I listened to her steps going down the stair, precise and rapid, you'd never think it was all worn and pitted to hear her heels rattle down . . .

I'm not clear which of us picked the other up. Mutual enough I suppose. I didn't lay her. She didn't lay me. We laid each other. Perfect. That was three months ago, maybe four. She's an unusual girl, considering her class anyway. Convenient too.

I didn't know then she was Corrado Dusa's niece.

Where to begin? (A problem as true in relationships as in writing a piece.)

I missed the commencement of the Dusa case, being drunk

117

at the time. (I missed the Cuba crisis, years back, for the same reason, emerging from a blacked-out few days to discover that the world had risked arriving in the same condition. I felt a bit cheated for a while.)

Just the same with Dusa. I got the first glimmering of it in a bar up Parioli. Something I overheard. It was that began to pull me round. The customary processes of recovery took their usual course and I only really surfaced to functioning level the day Dusa's first letter hit the Press. It got me down to the office fast.

Everyone there had their own theory. The strength of my position, apart from the fact that I hadn't been mulling it over for the past ten days or so, was my possession of an inside line in Bella. Only I kept quiet about that. I could have offered a sob-story piece to the glossy that is our news mag's stable companion—you know, *Sunday Times* stuff. But that's not my style (though I've done it of course, being a pro) or interest. Anyway it seemed best to keep quiet about Bella.

There was a change in the mood of the city. I'd sensed it walking across from Campo dei Fiori. It wasn't only the Police and Army evident all over the shop. It was the sensation of the *corrida*. Only who was the bull? Dusa? But he was absent. Perhaps the Republic?

I sat on the corner of the desk where my friend Antonio was sitting idle and said, 'It's going to dish us this, isn't it? Objectively, it must be aimed at the Party.'

'Christopher,' he said, 'I would like to believe it is the Americans, the CIA. I really would like to believe that because then we could say, yes it is nothing but the usual stupidity, but I'm afraid that it is not, that it is really what it proclaims itself to be, and that being so, I am totally lost. I find such reality wholly obscure, because the motives are malign and irrational.'

Antonio is an honest man. His father was a trade union leader imprisoned by the Fascists. Neither of them—I met his father several times, he died last year—could be called a victim of illusion. Experience inoculated them against the Millennium. Yet both believed rootedly, in a way I would like to believe, in the decency of man and the nobility of human

118

aspirations, and you could use such phrases of them themselves without a sneer. (It's the fact that phrases like this are still, despite everything, possible here in Italy, that has kept me living and working in the country. Despite everything, and by any calculations everything must include a hell of a lot, the possibility that such phrases have some meaning is alive here, and that is constantly amazing to a product of the English Public School system, and an Oxford that was focused on being either nostalgic or snide; or frequently both.)

'The letter is genuine enough though,' I said. 'It must be, yes?'

'Oh, genuine?', said Antonio. 'What is genuine?'

'I've missed things,' I said. 'I'm picking them up late. What's the Party's line?'

'Solidarity with the Government, condemnation of the outrage. Obvious and inevitable.'

'No, no,' I said, 'I mean, on the letter?'

'I don't think they've formulated one, but they can hardly dissent from the Government's view that it doesn't change the situation, they can't depart from support for the Government's refusal to negotiate. They daren't show themselves weaker than Schicchi.'

'And Schicchi?'

'Believes, naturally, that it is expedient that one good man die for the sake of democracy, Christian Democracy of course.'

'And is only relieved he's not the good man?'

'Precisely.'

'Not that he was ever in danger of being taken for that?'

'He may not be so sure on that point. We all have illusions about ourselves.'

'And where do you think he is? Dusa, I mean.'

'My dear friend, he is in Rome. There can be no doubt of it. And somewhere in the centre too. They will not have moved him far.'

'I've heard talk of an embassy. An Arab one possibly.'

'Perhaps, but it is unnecessary. Do you know what is the strange thing about this case? How open it is.'

'Open?'

'Yes,' Antonio lit the pipe he bought when on holiday in

119

England last summer. 'Yes, there are so many people I find who seem to know a bit about it. And of course it is opaque also. So many people know only a little, and some of them fail perhaps to realize their knowledge.

That is the sort of formulation Antonio loves. Open and opaque at the same time. You could answer 'Oh yeah', or you could take a closer look at it and end up agreeing.

'You know about the Dusa boy?' he said. 'Bernardo, one of the sons. He's said to have disappeared. Naturally that gives rise to speculation.'

'I've come across him,' I said. 'He's a would-be revolutionary. I shouldn't have thought he had the guts.'

'Well, he's disappeared. They're keeping it quiet. It would be parricide. Nothing would demonstrate the moral bankruptcy of the system more clearly. You want to dig into the case, don't you? You know that anything written here will have to be orthodox?'

'That's all right,' I said, 'basically, I am orthodox. You know that, Antonio. But if I come up with something that doesn't fit, there's other magazines I can sell a piece to, other names I can use . . .'

'Oh yes, and if you can get something on Bernardo . . . that would be a coup. I forgot, there was a call for you. Ed Mangan.'

'Oh God,' I said, 'Ed Mangan.'

'Yes, he is a terrible journalist, is he not?'

'Terrible. You know about Ed?'

Antonio shook his head. 'No,' he said, 'I have only read him. Enough.'

'But you haven't heard of his method. His famous method.'

'It never occurred to me he had one.'

'Oh yes, indeed.'

'Remarkable—I had thought his effusions the product of pure Anglo-Saxon flair.'

'Far from it. It goes like this. Ed once wrote a junk biography of Montgomery.'

'The Field-Marshal?'

'The same. Now in the course of what he called his research Ed was impressed by the Great Man's habit of keeping the photograph of the enemy general on his bedside table or desk. Monty used to claim this helped him get into their minds—PR crap of course. But Ed believed it. Swell idea, he says. So he starts the habit of collecting snaps of whoever he's working on and scattering them all over his hotel room or apartment. It's been said by unkind critics—most of Ed's professional colleagues that is—that this accounts for most of his blunders. He's got no eye for a face, you see, jumbles them up. He made a balls-up of a piece on Japan because he confused Hirohito with Chou En-lai, one wily Oriental being much like another to a Wasp like Ed. All the same he sticks to his method. If it doesn't bring success it still offers satisfaction. And that's the great thing, isn't it?'

'Right, Christopher. Who needs success if he can be happy with failure? Nevertheless the method is not so ridiculous. After all it's what one style of journalism demands, isn't it? That you get into the minds of your subjects. Your style, now I come to think of it. That's what you really did in the van Meer case, wasn't it? What about now?'

'I don't know,' I said. 'There's an amateurishness in any group that could use someone like Bernardo Dusa, yet the operation was carried out professionally enough. They haven't made an obvious mistake yet. Dusa's letter could even be a masterstroke, since the intention must be to set the State at odds . . .'

I arranged in the end to see Ed. You never know with a clown like that. He can have information without knowing it. So I arranged to pick him up in the lobby of his hotel, a modest dump in one of the streets down from the Piazza di Spagna— once he would have stayed automatically at the Hassler or the Excelsior. The porter didn't like the look of me—I was wearing patched and dirty jeans and an open-neck shirt, and I was debating whether to crush him with Roman dialect or Public School English voice, when the lift creaked to the ground floor and Ed bounded out. My first impression was that he looked rejuvenated; my second that he had aged in a surprising and rather horrible way. Something had gone from

121

his face, and that something was experience. 'Christ,' I said to myself, 'he's been born again . . .'

He showed himself over-pleased to see me. Americans often are. You learn it means nothing personal, and then you learn that it's significant to them. They really feel unhappy if they don't find themselves delighted to meet someone.

'You're the guy here I really wanted to see, Chris,' he said. 'I just can't say what it means to me you coming round like this. It's acumen and local knowledge I'm after. Let's go grab a beer.'

He talked all the way through the streets, back across Tritone, past the Trevi fountain, diagonally across the piazza in front of the Gregorian University where a few prickless priests-to-be were congregating, and all the time till we were settled at a table in the Birreria Peroni, just off the Piazza dei Santi Apostoli; it was dark and cool and still empty.

'Say,' he said, 'guess what's happened, Chris. My daughter's hit town, my little girl. What a time to choose, eh? What a goddam time. When I'm neck deep in this shit. So what do you make of it? I told the girls to meet us here, but we've time for a serious talk. So what gives?'

I get older and I get harder and I get more remote. I felt a spurt of anger. He was so easily what I could become myself. Just like that. I could see myself losing conviction in anything but the spurious excitement of the moment, back in the dead waste land of Anglo-Saxon empiricism.

'Oh,' I said, 'it's just a story to you, isn't it, Ed?'

He protested of course. People always protest at the sort of truth that diminishes them. He told me all about his change of faith, how he'd seen the light—I'm not sure the bastard didn't even mention Damascus; he must have, Ed couldn't have left that cliché unturned—and he held up his glass of Coca-Cola as testimony of seriousness; evidently the suggestion that we go grab a beer merely showed how old habits of speech survive the environment and society that gave rise to them. I called over my friend, the fat sweating waiter Pepe, who had now come on duty, and asked him for a large dark one for myself and another Coke for Signor Mangan.

'He is reformed,' I said. 'He is going to become a priest.'

122

'A man can be a priest', said Pepe, 'without frivolity.'

'See,' I said, 'your Coke proves nothing. In fact it proves the reverse of what you claim it does. I'd find it easier to believe you were politically serious if you still drank. Total conversions are always phoney. So I still say it's just a story to you and you're still an unreconstructed Cold Warrior.'

I was needling him on purpose and glad to. Even at the time I knew I was covering up my own uncertainty. It wasn't because of Bella that I felt this. She didn't mean anything to me that way or deep down. I was angry because I didn't know what to think.

'You're just a tourist, Ed. The journalist as tourist. I bet when you get yourself to hell you get a well-paid feature out of it . . .'

He took my needling tolerantly. That's one of the things about the born again. They've a good conceit of themselves.

'Look Chris,' he said, and 'here Chris' and 'shucks Chris' and went on to explain his virtues and expatiate on his serious involvement with world affairs.

'I guess I reckon Dusa's important,' he said, 'simply because he's a good man.'

But I knew what I wanted then. I wanted to believe they were going to be right when they killed him. I drank down a long gulp of the metallic beer and looked past Ed into the distance.

I stopped listening to him. He went on talking of course; people don't absolutely require an audience, some people at least. Instead, giving myself time to assimilate this realization, I looked round the big low-ceilinged room as if I'd never seen it before. And it was actually like that. Even the frieze—*nunc est bibendum*, what else?—looked new. But in fact this *birreria* had been a centre of my life in Rome from the beginning. I used to come here with an Irish actor who believed that beer could ward off the DTs. He was never certain if he wouldn't find himself locked out of the apartment in Parioli by his rich-bitch American mistress after our sessions. Consequently he spent a good many nights on my studio couch, a fact which nurtured my anti-American sentiments. Later my companion was an English poet, a pseudo-poet, oh very English, drenched

123

with the dew of Christ Church meadows, who came here to gaze on the young boy waiter of those days, but never dared do more than entice him to our table to take our order. Then they would exchange shy smiles. Even the memory of those smiles made me puke. For a long time after that I came here alone. I read the whole of *Das Kapital* at this very table. So the place represented a lot, the whole journey of my life.

'I put that point to Raimundo Dusa,' said Ed. 'Guess he didn't grasp what I was imputing . . .'

'Raimundo?'

'Yeah, he's Corrado's elder brother, an old buddy of mine. Used to be a diplomat. There was some kind of scandal. He's the old school though, keeps buttoned up. Ray's got no hope at all, just none whatsoever. He reckons his brother's a dead man, and if you ask me, wishes they would just get on and do it.'

But that was what everyone really felt. I knew that deep down. Nobody believed in an alternative ending, and there were many who saw Dusa's letter as a disgrace and hoped he would die before he could disgrace himself any more. I couldn't go along with that of course. I don't own the word disgrace for one thing, and second, second, I knew that what Dusa was writing was the truth. I almost told Ed that, just to see his face, but at that moment he stood up and began waving across the room which was now full and steaming of beer and the goulash sauce they were so lavish with. I looked over my shoulder and saw two girls and a boy approach.

The girls were full of expressions of American surprise, the pukeworthy sort occasioned by their tardy and incredulous realization that it is possible to deviate from the standards laid down by that Great God (or fallen angel), the American Way of Life. They were both classic examples of that, I saw at once. One the Brooklyn Jewgirl Mark One, the other echt Californian Popsy. The pair were so typecast it made you reflect again on the creative genius of the Studio system.

Ed's voice broadened to lecturing tones now he had a real audience, and he boomed on while the Jewish bitch settled and re-settled her duck-arse (piles?) on the chair and looked around the room with a tape-measure in her eye. I knew when she opened her lips, thick purplish lips they were, she would utter approved liberal sentiments, a Kennedy-worshipping cow if ever I saw one. And I've seen plenty, too many.

As for the other girl, Ed's daughter Kim, with her strawberry-pink mouth and everlasting legs, she made me creep with lust. It was all she was for, and it would never satisfy. Just looking at her made me feel savage—she was the bubble at the end of the American rainbow, what all that liberty and self-indulgence ended in; symbol and more than symbol of the catastrophe in which they've involved us all; Coca-Cola made flesh.

She looked back at me with her lips slightly open—it was hard to believe they were ever quite shut—and then stroked them with her beer.

She was a girl who would always caress herself.

But the boy; I've been dodging writing about the boy. He wore a thin dark suit and a set pale face and a lock of hair that kept trying to fall softly over his eye. He held himself very still and hardly touched his beer—you could see he didn't like it, taste and associations too I should think. He ate a few olives. I had seen him before. I knew that, but not where, and I knew his stillness meant he was special. Once or twice he moved his tongue very gently across his lips, just wetting them, as if to keep them from cracking. All the time he listened to Mangan and the girl Ruthie exchange approved liberal sentiments, with no expression on his face. No dissent at all. He might have been a young man in the Foreign Ministry. Even when I spoke up for the Palestinians against the Zionist Fascists, he stayed still.

The girl Kim called him Tom. She named him Tom every empty sentence she spoke. There was no response from him.

Ed went on explaining to Ruthie and Kim or to all of us, but really to them, the way he saw Italian politics. He drew on all his *Time* experience of the Cold War, and he placed the Dusa family and the Christian Democrats, and had all of the facts and none of the judgement. Kim's long fingers sought Tom's across the table. She blew smoke-rings at him, and she turned to me and smiled over the rim of her glass. She had a few refills. Every now and then she gave me a smile to keep

125

me in the game. In a pause she said, 'I just can't understand how people get hot over politics. Tom here gets hot. I know he does. It doesn't show, but I can just feel him simmer. I haven't found out yet what else he gets hot over.' She touched her pink lips with pink tongue. 'Do you get hot?' she said, looking at me straight. 'Christopher,' she added.

Ruthie leant over the table and said urgently, though not maybe to stop me answering Kim, 'Maybe you can tell us, Ed says you've lived here a long time,' she paused as if waiting for confirmation even of this, as if she had already formed the conviction that nothing Ed said could be accepted without corroboration.

'Seventeen years,' I said.

'I can't call you Christopher,' Kim said, 'it doesn't sound right. Chris? Maybe Kit. Kim and Kit, how's that?'

'Oh fine,' I said.

'Why do they make the poor man write these letters?' Ruthie said. 'Do they just want to humiliate him? It looks like it's pure sadism to me. Jesus, it's sadistic.'

'You could call it a process of education,' I said. 'They're showing him things as they really are. You don't know how these bastards of his party have exploited this country, these people. They've crucified the working-class. He's learning what it feels like.'

'Aw come on,' she said, 'it seems much like any place else. When I think of what my people . . .'

'Sure,' I said, 'your people. What happened to your people's going to be an excuse for the rest of history. For anything, Vietnam, Palestine, anything. As for this country—sure it's much like any place else—what difference does that make?'

I got to my feet and put a ten-thousand note on the table.

'That'll take care of the beer,' I said.

There is no difference between ignorance and wilful innocence. These people, these Americans, go about the world with their eyes shut. If they see dead bodies floating down a canal, they call for a relief organization. They don't see how greed is at the heart of all brutality, all injustice. How can they when their whole system is founded on greed and nothing else?

I stopped, angry and not wanting to be in the apartment

126

alone—there might be voices in that echoing solitude—I went into a little bar by the Pantheon and started drinking *grappa*. I downed two or three nerve-calmers quickly. A little man, a tenor who had lost his voice, came in and ordered a glass of milk. We nodded to each other. Sometimes he came and spoke to me here in his rasping dead whisper and told me about his daughter in Cincinnati. Or he asked me about my friend Katerina, a Polish violinist, who used to tell us here, in this bar, night after night, stories about her father who was a cellist. So many of them ended with the words, 'and he was so drunk it was as bad as the night he fell off a platform in Baden-Baden in the middle of a piece by Saint-Saens'—it had become a refrain. I found absurd tears pricking my eyes when I remembered this and I looked at myself sardonically in the long mirror behind the bottles. As I did so, I remembered where I had seen the boy Tom before. It had been in a wine-shop in the Suburra. I was with a Calabrian girl of mine called Margarita and she had pointed a boy out and said that was a sort of cousin, Bernardo Dusa, the politician's son. Bernardo was interesting, she had said. We should have a talk, some other time. But now she wanted to go home and fuck. So I didn't meet Bernardo. I couldn't believe then he was likely to be interesting. He looked as callow as they come.

There were two more letters from Dusa the next day. Their tone was more desperate still, the accusations against his colleagues now backed by threats of what he might disclose if they took no action to free him. The tone spoke of his fearful isolation. It brought him real to me. You couldn't read the letters and not feel that here was a man for the first time brought up against all sorts of reality that he had managed to deny all his life. They were stripping him naked. He had relied on his authority to protect him from all sorts of knowledge, and it was torn away. It was a rape before execution. Lines long dead in my imagination came back to me when I read these letters—they had that chill of knowledge that you get in the real thing—Lear and Dostoevsky and Dante. He was in the desert, with no shadow under the red rock. It stayed with me this realization—all through the grilling day. In the evening I took a tram up the Janiculum and stood under the statue of Garibaldi on his horse, thinking with rage of the lusts, lies and treacheries that seethed in the city spread out below. I sat at a *caffè* and ordered beer, only beer—the Consul used to proclaim that the Mexican stuff was full of vitamins, but nobody has ever made that claim for Peroni, except in jest or self-derision.

'Stop. I never knew the world was like this.' That was what Dusa was crying. Crying from the heart. I had known it at least since I was fourteen. I could not forget the captain of our dormitory, a tall elegant blond bully, the Housemaster's pet, a boy who really liked the CCF, a real creamy English boy with the false charm of the Chilterns, bathed in Home Counties security. One day, it was November, he drove us too far. We took him, five of us, after games that afternoon, all of us sweaty and muddy from rugby, and first thrust him down in a cold bath, and four of us held him there, crying already, while the fifth cropped his blond wavy hair. Then we tied him, naked but for the wet rugger socks which we hadn't troubled to remove, to the changing-room pegs, and left him there over tea. The socks made him look more ridiculous and lost than if he had been fully naked. There was no one to hear his cries. He was whimpering and abject by the time I came to let him go. All the time it was happening I was two people, sadist and masochist. He recovered of course, resumed his swagger or the appearance of it. Years later, when we were seventeen and the same height, he having stopped growing early, I having grown late, we became friends, even shared a study. He took my sister to dances. Once, when he was a cavalry subaltern and I an undergraduate, we met by chance in The Antelope in Eaton Terrace, drank a lot of whisky and went back to the flat I had borrowed and went to bed together. He couldn't meet my eyes in the morning, afraid of contempt. We'd made him so he couldn't ever believe in anything again. The destroyed can't afford illusions. America of course has never experienced defeat.

The light over the city turned dark violet. I switched from beer to vodka. It wasn't fanciful to see that Corrado Dusa is today exactly where Alastair Raven was that afternoon in

November, 1953. The politician and the prefect both brought low. Dormitory prefect only of course, and we didn't encourage Alastair to write letters about it. But Alastair could only be friendly, or, let's be honest, love those who had seen his nakedness; I expect he's married and lives a lie to his wife. There is that special bond between torturer and victim. They each know something of deep importance about the other.

So who is Corrado Dusa talking to now?

I could read his letters as a desperate attempt to involve the whole world in his disgrace and so in his love. The whole world except Gianni Schicchi, I suppose.

The night fell, moonless. I thought of Bella, who would understand none of this.

All the same, still thinking of Bella, inevitably I had Kim a day or two later. It was what she was for. She made me go through the whole performance though, since she was cock-teaser as well as whore. I came on her and Ed having a drink in Navona on the Sunday morning with the *Observer* and the *Sunday Times* which both had long articles on Dusa that Ed had to dissect. Kim was bored, dressed all in white, white jeans and a white shirt. She drew everyone's eyes, but they didn't stay on her the way eyes stayed on Bella or used to stay on my ex-wife, Sarah.

Maybe it was pity made me go through the performance. But there was loathing too. I wanted to humiliate her, for making me itch that way, but when, after lunch, she was naked on my bed and I realized that she deeply wanted just that humiliation herself, then something went out of me and my love-making was efficient, middle-aged and perfunctory. I don't know if she knew I had lost interest. A lot of men, I suppose, lost interest about the same stage and maybe she thought that was just how the sex behaved. She might never get what she wanted and go through life frustrated but unharmed.

'It's kinda cute your apartment,' she said, sitting up with the dirty sheet pulled round her on the bikini line of her breasts, the way she had learned from the movies. She accepted the obligatory cigarette, and blew out smoke and repeated what she had said. 'I guess it's a real bachelor's pad,' she said. 'How come you live like this though? Dad says Italian journalists make good money.'

'We do all right.'

'But you're English, aren't you?'

She wasn't really curious. You can always tell when they are. She was just making conversation to keep off silence, and when she went on to ask me if I had never been married, and I told her about Sarah, and if I had any children, and I told her about Julian, she came to a stop. No more questions. Social obligations had been fulfilled and she could return the conversation to herself where she felt at home, and a description of her sensations.

'I've got this thing about men, you know. I guess it's a kind of kink with me. Ruthie says it's the way I'm made. She says I'm a very physical girl.'

She stretched back across the pillow as she said this, letting the blonde hair fall advertisingly free.

'Well,' I said, 'your cousin Tom seemed pretty struck with you the other night. He couldn't take his eyes off you.'

She frowned, thinking visibly. It was incongruous, like watching an alligator dance.

'He's funny, Tom. I guess he's kinda shy. It's funny though finding an Italian boy that's shy. I never thought I'd find that. Not the way my ass gets pinched black and blue in the streets.'

I got her back to Tom and she told me of their visit to his home in the Abruzzi, and about his friend who'd been there. 'A real jerk,' she said. 'It was funny though, the way he just disappeared. Ruthie was sure he didn't want to go.'

Certainty came to me in that instant, like the first leaf-stripping wind of the Tramontana that tells you the summer is over; it came like the menace revealed by the lamplight in the street you had thought deserted; like that moment panic tells you to go on and not stop.

'He seemed a nice boy,' I said, 'your cousin.'

'Sure he's nice, he's a nice kid, but funny,' said Kim. 'You know, where he lives in Rome there's no telephone like. That's really weird. I guess I could hardly believe it at first. Why I'd be lost without a phone.'

★

130

Bella called me the next morning to say she had fixed an interview with her cousins.

'I've told them you can help. I've told them about those pieces you've done that you said to mention. They're a bit suspicious though, because you're a Communist. Or at least Nico is. Sandro doesn't count. He's sweet but not really in tune with the way people live. You understand? On the other hand the fact that you're a Communist is in a way attractive. They think you might have influence in circles they can't reach. So, they're not quite sure what you want of course, and they're nervous of giving you the sort of story you might twist. You can't blame them for that, if they're suspicious of everyone at the moment. They'd be nervous of journalists at any time I think. I know my father is. He always says they're trouble—maybe because he's a businessman, I don't know. And, Christopher, they don't know in detail what they want. They just hope you can do something for them. Only, you understand, they're desperate. I don't know why I say "they" all the time, because of course I'm in the same boat. I feel with them. But I have also told them that you are very intelligent and deep-down serious. Actually, Nico has a great respect for the English. So has Sandro of course, but he doesn't signify. What in fact do you want, dear?'

'I want the truth first,' I said. 'I want to know what has happened and what it means.'

'Ah,' she said. I could sense her vitality down the line, her reserves of energy and feeling. 'But you don't believe he can be saved, do you? You're sure he is going to be killed?'

'Yes,' I said, 'I'm afraid that's so. I could be wrong of course . . .'

'Sandro and Nico can't accept that yet . . .'

'But you can?'

'He's only my uncle of course . . .'

'That's not all though, is it? You're following your intelligence.'

'Yes . . . yes, listen Christopher, be gentle with them. Apart from anything else they are confused. There is Bernardo too, and they have had some unpleasantness with the Security Police about him. Sandro was almost in tears about it. Tell me

131

also. Since you don't believe he can be saved, what do you hope for?'

But I had no answer ready to that.

When I saw Sandro Dusa I wanted to hurt him.

'Nico is sorry he is late,' he said, stretching out towards me a heavy silver cigarette box. 'He has just telephoned to say that he will be here as soon as possible. The Bank . . .'

His voice tailed off, the way it always would when it left off mouthing inanities. I could see what Bella meant—he was so obviously soft and uncertain and vulnerable.

'Our cousin, Bella, says that in some way she believes you can help.'

He smoothed his hand down the creamy yellow of his trousers and fished out a slim gold lighter and snapped it at our cigarettes. He held his own cigarette gingerly, too close to the tip, between his second and third fingers.

'Help', I said, 'is probably the wrong word for what I can offer. I'm hoping for help from you two in turn though.'

'Oh,' he said, 'you are just like everyone else, that is what they really mean whatever they promise. Nobody wants to do anything to save him.'

He was perched on the arm of one of those heavy, ugly, oak chairs with ridiculous carving, and the big room was half-dark with venetian blinds drawn. The traffic in the Corso seemed a long way below. It was an apartment belonging to someone in Nico's bank that he had borrowed for our meeting. He had said, 'It is better that nobody should know we are meeting'. I had thought this excessive, but complied.

Now I said, 'I don't know if anyone has put it on the line to you. Maybe they haven't and maybe you are a political innocent. I should think from the look of you that's just what you are.' He made a vague deprecating motion with his cigarette. 'The thing is—the real world is nasty, don't expect too much. Look, this situation—I refer to the political development for which after all your father was responsible, the so-called Historic Compromise just round the corner—is regarded by all the politically responsible class, DC, PCI, PSI too, as vital. Vital. So they are not going to do anything that will risk cracking it. I don't know why I'm saying this to you. I'm probably wasting it and should keep it for your brother, but still here's how it is. (a) They're afraid, all of them, that any concession will simply encourage more acts of terrorism. That's what their friends in the CIA tell them. It's what the Germans say. It's the common-sense Anglo-Saxon view. (b) The DC are afraid that if they offer to treat, the Communists will regard it as a betrayal and will wreck the Government. (c) The Communists are afraid that if they suggest conciliation they will be associated with the terrorists. They have come a long way to be respectable, as some people would call it. They are not going to wreck that for one man's life, not when power is within sight.'

'Oh yes,' he said, 'but you see he is my father.'

His simplicity grated—they have no right to go on being children in the world we live in. Innocence is a reproach to reality. Another privilege of the privileged, and so an insult to those who suffer and those who know. And anyway there is nothing to say to it. It defies response. Fortunately there then came from the street the shriek of a police car siren to cut through his fascinated self-absorption, and then the door opened and the brother, Nico, entered and apologized for being late, but not too much. You can judge a man by the degree of apology and he passed the test. He looked at me straight, a composed reticent glance, irony implicit.

Sandro Dusa said, 'Mr Burke has just been making it clear to me that we are wasting our time, that there is no hope at all.'

I got another cool regarding look from Nico. 'Yes?' he said, keeping the note of interrogation light.

'That's so,' I nodded.

'But you still have an interest sufficient to bring you here?'

'Interest is hardly the same as hope. I'm a journalist, that's all.'

'And so would be satisfied with a story?'

'Of the right sort, yes.'

'And that would be?'

He spoke with the decision of a good bridge player trying to make a contract that depended on a finesse. We were all still on our feet, the heavy chunks of smoked oak acting as barricades, obstacle and bulwark at the same time. It was a negotiation, a parley, not yet (if it ever would be) a conversation. Dogs walking stiff-legged round each other, in smouldering distaste and distrust . . .

'How do you feel about your father's letters?' I said.

His eyes didn't shift. He slipped his hand into the breast pocket of his suit-jacket. It was a double-breasted suit with thin stripes, quite new; formal and forbidding.

'They make his colleagues ashamed,' I said, 'or so they say.'

'They go further than you may know,' Nico said.

'What do you mean?'

He paused a moment, glancing at me from under lowered eyelids, then walked over to the window, pulled aside the corner of the venetian blind and looked down into the Corso. I was aware of Sandro shifting from foot to foot and breathing little whistle-sounds.

'There's a direct line to us,' Nico said, still staring down into the street, attentively, like a man watching for a shadow. 'Father has been writing to us as well. What he says is . . . well, judge for yourself. Read this and please note, Mr Burke, I'm not imposing any conditions on the use you may care to make of this information.'

He handed me a flimsy sheet, covered with a condensed nervous script.

'This is from your father?' I said. 'You've no doubts as to its authenticity?'

'None.'

'And you're trusting me with it? Why?'

He made a deprecatory gesture with his hand. 'Bella's recommendation,' he said. 'What I've learned of you—for of course I've made other enquiries—oh, confidential ones naturally. The fact that you are English. A lot of reasons. Read it.'

'You realize', I said, 'that I came here to ask questions. There will be more now.'

'But of course,' he said. 'Later. Now read it.'

Dusa's letter began in warm affectionate tones, speaking of his deep love for his family, his complete confidence in their love for him. He stressed that this applied to all of them,

134

'without exception' . . . That must mean that he knew the truth of what I suspected, Bernardo's involvement in his capture. Did Nico, I wondered; Nico who was still gazing down into the Corso, as if rapt in a spectacle of the utmost drama; but I was sure he saw nothing . . . Dusa apologized for what he described as 'the exigencies of the political life which have from time to time and all too often prevented me from sharing to the full the intimacies and confidences which a father should share with his children'. Then he spoke of his present danger. 'All the same,' he continued, 'in all the circumstances of life one can learn something. Now I learn not only the depth of my love for you all, and the full extent of my duty towards you, but I am also offered the opportunity of assessing my actions, and those of my Party and colleagues, in a new light. Doing so, I see how far we have departed from our Christian and humane ideals, and, to my shame and shock, I see many of those ideals which I embraced so warmly when I embarked on my life in politics, now better displayed by those who presently hold me and my life in their power . . .'

He elaborated on this, and then said, 'Now, fully aware of this, and aware also that I have been deserted by those who have a duty towards me, a duty consecrated by comradeship and association, many of whom would not be in their present positions but for my help, encouragement and actions, I feel myself freed of my own obligations of secrecy, or at least in the process of becoming so liberated. So far I have been reserved and have revealed nothing of the many facts which I know, the disclosure of which would be harmful to the careers of many of my colleagues, even to the future of my Party; but I see no reason to maintain such silence unto death, especially inasmuch as I have become convinced that much that is shameful has also been unwise, and can yet be corrected. Naturally, I should prefer to make such corrections from a position in which I could ease their effect. Equally naturally, deserted and alone, I must use such weapons as come to hand in order to protect myself. If I have been abandoned, why should I remain loyal to those who have not scrupled to desert me? I therefore instruct you, my dear children, to convey this warning to Gianni Schicchi and the other leaders of my Party, and to let

135

them know that I shall reveal what they are themselves aware of, that this revelation will be disastrous for them, and that all that can prevent it is some real and effective evidence that they are prepared seriously to negotiate my release. Furthermore I point out that the conditions which I have now persuaded my captors to propose can hardly be called onerous . . .'

I hadn't thought he would fight like this for his life.

All the time I was reading Nico had remained still, his only movement the rubbing of finger and thumb on the winding-knob of his wristwatch.

'Well,' I said, 'quite a letter. No wonder you are perplexed, don't know what to make of it or what to do.'

Sandro said, 'Somehow we must use it to secure his release, to free him . . .'

I kept my eyes on Nico.

'The consequences,' I said.

'Yes,' he replied, 'the consequences. What would your Party think of it. Can you tell me that for a start?'

I shrugged my shoulders.

'Revelations about the DC?' Sandro said. 'Surely they'll leap at them? How could they fail to?'

'Oh,' said Nico, 'I doubt if we can be as certain as that. I am fairly sure that Mr Burke isn't certain at all, Sandro. Are you, Mr Burke?'

'You're right,' I said. 'Normally the answer would be yes, but just now, weighing the matter objectively, I would say they would rather no such revelations were made. That's my opinion . . .'

'Of course,' Nico said, 'they need not necessarily be made. The suggestion may be sufficient.'

'The suggestion has always been there. Implicit,' I replied. 'You may be certain of that. Schicchi has always been aware of the suggestion, aware and afraid. That's why we already have psychologists being wheeled out to talk of personality changes resulting from the use of drugs . . .'

'Then why won't Signor Schicchi negotiate?' Sandro's question was half a sob.

'Ah,' said Nico, 'he is held, I think, poised between two fears. And, unfortunately, one fear is balanced by hope . . .'

136

Had things been different, I could have admired Nico. I almost did even as they were. We ought to admire objectivity . . .

'So what would you want?'

A long silence succeeded; silence of the pall. Nico sat down. At a chair behind a desk. Of course. He leant back, face open to the ceiling, eyes closed, lips moving. He put his hands up to his face and drew his long fingers down his cheeks; lingeringly.

'We are on a chess board,' he said. 'A game is being played out, and like all games of chess it is moving towards a conclusion that seems ever more inescapable. Each piece has of course its pre-ordained mode of movement, its limit of freedom. Now at a certain point in the game, reversals become impossible. You have lost too many pieces. We have arrived there. In the End Game, as they call it. The king is one move, two at most, from suffering check-mate. All that can save the situation is to . . . stop playing chess, to sweep the pieces off the board, to say we will prove our supremacy by not playing games . . .' he threw his hands up. 'I am not sure that my analogy holds up,' he said, 'that it has in fact anything to offer. Bella would say that I am losing myself in words and ideas. What do you think, Mr Burke?'

'The rules say you go to Schicchi with this letter—well, a copy would be safer—and press it on him. See if he gets frightened enough to move. But he won't. The American State Department would never forgive him if he did; and as you know when the State Department frowns the Bank of Italy shivers etc. The old game. So I think you should tear up the rules. Sweep your pieces from the board. Stop playing chess.'

'And?'

'Give me the letter. Let me see if I can use it to tear things apart.'

He drummed his fingers on the desk. 'They are not negotiating because they want him dead,' he said.

'They would rather he was put to death than that they should be compelled to negotiate,' I replied.

'What will you do with the letter?'

'Publish it. Then perhaps . . . well, people will write demanding real negotiations. I don't write that sort of advocate's piece

137

myself, but I can arrange it. Others will make the demand spontaneously. If the demand is powerful enough, you never know. It's an outside chance . . . but if you take the letter to Gianni it will be buried.'

Nico handed me an envelope. 'Put it in that,' he said.

It should have felt like an important decision. Yet, in all of us, there was this lack of conviction that came from the feeling that the game was being played according to inexorable rules; rules that were fixed. They couldn't believe that their actions would save their father; I that mine would tear the Compromise apart and destroy the State.

I worked out this analysis later over a beer in the Apostles. I had never experienced this lassitude in a crisis before, this sense of impotence; and I also brooded on the curiosity that presented itself to my mind, that I, a good and loyal member of the Party, which was committed to amelioration of social conditions and a coherent programme of social and economic reform, should yet feel so strong an affinity with what I might have interpreted as nihilism, if a small voice hadn't insisted in me that it wasn't that at all; it was Revolution, the real, betrayed and cheated, but always desirable, Being.

We hadn't spoken of their brother, Bernardo, and I hadn't breathed my suspicions which were actually a certainty. There would be time for that later. And moreover, I just couldn't connect these two, the Poof and the Pundit, with my sensation of that boy; when you reflected, he had done what others merely dreamed of; killed his father. Or rather, sold him to the knacker's, which might be still more deeply satisfying.

Then Kim and Ruthie came into the *caffè* and straight to my table.

'Have you seen Ed?'

They sat down, not waiting for an answer; I'd been adopted as one of the gang. She stank, that Ruthie, physically and intellectually. And her talk . . . but, full of crap though it was, it led me seductively towards my area of interest; she was full of Tomaso and his mysterious friend. And, to do her justice, even she was breeding suspicions. She was suspicious of me too, and edgy. She kept putting her hand on Kim's and saying things like:

'Honey, I'm tired . . .

'Honey, not more beer . . .

'Honey. . . .'

I said, smiling with a resurrected verve, 'I'll take you to a restaurant. A fun place.'

She looked at Kim to tell her to say no, but of course she leapt at the word fun. Fun was what she lived for; she had no conception beyond it. So she wasn't going to play the little Dutch boy against a flood of fun. I was amused to have Ruthie tag along. She would have liked to get between us in the taxi, but of course Kim wasn't having that. I took them to the Baths of Caracalla, where there is a restaurant strictly for the tourists, with waiters dressed as ephebes and a hulking butch gladiator who comes round and bangs a plastic sword on your table and is photographed with blondes and blue-rinsed bitches . . . I ordered sucking-pig and Barolo and a bottle of champagne to start with and spoke to them in Roman slang so that they would give us something I could eat. The gladiator banged his sword on his greaves; oh Jupiter. Ruthie hated every minute, but Kim's eyes grew big with life. They were as large as soup-plates to start with. I felt her under the table and she leant over and kissed me and giggled.

I said to her, 'And how are you making out with Tom?'

She pouted.

I said, 'I'm really concerned to know. I appreciate one guy won't be enough for a girl like you. Believe me,' I said through her giggles, 'I'm not jealous, there's enough of that emotion floating around you already. Come on, Ruthie, you tell me, how's she making out with Tom? Here, this'll help you.' I poured her a glass of the muck they called champagne. 'Come on,' I said; but she just looked at me. 'All the same,' I said, 'all the same, Kim, I bet Tom doesn't fuck. I bet he has other interests. In fact I bet he's a virgin. It's a funny thing, chastity—you got any thoughts about it, Ruthie? You know how the knights used to value it. To say nothing of the good old English Public School tradition in which I was chastely bred. And why? Theory was, we all have a finite resource of energy. Sex takes it out of you—well, that's true enough. So if you want to be a big man you have to conserve it. What do you think of that . . . as a theory . . .?'

I talked on like this, fondling Kim all the time.

'Look at the gladiator, Ruthie,' I said. 'You think he's tough. Not at all. He's wondering who he's going to lay tonight. That's all. He amounts to nothing, all he's good for is laying. You agree with me, don't you, about chastity? Do you think Tom's up to something that he's so chaste? Do you think the boys who have Dusa are chaste? Do you think that's why they're committed?'

'Of course,' I said, pouring us all glasses of Barolo, 'by rights if we want to dominate, we should keep off this stuff too. Wine is a mocker and all that. But Ruthie, you don't really want to dominate, do you? You're like me, politically sentimental. That's why we're both taken with this piece Kim, isn't it? As for the Dusa case and guys like Tom and the real politicals there, you and me we're nothing but voyeurs. Isn't that so? That friend of Tom's you're interested in, what was his name . . . did he fuck? Did he drink? Bet he didn't. Not really. And then he just vanished, yes? You don't know where. Man of mystery? But not to the brothel, eh? You know I had a thought, I bet you couldn't recognize him. People like you don't really look at folk, do they?'

And then I shuffled a pile of photographs before her, and of course, in a fury, she picked him straight, Bernardo Dusa. I had ninety per cent of a scoop.

You may well ask—I could even ask myself—why I did it this way. She would have identified him of course if I had just rung her up, arranged to meet, bought her a coffee and laid the photographs before her. All I can say is I did it this way because I wanted to. She set me on edge. They both did. Really I wanted the gladiator to take her and I called him over to the table, but she got up and walked out. Kim stood a minute with her finger to her lips and made to follow her to the powder room, but I put my hand on her wrist and she turned her face to me, lips apart, and with that approach to grace she sometimes had, sank down beside me on the banquette. We didn't stay there much longer . . .

I woke with her beside me, the wrong girl and night and the hollow realization, brought to me straight by the tyres screaming round the corner that, despite everything, I hadn't drunk enough. I put my hand on her damp skin; no movement; even from her, living for the flesh and in it, in no other way, no response.

What brought me here to this decaying tenement, and why do I go angrily on?

I pad out of bed, across the dirty tiles, to the wine bottle, a flask of white, half-full, sour and comforting. I make almost no connection with my past and I sit there in the wicker chair, nursing my glass, nursing myself, and for a moment I would like to be Tom, and know that I was going to kill.

I could kill the girl in the bed.

It would be as insignificant as anything I have done. That stops me.

Another drink . . .

'The snake', wrote Louis Macniece, 'is back on the tree.'

I remember once going to Spoleto with my friend, Hugo. A friend of ours was playing Hamlet in a production that promised some excitement; in those days we could still get excitement from the theatre . . . that dates my story. (Is it a story?) I say a friend of ours though then I had only met him once. Hugo knew him well enough however. Carmelo Bene, of course—how could I have forgotten it was Bene? Well, we arrived. There was also my then wife, Sarah, and Hugo's lover from schooldays, whose name I forget but who later became a Buddhist monk. We discovered that the production was off. Bene had quarrelled with Menotti and been expelled from the Festival. At least that was the story they told us in the bar. Consequently we drove round Spoleto with some local boys and then took the night train back to Rome. Sarah and the other boy, whatever his name was, went to sleep and Hugo and I sat up talking Malcolm Lowry and drinking a bottle of brandy all the way back. At some stop a woman got on the train with a chicken on a string, which is of course a figure that recurs to the doomed Consul throughout the book, and especially before his death. Hugo and I were both staggered by the enormous symbolic importance of this coincidence, which was certainly one that would have delighted old Malc himself.

Another drink, looking at him.

What would that girl in the bed make of an old woman leading a chicken on a string onto a night train through the mountains? I'll tell you, it would mean nothing to her. That's right. She would be right. The reason I fuck her is in the hope that what she knows about life is in the end sufficient; all there is to know . . .

I wish I could believe any of that.

We live in a time that must have revolution, some revolution, or it will perish; of vacancy and inanity. That's it: we are our own Barbarians. Kim turns in the bed, with a soft moan. What pleasure that thought would give me if I loved her. There is a streak of new grey light comes across the piazza, and a scream of tyres again, and doors banging.

The feet, tipped with metal, come up my stairs. And the knock on the door comes, absolutely correctly, with the dawn.

After that, it's not played according to rule. They are polite; threatening in itself, admittedly. Three of them, two uniformed and the other in the grey suit of a serious man. Of the two in uniform, one was an officer, the other a gorilla. They took their time over pretending to establish my identity. I had suggested we go through to the kitchen, explaining that there was a girl in my bed.

'She's an American girl,' I said, 'she would be alarmed . . .'

They were civil and understanding, but they didn't suggest I put on anything more suitable than the towel I had wrapped round me when I heard the knock.

'You saw two of the Dusa brothers yesterday. Why?'

I lit a cigarette and poured myself another glass of wine. 'Yes,' I said, planting the flask on the table beside me. I gestured towards it. They declined.

'Why?'

'I'm a journalist, as you know. They're news.'

'I shouldn't have thought you were exactly sympathetic towards them. Yet I understand they sought the interview . . .'

'I would hardly say that. Unprofessional. And as for any differences, I'm naturally sympathetic towards them in their present position . . . it's a very human . . .'

142

'But, politically . . .'

'Politically, as I've no doubt you know, Captain, I'm a member of the PCI, and you know what their line is on this question. So, as an individual, of course I sympathize with the Dusa family—which of us doesn't—but beyond that, I agree with the Central Committee of my Party that we must rely on police enquiries.'

'And you would of course be prepared to help in any way with these?'

'Of course.'

The man in grey looked at me with mournful brown eyes. The uniformed men shuffled about, as if the action was too slow for their taste. Yet policemen should be accustomed to it. That's what their life's like after all; long periods of inertia interrupted by sporadic action.

He said, 'A case like this, it is necessary to cast a wide net. You know that. I have read some of your journalism, Signor Burke, with admiration if not always agreement. Your piece on van Meer, for instance, perceptive even if not in the final analysis wholly convincing. To me, that is. So it is like fishing a lake. You cast your net and you don't at all know what you may come up with. For instance, last night, you will have heard doubtless, we received a message that Dusa's body is in fact in a lake up in the Abruzzi mountains. Now, you can take it from me, it is absurd. A lake in the Abruzzi, why would they put him there? And indeed how? And it is unlikely that he is yet dead; you, Signor Burke, may know quite certainly that he isn't, with your privileged communication with the Dusa family. But of course we must investigate. We will find nothing. Probably the lake is still frozen. Who knows? Why do they do it, you may ask?'

'They do it to make us look silly,' said the uniformed lieutenant.

'Perhaps. Anything which makes us look silly undermines the State. To be quite honest, that is the basis of my personal dislike of journalists. It's not the facts which they discover that make me disapprove; it's their motive. States are fragile. They are too easily destroyed. But a lake in the Abruzzi? It is absurd. Do you know the Abruzzi, Signor Burke?'

143

'Not well.'

'A wild country. You could of course hide anything there. Tell me, do you know the other Dusa brother, Bernardo?'

'I only met any of the Dusa brothers today, for the first time . . .'

'A pity. He sounds the most interesting of them. You know he has disappeared?'

It was transparent. Impossible of course that any policeman, even one so obviously classed as 'a thinking cop' as this one, could actually find Bernardo interesting. I stood up.

'I'm going to make some coffee,' I said, 'I've been drinking wine too long. I woke feeling thirsty. Yes, I had heard something about him. It sounds a foolishness, as though he took fright at a shadow. That's all.'

Out of the windows, across the roof-tops, the East was reddening. Through a gap in the chimney-pots I could see the pine trees of the Palatine. I wished the policemen would go away; their patience is always exhausting.

'We've been checking up on his friends. You know how it is. I wondered if I might ask you to look at these photographs.'

He spread them before me on the table. Young men, mostly with beards; those without them possibly the same young men in unbearded state; the faces of the feeling, self-important young.

'Well?'

'Who are these?'

'That doesn't matter. Are there any you recognize?'

'They all look like every third boy in this quarter. You can see them all or their doubles down there at the Farnese Cinema every evening.'

He sighed.

'No doubt,' he said. 'Nevertheless, would you please look at these more carefully? After all, you yourself spoke of the importance of routine police work in this case. This is part of it. I'm being unusually patient, Signor Burke.'

I didn't say, 'You're being a damn sight more patient than the police who turned up here and slapped me across the face, turned the apartment inside out and locked me up for a couple of nights last October, after I wrote that piece about Moroni,

144

the DC Deputy from Taranto.'

Instead I sighed in my turn, sat down and, picking up a pencil, pushed the photographs about with it. The boy Tomaso was there, his face shining out from the others. I kept a bored Oxford look on mine.

'No,' I said, 'nobody.' Then I hesitated—I pushed at one of a rat-faced boy with a wisp of beard. 'Maybe him, but I don't know where.'

'You disappoint me,' said the Captain. 'I expected you to be more intelligent.' With his nail he pushed forward the photograph of Tomaso.

Through all that followed, the shoulder-shruggings, the smiling denials, the persistent questioning, the 'if you say so's' and so on, I wondered when they were going to wake up Kim and ask her the same question; and when they left, about two hours later, I still couldn't believe they hadn't done so. It made no sense to me at all, since it seemed likely that it was through Kim that they had made the connection between me and Tomaso. But did they take the next step and link him to Corrado as well as Bernardo, or did that idea still seem too far-fetched to them?

Kim woke. Stretched herself like an advertisement and showered, came towelled from the water, her hair clinging to her neck and shoulders, sat in a chair, her eyes heavy, looking like the wrong sort of morning, not beautiful at all. What she would be in time, sullen and fleshy. She babbled of a screen test she should have had, that had been postponed. She complained of this and that, and that and this. I saw in her America, perpetual adolescent, promoting its drugged moribund culture of sensation across the globe; great American word, global.

I said, 'Can you find your cousin Tomaso?'

'I told you he's not on the phone. It's crazy, not being on the phone.'

'Look, you see him though.'

'No,' she said, 'he said he would be away for five days. Said he would call me when he got back.'

'So he calls you?'

'That's right. It's crazy, like I said.'

'And he's away for five days. Get me in touch with him when he calls you. It's urgent.'

'OK, sure. I dunno, maybe I should go back to California. What do you think, Kit, I mean at least there when they promise you a screen test, they show up like. Right? Ruthie's no help either. This guy said he was like a producer too.'

I went round to the office, past the rows of policemen that still acted as barriers and checkpoints all over the city.

Antonio said, '*Ciao*, Chris. I'm just sending down to the bar for a coffee and cheese sandwich. What about you?'

'I'll take the sandwich, but a beer with it.'

'Fine,' he said, 'what about the Abruzzi lake then?'

'A joke, quite a good one.'

He shook his head at me. My reaction was too English, frivolous. Antonio, despite his deep inherited respect for the English—didn't we help Garibaldi?—still can't accept our frivolity.

'No,' he said, 'it is not like that, you understand. On the contrary, it's very serious, a test, don't you see? They are experimenting with their credibility. The number of troops the Government sends to search the lake, which, by the way, is certainly still snow-bound and under several centimetres of ice, will serve to indicate how unnerved they are. That in turn will help the PDP to determine how far they need be prepared to compromise.'

'You think they may be ready to compromise?'

'In the end they are politicians too; their demands will be moderated. But such compromise does not exclude execution.'

The beer, coffee and sandwiches arrived. I took a swig; metallic.

'How did you get on with the brothers Dusa?'

'They have had a letter from their father. Direct.'

'And you've seen it?'

'Not only that. I have a copy.'

'With you?'

'Here you are.'

I sat on the edge of the desk, holding my beer glass in both hands, for the moment happy not to feel the need to drink.

'This is magnificent,' said Antonio. 'And we can publish this? Yes? Superb. You realize, it blows everything up; it may even save him . . .'

So even Antonio was inconsistent. He was certain, at one level, that he had been right all along: they would kill Dusa. And in one sense he didn't mind at all. Dusa might be the best of the bunch, but it was a bunch that had served the Italian people pretty ill. On the other hand, Antonio was also a man of simple decency. He couldn't condone terrorism, even where he applauded the cause. In his heart he was afraid of where even the most idealistic movement could lead us, once it took to violence. And he feared violence, whereas I . . . I could not look on it without envy. And I wanted to understand it, while Antonio knew it already, felt it within himself and controlled it . . .

Meanwhile Antonio said, 'I forgot, you had a telephone call. This number . . .'

I glanced at the paper: Bella's number, but for the moment I ignored it. The revelation of Antonio's divided response was too important. I said, 'All the same if we help them to negotiate where does that leave the Party? Won't it strengthen all the extremists and attract still more of the young away from the Party and towards them? Isn't that one of the things we have long been afraid of, and isn't the fear even more urgent now . . . ?'

Antonio filled his pipe. 'Everything you say is true.' He gave me a frank, manly—yes of Antonio I can use the word, manly—smile. 'Only if we are in a position, you and I, to do something which could save his life. Well, are we going to be able to look at ourselves in the shaving-mirror if we don't? And I'm the wrong age for growing a beard. You have to be very young or very old to go in for that sort of self-deception without harming yourself . . .'

I saw his weakness, even though I found myself unwilling to argue it with him. Affection prevented that. All the same it should have done something to my respect for Antonio, to find that here, in what was not even the last resort, he was ready to put his own peace of mind, even what you might call a sense of honour, before what his reason told him was politically, and therefore historically, right. What did it matter whether he

147

could face himself? Apart from immediate considerations, all the logic said Dusa had to die. Things had gone too far for any other outcome to be anything but a farce.

Which didn't mean that it mightn't be right to use his letter. After all, I didn't believe it would do anything to budge Schicchi.

I said, playing it from both ends, 'OK, Antonio. Here's Dusa's letter. You take it and use it how you think best. As for me, I'm going to call my girl. That's who this call was from.'

'Oh Christopher, you and your girls . . .'

Antonio knows me too well; or thinks he does.

Bella said to me, 'Can I trust you?'

She had picked me up in her car and said, 'My office think I am going to the dentist. I thought we could go out of Rome.'

She had driven me along the Appia Antica, first past the high-walled, iron-barred, Doberman-and-electronic-device guarded villas of the profiteers, then past the whores sitting in their Volkswagens—the years when they sat in the autumn by bonfires were long past—then turning left, through scruffy and straggling suburban villages and up into the little hills, the Castelli. The sun was shining, flowers were everywhere, lakes were deep blue. We stopped at a Trattoria called 'Il Paradiso' and ate *fettucine al burro* and lake trout, and drank the house *vino scelto*. Rome seemed a long way away, though we had driven for only forty minutes.

'I used to live here,' I said, 'when I first came to Italy.'

It had been a different Italy, a different Christopher. I had stayed with an American poet and his Irish girl, in a villa overhung by mimosa trees. The garden had been full of roses, the house covered with geraniums, hyacinths too. I remember the girl coming in from the rain, her arms dripping with flowers. I had been writing poetry myself then, that self long buried. Right enough. You look back to Ancient Greece and in one century, I forget which, you find just fragments of the soldier-poet Archilochus, and any version of him is a reconstruction of fragments, and there's nothing else; or you look even at Catullus and see how little there is, and nothing else that begins to be like him, and then you look at now; at all the verses published by all

148

the University Presses of the USA, and you begin to feel sick. You feel very sick if you have any decency, and even sicker when you compare these and their distance from any physical reality with what is physical reality for most people. And then, you look at the system that supports all these pricks who write these verses and ask what they contribute themselves. And then you are not surprised by their distance from reality but you are still more disgusted. I started to feel that way about myself. It was about then I joined the Party.

I started explaining all this to Bella, but I didn't get far. It wasn't her sort of thing.

'What happened to the poet and the Irish girl?' she said.

'She bred children, he continued to write verses.'

'Were they happy?'

'How should I know?'

That's the thing about Bella; she still believes in questions like that. So, of course, did my wife Sarah.

For a long time I have been a good Party member. I've accepted—having first accepted that the Party was the Way—I've accepted step by step its retreat from a position where it was demanding a new start, to where we are now. I've accepted the Gramscian theory that we must accommodate the non-proletarian classes—how should I not, having inserted myself into the class of intellectuals with our historic function?

And it's all going wrong.

I couldn't tell Bella anything of that.

Instead we talked about her cousins. I asked her what they thought had happened to Bernardo. She said, 'They are afraid . . .'

'Of what he's done or of what has happened to him?'

'Of both. But perhaps more of the former . . .'

She looked me straight in the eyes as she said that, and then quickly at her plate again and began taking some flesh off the trout's backbone, with neat, certain movements.

I said, 'You think his disappearance is connected with his father's capture, don't you?'

'It must be,' she said.

She didn't have much time for Bernardo, thought he was silly, given over to theories; vain and weak also; anyone who

149

flattered him could do what they liked with him; and he had no sense of family decency or duty.

'He's a bit of a rat,' she said.

Of course I'm nearly schizophrenic. I know that, have done so for a long time. I must be. Else how could Bella's complete indifference to everything I think important, that is, her absolute mindlessness, make her seem more attractive to me. Her mouth never looked more desirable than when she was uttering these meaningless and conventional platitudes.

Then she said, 'Christopher, I want you to do something for me. There's someone I want to see. He's in a lunatic asylum. Will you come with me? I don't want to go there alone.'

She told me about her Uncle Guido, and I knew why I had been chosen to accompany her. Foreigners don't really count. Even one as Italianized as myself isn't one hundred per cent real.

We published Dusa's letter to his family. It aroused a good deal more speculation. Would there be a successor which actually named the scandals? Were the revelations for real? We were inundated with calls, pretty fierce ones coming from DC headquarters. The police descended on us. I had telephoned Nico Dusa and he had thanked me and told me to say straight out that he had given me the letter. We published that fact too. He was afraid that they would stop up the channel and no more letters would be received direct from his father. On the other hand he agreed with me when I pointed out that they could scarcely welcome an allegation that they were coming between the captured man and his family because they were afraid either of the truth or of the public sympathy which was attaching itself to the beleaguered family. Where the family was concerned the DC bosses were on tricky ground. They couldn't say openly what they no doubt had come to believe: that the ground had shifted and, in a sense, Dusa, his family and his kidnappers all now wanted the same thing—negotiations and a settlement; that they were therefore objectively on the same side, and that the DC hierarchy, the PCI bosses and of course the Police were united against them. No, they couldn't admit to that; they had to continue to treat Dusa as their potential martyr and actual hero while doing all in their power to obstruct the course of action which he was so impassionedly advocating. Of course they talked of torture, drugs and brain-washing; that wasn't the way his letters read. They were authentic Dusa, cool, crafty and compromising; in every sense of that word.

Certainly negotiations of a sort were under way. But they were the wrong sort of negotiations; negotiations about negotiations and confined within the politically respectable class. Which I myself was on the point of leaving.

I was going home in a night that was still warm, through the narrow streets, now cleared of motor-cars and strangely silent, around the Pantheon. A part of a city that had become myself—there, in that apartment block, my friend Tony had gassed himself, there, in that bar, I used to drink through the night with a girl-friend called Vlashka, an improbable Pole, there I saw the *carabinieri* beat a young man to death, and ran away in fear which turned to shame on the steps of that bar there, but when I got back, all had gone and I could never be certain it had really happened; a lot of things in my life have long been in that indetermined condition.

Through a narrow alley, above which the houses almost meet so that it is only too easy to steal your neighbour's shirt from the lines of washing stretched across the gulf to dry. Rome, which goes on and on—that doorway there has seen, even to my knowledge, three men knifed to death: one in the *quattrocento*, one in the days when the French revolutionary troops threw out the Papalists, and one the week before last. All for the same reason; they knew things dangerous to know and could not be trusted to keep them to themselves.

I turned into my own doorway, rounded five flights of stairs and heard breathing. It sat ahead of me in the dark. Not, as it might often have been, a girl. Slightly asthmatic. There was no staircase light. The moon was too far round to creep in at the slit that served as a window at this level. I stopped. The wheezing was held in check.

'Who's that?' I called, softly.

'You come back late, Signor Burke.'

151

The words were forced out, grudgingly. A dry salvaged voice.

There was a shuffling. The figure was rising to its feet. Though a couple of steps above me, it came only level with my chin. I was aware of the outline of a hat's brim just below eye level.

'What do you want?' I said.

'Oh I don't want anything. Not for myself. I thought we might talk. Yes, I am alone . . .'

There was something caustic about the voice, a note of superiority despite its flat, rather common, timbre.

'Might we?' I said. 'You think I should want to?'

'I'm sure of it.'

'In that case you might let me past to open the door.'

'You forgot to lock it,' my visitor said, 'but I thought it more polite to wait on the stairs.'

I pushed past him, almost without the tension that the possibility of a knife in the ribs was breeding. All the same, I felt the hair rise on the back of my neck.

He was as small as he had seemed, and slight, in the shabby suit of a decayed clerk. The hat, a Trilby as I had thought, stained and worn.

'I'm called Enzo Fuscolo,' he said. 'You won't have heard of me, I think.'

'No.'

He was looking at me searchingly.

'You don't remember a bar in Parioli, just off Piazza Ungheria, ten days ago either?'

'No.'

I took a bottle of whisky from the cupboard and two tumblers.

'Not for me, thank you,' he said.

'As you choose.'

I poured myself one, which I needed.

'No,' he said, 'I was talking to Raimundo Dusa . . .'

'Oh.'

'Ah, I have interested you at last.'

I sat down in one of the deck-chairs with the tumbler held in both hands. I stretched out my legs . . .

152

'Up to a point,' I said. 'There are a lot of Dusas around these days. Too many of them, all except the ones I might be interested in meeting. Speaking as a journalist. Perhaps you are going to offer me an interview with one of them . . .'

He smiled. His smile worked on only one side of the face, the side that wasn't marked by a long scar that ran almost up to his eye.

'Not exactly,' he said.

I had the uncomfortable feeling that he was sizing me up, and playing with me at the same time. There was now no sense of danger, and, as I reflected later (with some surprise) not even any real sense of puzzlement either; and that was certainly odd, because I had after all no idea who he was, where he had come from or why he was there. Yet I sat sipping my whisky, and had surrendered the initiative to him, even though he had come to my apartment in this way. I ought to have been challenging him to account for himself; but I wasn't.

'It's understandable, of course, that you are not interested in Raimundo Dusa. Why should you be? He is a dead man, quite dead. Even as a symbol of a sort of Italy, a sort of civilization if you like, that is vanished, he is of no interest. Of no importance. Nothing, after all, is as dead as a dead Liberal. I'm sure you agree with me on that point.'

He smiled again.

'Yes, Raimundo is a dead man. Whereas, I, I, Enzo Fuscolo, am a ghost. Much more significant. And, Signor Burke, I know quite a lot about you. We have watched you and identified danger. You are consumed by what? Hatred? Disgust? It doesn't really matter what, does it? And it doesn't matter either who I mean by "we", does it? Not for the moment anyway. I know all about your interest in the Dusa case too. And that is what is really urgent, isn't it . . . ?'

He paused, an open invitation to speak. I waved my hand and stretched out for the whisky and topped up my glass . . .

'And there are only two Dusas who count. Corrado and Bernardo. Yes? And, as a journalist, you would like to meet them, talk to them, wouldn't you? Not that I'm promising you that, yet. No. Still, one thing you must admit about this case.

153

It reveals, doesn't it, how the personal and the public penetrate each other . . .'

He was speaking like a man who had been silent for a long time.

'And that fascinates you, doesn't it? The case is beginning to obsess you. It's like a microcosm of Italy, and, for a long time, Signor Burke, you have been obsessed by my country. And what happens when personal inclination and public—what shall we say?—obligation, even interest, pull in opposite directions? That interests you too, doesn't it . . .?'

I sighed: 'I don't follow you at all. Not at all. Look, it's late. I assume you have come here for some reason other than just letting me know that you know a bit about me.'

'Oh yes,' he said, 'but it is necessary to get one's orientations first, and, as I say, that is difficult when there is a sort of clash between personal inclination and public duty. You see, Signor Burke, I have a problem. I would like to lay it before you . . . I have your permission?'

'Of course.'

'Suppose . . . we will set it out like this . . . suppose. You have a man of fairly humble birth but with ambition and with a certain ardour of soul. He is an idealist, this man. He commits himself to a cause, to what he conceives to be a great cause. He is no time-server, as so many who lend their voices to the cause are, but a true idealist, a true believer. Because of his constancy he is broken when the cause dies. When it is overcome. He nearly dies—for the cause—but he does not quite die. He lingers, partly alive. I say, only partly, because, in his ardour for the cause, he has destroyed all other natural affections. He has no family, for they have disowned him, no friends, for his true friends are dead, and those he thought friends have proved traitors. He survives, just a shell. True, he continues to work for the old cause, but he does so without hope, for this cause is itself in the same condition. So, there we are. The man's life is in effect over, and if anything sustains him, it is bitterness, his sense that what was good has been betrayed. Then he comes on a young man who seems to him his own youth reborn, someone with the same innocence and the same ardour, the same commitment to action. Only this

154

young man's ideals are perverted and they, the old man and the young one, find themselves separated. Time passes. The old man lives a life which would be quite empty except for his memories and the fact that, from time to time, men of power find it useful, even necessary, to employ him. This means that he remains—oh, only vestigially—engaged in affairs. He has in a sense a patron. This patron, who certainly uses him reluctantly and who has no more cause to love him than he to love the patron in turn, becomes a man of great power, even though the new political structures make it necessary for him to disguise the power he wields, which is of course one reason why he makes use of our . . . what shall we call him, Signor Burke? We cannot call him, "our hero". There are no heroes in our modern world. Let us be conventional. Let us just call him X. Yes, in the end, I like the idea of calling him X. And the patron we shall call Y. And the young man Z. XYZ. It is after all appropriate. What are politics but the algebraic expression of life, of our ideals and desires? You can't find that too metaphysical?'

I did, of course, but merely waved my hand.

'Now it comes to X that Z is getting into what he would call bad company, but there is nothing of course that X can do about it, except watch. After all, how much that is important in life is reduced to the act of watching . . . I hope I'm not boring you? There comes a moment of drama. Y is kidnapped; he disappears from the scene. X, through his silent attention, knows what few others know—but what I have reason to suppose, Signor Burke, you suspect—that Z is one of those responsible. He knows too where to find Z. But he also knows that by reason of their long separation and the ideological waste land between them that Z can no longer trust him. And he also has reason for wishing to communicate with Y . . .'

I looked down at the brown liquid and swirled my glass. It swung round, the whisky, dissolving the reflection of the naked bulb; settled slowly and the reflection re-formed itself.

'OK,' I said. 'And what about son of Y?'

'Son of Y?' Fuscolo laughed. His laugh was a titter, like someone in the audience rustling sweets in a horror movie. 'He might be more difficult to contact, don't you think?'

'Would your young friend know?'

'That question is unworthy of you, Signor Burke. Naive.'

'OK. But why do you come to me?'

Whatever he said wouldn't be the truth. Corruption came off him like methane from the marshes. He stank like the corpse of an old coalition.

'Like X, Signor Burke, you are not deeply involved. And, I understand, that like X, you can no longer believe, because you know men for what they are.'

'Flattery,' I said, but I felt myself warm to him. There can be no flattery like the voice which tells you you have been through Hell. It gives us the message that we would like to believe of ourselves. And the man who has been through hell has nothing to fear. Only I knew, what he might not believe, that all I had done was put my nose through the gates.'

'Can you tell me where to find him?' I asked.

'Of course. The American girl has complicated things. She has come close to unnerving him, but yes, I can put you in touch. That, after all, is what I came to do . . .'

The next morning was bright, a day of early summer with deep azure sky, but no extreme heat. Bella came to me in a white dress and sandals. Her lips brushed my cheek. We were at Canova's in the Piazza del Popolo. She glanced at my Negroni and asked for a *cappuccino* and a doughnut.

'Is this breakfast?' she said, 'or what?'

I spread my hands. 'As you like.'

'No,' she said, 'I like to lead a well-ordered life. I had breakfast and this is now elevenses. When I went to England the family I stayed with made a great thing of elevenses. Heavens, how boring they were. They lived in Barnes.'

'And had two point three children and a Wolseley; no, these days it would be something different, probably a Fiat or even an Alfa, if they liked Italy. I know.'

It was what I had run away from, after all; the willows by the Thames, the Atco mowing machine, Charrington's Toby Ale—Sarah's parents had lived just like that, though actually in Richmond. England was now for me a country that existed in memory and on celluloid. I felt a foreigner on my infrequent visits. Why, the last man I had voted for was Gaitskell. For a moment I could feel sentimental thinking of it: November mists, racing at Kempton with the far side of the course invisible, television in a room with a fitted carpet. It was a pool out of the main current of the river that was history. But what was happening? The river, as rivers will, was changing its course, eating into the other bank, eroding it, cutting a new and faster channel; the pool was left to stagnate; a sandbank grew up between it and the river.

'One thing I liked about England though,' Bella said, 'was that there were no politics. You couldn't imagine anyone killing anyone else for politics. Why, the family I stayed with wouldn't even watch politicians on the television. I liked that. On the other hand they would watch golf and tennis and cricket by the hour. Heavens, but it was boring.'

She frowned. 'All the same,' she said, 'no politics. When I think of poor Uncle Corrado . . . you haven't heard anything more, have you?'

'The DC Party Executive are meeting today. There's a certain move. It's said that Mastagni is going to make a speech in Venice tonight . . .'

'Mastagni . . . I thought he had quite retired . . . I get confused with them all . . . he must be eighty-five?'

'Oh yes, he's a back number. Still he has a certain "moral authority" as they say. The theory is he can no longer have any private personal ambition.'

I wasn't actually convinced by that. Mastagni had been one of the early DC barons, a close associate of de Gasperi. Of his generation rather than Dusa's and Schicchi's. He had been in all the Governments, right up to the time when Dusa had first made the opening to the Left. Mastagni had been Prime Minister a couple of times at least, but he had made the mistake of associating himself with Tambroni's Ministry which had been ready to rely on the support of the Neo-Fascists, a move which had seemed sound enough in the context of international politics—it was the Dulles era after all—but which had rebounded domestically. Mastagni had been out, regarded himself as the scapegoat. Still, from without, he'd kept influence, saw himself almost certainly as the Italian

157

de Gaulle, though he had of course nothing like the General's war-time record to bolster his reputation. Perhaps he was seeing this particular crisis as the last chance he had to spring back into power; his 1958 in fact. Therefore it could be certain that he would have to take a line that diverged from, say, Schicchi's. I had discussed all this with Antonio. He saw it my way and stressed how I shouldn't forget that Mastagni, being a baron, had retained a local fief.

'What's more,' Antonio had said, 'in the current electoral situation, a man who can deliver a region, as Mastagni can still deliver the Veneto, isn't to be sneezed at. He can hardly fail to retain influence, even power. It's a question of how he sees fit to use it, which side he comes down on. But wait! We may, perhaps, be looking at it too simply. Eventually he might find it more effective, from the point of view of his own interests, to stiffen the Schicchi line rather than rebut it. On the whole, however, I incline to think he will take the alternative line. It is more dramatic, and old men cannot resist drama . . .'

I had then telephoned Nico Dusa to give him the news if he hadn't already had it, and test his reactions . . .

'Is this, do you think, the response to Father's letter, which we were very glad you published, just like that?' he asked. There was a new note of eagerness, amounting to hope in his voice.

'It could well be.'

'I suppose few people have more that they might wish not to have revealed than Mastagni,' he said.

'There is that, and he is an old man, and like all old men, in a hurry. Only the young can really afford patience . . .'

'It is lucky then that Father's captors are young . . .'

Bella lit a cigarette. 'I can't believe that any of it will work,' she said. 'If he is to be freed it must be done in a different way, at a personal level, I am sure of that.'

'You're probably right,' I said.

Hers hadn't been Ed Mangan's view. That was probably a recommendation in itself. He had called me in great excitement, proposing a trip to Venice to hear what Mastagni had to say.

'It's going to be a great occasion,' Ed boomed. 'That old guy is just at the point when he may see the light. Besides, I remember from the old days', Ed's voice took on a lingering note of nostalgia as he pronounced the phrase, 'Foster used to say he was worth the rest of them put together. And, from this distance in time, Chris, you know old Foster shines forth among our Secretaries of State. People knocked him at the time, but, my God, if we had a man like John Foster Dulles now . . .'

His voice died away in admiration. I didn't ask him how he reconciled this with his new political stance. There would have been no point in it. The born again can square any circle, any time, no problem.

'All right,' said Bella, 'it's kind of you to come, Chris. Let's go.'

'Why not?' I said.

In the little yellow car, my hand resting on the top of her thigh, I asked again, what she hadn't answered the day before. 'Tell me about this uncle . . .'

She pulled her lower lip back with two square-ended very white teeth, changed gear and shot past a bus on the inside just before it began to pull towards the pavement and a stop.

'It's difficult,' she said, 'I've never seen him. It's not at all my sort of thing wanting to see him. He's been shut up for years—thirty, forty, I don't know. He is, Daddy says, a complete imbecile. Daddy can't bear seeing him, hasn't been for—oh I don't know how long. Uncle Raimundo goes, Uncle Corrado did, sometimes, I think. I never have. I didn't know he existed for a long time. And then, when I found out, I was horrified. And then curious . . .'

She paused. 'I'm not quite sure where to go next . . .'

We were across the river now, on the lower slopes of Monte Mario. Concrete villas sheltered behind high spiked walls. Then we turned a corner and were in an area of apartment blocks, too close together, pressing on each other, but with trees—cypresses and pines—fighting for life between them, and the balconies hung with red flowers. You had the feeling that life here was a struggle for breath, but an expensive one. There were no children playing in the streets. Every second gate had a sign *Cave Canem*. The bars at the corner of each street all proclaimed that they were also *pasticcerie*.

'It's somewhere up here,' she said.

A long blank white wall suddenly stretched out. Alone among the walls in the quarter, nothing grew on it, neither flower nor greenery.

'This must be it,' she said. 'It was built as a convent, I think.'

We had to wait a long time in a dank little room, with religious tracts on the cheap table from the department store, and a crucifix on every wall. The life went out of Bella as we sat there; her fingers moved over her dress, smoothing invisible creases. A nun had shown us into the room, with murmurs of inquiry and mutterings over the unsuitability of our visit. I lit a cigarette in defiance of the notice prohibiting it. Ten minutes passed, perhaps a quarter of an hour. The clock on the wall was electric, giving off a low throaty hum, no tick; like an insect. The door opened and a man came in.

He introduced himself as the Director, offering a handshake firm by will rather than nature. He exuded unreliability like the manager of a suburban cinema, touching his wisp of a moustache and saying, 'You have come at an unfortunate time. That's one thing. Your uncle Guido has had one of his bad turns. Sometimes he is conversable. Not just now. Really you would gain nothing by seeing him. Anyway, *signorina*, there is another consideration. Do you have anything in writing? From your father perhaps or one of your uncles? By way of authorization rather than identification, you understand. I would hardly require the latter—apart from your word for it, I can see clearly enough that you are a Dusa—but we do have an understanding—the clinic and your father and his brothers —that we admit no one else without express authorization. You comprehend? I am sorry. Desolated. But that is how it is. And anyway, as I say, the time is hardly suitable. He is not well. Come back next month with the proper authority.'

Bella pleaded, argued, fluttered her eyes. Pointless. The Director could not be moved.

'All right,' she said at last, conceding, 'but tell me something Doctor, this sort of illness of my Uncle's . . . how does it come about?'

'For me', he said, 'it is first and foremost an illness of the spirit. He does not wish, has never wished, to recover. It is an illness of withdrawal, which can become total.'

'And how do you treat it?'

'How can we? We keep him physically well. That is important. Occasionally, from time to time, in the past, we have stimulated him. With a little electric shock, you understand. Oh quite a small one. Enough to rearrange and enliven the brain. It can be effective. Six months ago he was reading the newspapers. But it does not last. Then there are drugs, they are necessary too. But for a beautiful girl like you, *signorina*, this sort of talk, this sort of place, cannot mean much. You are in your Springtime, your unthinking Spring. Enjoy it, young lady. Take her away, *signore*, and let her smell the flowers.'

'Is there any chance that he will recover?' Bella persisted.

'Oh if he wanted to get well, perhaps he could, even now. But . . .' He spread his hands, palms open, and smiled.

We got no further. He was all compliment and evasion. We left, Bella pale and defeated. I'd never seen her look like that.

We made our way down a long whitewashed corridor, behind a nun jangling a bunch of keys. Doors off the corridor had little spy-hole windows. Then to the left there was a courtyard. Three or four figures, dressed in blankets, were shuffling round it, watched by two lounging, sallow-faced men in white jackets, one of whom wore boots to the knee. Their faces were quite without expression as they watched the patients.

The booted one, who was holding a piece of water-melon in his huge paw, shouted, 'Come on now, no stopping, no lingering. You're out for exercise, not to sniff the flowers.' He spat out some melon-seeds and rubbed his mouth with the back of his wrist.

'Exercise is very important . . .' said the nun. 'It is part of the Director's programme of physical fitness. You have no idea how unfit and useless the patients used to be until he took over.'

She unlocked a metal grille and led us into a narrow dark

room under the gateway; then opened a small double-locked wicket-gate, let into the huge double gates, and we stepped into the sunshine.

'I'll drive,' I said. We drove down Monte Mario in silence. Then she said, 'Stop a moment, there's Uncle Raimundo . . .'

I put the brakes on. She called out. A grey man in a shabby linen suit turned from the window of the antiquarian bookshop he had been contemplating, and raised the cane he had been leaning on. His skin was all papery, and when he spoke, his voice was hoarse.

'Where have you come from?' he said.

IV

RAIMUNDO

My diary lapsed, became a series of jottings, a feeble ill-rooted
plant; like our State. That is, in a sense, the whole problem of
Italy, that we have never authenticated our State. And so,
those with a grievance or a mere temperamental disaffection,
resort to the bomb, the gun; just as my native Calabria was
always rich in political brigands in the days of the Bourbons;
and then, after the Risorgimento, the same brigands re-
appeared, now calling themselves *Borboniste*.

But perhaps the cause of my falling silent was more
immediate. I think it may have been the letters Corrado began
to send us from his prison. They challenged me, those letters,
and in the face of such a challenge, I relapsed into my numbed
condition.

I couldn't believe they were anything but authentic, and yet,
on reflection, how they substantiated what I have written in the
first paragraph of this, my long delayed but at last resumed
reflections on, and account of, this terrible business. For what
did Corrado do, in these letters, but deny the State that he had
helped to create? Instead he was turning back to that eternal
Italian reality, the only thing we are prepared to trust, the
Family.

Even though the Family, in the person of Bernardo, had
acted the part of Judas.

(But of course Christ forgave Judas more easily and completely than he forgave Caiaphas, and so Corrado with
Bernardo.)

I am different, spoiled perhaps, victim of a residual faith in
humanity. I have these principles, certainly vague and feeble
enough, but nevertheless there, implanted in me by my liberal

education, and these in fact deny the over-riding virtue of that Italian reality, the Family; and instead assert the claims of the State. For whatever else it may contain, however it may itself be corrupted, it is the State, not the Family, which exists as the means of guarding civil life; and that is, after all, what we (if not the anthropologists) mean by Civilization. It is a product of the State. Without the sanction of the State, we are back in the days of the robber barons. Isn't this what Aquinas meant by his justification of the State, that, for fallen man, it is the *sine qua non* of civil life? And here was Corrado, in these letters, denying the validity of that State to which he had apparently consecrated his life; denying its ambiguous Reason, and refusing to push that consecration to the point of self-sacrifice.

Ah, but there is another, more throbbing, note, the voice of humanity.

What could be more moving than the pain of Corrado's letters, their revelation of a soul which felt itself so hopelessly abandoned—and yet kept hoping—kept hoping and scheming and refusing to surrender? And the letters were complemented in my sympathetic imagination by the sight of my American across the courtyard engaged on his wholly private battle with despair. In my dreams, shot through with images from the *Inferno*, the American's face continually merged into Corrado's, and both, who had thus become one, were sucked into a morass of grey mud, watched over by serpents; they sank down, mouth opened in a scream that would be choked by the mud, and at last only the tips of their straining fingers showed above the glistening surface.

I took to my bed for three days, after the first letter. I tried to sleep, drugged, through the telephone and the silence that followed. Occasionally I rose to feed the cat, make myself tea (was anyone giving Corrado the tea on which he had come to depend?) and then I looked always across the yard to this American, whom in a sense I had come to adopt. If he came through, then . . . I watched him as more faithful men have watched the sky for ominous birds. He sat at his jerkily-moving typewriter, he raised his glass; once the boy visited him, and I saw him fish in a jacket with that unmistakable movement that precedes the exchange of money. Once too, he smiled across the courtyard to me, a smile that contained a wealth of that irony that can come to a man who goes on without hope; it is a very arrogant irony of course.

Then Sandro came to see me.

'We are worried about you,' he said.

'I am the least of your worries,' I replied.

He drifted around the apartment; he looked at himself in half-profile in the ormolu-framed glass; he leant over the balcony, his cheek caressed by honeysuckle.

'Do you know the most extraordinary thing, Uncle?' he said, turning towards me, his eyes wide. 'It's that Father seems so much closer to me now. I've always been rather in awe of him, you understand, because, to be quite frank, I've felt he despised me. I was a disappointment to him. Nico and Bernardo were both more to his taste. And do you know something else? I've started to go to Church again. I've been to Mass twice, with Mother. I had almost ceased to believe. I mean, nobody I know, none of my set, believes in anything; neither religion nor politics, you understand, but this has shown me that you can't live like that. So, you see that's how it is. Of course Bernardo has always found me and my friends trivial. Frivolous. Maybe we are. But what Bernardo has done has really frightened me, you know. I hadn't realized how deeply he was committed. That's frightening . . .'

He smiled at me, a smile that was still gentle and sweet, but trembling at the corners of his curving lips; Bernardo had taken innocence from his brother.

I said, 'There was an English writer called Chesterton—you won't have heard of him—who said that when a man stops believing in God, he doesn't believe in Nothing, he believes in Anything. On the other hand Chesterton was a Catholic convert himself, and there are plenty of people whose way of life disproves the truth of this observation. It is after all perfectly possible to believe in nothing, or at least in nothing much. There are in the end, my dear, two categories of men, those who must have a faith and those who get through life without one. Don't deceive yourself as to which class you belong to . . . How's your mother?'

Sandro's face grew grave. 'Her faith is wonderful,' he said, then smiled again, a younger smile, 'but I must confess, it's the devil and all to live with.'

Sandro might be saved by humour—we would all after this have to find some means of reconciling ourselves to existence. The things which make life and sanity possible are those which stultify reflection or aid mockery. Only very occasionally do you find the exceptional man like Corrado, who, as his letters revealed, could live in Hell with eyes open and acceptant mind.

I should have said some of this to Sandro, but didn't. And yet I couldn't of course recommend to him the incessant activity of my dear Ettore or the blind, nonsensical, life-denying commitment of Bernardo. I could only hope, with a hope as tenuous as a sunbeam, that, when it was finished, he would find his way back to the surface of existence, and float there elegantly; but I could not believe that he would be able ever again to invest a tennis-court with the full meaning of life.

These next days come back to me in fragments. I renewed effort, consulted with Nico, called on a Cardinal, went, at Nico's request, again to see Gianni Schicchi. To my surprise he agreed to receive me at once. Was he, I wondered as I put down the telephone, and wondered again, as the official led me out of the lift along a gilded corridor, coming under the sort of pressure that would cause him to seek an excuse to change his line; a change which would only be discernible in retrospect, for to be effective it would require to be clandestine and sudden. One of the great political arts is that which enables its master to turn right about without being seen to move. De Gaulle brought it off over Algeria, and Gianni was a keen admirer of the General.

The fat bottom was turned towards me, as if he had already made the about-turn which I had been brooding on. He remained a few moments without moving, continuing to gaze out over the piazza which was shrouded by a sudden squall of rain; bare-armed tourists scurried for shelter on the distant pavements.

I was reminded of Mussolini sitting at his desk apparently absorbed in work until suddenly and belatedly aware of the visitor before him attending on his pleasure; then the Duce would leap to his feet with vociferous apologies.

166

How tired one gets of the acts that great men feel obliged to put on.

'Well, Gianni,' I said.

(This time I was going to approach him as an old friend, indifferent, as it were, to his authority and influence; in that way I might hope to be able to make the appeal to his humanity . . . as I had promised Nico . . .)

He swivelled, on his heel, like a cavalry officer indignant at receiving some rebuke. The nerve in his cheek twitched.

'What your brother is doing is unforgivable,' he said.

'Would you repeat that to Elena?'

'I wish', he said, 'I could believe that they had drugged him. The doctors tell me there is no drug could make him behave as he is doing, blind to honour. They find no evidence, but, I assure you, when the time comes, there will be evidence enough. Our honour unites with expediency to demand it.'

He sat down, motioning me to do the same, and leant forward, placing his forearms on the desk that divided us. He dropped his voice.

'Raimundo,' he said, his tone now warm and confiding, 'how do you feel about it yourself? Aren't you just a little ashamed of these letters? As for me, I was astounded when they began to appear. Listen to me, Raimundo. I speak from my heart also. How should I not? My feelings for Corrado have always been warm. We have been colleagues for forty years. We have had our disagreements—of course we have—they have only added to the respect we have always felt for each other. Do you know how I feel? I feel betrayed. Betrayed and soiled.'

There was no reply possible, except 'liar, comedian, ham . . .' I said nothing.

'Listen,' he said again, 'we knew, all of us Party chiefs, that this sort of thing might happen. We had considered the matter with the greatest care, and we had concluded that, in no circumstances would we negotiate with the brigands. In no circumstances. There is a document to that effect. I'll show it to you. Your brother's signature stands at the head of the list. I assure you, had they taken me, Corrado would not lift a finger to release me; not a finger; and nor would I expect it. That is, nothing would be done beyond what we are already doing—prosecuting police enquiries to the utmost. That is the first and particular point on which Corrado has reneged. Under horrible pressure I admit, but nevertheless, reneged, you understand. But that is not all. It is very far from being all. Raimundo, listen to my next question. Why was that document signed? Why? It was signed, as you know, as a moment's reflection will assure you, because terrorist activity strikes at the very roots of the tree which is the State. If we surrender to it, and negotiation is surrender, for it legitimizes the activity, where are we? Where do we find ourselves? We are in anarchy. That's right, anarchy. Everything we in this Party have devoted our lives to establishing, a stable, orderly and just society, is in the melting pot. You cannot confute that. Furthermore, Raimundo, at this precise moment, we are engaged in what are, equally undeniably, the most delicate and perilous transactions in the history of the Christian Democratic State. We are drawing the fangs of the Communist snake. To do that—and I confess that I originally opposed it when your brother advocated this Compromise, aptly named Historic, I opposed it not merely ideologically (for I am aware that ideology must be flexible) but because I thought it too delicate an operation—so, to do this, to carry it into effect, what is required? I shall tell you. Absolute mutual confidence, absolute good-will. And what is the purpose of Corrado's capture at this very juncture? Simply to upset that confidence and good-will, there can be no doubt. Therefore, what must we do? We must refuse to be moved. We must display true solidarity, not only with our new partners, but with our own past. For what are Politics but a Concordat between past, present and future . . .'

Perhaps I exaggerate in memory. Perhaps he was not quite so rhetorical. But I think he was, I think my rendering is authentic enough. What could I say in return? My intention to appeal to humanity had never seemed more frail and ridiculous. It would shrivel up in that atmosphere like a little country rose exposed to the desert's heat. To hope that a still, small voice might be heard amidst the clash of World-Historical Forces—as well ask for sympathy from an anaconda.

I said, 'What you say, Gianni, is very impressive, and up to a

168

point convincing. But there are other aspects from which the case may be viewed . . .' I paused to light a Toscano, and he broke out again . . .

'Also, and I implore you to bear this in mind, there is the appalling matter of Corrado's treachery. He threatens to reveal hideous secrets that he asserts we have. Threatens us, his companions. Yet of course he has stopped at threats. For such secrets exist nowhere but in the lurid imaginings of gutter journalists. In their mouths I laugh at the idea. But in Corrado's? In his they are granted authority, credibility. That to me is black treachery. To give his authority to a lie. He can reveal nothing, for there is nothing to reveal; but the threat to do so is enough. From such a quarter and at such a time . . .'

I said, 'And yet, his letters could denote loyalty too. There is after all nothing to stop him from inventing such secrets as he chooses. And there is one point that you seem to have overlooked, and that is Corrado's success in moderating his captors' demands. Look how high they started and see what they have come down to. In his last letter the figure for exchanges is reduced to one, one solitary prisoner in exchange for Corrado. That doesn't seem much to ask.'

Gianni threw his hands up, brought them down to his desk and gripped a pencil between them. His knuckles whitened; he stared at me a long time.

'I am surprised at you, Raimundo, I had thought better of you. Your diplomatic brain must be rusting, I fear. The modesty of the demand matters nothing. The true demand remains immodest. For the true demand is this: that the sovereign State treats these brigands as diplomatic equals and parleys with them. So numbers are irrelevant. Any negotiation impugns the true authority of the State. It cannot be done . . .'

'Very well,' I said, 'I accept your point. For the moment. Nevertheless, you in your turn, Gianni, have overlooked something. You have overlooked the fact that you are acting predictably. And what is predictable has probably been predicted; I imagine their political intelligence is sufficiently acute to have anticipated that you would act in this way. Accordingly your refusal to negotiate must be what they expect, part therefore of their plan. It may even be what they desire. Negotiations by way of contrast would take them by surprise, even confound them. As it is, let me suggest that you have been outwitted. You are playing the game their way, according to their rules. It may therefore be that the State— and believe me, I too respect the authority of the State that I served for so many years—may well be more threatened by your refusal to negotiate than it could be by any conceivable negotiations. For you are assuming that they truly wish to negotiate, whereas they may rather desire to show you to be at the same time inhuman and ineffective. Corrado's kidnapping has certainly been a blow aimed at the foundations of the State. What will be the effect of his assassination, which among other things will reveal that the State will not protect those who have consecrated their lives to it?'

I have never been so eloquent. All I got in response was a shrug of Gianni's shoulders, and a curt, 'We shall see . . .'

As I left the room, he raised his head from his desk and said, 'We must pray.'

'My sister-in-law does so continually. His Holiness assures her that he shares in her every prayer . . .'

'Ah yes, commend me to her. His Holiness, we all know, is a saint. The rest of us, alas, are merely human . . .'

I came away feeling hollow and perplexed. There was no hope of DC action; there never had been, but illusion, even the faintest most iridescent illusion is sustaining. And I could not believe, as of course I had never believed, in the possible success of police investigation. On the contrary, the closer the police came to Corrado's capture, the closer he came to death. Hadn't that thought been in my mind when I had denied all knowledge of the Caravaggio Christ? It hadn't merely been a feeling that I should protect Bernardo, which had caused me to deny him? I was sure of that, wasn't I? Though how, I wondered, did Elena and the rest of the family stand on that point? Would they willingly save Corrado at the expense of Bernardo? Corrado would not himself accept life at that price.

Possibly it was my memory of the Caravaggio Christ, fanned by a ridiculous hope of seeing him again, but rather I think, a desire to wash the taste of Gianni Schicchi away, that made me now direct my steps towards the little wine-shop in the back-room in Piazza del Pasquino, where I hadn't found myself since before the tragedy; I was accustoming myself to think of it as 'the tragedy' now, preparing myself to accept my brother's death. And had there been some fatal classical flaw in him which had contributed to the course of events; or were we all simply at the blind mercy of the Fates?

Before, I had too easily accepted the comfortable delusion that tragedy was dead.

Fr Ambrose was there, huge and brown-gowned and sweating.

He gave me a warm and firm handshake, an English action of silent consolation rather than the perfunctory greeting of the *caffè* table. He called for wine, and said nothing more till our hostess placed the half-litre of white on the table.

'It's rather a sour barrel,' he said. 'You know that young lawyer, Eustachio, don't you?'

'Yes, certainly.'

'He's been in, much excited.'

'Oh yes.'

'Do you remember one day two young men here talking revolutionary stuff?'

'Yes,' I said, 'but you can find such all over Rome.'

'Oh quite. Eustachio got excited because he saw them again. He had convinced himself that they were involved in your brother's abduction. It doesn't seem likely to me. Obvious reasons. Still,' Fr Ambrose stretched out his huge bear's-paw and curled it round the flask and poured us each a half-glass, 'Eustachio who is a bit of a rat perhaps, with all the persistence of the rat tribe, went round to police HQ, had, through connections, no problem in getting himself shunted to the right department and made his report.'

'Just that? That he had overheard subversive language?'

Fr Ambrose shook his head, huge, ursine also, avuncular . . .

'No, no, I've been telling the story badly. I never had any gift for narrative. Eustachio has seen them again, possibly followed them, at any rate convinced himself that he knows where to lay hands on them. That's what he went to report. And what do you think happened?'

'They weren't interested?'

'No, exactly like that. At first, apparently, they were extremely interested. Eustachio was ushered through various echelons, his excitement mounting. But when he reached a level, which he has convinced himself was near enough to the top, he found polite lack of interest. Very good of you to take the trouble, *dottore*, the matter is in hand. Of course his conclusion is the exact opposite. The matter has been sat on, there is a cover-up. So . . . mind you, he wasn't exactly offering firm evidence, you know. Just a hunch when you come down to it . . .'

Fr Ambrose, secure in his Faith, is infinitely sceptical beyond it. There is no action of which he can believe men incapable. He places no faith in any institution outside the Church, and even where that is concerned, he knows how the human capacity for mischief can corrupt even the most worthy and noble. He believes firmly in God, and also in Man's innate tendency to disregard, deny, twist and foil divine intentions. Accordingly, in his view, Eustachio might be deceived by himself as easily as by others; the matter was equal; nothing could astonish Fr Ambrose.

As for me, I had no difficulty in believing that there were those in power who would willingly, and from a diversity of motives, aid the terrorists. Terror is never without friends in police circles. Nothing after all works so surely towards the power of the police as a good terror; terror spawns counter-terror. Any secret service worth its salt must encourage conspiracy, its *raison d'être*. The Inquisition cannot do without heresy. So it follows that those organs of State whose duty it is to protect the State's security are also those which have a vested interest in promoting insecurity. The young man in the dark suit, Caravaggio Christ's companion, could be a police spy; a police agent could have master-minded Corrado's capture; Caravaggio himself might be a dupe.

I said to Fr Ambrose, 'It's certain of course that, after the Revolution, the Police and Secret Service will be staffed by the idealists of today; if, that is, they can elbow out the careerists who will change their opinions to protect their positions.'

And thinking of Gianni Schicchi, I said, 'The same ambiguity exists at the political level too: what if the PDP and Gianni

172

Schicchi are in unacknowledged agreement; both bent on a course of action that will make the Historic Compromise first impossible, and then unthinkable?'

The next morning I telephoned Elena. She replied with the bleak courtesy of a widow. I promised to go and see her in the late afternoon. Why?

I sat at my desk. A long time. Outside (I thought) the sun rose to make the city its gridiron, but, in fact, when I looked outside, the air trembled. There was even a little puddle in the courtyard. The swifts flew gleaming in and out of the chimney-stacks and television aerials. Sasha rubbed himself against me, calling for milk. A simple Horatian desire, a cat's life. The telephone rang. Ed Mangan in great excitement. Apparently Mastagni was due to make a speech in Venice. It was expected that he would urge negotiations. Ed was flying to Venice to hear him. Why didn't I come too? My presence would have enormous effect. I told him Mastagni was a *vieux con*; perhaps he didn't understand, for he replied that 'Foster had thought a hell of a lot of Mastagni'. An Americanism leapt to my lips: 'so what?'

I had not been to see poor Guido since before the event. I ought to go. I set off, calling a taxi. It was a summer morning of rare delicacy, after that light rain of the dawn hours; it gave everything a freshness, tender as a Renoir. (Oh those long-haired girls cradling baskets of flowers beneath the cherry-blossoms.) The taxi stopped in a jam of traffic, hung over by a wealth of flowers. The air suddenly filled with the scent of roses.

I could not continue; for the first time ever, I was unable to descend to Guido's shadowy world.

It was a relief to walk, down the hill, away from the asylum. Everything seemed to beckon, to invite the spirits to rise. A little boy ran across the road with a golden spaniel at his heels and with a quick leap landed on the rim of a little fountain and splashed water on his face, while the dog yelped below. Two girls in white frocks sauntered out of my imagination and down the steps of an apartment block with slim baskets dangling from their wrists, indolently towards flower stalls and fruit stalls and vegetable stalls at the bottom of the hill. Their voices came to me, clear and liquid with laughter, as they conversed of trivial and wholly alive and real details. How absurd it was to pretend that great questions of public policy had a reality that the price of bread or the efficacy of a brand of hair lacquer somehow lacked; in truth it was the other way round. So much for Hegel.

I heard a voice calling my name behind me and there was Bella waving from the window of a little yellow car, a man I didn't recognize beside her in the driving-seat. She was a girl for that sort of morning. These other girls I had been watching with an ache that contained nothing of identifiable sexual lust but certainly a longing, a nostalgia, for that world of immediate primary sensation, and for a life where all the questions could be answered (perhaps even in the pages of the glossy magazines) belonged so clearly and certainly to Bella's world, that they might have been acting as her precursors, so delighting my imagination that it had developed a force capable of conjuring Bella herself into my presence, as if on a magic carpet. Certainly all three could immediately (on a more prosaic level) have found themselves engaged in a warm and animated conversation, which they would have found perfectly satisfactory, and they would have found it absolutely unnecessary to bring in any extraneous references to Renoir to give it reality; all would have come naturally to them.

'Where have you come from?' I asked.

Bella said, without a blush, 'I've been trying to see Uncle Guido, but they say he's not well enough to be seen. Is he often like that?' she asked, unaware of the shadow passing over the sun.

We talked of the asylum, my answers as evasive as I was sure the Director's had been, and then we consulted watches and, deciding it would soon be lunch-time, proposed and agreed that we should all go for lunch together, somewhere where we could sit outside, and one of us, Bella, I imagine, offered the suggestion of a restaurant not too far from there, a restaurant therefore in a quarter I would never have been accustomed to frequent; but of course she had friends, boys and girls of her own age, who lived in their solid bourgeois apartments with their parents in all the respectable areas of Rome which were merely designations on the map for me; and of course you found many good solid restaurants there which catered for the inhabitants of the quarter, and in fact served more authentic and worthy food than most of those in the Centre, so many of which were corrupted by serving principally tourists.

We were sitting at a table outside, but under the awning, so that the sun came to us, its rays diffused in a general atmosphere of warmth, which I could imagine being given off by Bella's perfectly rounded and bronzed arms, and we had ordered our *pasta* before I realized that I had seen Bella's companion before. She had introduced him as an English friend, Christopher Burke (avoiding saying, what I learned as the meal progressed, that he was a journalist, doubtless in case I should somehow suspect that she had taken him to poor Guido's asylum at least partly in that capacity; for who these days can trust journalists with anything?). He tilted his wine-glass and I realized that I had seen him in that bar in Parioli, the day I had talked with Enzo Fuscolo. And when he looked sideways at Bella, it came to me that they were lovers.

I was jealous, of course I was jealous, and when Bella said, 'It was Christopher Nico gave Uncle Corrado's letter to. It was his magazine published it,' all I could reply was, 'Good of you, Mr Burke.'

'But you don't think it was worth doing?' he said.

'Perhaps.'

'There's been some response, you know,' he said. I was pleased to detect the self-justifying note in his voice. 'An affair like this of course has so many complications . . . You know about Mastagni's initiative . . .'

'I know it's rumoured he is about to make one. I must tell you I don't set much store by it . . .'

'He still has influence,' he said. There was a petulant look to him, like an adolescent who feels he is not sufficiently appreciated. I recalled his appearance in the Parioli bar and again in the little bar by the *Messagero* offices, and I wondered if only that was at the root of his dissatisfaction.

'Mastagni,' I said. 'Who could believe in someone like that? A windbag. It's true', I said, 'that this morning an American journalist friend telephoned me in great excitement about him, but I had understood, Mr Burke, that you have lived here a long time. You can't surely be deceived by that sort of empty rhetorician, can you? We can be quite certain of one thing; no one has ever achieved anything by putting his faith in Giuseppe Mastagni.'

'Was your American journalist Ed Mangan?' he said.

'You know Ed too?'

'Oh yes. And of course I agree with you about Mastagni. It's only that one wonders in a crisis like this whether . . .' His voice tailed away.

I said to Bella, 'How's your father?'

It was a sort of reminder, my question. I was sure Ettore could not approve of her liaison with this journalist who gave off a whiff of bad cheques and broken promises.

'This veal is very good,' I said. 'Clever of you to know this restaurant, my dear.'

Burke suggested we have another litre of wine.

'Not for me,' I said, 'but go ahead.'

When Bella, after we had finished eating, went over to another table, where she had seen friends of hers sitting, friends to whom she had already waved on their entry to the restaurant, where they were evidently well known, Burke leant over the table towards me, and speaking in a lowered tone, so that his voice was hard to hear, muttered, 'Ed Mangan's not the only guy we have in common. I believe you know one Enzo Fuscolo . . .'

'Oh,' I said, and glanced at the wine-flask which he had lowered considerably.

'He called on me the other night. He said he knew you. I hadn't met him before . . .'

'Was it', I said, keeping my voice level and dead, 'connected with this business of my brother . . .?'

'Everything is, these days,' he said.

'I wouldn't trust Enzo Fuscolo in anything . . .'

'He doesn't exactly inspire trust,' he said, 'but he might have information . . .'

'Anything he gave you would be tainted. In your own interest I would advise you to have nothing to do with him . . .'

Why did I say that? Was it so that I could see his eyes glaze over and his jaw set?

'I don't want to hear anything he put to you,' I said. 'I regard Fuscolo with a mixture of contempt and distrust, and I advise you to do the same.'

'So you are not interested in his information?'

'No, because I cannot believe that his motive could be good. I . . .' I paused. 'He's a dangerous man, Fuscolo,' I said. 'And he has always had unpleasant associates . . .'

One thing I was sure of: Fuscolo would be too much for such a one as this Christopher Burke. His corruption was the fruit of an old wisdom, and he had a capacity for self-denial, self-abnegation, which would find easy mastery over the callow egoism I saw before me. For myself, Enzo Fuscolo's re-appearance in my life resembled the terror of empty places that should be holy; he was a Black Mass of a man.

'You're very certain that he has nothing to offer.'

'*Timeo Danaos et dona ferentes*, that's all.'

'So if he said he knew one of those responsible for, at least one of those involved in, if responsible is perhaps too big a word, involved in your brother's capture, that's to say . . . you still wouldn't be interested . . . ?'

'My answer would still be the same . . . but I might suggest to you you call in the police. I'm sure, Mr Burke, you have some friends who could help you there . . .'

I was arrogant of course, as well as jealous and distrustful. I insisted on paying for the lunch—a point I carried without meeting any strong opposition—and, refusing a lift in the little Volkswagen, set off on foot. After a bit I hailed a taxi and directed the driver to the Borghese Gardens and sat on a bench there.

It seemed to me as if I was willing my brother's death.

I could take no action except what I knew would prove ineffective, and I felt this overpowering reluctance to follow either of the possible leads I had been given.

The pine trees stood out black against a cloudless azure sky. Over to my left the honey colour of the Villa Medici flickered through the trees. Two young mothers pushed prams past my bench, cooing to their babies. In the distance, over in the Piazza di Siena, a band was playing; the Grand March from Aida. Verdi had had an idea of Italy as, I suppose, an Imperial power; it had been merely rhetorical. For Mazzini, on the other hand, Italy's mission had been spiritual. We were to assert true values against the two denaturing forces of the nineteenth century—capitalism and socialism. But who had ever really learned from Mazzini, anything except fervour. How did Corrado's captors stand on the Mazzinian ideology? How did I stand myself? And how did Corrado?

In a curious way Corrado might claim to be his heir, the closest Mazzini had to an heir in real politics. But in this, as in so much, he was alone. For the rest of his party, talk of spiritual values was nothing but rhetoric. Theirs was the politics of the percentage, the cut, the fast buck. They were *mafiosi, camorriste.*

Just the faintest zephyr brushed my cheek, bringing with it the tender aroma of honeysuckle. The sound of traffic was stilled here. If I lifted my eyes to see through the tree-tops the undulating blue of the Alban Hills, I could fancy myself in another time.

And would that have been any better?

Had we lost a chance, twenty years back, when the wind from the West was fresher, purer and stronger? Had we? Surely not? What was vital and valuable in America could never be transported back to Europe. What was America after all but the repository for the hopes of those who had failed in, been rejected by, Europe? And for all the rhetoric of freedom all they had really learned there was how to gratify the greed which circumstances, culture, history had suppressed in Europe. They had destroyed the America of 1776, and so all the attempts to Americanize Europe, which had been so busily pursued since the war, came to little more, in the end, than a spiritual debasement; against which, precisely, the kidnapping of Corrado, rightly (whatever his own reservations), seen as one of the authors of this Italian Miracle, was certainly a protest. Only, I feared, even its authors would only offer more of the same. What else could Mass Society be persuaded to accept? We had gone so far beyond any other human experience.

I heard a voice say, 'Well, if that doesn't beat anything . . .'

The speaker was an American boy, in shorts and T-shirt. I followed the direction of his gaze.

A man was approaching along the broad walk. He moved with a certain stately deliberation, as if he was wearing high heels to which he was hardly accustomed, or perhaps even as if he was taking a rather pompous part in some historical pageant, and, like an unskilled actor, overplaying his part. His plump and fleshy chin was tilted upwards as if supporting this impression which was however impaired by the cigarette-holder that he was gripping between his teeth. He looked neither to right nor left, and yet irradiated his consciousness of being an object of attention; the progress was hieratic. He lacked only attendant acolytes to be a bishop in procession. Yet acolyte there was, and it was indeed it which ensured attention. Behind him, in identical posture and attitude, even to the cigarette-holder with lighted cigarette and smirk, paraded, on its hind legs, a grey poodle dog. It kept its distance, perhaps a metre behind its master, and walked no less self-admiringly, entirely conscious that it was making a memorable spectacle.

The American boy said, 'I've seen monkeys but that's the frozen limit. That really sends you like.'

He watched open-mouthed as the pair, master and dog, proceeded past us. He watched them as, still without deviation or acknowledgement of the interest they were arousing (in this reticence of course emphasizing that the ecclesiastical comparison was the correct one), they passed us by and continued up the avenue, the crowd, admittedly a thin one, stepping aside in awe or wonder to let them by. And they disappeared from sight to a point where I supposed the master would snap his fingers and the dog, abruptly descending to its natural level, would trot up, muzzling his hand in search of the titbit with which it would surely be rewarded for its performance . . .

The American boy shook his head in long amazed silence, crumpled up the paper bag that had contained his lunch and dropped it in a bin that advertised Coca-Cola on its side . . .

Descending the Via Veneto I stopped where I almost never stop, at the Cafe de Paris for an ice and a cup of coffee. What I liked about it, for that moment on this afternoon, was its

179

denationalized irresponsibility. There, for a few instants, anybody was allowed to be what he fancied, so long as he could pay for what he ordered.

Certainly in a sense everything this *caffè* offered, the pink table-cloths, the shade from the sun, the trees, the scurrying waiters, the heavy metal ice-cream holders, the high babble of vain conversation, mingling with the cigarette smoke as it rose to lose itself in the broad leaves above, everything belonged, one way of looking at it, to a world of illusion; we had all come here to play, at just that game, not being ourselves. For the waiters, perhaps, the situation was worse—which could be the real world for a waiter—his customers' or his family's?

A girl was watching me from the corner of the news-stand. She had twice tried to catch my eye. I could sense her attempt, even though I had not raised or turned my head to look at her, and though the corner of my eye had registered nothing beyond the fact of girl. She was looking at me as she would look at others throughout the day, week after week; picking on me, presumably, simply because I was alone. Perhaps my air of dandy in decay suggested something; not, certainly and obviously, attraction; just availability and a willingness that she might presume.

At last her will prevailed. I looked at her. She was, to my astonishment, beautiful. Very young, with a bronzed skin and a magazine face, regularly featured, with rich curving lips and big eyes. Her short hair was red-gold and she stood with one leg drawn up, the sole flat against the news-stand behind her, in a gold dress like a legionary's tunic, her eyes fixed on me. The smile she offered could almost have been called ingenuous.

Equally astonishingly, nobody else was looking at her. She might have been my own private mirage.

My blotchy hands shook as I took out some notes to leave on my plate beside my bill.

I got up and walked away. I was trembling.

I had walked perhaps two hundred yards, fast, downhill, when I stopped, leaning for a moment against the trunk of one of the big plane trees.

Later, I said to her, 'Let me give you dinner.'

Her smile had all the knowing charm of a spoiled child, irresistible to me in its admission of human imperfection.

'My boy wouldn't like it,' she said.

'No?'

'It's not the same,' she said, 'business is one thing . . .'

She put her foot up on the chair to buckle it, letting me see her lovely line of long leg, reviving in me for an instant the belly-catching desire, as painful as it was sweet (the two sensations being in fact hopelessly commingled) which had, an hour or so back, caused me to turn and march up the Via Veneto again. I had found her gone from the news-stand, and then, my heart pounding at the realization of what my cowardly prudence, my moment's failure of nerve, had seemingly denied me, I had caught sight of her going away from me along the Via Ludovisi. With no regard for anything, I had given chase.

The cheap hotel was shaded and breathless.

She said, 'He's jealous. You know, we talk often enough, he and I, of a film contract, but he's terrified if he thinks I meet a producer.'

'How long have you been doing this, Renata?'

'Six months . . .'

'And how old are you?'

'Do you really want to know? It might embarrass you.'

Her smile had not yet been quite corrupted—the coquetry might have been offered across a village fountain.

'Well, you're a man of the world, a gentleman. That's why I selected you. A girl has to be careful. I'm sixteen . . .'

She sat down on the bed beside me.

'That's why I go there in the afternoon, I wouldn't dare in the evening. Not because of the men, you understand. I choose them carefully enough. No, it's the other whores. They won't stand for a girl like me, only a semi-pro. One of them scratched my dress off the only time I tried it, and I had to run through the street in my knickers and boots, clutching it to me.'

She laughed at the memory. I put my hand on hers.

'Tell me about yourself.'

Her story was simple enough and hackneyed; no doubt suitably doctored, but not, I think, excessively. The claim to

181

pity was hardly blatant. The family came from the South, her grandfather arriving in Rome from Cosenza. She was vague about dates but I suppose this was sometime during the twenties. He had been a skilled artisan and apprenticed to an uncle, who had himself married the daughter of an old Roman family of artisans. They had lived in the Via dei Cappellari, that narrow and pestiferous street, reeking of history, just next to the old prison. But the trade had been overtaken by modern methods of mass production; the little workshop had failed to last her grandfather's time. The property had been developed; restoration, that so often sounded the death-knell of living Rome. The family had been moved out to one of the *borgate*, the gaunt, ghastly barracks where we now house our superfluous proletariate, well out of sight of the tourists. Her father, talented but easily discouraged, had been a drifter. Renata was vague about him; perhaps affection kept her so. But he had clearly lived at least on the edge of criminality. Her mother, like all Italian mothers, was pious—how could any of us tell a life-story that omitted that insistent detail?

There were of course numerous brothers and sisters—she, Renata, was the second youngest. They divided into the good and the bad—two of her sisters worked in shops, one in a factory, one brother was a clerk, the others were unemployed. As for her, she had done well enough in elementary school; only, there was no point in it. No point at all; it could only lead to drudgery. Look at her sister Nina, twenty, married with two kids, herself working in a grocer's shop, while her husband sat around the mean *caffès* of the *borgata*. What sort of life was that? And Nina also had been beautiful.

She put her long forefinger to the corner of her lips, which, after she pronounced these words, the epitaph of a brief summer, remained slightly apart. She would not yet let life pull down the corners of her mouth or roughen these soft and shapely fingers . . .

And meanwhile, all through her childhood, the cinema and the magazines insisted that there was a different world, a world indeed of which she had already caught glimpses. When she was twelve or thirteen she used to play truant from school and take a bus to the Centre and gaze at the beautiful women.

How had she started? Well, it had been her brother Mario who had started her. Mario was very like her—they had often been taken for twins. So he had early found himself an object of attraction; there were always men on the lookout for pretty little boys . . . (for a moment she caressed the memory of those first evenings when Mario, giggling in a corner with her, had told her his experiences). Naturally he had not refused. It was always so much easier for a boy, so much less shaming, because, well, people didn't find it out so easily. Not that she felt ashamed—it was a service, wasn't it? Anyway Mario had shown her how to set about it; and it was Mario who had introduced her to her Toni. She and Mario and Toni were a group. I must understand, Toni protected the pair of them. That was it. She hadn't had a choice; and she smiled and kissed me on the cheek.

What after all had she and Mario to sell but their beauty? And again her fingers flickered to her cheek for reassurance . . .
Of course, if she could get into films . . .

Her phrases came to me like the steps of an old dance routine in a dingy theatre, where the plush has faded, the lighting sheds no illusion, and the dancer believes neither in the dance nor in the audience. Yet the hackneyed echoes of nineteenth-century novels, the sad material of too many poor movies, merely emphasized to me, what all the events of the past weeks had been bent on proving, that life is a charade played for real. On one level we may know, with utmost certainty, that it is quite meaningless; even so, pain, stabbing the heart, denying the body sleep, mockingly insists on the significance of actions.

How can you deny the reality of something which hurts?

And, as for Renata, it was all real to her. She wasn't living her life, where others might read it, in poor novels to which they gave only a cursory voyeur's attention, but in her undeniable emotions. And people still lived and hurt as she did. Her path of escape would narrow, might become no wider than the thin corridor that ran along the inside of the cloister to Guido's cell. Of course she might escape—as her greenish eyes sought a way out, she might indeed be one of the 'lucky ones'—make her way from indigent materialism to a luxury

183

that would be as empty, as devoid of anything but the will to possess. The will to possess that is the poison ivy of the heart. She had beauty and youth; she would lose them both, and, while employing them in this clumsy search for escape from the mean realities of her family's life, she would destroy the capacity for love, the growth and realization of which can alone cheat (or give the illusion of cheating) what else we learn of our wolfish natures, can alone compensate for the loss of youth and beauty . . .

And of course her drab story was exciting too, because simply to look at her excited me.

'You don't know anyone in films?'

Her voice quivered with desire, as my hands had done. And of course there was no reason why she shouldn't make that sort of escape. She would make a fine slave-girl in a Roman Epic. But to help her to that world . . .

'I don't know,' I said, 'I'm old, out-of-touch, incapable. As you know.'

I rose, a little unsteadily, from the bed, and crossed to the window, pushed the shutter aside and looked out. The day was touched with evening; for a moment, silence; as if in the country. The soft zephyr on the face. I should have been at Elena's an hour back—I had forgotten all about her. I glanced at my watch. Mastagni was due to speak in the next hour. I looked round. Renata was straightening the bedclothes. She said, stretching over the pillow, 'You're not so old . . .'

'Flattery . . .'

I took some more money from my pocket.

'Here,' I said, 'do something for me. Don't take anyone else tonight. Go and see your Toni. Have a good dinner and make real love to him. I'll think about films, there are people I used to know. Here's my card . . .'

I couldn't fail to detect greed in the way she snatched it.

'Dr Raimundo Dusa,' she said. 'Fine. I can call you?'

'Call me when you like,' I said.

I descended the rickety stairs, past the stiff Sardinian concierge, and out into the gathering twilight. I found a taxi and gave the driver Corrado's address.

'I must be mad', I said to myself, 'to give my address to a

young whore. I who try to keep everyone out of my life.'

But the truth was, I didn't care, and, as the taxi wove through the traffic jams of the warm night, her face stayed with me, cutting across the neon signs of the bars, and I pictured her move with the resentful elegance of the caged cat. If nothing else, she would enter my dreams, my long nocturnal imaginings, where life moved faster . . .

I had arrived at Elena's before it struck me how Renata had shown no recognition of my name; yet Dusa is uncommon enough.

Nico was alone in the drawing-room when I was shown in, standing aloof in the shadows, engaged in cleaning a cigarette-holder. He looked up from the task a moment, 'Mamma will be down quite soon. I made her rest for a bit. She's at the end of her tether.'

'It's hardly surprising.'

I sat down. The heavily furnished room was gloomier than ever. An ormolu clock of the Second Empire period ticked dully. When it chimed the quarter the note sounded hollow.

Nico glanced at his watch. 'The clock's slow,' he said. 'What time is Mastagni due to speak?'

'About now.'

'We can't expect anything from him, can we?'

'No.'

How many silences there are, which stretch their slow length through our lives: the silence of embarrassment, the silence of boredom, which shows itself in the glazed eye, the restless fidgeting, the silence (true perfect silence) of satisfied love, the long heavy silence of death, the sharp silence of apprehension, when the senses stand on the alert.

Which was ours now.

Nico had aged and hardened during the ordeal. I remembered what Corrado had said of him, that he was the Italy of the Past, cynical and shrewd, who would make an admirable Governor of the Bank if things held steady . . .

I got to my feet and strolled over to the window and stood a long time looking obliquely out on the terrace. I could see wasps flying in and out under the eaves up to my right.

'You've got a wasps' nest there I think.'

'We tried to clear it out. I thought they had gone. We'll have to do it again. I'm sorry, Uncle,' he said, 'I'm not really able to think much, to make conversation with you, or anything. I should have told you at once, we've had another letter from Father. I don't have it here, Mamma took it upstairs . . . but . . . it's concerned wholly with his funeral arrangements. He has given up. He says that it is to be private, that no representative of the State, or of his Party, which has abandoned him, is to be present. He absolutely forbids it. He wants only to be surrounded by those who have been true to him, whom he loves, his family. That's why I made Mamma lie down. It's all over, and that clown Mastagni is making his important speech. Too late. Too late. Even if he does say something. As for the rest, I sent Sandro out. I couldn't stand having his pained futility beside me. I told him to go to play tennis.'

'That was cruel, Nico.'

'They have done nothing, nothing but talk. We have all done nothing but talk, even you, Uncle. I have done nothing but talk myself.'

'But what could we have done . . . ?'

'Oh I know . . .'

He crossed the room and switched on the big old-fashioned wireless set. 'There will be some news,' he said, 'soon.'

There was only music, and he turned it low. Richard Strauss, I think . . . odd how the mind continues to register the unimportant detail.

'I wish it was over,' he said, 'and we could begin living again. What do you think Bernardo is doing? Is he, too, still alive? Or have they disposed of him? Sandro and I went to see an English journalist Bella has taken up with. Did you know that? Useless. I can hardly think beyond the personal. Do you know at one time I was resentful that when I suggested to Father I might go into politics, he didn't encourage me. How would I stand if I had? And how do they feel, you think, these zealots who have him and who are going to kill him? For what? An idea? An ideology? To give it a grander name. We have had too much of ideology.'

His whole torment was that of the man of business, the

186

practical man who is the exemplar of our civilization, suddenly confronted by the realization that there are those who don't play by the same rules, who are indeed governed by an idea, which they are ready to turn into action.

'What do they want, what do they really want?'

'I doubt if they could tell you,' I said. 'Surely Bernardo tried and failed?'

'Oh often enough.'

'Yes, when it comes to that all they can do is spout out words, slogans, which one must admit are perfectly meaningless. But, and this is where the practical man like you, Nico, or like your Uncle Ettore, goes astray, fails to understand them, their motivation is not merely verbal. No, and it's not absurd either. Possibly the only member of the family who can really understand it is your father himself. But I have glimmerings. You see it's based on feelings, and though I don't have any feelings strong enough to precipitate action, yet I sufficiently share these feelings to have some understanding of how they could lead even to such dreadful action as this.'

I took a turn about the room, lit (unthinkingly) a Toscano, wondered if it was worth saying anything. It was almost dark outside now, the scent of the oleanders strong. A family should have been rising from their supper together.

'So often those who turn to violence are among the best,' I said. 'That's a common enough phenomenon, even though it's equally true that any movement of this sort is sure to attract its share of psychopaths and those wretches whose only pleasure lies in destruction. And one must realize too that moments of this sort are essentially responsive. That's obvious. They are a form of reaction to things as they are. Look how we live today, in this Western Europe which is increasingly a copy of the United States. On the one hand we have no values except material ones. We have abolished religion—oh we pay lip service to it, nobody more so than the barons of your father's party—but, in effect we have abolished it, because none of us in the West—I might more truthfully say in all Europe and America—believes that there is anything beyond this life.'

'Surely that's not true. There are many who still believe in life after death. Look at Mamma.'

I waved my hand. 'There are survivors,' I said, 'certainly. That doesn't change the fact that we expect complete gratification in this life. We all seek earthly crowns. And we have come to identify the *summum bonum* with material satisfaction. That's the whole point of the consumer society. Now what's the consequence?'

I was not sure that Nico was really listening to me. He had begun fiddling with the knobs of the wireless again. It was, as I said, an old wireless, an electrically powered one, and tuning was always a problem. We had given it, I remembered, to my mother in 1950, Holy Year. Had it been that she might hear the Pope's broadcasts? Yes, that was right—she had suffered from shingles, and had been unable to attend Mass at St Peter's, or at San Giovanni, and we had bought this fine German set as, I supposed, compensation.

'There are two consequences,' I said. 'First, many feel a lack. What is offered seems inadequate, not so much in quantity—these are usually people who have been well enough supplied with material goods—but in quality. They feel there must be more to life than this getting and spending. At the same time, consequence two, there are still many in our society who have what seems a quite inadequate share even of what is offered. They ought therefore to have more; social justice demands it. And curiously the same people experience both feelings, simultaneously, even though it is perfectly obvious that they are incompatible, contradictory. Hence perhaps the violence of their acts.'

'It doesn't make sense to me.'

'No, but sound banking doesn't to them. For them money is a symbol which is worshipped as a god. The curious thing about this terrorism is that it is completely modern. We have seen nothing like it before, which may be why it is so hard to deal with.'

'I don't follow that, and I can't quite agree either that we have no ideals in conventional society. We do surely— democracy, liberty, social justice, they're not just abstractions.'

'Aren't they? Are you so sure? But what I was going to say about the novelty of this terrorism is simple enough. Of course we've had terrorism in the past. But that terror has always been aimed at something specific, clearly identifiable—an independent Italy, Poland, Ireland, the establishment of a Calvinist State, or the re-establishment of a Catholic one. The object is plain enough—you can tell when it has been achieved. But now, this time, it is quite different . . . these young men, they are pursuing a chimera, something that will never be achieved, the Just Society, and so the failure will always be evident; the Revolution never comes, for it is always perverted . . .'

'And for this chimera, as you call it, they will kill my father?'

'Yes, Nico, they will . . .'

I put my Toscano to my lips, but, forgotten in my eloquence, it had extinguished itself. I got nothing but a cold sour taste. As I took out matches to relight it, the door opened and Elena came in.

'Tomorrow,' she said, 'I shall go to see His Holiness. He has granted me an audience.'

The wireless crackled to life.

'Here is a report from our correspondent in Venice of the important speech made this evening by the Honourable Mastagni . . .'

It had, said the announcer, been an evening pregnant with excitement. The political temperature was running high in the whole of the Veneto, and beyond it, all over Italy, as the veteran statesman took to the rostrum to make what had been heralded as a significant intervention in the Dusa affair . . . He had spoken for more than an hour, to repeated cheering . . .

But the veteran orator's language had been even more than usually opaque. At the end nobody was quite certain what he had meant. Whether it was a clarion call to action or whether he approved the Government's course and merely thought they should be more ready to shout loudly . . .

'It's quite clear', said Nico, switching off the set, 'no one has bought him yet. The Honourable Mastagni is still for sale.'

TOMASO

Tomaso spent these days waiting. He was off duty and commanded to 'be himself'. It was an order he found puzzling. How could he be what he didn't know?

Waiting, he would have passed much of the day lying in bed if he had not been afraid of what that implied. He very strongly didn't want that, and he found the narrow cell, with the peeling plaster and the naked bulb, turned his thoughts in that direction. He couldn't help it; there was nowhere to sit or lie but the bed.

So, he went out into the streets.

His room was high up in a tenement in the bleak area near the railway station, an area that had never recovered from what it had been built to do, which was to house the first workers, clerks, builders, navvies, waiters, small employees, lured to Rome by the city's sudden expansion after 1870, its transformation from being a souvenir of the Ancient World remoulded by the Renaissance Popes into a celebration of what was in so many ways a vainglorious fraud, the liberal monarchy of the Piedmontese. But it was still a quarter of transients, where questions were politely left unsaid.

Tomaso would go down to the bar on the corner early in the morning, and sit there with a newspaper before him on the rickety metal table till the sun was high. Long before then there were always half a dozen or so unemployed youths hanging round the pin-ball machines, gloomily joking, eyeing the girls who swung past on the pavement. The boys bulged in their jeans, bracelets shone on their wrists; the studs gleamed on their leather jackets. For the first days Tomaso was afraid that they would speak to him. The thought was deeply embarrassing; how could he reply? But it never happened; they were too sunk in the apathy of their own being.

He sat there and watched a yellow dog, squirming round the newspaper kiosk. It lifted its leg, with a gesture that was at the same time furtive and precise, on each of the four corners of the kiosk. Then it began rootling among the cabbage leaves in the gutter.

Someone passing Tomaso's table said, 'In my opinion he is already dead. These letters are not his . . .'

The words hung behind the speaker like the curtain of plastic strips that trailed over his shoulder as he entered the bar.

In two days Tomaso would be back on duty.

He found himself remembering the only time he had been in hospital. The antiseptic atmosphere had appealed to him, and he could have fallen in love, in the most conventional way, with at least one of his nurses, if he hadn't reflected that she wasn't always the brisk efficient girl in uniform, but, out of it and in other clothes, would have the same complicated importunity as he was sure other girls had. It was a frame of mind that might have led him to consort with whores, if he hadn't been repelled by the certainty of squalor.

And yet he hadn't made his bed since he moved into the narrow room.

The best moment of his life had been when Dusa had said 'yes', he would write the letter. The Professor had assured him there would be no problem—Tomaso hadn't been certain.

What struck him though was the dignity with which the decision had invested Dusa.

At the moment he said 'yes', he was sitting at an oblique angle to the table they had given him. For some minutes, ten, twenty, Tomaso couldn't be sure, he had sat brooding, his head couched in his hand, one elbow resting on the table. Tomaso could see his lips moving. There was an odd quirk of humour to the mouth that he hadn't been prepared for, a twisted irony in its lines. He hadn't noticed the irony at first, and now, with only these lines visible (the rest of the face being hidden), lines that became, second by second, as it were, less lips than some sort of representative spirit twisted in an arabesque of ironic enquiry that cast doubt on their actions, now Tomaso, who had been certain that Dusa was praying, wondered if this man approached his God also in irony; and then it came to him (he recorded all this searchingly in his diary, that diary he had been forbidden to keep, and so nourished as a secret vice) that History itself, the one true God, was an Ironical Spirit; his world-view lurched.

Dusa's other hand began to move. It was a long, composed hand, and had been extended not quite flat, fingers bent by arthritis, on the rough blanket that covered the little table; it lay there like a hand in a *cinquecento* painting. Now, slowly at first, the fingers began to move, like a man trying out little series of notes on the piano.

He said, with just a touch of lightness in his voice, 'And you really have a means by which you can guarantee that my letters will reach my wife, and you will permit me to write directly to her, and to my family also?'

There was a note of longing in the soft modulation of the word 'wife'—'*moglie*'; yet it was nostalgic rather than expectant. Tomaso knew then, with the certainty of a drum-beat, that Dusa would fight, contrive, invent, rehearse, lie, plan, counter-plan, urge, beseech, threaten—all without true hope. All the same he lifted his head and said, 'Yes'.

They had given him a different shirt and Tomaso could see sweat-stains under the armpits. Dusa looked round the white walls of the box in which he was confined, a box that had been inserted into the room, and one which was of course sound-proof, and again let his hand drum lightly. Writing would keep him alive; he would be more himself again writing.

Half-way through that first letter he had looked up from the sheet, and said to Tomaso, 'I think you are a friend of my son Bernardo.'

Statement not question. Tomaso nodded. Dusa's face retained its immobility of a Red Indian carving, but he raised his chin perhaps two centimetres and kept looking Tomaso straight in the eye until the boy could no longer hold his gaze.

'He should have done it some other way, he should have known how to. My driver, Giovanni, he used to bring Bernardo sweetmeats when he was a child. All the other servants preferred other children, but Giovanni used to say that "Bernardo has his own quality". He should have remembered that. Between us, Bernardo and myself, it has been reduced to politics, but he should not have forgotten Giovanni . . . Still, he is safe, I hope; when you see him, give him my blessing. And my love . . .'

192

'I don't suppose he will come to me here?'

Tomaso shook his head.

That first letter had been Tomaso's triumph. He knew that. He almost suspected it had been the reason he had been brought into the group; as a boy who could get Dusa to co-operate. Why that assumption should have been made he couldn't know. From early on though, the Professor had said, 'It's Vlad here who will get him to play it our way. You wait and see . . . We each have our different qualities . . .'

Tomaso got to his feet and went to the *cassa* and paid for another coffee, then went to the bar to collect it and returned with the cup to his table. He liked the small scruffy *caffès* which didn't insist on table service as the big bourgeois ones did. He found he was drinking a lot of coffee, and eating nothing.

For all his time alone just now, he was free from too much reflection. It was a life of primary sensation, wary as a beast. He took note of the movements of the street, which kept coming between him and the words in the newspaper in front of him; these anyway seemed remote. They read like messages from another world where everything could be expressed in abstractions . . . Tomaso moved his foot slightly, a small cramp nestling like a crab in his toes . . . Forty-seven hours till he returned.

An argument had started among the youths over by the pin-ball machine. Tomaso saw hands flashing, cutting the air, striking the perspex top of the machine, being extended in gestures of incredulity; voices were raised; it was apparently a simple dispute over procedure. He felt a small stab of envy; he had never belonged to such disputes. Instead he kept watch, holding himself taut in his thin black suit and white shirt, with no tie; for the first time in years he needed a haircut.

Women were emerging from Mass in the church opposite, some of them clearly workers who had gone to church off an early morning shift. Unlike the old women in black, these removed the headscarves they had been wearing as soon as they were free of the church portals.

A police car stopped with sudden violence at the door of the *caffè*, and three policemen bulging in their summer uniform, the leather of their gun-belts gleaming and the revolvers themselves bouncing against their hips, like butcher meat suspended on hooks, debouched from the car, and flowed with a swelling motion like a sea-wave into the *caffè*, one of them even stamping on Tomaso's toe as they forced their way past. For a moment the boys round the fruit-machines moved with a self-conscious casualness; their indifference to the police entry a matter of will and nerve. Tomaso himself hesitated in the movement of his hand towards his coffee-cup; he couldn't be sure that the cup would not rattle on the saucer.

But the policemen themselves had no interest in anyone in the *caffè*. They crowded round the bar, shouting for lemonade and sweet cakes. Their talk, loud, complaining and then ribald, was of work schedules and girls. They were men by themselves. The slight tension was dissipated.

Tomaso felt a hand rest very lightly on his shoulder. Looking up at a face in shadow, seen from this unusual angle, he didn't at once recognize Enzo Fuscolo, whom he hadn't anyway seen for a long time.

'Marchese,' said Fuscolo, and sat down opposite him.

His presence brought back to Tomaso the steam from Lenya's samovar and the curling yellowish smoke from the brown-papered Russian cigarettes with long cardboard mouth-pieces that she used to smoke. And then a thin voice discoursing of a desert wind . . .

The little man sat on the chair opposite him. Its legs or perhaps the pavement were uneven, for, though his move-ments were of the very least, minimal, the chair constantly seemed in motion. Without looking at the bar, he summoned the boy who had been serving drinks there. He raised one finger to him, and said, 'A glass of mineral water and a coffee for my young friend.'

Tomaso could find nothing at all to say. It seemed absurd to ask, for instance, how Lenya was. On the other hand, he could hardly resume the conversation about, say, Nietzsche, which they had left off five years before. Yet this was exactly what Fuscolo now did.

'When the lesser men begin to doubt whether there are higher men,' he said, 'the danger is great . . .'

194

Tomaso remembered him saying that in Lenya's kitchen. He had been explaining why, in spite of their opposition in politics, he had found Khruschev's denunciation of Stalin 'absurd'. 'Take my word for it, Marchese,' he had gone on to say, 'this is the beginning of the disintegration of the Soviet Empire. Oh, it will take years, decades, no doubt, but there it is . . . it has begun . . .'

'Do you remember when we used to talk?' said Fuscolo.

'Yes,' Tomaso nodded his head, the word coming out as scarcely more than a breath.

'We had some good talks. I was sorry when you went away, though I recognized of course that you felt it imperative. I had enough respect for you to grant you your right to what was imperative. So I made no move to follow. Lenya is dead now.' He sipped the water which the boy had laid on the table before him with a gesture which had something in it beyond the distaste that any waiter may legitimately feel for any customer. 'Cancer,' he said.

'All the same,' he said, 'I haven't exactly ignored you, Marchese. If I was to speak to these fat fellows by the bar about you, they wouldn't know what to do, would they? You know what I mean, no need to spell it out. What you are doing is certainly in accord with the Nietzsche we used to discuss, isn't it?'

Tomaso for the first time looked at him, 'What can you know?' he said.

'Well,' said Fuscolo, 'what can't I? That rather more exactly puts the question. It's what it amounts to. Oh, you have done very well. You have destroyed the great men. The State lies in ruins. You have made a joke of it. But you are not just humorists, are you? You . . . what will you do next?'

Somewhere, not far away, probably at the junction with Via Cavour, there was a traffic jam. The noise of horns had been growing in stridency for some minutes. Now it had become almost continuous. The policemen at the bar came to the door and stood there looking in the direction of the noise. They jostled each other, one of them leaning his hand on the table to steady himself, and then turning to apologize to them. All the time Fuscolo continued to fix the boy with a gaze that he could

195

not meet.

'I mean,' said Fuscolo, as the policemen turned back, joking about the incompetence of their colleagues in the traffic control section, 'I mean after you have killed him . . .'

Tomaso got to his feet, kicking his chair over backwards as he did so. He began to walk rapidly away, with no idea of where he was going, merely to put a distance between them. But that made no sense. It didn't alter his consciousness that they had been betrayed—it had to be betrayal—that all was in ruins, and that somehow, because of his remote connection with this man, or because of some other connection—Kim's blonde hair and pouting lips shimmered before his eyes—it was his fault. He hadn't gone as far as the corner, when he slowed down, his feet dragging, and when he felt a hand rest on his elbow he was almost glad.

'What are you going to do?' he said, unaware that he was asking the same question.

'It depends', said Fuscolo, 'on how you develop your ideas. You can't imagine that it distresses me to see the State in ruins, this Liberal-Christian experiment. After all, what have I, what have you, to do with what merely is, what is no longer, and can never be, in the condition of becoming? Like you I feel a cleavage, a deep and unbridgeable chasm, that separates me from everything that is customary or reputable. We are the same. Do what you will, Marchese.'

For some minutes they walked in silence, till they arrived opposite the blank wall that ran along the side of the railway station. Then Fuscolo said, 'The bourgeois State is doomed. A consequence of its denial of the principle of superiority, its attempt to be all things to all men. The result is nothing. Not nihilism which is vibrant, but simply nothingness, torpor. So I approve of what you are doing, but, I ask you, Marchese, what happens next?'

Tomaso shook his head; he had to get rid of this terrible Old Man of the Sea who understood everything and nothing at the same time. Fuscolo pulled at his arm.

'You don't, I hope,' he said, 'any longer indulge yourself in fantasies about social justice? Surely you are concerned with the prime problem, which is the liberation of the spirit of free men. Who can always, at any time, anywhere, be only a minority. Who must control, exercise sovereign power.'

The little man licked his thin lips and pressed his mottled and scaly hand on Tomaso's dark sleeve. The day yawned before Tomaso, empty as the hills of his Abruzzi, with this mad voice cawing like the ravens that flew circling the ruined castles of long-dead barons. And across the city, Dusa sat in his white shirt in his white-lined box, writing.

Tomaso said, 'It is all nonsense what you are saying, mad nonsense from the past. I have to go. I have an appointment. No, not what you think. There's no point following me. I'm going to see a girl, my girl.'

And with no forethought or real exercise of the will he had thrust out his hand, stopped a taxi, and then heard his voice giving the name of the *pensione* where Kim was staying.

It was only to get away of course, but, even so, once in the taxi, having looked back to see Fuscolo standing there, oddly forlorn on the pavement's edge, he didn't countermand the order; though when he entered the hotel in the Via del Babuino he found himself half-hoping she was out . . .

The woman behind the desk watched him as he made for the stairs; her voice had held a note of contempt. He knocked on the door. Kim's voice answered, muffled, and he pushed open the door which had been off the latch.

The room was half-dark, the shutters closed and the long curtains still drawn. Even so he could see that the mess was frightful. There were clothes strewn everywhere, thrown down anyhow, and the air stank. Ash-trays brimmed and someone had knocked over a bottle of scent. A bottle of brandy (Stock 84) stood open and three-quarters empty on the dresser.

He switched on a light. Kim was lying on the bed, her legs drawn up to her mouth, like one just waking. She wore a short nightdress that was crushed and streaked with something yellow. Her hair hung over a face blotched and red with crying. One lip was puffed up and her left eye was bruised, bluey-yellow and blackening.

'Kim,' he said, 'Cousin, what has happened?'

She put her arms round him and kissed him hard on the mouth, lurching on him hard so that, to keep himself from falling over, he had to put his hands on her naked bottom. She stank of brandy.

'It was Ruthie,' she said. 'She beat me up. She just beat me up. Ruthie. Me.'

She was sobbing and for the first time Tomaso couldn't resist. He took her in his arms and helped her to the bed. He leant over her and kissed her again, and she pulled at his tie and began to unbutton his shirt.

Later, as she lay asleep, crushing his arm, and wisps of hair tickling the corners of his mouth, Tomaso watched flies crawl over the ceiling. He could feel the afternoon hot and drowsy beyond, imagine the heat stretching itself down to Piazza del Popolo, just freshening as the city opened out to the gardens above. Had she merely wanted reassurance? And he release? He stretched out his finger and lightly touched her sleeping and bruised lip. She shifted slightly, moving one soft damp leg on top of his. He let his finger run off the lip and rest on the tender cheek. She gave a little moan. He fell asleep, dreamless as not for a long time.

When he woke it was evening and Kim still slept. He thought, as lovers so easily think, that she slept like a child, and he warmed, as again why not for nothing is more natural, with a protective pity. If he hadn't been afraid of waking her, he would have risen and cleaned and tidied the room. But anyway, it was better and warmer to lie here, perhaps for ever.

She stirred, woke, smiled. They made love again. Night closed in on them, boy and girl, asleep, entwined.

Tomaso woke at four. It was still hot and he felt still a glow of sweat, but now the fish swam in his belly. In the distance, in the Borghese Gardens, an owl hooted. Tomaso disentangled himself and padded to the window and opened the shutters and leant out over the city. A police car screamed through the streets, leaving a long silence behind it. He crept back to bed but comfort and sleep had fled.

In the morning Kim, shaking a little, was full of projects. She showered and washed her hair and talced her body, and came back, dressing-gowned and fragrant, to kiss him and drink the coffee which he had ordered. She made up her face and brushed her hair with long sweeping strokes, and put on a short simple white dress with pink horizontal stripes.

'Christ, what a mess,' she said. 'Let's get the hell out.'

They walked, their little fingers linked together, through narrow streets towards Navona. Near the Pantheon they stopped at an old jewellery shop. Kim admired a bracelet of old slim gold, and they went into the shop. Tomaso bargained and bought it; he slipped it over her hand.

'Don't let's go to that big piazza,' she said. 'That jerk Chris goes there. I don't want to see him. I don't want to see anyone else.'

She pressed herself against him. He held her a moment, kissing. They had passed perhaps a dozen news-stands and he hadn't bought a paper.

They sat in a *caffè* by the Pantheon and drank freshly squeezed orange juice, hardly speaking but always either holding hands or just lightly and repeatedly touching each other. Swifts buzzed black across a sky the colour of corn-flowers . . . Japanese tourists swarmed, yackety yack about them . . . a German made a scene with the waiter . . . two old women, in black cowls, shuffled past . . . a Franciscan elbowed them into the gutter . . . *carabinieri*, gorgeous in blue and red, like over-fed macaws, strutted by, silent in self-importance . . . Kim played with Tomaso's fingers until he lowered his eyes which had been fixed on the Pantheon's shimmering dome and smiled at her. 'Take me away,' she said. 'Take me out of town. Take me to the beach . . .'

'Today?' he said.

'Right away. Maybe we could go to Capri? Could we go to Capri?'

You could not imagine how that dome was suspended. Surely that circle of wall could not support that soaring structure? And yet it had, for almost two thousand years. Perfectly. That was its message; you could achieve just that, perfection. Which the Japanese then came to photograph.

'Capri?' he said. 'Capri?'

'Yeah, they say it's great. And lovely. Just lovely.'

'It's not possible,' he said.

He felt the movement of her fingers stop.

'Oh,' she said, 'I thought you were different, Tom. What's so special that you can't?'

He could see her hand twisting the slim-gilt bracelet.

'Maybe next week,' he said, 'but not immediately. Maybe in four days.'

A little gust of wind blew a paper bag past their table. It flipped into the gutter and rested there, as if wind and movement had never been. Tomaso retrieved Kim's hand . . .

'In four days,' he said again.

'I want to go now,' she said. 'I don't want to see Ruthie again, I just never want to see her again. Don't you want to know about it? Don't you? She crazy, that's what it is. Crazy jealous. You didn't know she was like that, but she is. She sure is. Does that make you sick?'

They went in the end to the beach, taking the metro to Ostia for the afternoon, buying swimsuits there and lying all afternoon in the baking sun. They drank beer and ate prawns and then strolled to a *caffè* and ordered large and elaborate ices. Kim kept her dark glasses on to hide the damaged eye. When they came back they had a plate of spaghetti in a cheap *trattoria* and went to bed early. Tomaso was back on duty the next morning.

He said to her, 'I have to be away for two days. It's an appointment I can't break. But, after that . . .'

He woke early. Her words came back to him, 'Ruthie keeps asking about that friend we met at your mother's. She wants to see him again. Maybe if she did we could make up a foursome and Ruthie would be all right again . . .'

He slipped from the room, Kim still asleep. The morning was still cool and empty; rose-fresh and dew-damp. Tomaso's dark suit and pale face had the morning's simplicity uncorrupted by action. He walked quickly with the light step of youth, up the Via San Sebastianello to the Pincio. For a moment he was confused there, becoming as it were an island in a wave of girls. They swept past him on roller-skates, their hair stretching out behind them; they swooped like swallows round the paths that were lined with the dead statues of the dead heroes of the Risorgimento, and the first dead Parliamentarians of United Italy. Tomaso, taken by surprise, hesitated. There came a last swooping dive and the girls were gone, as a sky is suddenly emptied of birds.

He walked across the gardens. You could check there if you were being followed. At the far side, he loitered in the street, then, at the very last moment, ran for a bus. Its doors were on the point of closing but he just squeezed in. It carried him down Via del Tritone and he got off and dived into the tunnel under the street. Out on the other side he made his way by side streets to Piazza Venezia. It was just eight o'clock. Outside the second of the three *caffès* there he paused, as if waiting for a bus. A little grey Volkswagen stopped, and he got in.

The driver, a chubby young man in a yellow T-shirt, said, 'Clean, Vlad?'

'Think so. Yes.'

'We'll make sure.'

It was as if Dusa hadn't moved since he last saw him. He was sitting in the same attitude as if already detached from his surroundings, from what was happening, from his life. The large pad of schoolboy's white paper was still at his left hand, half a dozen pens and pencils to his right, the tea-cup at the edge of the little table.

They had grown accustomed to each other. From the time when Tomaso had persuaded Dusa to write the first letter, he felt that the politician looked forward to his spells of duty; and he found this disturbing. Today he could hardly keep his eyes off the naked yellow bulb that hung directly above Dusa's writing-paper.

Dusa said, 'I have been thinking about you a lot. You are an idealist.'

There was a single fly, a puffed-up and squidgy bluebottle, buzzing round that naked bulb. It hummed like an electric typewriter.

'One way or another,' Dusa said, 'we're coming near the end of the period of waiting. Things must come to a point of resolution. Now, either Mastagni makes his appeal, which was certainly timid enough, much more effective, putting my former colleagues in a position from which they can decide to amend their strategy and accept negotiations, or, I suppose,

201

everything is finished. The issue's clear enough at last. That's why I have been waiting to speak to you. As if you were my poor son Bernardo; and perhaps, by your intermediation, directly to him. For, naturally, Bernardo has greatly occupied my thoughts. Very painfully, to be sure; and yet, after all, he resembles me more closely than any of my other children does. I can understand him better than I can understand poor empty Sandro for instance. You won't have met my youngest son Sandro, I suppose?' Tomaso shook his head. 'He's a good boy, but, as I say, empty.'

Dusa gave a little smile that might have been meant to carry comfort. 'You mustn't think death is so very important,' he said. 'Of course, if you don't believe in God, if you have not been a faithful son of the Church, I suppose it might loom disproportionately large. But I see we are at the conclusive moment and I do not intend to embarrass you, my son, in any way. What would be the point, even though you were to me the man who has to point the gun. The decision wouldn't be yours. All the same I am glad to see you again.'

He stretched out his hand and lit a cigarette . . . 'I stopped smoking thirty years ago at the first mention of a possible connection with cancer. Now you see . . . I am grateful to you all, I want you to know that, first, even though it is impossible that I should not also at the same time resent what you are doing to me, even more particularly to my family. To forgive your offences against me is possible . . . to forgive those against my family, that demands more charity than I can summon up. All the same I am grateful . . . but I am curious about you. Tell me about yourself . . .'

He gave a faint smile and gestured with the cigarette, 'I do not of course mean police questions, who you are and so on, even though you will admit that in present circumstances the probability is that I could be acquainted with all such dangerous facts and the danger would be extinct. But that doesn't interest me . . . I am interested in why, what you really believe, in (I suppose) what you hope to achieve . . .'

'How can you face death like this?'

The words were blurted out; Dusa raised an eyebrow. 'I've had time to prepare,' he said.

Tomaso got up and began to walk about the room. 'I've never suffered myself,' he said, 'but I've seen signs of deprivation. Look at Italy, unprecedented prosperity, and still great poverty for many, and that's not the worst of it. The dishonesty, the lack of purpose, the selfishness, nothing but greed and lies, how could you have encouraged it? Whose life has any meaning, any significance at all? Not even the rich. All my life I have felt like a skeleton here. Always. I used to feel the same way, but think differently. There was a man I used to know who read Nietzsche. He was an old Fascist, he had really believed in Mussolini, he tried to convince me that there were superior beings, men set apart, and that nobody else mattered, they were just the mob. But then I remembered the peasants on our estate, and I saw their children in the *borgate*, and I knew that what he said was all lies, all vanity. One man is as important as another, everyone should have a chance, and we have a system that makes nonsense of that truth, and so we have to smash it, to smash it do you hear, and that means first of all destroying the State. Well, for a long time, our people hoped that the PCI would do that, it's what they promised to do, after all, but they have been corrupted, and you, you,' Tomaso's voice faltered, he struck the table with his fist to help him go on speaking, 'you are the first instrument of that corruption, for you have invited them into the structure of this bourgeois State, this State committed to exploitation and deprivation, that's why . . .'

He had never spoken so much, he who had always been silent, feeling these things but letting others speak.

'All action', Dusa said, 'contains the seeds of its own corruption. Should we then abstain from action? It's been brought home to me that I have lived my life with the wrong goals, and yet, my son, my goals have not been so different from yours. It has been brought home to me that I have lived it in the wrong manner, and yet my commitment to action has not been dissimilar to yours. I have come to see that, aiming for good, I have made a mistake in the way I have defined my life, and yet . . . have you any conception, my son, of what power is . . . ? Power is the greatest cheat of all, the ultimate

203

delusion. I have not been the chief of the Christian Democracy. My word has never been effective, just like that. I have fought battles there, winning some, losing others, more often perhaps losing. I cannot tell. Victory is never what it appears on the prospectus. Power is a drug, a pleasure, but also and always less than you think. Your target is never achieved, it recedes. Action corrupts, yes, my son, you are right there, but it is itself corrupted; and political action is and always must be a matter of constant compromise. I have no doubt you would call them shabby and seedy, these compromises. What gets done is so much less than is planned; and it is for this, and in this, that I have passed my life. When I tell you that, can you be so confident that your own purity of will and deed can survive?'

Dusa spoke without moving at all, his words coming to Tomaso as a sort of automatic language, disembodied, out of nature; yet the two of them might have been holding hands round a table and listening to a spirit speak, the words seemed to have so little connection with Dusa; even his mouth hardly opened, the words sliding forth. When he fell silent, only his fingers shifted slightly like crabs edging across the wooden surface.

'You see, my son,' he said, 'the limits of action are abruptly reached. Oh, when one has no power, then certainly anything is possible. But when you are given actual political power, then you quickly discover what a cheat it is. Look, I pray you, at the Russian Revolution. I have never believed that Lenin and Stalin were evil in will; on the contrary, what they willed could only be what we should all desire: prosperity and justice. Their wickedness lay elsewhere: in their ignorance, in their ridiculous and fundamentally childish optimism. They knew nothing of the limits of action, of the complex obscurities of the human heart. How could they know anything of Man, who had rejected knowledge of God? . . . If I could only convince you, my son . . .'

He lit another cigarette, drawing smoke deep into the lungs it would no longer be able to corrupt.

Tomaso said, 'But greed doesn't have to be encouraged, and a system which does encourage it can only perpetuate injustice.

And that is our Society today, the result of our type of State. Isn't that true?'

'Yes,' Dusa said, 'it is true. I do not believe however it could be otherwise.'

There was no means of knowing the time in the box. Tomaso felt himself in limbo; there it was always either the *cafard* hours of twilight or those barren wastes that stretch towards morning.

Dusa picked up his tea-cup, and sipped again a liquid which had long been cold. 'I wrote again to my family while you were off duty,' he said.

Tomaso nodded with the deference of the functionary in whom there is respect but no flattery.

'About my funeral. I said that I do not want any of the men of power to attend; only my family, my loved ones . . . if I had taken another route, and yet, almost any way can be corrupted. The Saints after all are in their proving the most fiercely assaulted . . . when you see Bernardo, if you ever see him again, you will give him my love. You will assure him that it still extends to him. A deep love. You will do that.'

There was no question in his voice. Tomaso nodded again.

'Of course,' said Dusa, 'I ask myself if my life could have taken another course, if I assumed the wrong responsibilities. I cannot make up my mind. On the one hand, for my sake, for my family's, obviously this is true; I have been in error. On the other, when I look back and consider Italy as it was under Fascism and at the end of the war, I ask myself how any man of good conscience could have stood apart. How? The country was bleeding, broken. I could not believe in any politics that were separated from the ministrations of the Church, and yet . . .' he lifted his hands, spread them wide, 'here we are.' The hands fell with a thud to the table, a discordant thud with something of a rattle in it.

'Do you have a girl?' he asked.

'Yes.'

Tomaso's lips remained parted after speaking the word, as though it had surprised him . . .

'And is she one of your . . . colleagues?'

He shook his head . . .

'My wife has always hated my public life. She hates the Party, she hates power. And fears it . . . what about your girl? Will you be able to reconcile the public life you have embarked on with the responsibilities of love? Or will you, like me, betray love . . . if you betray love, you betray wisdom. I won't say you betray God, though that is true also . . .'

The door opened. One of the comrades entered, carrying a tray. He put it before Dusa. There were a pot of tea, a cup, a slice of lemon and some biscuits on the tray. He said, 'We would like you to have a bath after your tea.'

Dusa lifted his head.

'A bath?'

'Yes, that's right.'

Tomaso found he couldn't meet their prisoner's eyes. He kept his own fixed on the rough hessian that covered the floor. He shuffled his feet making a small scratching sound as he did so. He could hear the tea being poured into the cup. There was no sound of tea-pot knocking against the china.

Dusa said, 'I have one last request to make. Would it be possible for me to speak to my wife . . . ?'

Tomaso lifted his eyes. They met his comrade's, blank and wondering as his own must be.

'We would have to take instruction on that,' the comrade said.

RAIMUNDO

June 10 A morning of the most perfect gold and blue; I woke idle as Sasha who was already spread out in the sun like an emblem. For at least five minutes I basked in well-being, mindless of my brother. The result of my encounter with Renata?

Almost certainly. I could still smell her tawny skin, feel myself warming to her bronze-gold beauty. I felt no shame, but then the ache of an old man's lust, embroidering fantasies. Will such idle dreaming ever stop?

All this, as I lay in bed listening to the wakening traffic of the day's unfolding.

Elena telephoned. She was going to have her audience with His Holiness as she had already told me on my visit to the villa yesterday. Had I anything else to suggest? This was the last chance. What could I say? I could not bring myself to tell her what I knew, that the whole business was vain; she might receive a comforting gesture; no more. So, wearily, I said, 'You can urge him to bring all possible pressure, even at this very last minute, to bear on Schicchi and the gang. That, I'm afraid, is all. Unless they can be brought to negotiating point, everything is hopeless.'

It is indeed the very last minute. Just now, 11.30, Nico has called me to say that the terrorists have just issued a new communiqué. Even at this moment of utmost urgency, they have lost nothing of their wordiness:

'*Comrades,*' it starts, '*the battle begun on May 10 with the arrest of Corrado Dusa has now arrived at its point of conclusion.*' It talks of the Christian Democrats having replied to their own offers of '*positive negotiations*' with '*counter-revolutionary violence, hundreds of preventive arrests and special arbitrary laws, and*' (using a phrase the delicate perversion of which I almost admire) '*political genocide*'. They vapour about what they call the '*lurid collaboration*' of the PCI—the sting is at least what the Communists' inhuman obduracy, dictated solely by their political ambitions, seems to merit—and they spout the usual cant about '*the State of the Multi-nationals having been stripped of its grotesque mask of formal democracy*'. Concluding that '*no amount of anti-guerrilla psychological warfare can disguise the victory of the revolutionary movement and the incandescent defeat of the imperialist forces*' they say that '*the only language the servants of imperialism have shown themselves to understand is the language of the gun, and that is what the Proletariat is learning to speak. Thus we conclude the battle joined on May 10, executing the sentence to which Corrado Dusa has been justly condemned.*'

'Do you think it means?' Nico hesitated . . .

'It depends. It could just have a future sense, still, I think it does not necessarily imply that they have done it. It could be the last turn of the last screw.'

'Precisely. My opinion exactly. Sandro is of course certain that Papa is dead—he is lying on his bed in tears. Even if our fears were fact, what would be the point of that? As for Mamma, she is still at the Vatican. Well, I suppose there is nowhere she will receive better comfort. They are certain to have heard the news there too. I hope they tell her. But, listen, Uncle, is there still anything we can possibly do with the Party? What about Mastagni?'

I could not bring myself to say, 'there is nothing'. Nor could I say, 'Everything is confused. People think they are still playing a part when in fact the curtain has come down on the Comedy.' Instead I said, 'I'll try to see how things lie, but don't hope, dear boy, don't hope. What about your English journalist? Can you get any information from him, Bella's friend? A Communist shift of direction is the only thing I can imagine which might . . .'

'I have already tried. He was drunk.'

When he put down the receiver, I called Ed Mangan; at least he had gone to Venice to hear Mastagni, and though I had no faith in him . . . quite simply I couldn't think of anything else to do . . . he might know someone at the State Department, my own contacts were all out of date . . . an attempt to call Gianni Schicchi was rebuffed . . . the chiefs were in conclave . . . Ed was out, I left a message.

12.00: the telephone again.

'*Dottore*, it's Enzo Fuscolo speaking.'

Almost I put the receiver straight down.

'Listen,' he said, 'I want to see you. I have information. No, of course not, over the telephone. At two o'clock I shall be in the big bar at the Termini. I can't get there any quicker . . .'

Of course I assented. What else was there to do?

It would give me an excuse to leave the apartment. Meanwhile I prowled round, looking at my long line of bookshelves with distaste. Even the wisest, most profound of the philosophers and novelists there couldn't in any way help me at this moment. The scene Plato recounts in the *Phaedo* may have been grimmer for Socrates' friends than for Socrates himself.

I hoped they would use a gun; they usually did.

And they would park the body somewhere dramatic.

I turned on the wireless; its inanity was intolerable.

The doorbell rang. It came to me, for no reason except hope, that it might be Bella.

Instead it was a boy whose features and colouring I couldn't at once make out as he stood in the shadow, and I was at first aware of slimness and curls framing his head like an aureole. He was leaning easily against the wall, and disengaged himself with a movement that was both languorous and graceful. For a moment I wondered if he was miraculously an emissary from Them—how else could I now think of them but as just that, personal and remote—and I fell back a step, and he came forward into the light. His teeth flashed in a confiding and warm smile. I saw my absurdity and also, from the likeness, who he was.

'She's a silly girl,' he said, 'she didn't recognize your name, but when she showed me your card, I realized at once who you must be. I checked up to make sure of course. Mind if I come in?'

He didn't wait for an answer, but slid past me.

'Nice place you've got, all these books,' he said, perching on the arm of a chair. 'Renata liked you. She went on talking about you at supper, which I gather you stood us, thanks. Then she showed us your card and of course I got excited. You can't blame me for that now, can you? Of course she's absolutely ignorant of public affairs—she hardly knows who your brother is. Toni, that's her boy, was excited too, but I said "hands off", he's a bit of a bastard Toni, though he is a mate of mine.'

'Ah yes,' I said, 'I understand.'

'That's a nice piece,' he said, picking up the old silver cigarette-box and weighing it in his hand. 'Worth a bit that. I do things in that line from time to time.'

He smiled at me, a smile that was mischievous, radiant and frank and deceitful all at once. The likeness to Renata was astonishing, until he smiled. There was nothing of her innocence left in him, though he looked like an angel fallen from a *cinquecento* ceiling.

'Matter of fact, it's a coincidence, you living here. I've just been calling on a friend of mine, an American, who lives in a *pensione* just across your courtyard, but he's out. Actually I

209

wasn't very pleased about that. He owes me some money, you understand. I'm fond of him, but I get touchy when people owe me money, and I was very much hoping he would pay me today, but he's not there. So I thought I'd drop round and meet you.'

He sat absolutely still, composed, sure of his youth and his beauty, in a soft cream-coloured sweatshirt with a broad green stripe and pale coloured jeans, and smiled at me again. 'Do you like boys too?'

I couldn't see him as one of the proletariat who was learning to speak the language of the gun, and probably the earnest young men who were going to kill (were killing? had already killed?) Corrado would have found difficulty in so recognizing him either; and yet there could be no doubt, he was an authentic child of the gutter, using such gifts and weapons as he possessed to make his life: his beauty and his body. And was he perhaps for the moment happy? He looked happy. Not that I was ready to sentimentalize him. There could be no doubt that blackmail and extortion were in his mind, as they had been in that of the boy Toni he had so easily disparaged. And I suppose that such thinking revealed him as having some sense of morality at least.

'Oh boys,' I said, 'not that way. No.'

'Later maybe. Another day.'

He leant back and crossed his arms and tensed his legs and then crossed them too, and smiled at me again, quite sure of himself; I couldn't help smiling back.

How easy it would have been to say yes. What, after all, is the difference between a boy and a girl when all you seek is the reassurance of life, the reinvigoration old age like mine cries out for? Indeed, that tortuous Jesuit inside me could make a better case for saying 'yes, come with me' to Mario than to Renata. There was less to spoil. If one is using another person for their body, giving nothing back in exchange except money, then it would perhaps be less wrong to exploit Mario, who was, I was so sure, without any innocence, who had indeed by Renata's account been the agent of her corruption. And Renata, on the other hand, I could feel sentimental about; oh yes, oh yes.

But do such questions of right and wrong ever in fact enter such relations?

Mario said, 'You know, it's funny. I mean it's funny the way life links people together. Because I've watched you from over there, from my friend's room. He's watched you too and been curious about you.'

He knitted his brows, suddenly looking vulnerable.

'He's in a bad way, my friend,' he said. 'I think he would like to kill himself. You know that's something I don't understand. He's got money, you know. He drinks all the time, bourbon whisky, and then he cries. He goes with boys and then drinks himself into stupidity because of it, and when he wakes up he is bad-tempered and often very sick. I don't understand though I'm fond of him too, you see. Sometimes he gives a whole lot of money, and other times he tries to get out of paying, and wants to make-believe all sorts of things. He's always laying little traps and tests for me. It's very difficult, you understand.'

I was not sorry to have him there, graceful and empty and alive. He had his own knowledge and wisdom too, acquired by something more than theory. He knew men at their most lonely, the inhabitants of mean rooms in cheap hotels, where the walls were dirty, the ceiling stained and the wise went drunk to bed rather than examine the sheets. He knew the cry of despair, the moaning that can sound through the cat's hours of the night, the desperate clutching that tries to cheat emptiness, the self-contempt that lurks in the abashed morning eye. He might not understand the springs of motive, but at least he knew something of the twisted complications of our natures; knew it from experience. Of course he lied, cheated and stole, all with a smile, and the love he offered was merely counterfeit; and his roses would soon wither in a nipping autumn, but still, when I looked at him perched there, golden, confident and mocking Cupid, I could only see the beauty of a boy who believed in nothing but himself, and who would never kill for some high-sounding idea, for the best of reasons, for some noble abstraction. There was something to be said for a lack of interest in the Rights of Man.

'Still, Renata's a nice girl,' he said. 'You'd like to see her

211

again? An arrangement of some kind maybe. And me? You said no, but perhaps another day?'

He flashed a radiant smile that dimpled his cheeks.

'So,' he said, 'why not?'

'I'm an old man, among other things.'

'You're not so old. Besides, I'm a . . . I've forgotten the word. Someone once told it me. A boy who likes old men.'

'You could say a gerontophile; you're too pretty for that.'

'Oh yes, I'm pretty. That's maybe why. Old men are gentler, they love me the way I love myself. The younger ones are angry and resentful. Understand?'

'And your American friend? How does he love you?'

'Poor Max, he has no light in him. You mustn't think', he said, his lips pouting in seriousness, 'that because I laugh and talk of things like this I am simply frivolous. I know what it must be like for you now, with your brother held as he is. I've suffered myself; my family . . . but there's no point talking about that. These people, the terrorists who are holding him, what do they know about anything? Do you know—what they are like? They are just ignorant. I've thought about these matters myself, and I'm sure of my judgement. They don't know anything except big words and ideas. But you're helpless against them nevertheless . . .'

In a little the telephone rang. Ed. Excited. Calling from a bar. He would be round soon as a taxi could bring him. Say ten minutes. Good. I made apologies to Mario, and took some money from the drawer of my desk . . .

'Compensation,' I said, 'and you missed your American.'

He took it with a smile but no thanks. I hadn't expected them; it was Fortune had won him the money.

'And I'll come again. Yes?'

'If you like . . .'

'You need a friend. When they have killed your brother, you will need one more . . .'

'I have other family.'

'Oh yes, but family is different. You'll see.'

He darted forward, kissed me lightly on the cheek, like a faint sea-breath on a Capri afternoon, and left.

At my age one might as well act absurdly as not; one fears

nothing of the criticism of others; my own is quite sufficient. And there will be no responsibility, no obligation towards Mario, whereas his sister calls forth protective and quasi-paternal feelings, mingled with the lust. All the same I can see their entry to my life as another step in the process of dismantling my defences which this horror has set in motion; I am continually being forced to admit experience again.

Ed was breezy, hugely excited, like a policeman, newly appointed to the Vice Squad, entering his first brothel.

'We're on to it. It's going to break.'

He threw himself into a chair, only to leap up again almost at once, as a girl followed him into the room . . .

'You haven't met,' he said. 'Ruthie, this is Ray Dusa; Ray, Ruthie Landeswitz. Ruthie's a girl-friend of my kid daughter, Kim. They've come to Italy on holiday, but she's sort of got hooked on your brother's case. Fact is, Ray, she's put me on to the scoop of a lifetime, only there are a few problems to clear up. But that's number two.'

All the time he was talking he was bounding around the room, as unable to keep still as a baboon in its zoo cage.

'That's number two,' he said. 'That's right, Ruthie?'

'I don't figure out how you number things, Ed. I'd have put it first myself.'

'Let me tell you how, let me tell you both. You wouldn't have a Coke, Ray, would you?'

'No, I wouldn't.' My apologies however were so disregarded that I couldn't but feel the request had been automatic, a sort of nervous reaction, hardly consciously expressed. If I had put a glass of anything in his hand, he would have drunk it without noticing that it wasn't what he had demanded. As it was, he passed over its absence, without comment.

'It's Mastagni,' he said. 'I've just had an exclusive with one of his aides. The old boy's going to turn up trumps. He's going to demand negotiations, serious ones, and when I say "demand", I mean just that. Nothing less. I tell you, Ray,' he hammered his fist into his other palm as if the action could dissipate my scepticism, 'there's a meeting of the Executive Committee of the Party going on right now. This instant. The old boy's going over the top. Right over . . .'

The telephone rang. Elena.

'You won't believe it,' she said—there were sobs in her voice, 'His Holiness . . . it is incredible . . . His Holiness has told me he is about to announce a personal act of intercession on Corrado's behalf. He will tell the terrorists that he is willing to offer himself in exchange. Can you imagine that, Raimundo? Can you conceive the magnanimity?'

It was too much. They were both too much. Little Mario had more sense, being devoid of optimism, and suspicious.

I said, unforgivably, to Elena, 'And what makes you think they will accept?'

Silence.

'I'm sorry, my dear, but to them, let me tell you, this will be simply a Public Relations move, nothing more. Why should they accept? They can't. Even they wouldn't be able to kill His Holiness, so they would have thrown away their bargaining power. I quite understand that you are elated, I see that the offer is wonderfully noble, but don't delude yourself. There is no prospect that they will agree. Ask Nico. You'll find that he shares my opinion.'

Silence.

'Listen, Elena. They have taken Corrado for a political purpose. We don't know exactly what that is, whether it is as they claim or not. That doesn't matter. They may, even at this last moment, hope to achieve something in negotiations, to force the State to grant them recognition, make certain concrete concessions also. That is our only hope, that there is perhaps a faint, a very faint, chance that even now when the clock's hands stand at eleven fifty-nine, negotiations will be offered and will be successful. On the other hand it may well be that they have always, from the very start, intended to kill Corrado and that the offer of negotiations is no more than a piece of propaganda, which they are certain the State will decline . . . In that case . . . either way, they will have nothing to say to His Holiness's offer, except no thank you.'

When she spoke, which was after a silence long enough to make me wonder if she was still holding the telephone or if I had been speaking simply to vacancy, it was to say, in a voice that was cold and dead as a crypt, 'Of course, Raimundo, you have no faith, you are a mocker. And I have wondered whether your mother is right, whether you have not always been jealous of Corrado, and now are not distressed by what may happen.'

She put down the receiver before I could deny her even once.

'Did you gather the gist of that?' I asked Ed Mangan.

'Sure I did. It's great, but it's not going to be necessary. Mastagni's the boy'll fix it.'

'You saw this morning's communiqué. He may be dead already. What of your Mastagni then?'

'You don't want to believe that. That communiqué was bluff. I tell you, I know. Foster always used to say Mastagni was the only man in the Mediterranean he could trust not to sell his grandmother to the Commies. Mastagni and Karamanlis . . .'

I was back in the awful boredom of receptions, dinner-parties, Press Conferences, briefings in Washington, at the UN, at NATO Headquarters; the dreadful American insistence that the world was theirs, to be read their way. For a moment I felt a shiver of sympathy with Corrado's captors who were denying that, and the forces of money and materialism, and exploitation, in the sacred name of democracy. Americans have never understood what Vietnam did to the world, how it made democracy a dirty word for the young. Though the young may still use it, they do so with a very different meaning from the one it had on the lips of John Foster Dulles or that soiled hero, John F. Kennedy.

'It's childish', I said, 'to pretend that a man like Mastagni, corrupt to the core as a result of his half century and much more of egotism, can effect a miracle. Tell me instead, my dear Edward, of your scoop.'

But he had crumpled. He couldn't take scepticism; like all his generation who had come from the West to set old Europe and Asia to rights, he depended on admiration and love; an adolescent condition, that I couldn't help again reflecting little Mario was superior to. So now Ed slumped in his chair, and said only, 'I wish to hell you had some Coke.'

The girl took it up. She said, 'We've really got to talk to you, Dr Dusa.' Her voice was low, quick and breathy, with an odour of mentholated pastilles, 'You see, I've met two of the kidnappers. I'm quite certain about it. Only there are all sorts of problems, personal ones you could say. You see it's like this,' and she began to tell me, circuitously and in unnecessary detail of a visit she and her friend Kim had paid to Kim's cousin in the Abruzzi, and how he had had another friend there who had disappeared; she now knew that the second boy had been my nephew, Bernardo, and the other was called Tomaso. 'Look,' she said, pulling a small book of photographs out from her canvas bag, 'they didn't know I was taking this, but that's Bernardo, isn't it, and this, you see, is Kim's cousin, Tom.'

She pushed the snap towards me.

'Like I said, they didn't know I was taking this. Or I'm sure they'd have stopped me. That is your nephew, isn't it? I haven't known what best to do, not since I began to be suspicious. So I went to Ed here . . .'

I had recognized the other too, of course, and had known I would, had known ever since that policeman had shown me the photographs of Bernardo's acquaintances, that the Caravaggio Christ was the one who mattered. He could have been watched if I had spoken then; he could have been tracked, the right connections made, and Corrado freed. I still didn't believe it. My decision to do nothing then had been as wise as my distrust of police activity was total. Negotiations had been the only way in which my brother might have been freed, and the failure to embark on them, and consequently, the responsibility for his death, lay with his colleagues in the Christian Democrat Party; and especially with Gianni Schicchi. That was what my reason told me; to alarm the terrorists would have been to write Corrado's death warrant.

But now?

I said, 'Yes, it's Bernardo and a friend. Does it prove anything?'

'Oh,' she said, 'it was a good bit after the kidnapping, and Bernardo was kind of hiding out there. Then he disappeared like. Right? And Kim's cousin, Tomaso, he disappears for a couple of days at a time. It all fits. I know it does. I can't be fooled any more.'

216

'So that's Ed's scoop?' I said. 'It's too late to save Corrado, but you'll have to go to the Police. You'll have to, though you won't get far, I'm certain of that.'

I was amazed by my passivity. Did I no longer want Corrado to be saved? Was my mother right? Had I reached the point when I was at one with the terrorists, objectively on their side, hoping that they would now get away with it? Certainly I could feel little animus towards them compared to the intensity with which I regarded Gianni Schicchi and the rest of the gang. It seemed to me that the terrorists were acting with a radiant honesty, whereas Gianni . . . I looked at my watch—a quarter to two. 'I have an appointment,' I said.

They accompanied me down to the street, Ed Mangan still swearing that I was wrong, that he knew, he just knew, Mastagni was going to fix it—we'd have the results of the Party meeting late that night, and then we'd see.

'So,' he said, 'Ruthie'll hold off going to the cops. We can't risk jeopardizing Mastagni's initiative by starting off police activity of that sort. When your brother's free . . .'

'Ah yes,' I said, and took a taxi to the station to keep my appointment with Enzo Fuscolo, an appointment that promised to be as meaningless as the conversation I had just had.

Why does one involve oneself in action, save to kill time?

V

CHRISTOPHER

It ought to be more of a puzzle to me how I muck things up time and abloodygain. Thank God, as I've said before, for the Italian Labour Laws, which offer journalists like me an absolute security of tenure. Otherwise, even in a profession like mine, I'd have collected a heap of trouble. As it is, despite calamitous lurches from waggon to gutter, I survive.

Not bad, that, actually, to survive these days.

More than Dusa managed.

For all his cleverness, and he was as astute a bugger as you could ever hope to come across, they did for him.

And they did it with a perfection of timing that you can only call masterly.

I spent a lot of time reconstructing this scenario that follows, piecing the jigsaw. Some of it is straight personal reportage; the rest imaginative, but hardly anywhere inventive, reconstruction.

On June 10 there was great activity on numerous levels.

Level one—I place them in descending order, starting therefore with the Pope.

Level one, therefore. In the course of an audience with the soon-to-be widow Dusa, His Holiness attempted to avert the catastrophe with a gesture of the utmost sublimity. He offered the terrorists his own Holy Person in exchange for the faithful son of the Church, Corrado Dusa. It was an offer that naturally grabbed a few headlines, but probably didn't keep the PDP High Command occupied long. I doubt actually if it even raised a giggle from them. What the hell, after all, could they want with the Pope? They couldn't, as good Italian boys, sons of devout mothers, credibly threaten to shoot him.

Could they?

Action on that level therefore fizzled out fast.

Level two—but after the Pope I find my scheme breaks down. Who is to determine the respective levels of the boys who were holding Dusa, the DC and myself?

Take a look at the DC first.

Mastagni had finally stirred. He was prepared to go a little further. There had been no satisfactory response to his Venice speech, which had of course been as clear as a Thames Valley November afternoon. Nobody had offered him a job of any kind. So he had to push the door a bit harder. He allowed it to be understood—not, you understand, by the plebs, it was hardly time for that yet—but by the people who matter, that he might feel the urgent exigency to push things further, and perhaps come right out into the open and say that grounds for negotiation might be discovered.

The delicate hint was sufficient.

He was invited to a Party conclave to discuss his unmentionable suggestion. Of course that wasn't what they discussed at all. Instead they talked about just what he would have to be granted if he was to be persuaded not to make this foul proposal.

These things take time, and this for the most obvious and highly respectable reasons.

All the jobs were already taken. There was nothing free for the old boy. (They couldn't of course just offer him Dusa's, since they had still to pretend that efficient police work would any day now result in his liberation and consequent return to the post he held with such distinction, blah, blah, blah.) It was a question therefore of someone being ready to vacate his own seat, or rather being persuaded that someone else, his dear and good friend, the Honourable Y for instance, should be sacrificed. Now of course that might not be too difficult, everyone in the Power Game having his pet X, Y, or Z whom he was reluctantly prepared to place with reverence on the sacrificial altar; but things are never quite so simple. Two obstacles presented themselves.

In the first place, for A to sacrifice X was to risk weakening his own position *vis-à-vis* B; and so on.

Secondly, how could it be fixed that the demoted X or Y should not himself come out into the open and advocate negotiations, or, as it was already being put, play the Mastagni card.

Predictably, bargaining was tough. (Fortunately the DC is as leaky as my shoe.) These boys are limpets though. Still, by ten o'clock in the evening of June 10 they believed that a satisfactory agreement had been reached.

K would vacate his place, move three steps sideways to take over from M, who had nobly agreed to accept demotion, provided he was simultaneously granted the land concession he had been seeking for his wife's cousin. He would therefore supplant S, who would move sideways to dislodge V, who would then move one step down and replace Y. (Y was very young, and there was little fear that he would throw a tantrum; instead he would accept his new position philosophically, in the assurance that his noble self-sacrifice would gain him credit for devotion to Party and the Public Service, credit which would stand him in good stead in the years of office to come.) Anyway, Y would be compensated with an embassy. It didn't matter what the supplanted ambassador felt; he was too distant from power for his views to be of the least importance, and, besides, it was remembered that Corrado had been his patron. He was the only one of Corrado's protégés to suffer in this reshuffle; it was necessary for the moment to bind the others to the Party; they could, if desired, be disposed of later.

So that was settled; and then Mastagni, feeling power surge back into his geriatric veins, said it wasn't good enough. If K's job was the best they could offer he would have to go ahead with the public proposal of negotiations.

All to start again.

Such is the devotion to duty of our public men that they were ready to embark on new discussions straight away. But Gianni Schicchi consulted his watch and announced that it was late, they weren't likely to think straight at that hour of the night, and proposed that they resume in the morning.

That was a card Mastagni didn't dare to trump, but he began to wonder whether he had over-called his own hand. He had forgotten the time element in the excitement of returning power. Gianni Schicchi hadn't. Gianni alone, it seems, had taken note of the last communiqué from the PDP, or rather hadn't allowed it to be driven from his mind by the excitements of real politics, and Gianni reckoned that it was just possible the terrorists would indeed have acted on their word. If they had . . . well then it was pointless to make elaborate concessions to an old incompetent like Mastagni . . .

You may think this is all ironical, jaundiced stuff. Of course it's true I don't actually know what was going on in Gianni Schicchi's mind any more than I know the precise contents of a sewer, but in both cases, my guesses are what they call informed . . . It's certain that at around ten o'clock the word was that Mastagni wasn't satisfied with the goods on offer, and that a new round of customary discussion was being embarked on. The waiting journalists (Antonio among them) sent out to the bars for salame sandwiches and beer, and then, just as these arrived, the doors were flung open, and the chiefs were being escorted to their cars. The journalists flocked after them, and three waiters were left stranded, with trays outstretched . . .

As for me, at about that hour, I was getting up from a bed into which I had collapsed sometime in the afternoon. The other occupant, a black American actress of little talent, had been urging the move for some time.

How had I got there, and in that state, in the middle of the most exciting journalistic crisis of my time?

Two reasons: first, it had got on my nerves. I had decided that it was a bore; like Hamlet, it had all been going on too long.

Second—level three as it were—I was suffering from emotional irritation too. The previous afternoon, as we saw her dismal old uncle (an unreconstructed sod if ever I saw one) off from the restaurant, Bella had turned to me and said, 'That's it, Chris. I have been thinking and I have decided. It's finished.'

'What do you mean?' I said, though of course I knew very well.

'It's over, understand?'

'No,' I said; obstinate.

I stopped the car and looked over at her. Funny, I'd never

221

noticed what a chin she had, maybe she usually ducked out of profile. Anyway she did that now, dropping her head and turning it half-round so that her hair fell over her eyes and softened the line. But it was too late; I'd got the message of that chin.

Her fingers were picking at each other, but when she spoke her voice was firm enough.

'I wasn't a virgin, you know that, when we met. Still, I hadn't had as many boys as I let you believe. Just two. On ski-ing holidays, which I always felt didn't really count, you understand. And I won't pretend I don't enjoy it with you. You wouldn't believe me if I did. But the fact that I like it is maybe part of the reason I'm calling it off.'

'Mortification of the flesh, Bella? In this year of grace?'

'If you like. Self-restraint. You see I know it wouldn't last with you, nobody ever has, have they? But, after you, there would be somebody else, and another, and so on. It's all no good.'

'None of that means anything to me, I don't see that it matters,' I said, taking my hand off the steering-wheel and putting it between her legs.

'I am sorry you can't, but it does,' she said, and very precisely removed my hand from where she had often been happy enough to let it rest and explore.

'You're upset', I said, 'because of our visit to the asylum. Meeting your uncle too. That's all. And of course your Uncle Corrado? It's all set you thinking of your father.'

'Not really my father, the others, yes. Uncle Corrado most of all. You see, I can't help thinking that if we all of us didn't go in for this permissiveness, well you might not have terrorism either. It's a matter of respect.'

'For Christ's sake,' I said, 'people have always fucked. And will. You're talking balls. I can't listen to it. You'll come round though.'

'No, I won't. I've made up my mind.'

And her chin tilted again, and this time she left it up there, as if she didn't mind me seeing her in profile at all.

I said, 'Are you really trying to tell me, Bella, that because you and I fuck, that's got something to do with urban terrorism? Are you really saying something that half-witted?'

'No,' she said, 'of course I'm not. Not directly. And you know I'm not, and that my reasons aren't as silly as you are pretending. What I'm saying is very general, and I'm not falling into any sociological mess, saying *we are all guilty*, just as if we were taking part in a television chat show. Only it's like this. We don't love each other. And where there is no love, there is only self-indulgence, the desire for sensation, nothing more.'

'Giving pleasure to your partner. That's something more.'

'You know it isn't. The whole act becomes an end in itself. Action for the sake of action. *Tout court*. And that sort of thing is sterile, you understand, sterile. Nothing can come from it. So, I've decided. It's a small step from living for sensation to living for violence and destruction. Even love-making can become cruel when there are no consequences.'

'Christ,' I said, 'are you coming out against birth control now?'

And she fucking was.

'Well,' I said, 'you've gone crazy. You'll soon be up there with Uncle Guido.'

'I knew you would try to make a joke of it,' she said; but there was no smile in her response, and the chin was still tilted.

'No,' she said, 'this affair has changed my whole way of thinking, my philosophy. And I've been talking to my cousin, Nico. You don't like Nico, I think?'

'No,' I said. 'I thought he was a young prick actually.'

'He didn't like you either. We started talking about particulars, about what might make people behave like these terrorists. And remember, Nico and I both know a bit about them. We know Bernardo. No secrets—yes? We all believe Bernardo is one of them. So it's like this. There's a problem. What could have made Bernardo do what he did?'

'Fucked around, did he?'

'What is the point? What is the point? Listen, Christopher, I give you one last chance, or I get out of the car.'

'No point in that anyway. It's your car.'

'All right, listen. And stop being clever and cynical, understand. Bernardo talks a lot but he is not clever, I think. He believes he has ideals. Truth, Justice, Liberation, et cetera, et cetera. He believes people are exploited. Maybe it's true. Maybe they are exploited. Maybe they are deprived. Maybe capitalism is wrong. I don't know. My father's a capitalist. Maybe he exploits people. He doesn't exploit me, not his family. He loves us. But maybe it's all wrong. So? So? How do we make it better? Do we smash the system and say, start again from nothing, or do we just try to make it more moral, to behave well ourselves? Bernardo says smash it. And then? I think deep down Christopher says smash it too. Maybe that is part of the reason I can't go on with you. I'm afraid of that.'

'If you're afraid of it, maybe it's because you're refusing to admit how it attracts you.'

'No, that is silly. Nico says you can't create out of destruction. Good can't grow out of evil, peace out of violence. I believe him. He is a poet, he makes things.'

'He's a banker too,' I said.

Well, that was a last line. It was a last line of sorts. What she was doing was just retreating. She had put her head out of the *attico di gran lusso* and taken a look at the real world and didn't like it there where you can get hurt; so she was taking this excuse to creep back into her fur coat. I was angry. Naturally I was angry. It wasn't just that she was a good lay—a marvellous lay and a girl I liked too—there was more to it than that. I'd made my break from that world, the softer English version, of the Surrey pine-trees, the Saturday golf at Walton Heath or Worplesdon, the Rover purring on the gravel under the copper beech, the gin-and-tonics, the loud pink laughter; it was a world that was less obviously exploitive than this cruder, gaudier Italian one, where money was even flasher. But I'd got out. I wasn't happier; you can be really happy with *The Daily Telegraph*—my father was—but at least I was no longer living a lie, battening on others, one of Them, the exploiting class. And now to see Bella running away from the one thing by which she had expressed her revolt, sexual freedom, made me want to puke. It's been the only great subversive force of the last thirty years, sexual freedom, and she was turning it in. She wasn't running away so much as locking the door.

That was it. I took the keys out of the keyhole, and pressed them hard down on her crotch, hurting her a bit, I hope. She squealed anyhow.

'OK,' I said. 'You should get some of these made for the chastity belt. And you'd better marry your cousin, Nico. He'll keep you in the style that'll let you forget how most people live. And I hope you fucking well choke on it.'

So much for that. Back to the scrubbers. Back to the Stock solution; all night. Sometime the next day I thought me of fat Bertha, went off to explore her deep fatness, and then passed out to wake to her tongue in my ear urging departure. Fair enough.

All that of course is fact, hard true reporter's fact, even though the dialogue may not be absolutely verbatim. Old skills dying hard, it's actually pretty well verbatim.

Level four has to be speculation, but it's the speculation that has resulted from a lot of hard digging. Conversations with Antonio, interviews with contacts, even (through one of these contacts, whom of course I can't name) a long telephone interview with the PDP's spokesman who called himself Joe; as good a name as any.

So you can take it that this is as authentic an account as is likely to emerge of this affair which, looked at one way, was a joke: a gob of spit on the walls of that grotty white sepulchre, the Republic.

They'd decided to kill Dusa a long time back. The hard ones, the Professor (who I think actually is a professor), a bearded bloke calling himself Angelo and a trim-suited lawyer called Dr Marco Schiavetti (whom I can name since he was killed in a car-crash last week—what sort of crash?) had always regarded the negotiations as a blind. In fact they were almost knocked off their stride by Dusa himself—there seemed to be a moment when the pathos of the letters might have so strong an appeal that they would be faced by the unwelcome fact of an offer they could hardly refuse. Still they had a fall-back position; they were ready to shout treachery and ill-faith.

Dusa let them down of course. He let everybody down, refusing to play the part that had been written for him. That only steeled their resolve. They had hoped, and expected, that he would crack—their psychological expert had assured them, that, deprived of the authority in which he was accustomed to dress himself, he would really crack and spill whatever beans they demanded; merely to make some sort of human contact. It didn't work out like that; and, for this failure, they blamed Tomaso. They were quite right to do so. The interest he aroused in Dusa kept the politician sane. Of course it was Tomaso who had ensured his co-operation in the first place, but this meant less to the Professor than the certainty he came to acquire that Tomaso had helped Dusa preserve his dignity; Dusa, he felt, would have co-operated anyway.

Needless to say, they didn't take the Mastagni development seriously. They knew him after all for a windbag, and couldn't believe . . . still, his manœuvring may just have determined the timing.

When, after all, could they strike more insultingly and with greater effect than when the high chiefs of the Christian Democracy were assembled in conclave debating their proposals and communiqués? What could more blatantly show the irrelevancy of the DC to any sort of reality than action at that moment?

They gave Dusa a bath, dressed him in the black suit he had been wearing when he was captured. They had watched him dress himself, putting on a blue-striped white shirt, newly laundered, made for him by a smart Bologna shirt-maker (but the quality was not unfamiliar to most of the Partisans). Old-fashioned as ever, he clipped in cuff-links. He knotted a blue and white dotted tie — Dusa had never been seen in public without a tie, I doubt if even his children had seen him without one. He got it on all right, the dressing, except that his socks were inside-out.

I don't claim to know what they said to him, where he thought he was going; but I can't believe he didn't know this was it. They were going to kill him; he was dressing for death. They wouldn't have told him a lie; they had too much respect for truth.

And maybe human dignity.

They marched him downstairs in silence. He hadn't got his briefcase — the papers it had contained were the only thing the Partisans could use. Someone carried his other belongings. His watch was wound up and at the right time.

They asked him to get into the back of a hatchback Renault 5. He did so without a struggle. Then they opened fire, two guns at least, ten or a dozen shots. It was finished.

Disposal of the body. They had nerve, these partisans. They drove it to within a hundred metres of the DC headquarters.

Inside the Palazzo, the time now 11 o'clock on June 11, the Party Chiefs had re-convened. This time Mastagni was speaking; he had decided to change tactics. No longer waiting patiently for others to decide what he should be granted, he was instead pushing at the door. In his slow, patient, sing-song old man's voice, he was urging the claims of . . . wait for it . . . humanity.

He said (and I quote, as one of the secretaries gave it to me), 'Gentlemen, there are times when even matters of high policy, sagely constructed on the basis of the most serious and illustrious principles, must yield precedence to the sacred principles' . . . he crossed himself . . . 'of our peccant humanity. Our brother lies in danger and in anguish. Our hearts throb in response. Our souls aspire towards him. Though policy may urge that we harden our hearts, stop up the soul's breath, instinctive humanity will have none of it . . .' He closed his eyes, 'Besides, who knows . . .?'

'The Americans will not like it,' said Gianni Schicchi, 'and we have to put through the renewal of the German loan next month. They will require evidence of strength of purpose . . .'

Mastagni kept his eyes shut, holy effulgence in his cheeks.

And then the telephone rang on the President's desk. They were off the hook. The decision had been removed from them. Their secret prayers had been answered. They observed reverent silence.

It was broken, after some two minutes, by Gianni Schicchi: 'The State must celebrate its servant, Corrado Dusa. San Giovanni in Laterano, yes? And perhaps His Holiness' health will permit him to officiate . . .?'

I don't often laugh, but when I had pieced all this together, with final help from Antonio, and he had gone off, wet-eyed himself, leaving me in a little bar behind the Corso, with a

Fernet Branca before me, I laughed and laughed and laughed; what the French call a *fou rire*.

They had parked the Renault 5 equidistant from the DC and Communist party headquarters, just out of range of the PCI's closed-circuit television scanner, and beyond the fringe of the riot police squads. It was as close as possible. And then they'd walked away for a coffee. Two fingers to the State.

And I laughed with admiration. I'd lost Bella but I'd won that laugh. My own journey had won me that laugh.

TOMASO

The moment for Tomaso had been when he heard the familiar voice say, 'I wish to repeat and finally to make clear to you, Honourable Corrado Dusa, that this is not a murder, but an execution. It is indeed and in truth the execution of the sentence of the People's Court for crimes against the Italian People and their democratic rights . . .'

Tomaso wanted to say, '. . . but these are only words'; yet with what else but words had Dusa himself constructed his life? Only, he had no words now. Instead a curl of a smile hovered at the edge of the mouth. For the lightest moment he touched his lips, which were cracked with the unseasonable cold he had developed, with just the tip of his tongue, and then he bowed his head, almost as if he accepted the just sentence of the Court. But it wasn't really like that—it was a measure of his indifference now it had come to the point. The long battle was concluded. He could do no more. So, with Southern resignation, the almost Eastern acceptance of Fate that history has imprinted on the Mezzogiorno, he surrendered to the effective, the dominant, Will.

He showed the same deference when they told him to get into the back of the car; only when Angelo and Birgitta presented the muzzles of their guns to him, did he momentarily close his eyes as if to ward off the significance of what was about to happen.

Tomaso had to watch. It was the culmination of fifteen months' planning and fear. Dusa's hand moved, independent perhaps of conscious will, in a vain gesture of self-protection. The guns spat. Even in the confined space of the hatchback's boot, the body kicked, convulsed; then was still.

Nobody had spoken since they left the room into which the plaster-board box that had contained Dusa for so many days had been inserted in late April. They all knew what they had to do. And for the moment they didn't even exchange glances.

All the same, now it was over, Tomaso sensed Angelo relax. Birgitta blew down the muzzle of her little Beretta. She slipped it into a shoulder-bag that advertised Cinzano Bianco.

The act they had just performed severed them from their past.

Consciousness of this crept over the morning of the horizon. Tomaso moved, on legs that were not exactly unsteady but unwontedly aware of themselves, towards the door of the garage and opened it a crack. An old woman in a black dress ragged at the hem was fingering through a dustbin on the other side of the little cobbled street. She hadn't heard the sputter of the silenced guns. It was just five o'clock in the morning.

Had she been up all night? Where did she sleep? It was to prevent her sort of fate that they . . . Tomaso drew back from the door. The morning breeze, stirring a grey light, was still cool.

Angelo said, 'We've two hours to kill. Some coffee'd be a good idea.'

Tomaso shook his head, not so much to the coffee, which in fact he wanted, now he thought about it, but simply in general negation.

('I felt proud,' Enzo Fuscolo had twice said to him, describing how the other Partisans at the end of the other war had tried to hang him.)

He approached the door again. The old woman had found something in the bin, a brown paper parcel, from which she extracted a piece of pizza. She thrust it between her jaws which almost certainly contained no teeth, and began to tear at it.

'You have to admit, he died better than he lived,' Angelo said.

The Professor flashed an open hand, fingers rigidly twisted, across a screwed-up face.

'What does that signify?' he cried. 'Nothing. Life, not death, is the test.'

'Still, he might have been a nuisance,' Angelo said, his accent becoming, as it usually did in moments of emotion, more strongly Roman. 'It was nice of him to be co-operative.'

'Vlad,' said the Professor, 'you understand what you are to say when you telephone Dr Nittri at the University. That he is to go personally to the Dusa house, not telephone. He is to go there to tell them the news and where the body is to be found. What we must now do is prevent the State from making this man a martyr; we must show how they have alienated the mourning family, because they have refused to listen to the claims of humanity; in this way we demonstrate how the State, for all its vaunts, is no more Christian than it is democratic.'

'Christian,' Angelo spat.

'Nevertheless, it has been a stage in the evolution of humanity and human society. That is all,' the Professor said.

The old woman had finished the pizza and begun rootling again in the bin. Upstairs in their larder they had a lot of bread and tins of tunny fish and beans.

'And then of course you resume normal life, which anyhow has not been much interrupted. Dani and Marco will attend to what has to be done here.'

'I'm going to make that coffee,' Angelo said. 'Mornings without coffee . . .'

Dani put a green loden coat over Dusa. Then they locked the garage door again and went upstairs.

Birgitta said, 'It's funny to have lived through a day like this, to have had the sort of experience that you know will form your life for ever.'

'That's surely happened to you before,' Angelo said, 'you're not a virgin, are you?'

'There is more than one kind of virginity . . . I thought you knew that, Angelo.'

It was half-past nine when Tomaso made his way through the echoing glass and marble of the Termini Station, which was full, as usual, of tourists, soldiers coming and going on leave, priests arriving for congresses, small town businessmen who could not afford to fly from Milan or Turin or Pisa when it was necessary to visit a Ministry to obtain some essential but otherwise worthless permit. Tomaso moved through the crowd like a ghost or a saint; one who had no dealings with them. If his sensibility had been differently formed he might have felt himself a visitor from another planet.

All these people—even the priests who had heard innumerable confessions delivered *in extremis* and who had administered the last rites more often perhaps than they would be able to recall—were virgins. Not one of the soldiers who stood about hopelessly wishing they could afford to buy even one bottle of beer between two of them, was really anything more than an actor in the game of war; most of them of course were only clerks.

For a moment he paused, in the fancy that he had caught the eye of a *carabiniere*, who was standing in the middle of a crowd of circulating Japanese tourists rather like a statue of Napoleon in a piazza. But no, the dark brooding eye of the policeman swept over Tomaso in utter vacancy; probably his anguish was fixed on thoughts of a beefsteak or plate of *fettuccine*.

Tomaso found the telephones and dialled the number he had been given. When told what he had to do, Dr Nittri said, with a painful weakness in his voice, 'Do I have to go? Can't I telephone?'

Tomaso explained again that that was impossible. In the first place the Dusa telephone was tapped. Accordingly, if Dr Nittri telephoned then the agents of the State would know as soon as the family, which was undesirable.

'Besides,' he said, 'surely you realize that humanity demands the *signora* learns of it in person, that the family has the information before the authorities for this reason also.'

And he repeated again the information that was to be given.

Dr Nittri at last acceded, not without a self-pity that brought the first smile of the day to Tomaso's face.

He replaced the receiver and went to the *cassa* to get a second *gettone*. At the same time he ordered a cup of black coffee, and went to the bar and drank it. He had not in the end been able to touch the coffee Angelo had made earlier. He returned to the telephone and dialled the number of Kim's *pensione*. The woman at the desk said, 'She doesn't answer the telephone.' Tomaso could not settle; it was necessary he spoke to Kim before the news was public. He was sure of that; of course she would not be much interested in it—that was hardly the point.

The *carabiniere* was looking at him again, though still remaining Napoleonically unmoving. Tomaso left the station, walking on his quick, light, narrow feet, a slightly floating gait, detached and protected by the chastity of his dark suit; like a shadow moving across the waters. He was surprised by the deep blue of the day outside the station.

10.59.

He couldn't, of course, go home, back to the mean room where he slept, even though he had now been awake for almost thirty hours. And it was equally impossible to sit down at a *caffè* table with the morning newspaper that would not contain anything but speculation on the affair that had now advanced, irrevocably, beyond that empty stage. Tomaso sat, for a moment, on the edge of a fountain, dangling his fingers in the water; but when a middle-aged man with sandy hair and an open, flowered shirt that revealed wisps of curly grey hair sprouting from the chest, approached him with conspiratorial smile, he began walking again.

Suddenly—he had reached the street of the airline offices, the Via Bissolati—he felt the mood of the city change. The word was out; they knew. The matter was accomplished. He turned up the Via Veneto, because it was so utterly a part of the city with which he felt no affinity at all, and sitting down at a table, covered with a pink cloth, asked a waiter to bring him a cup of coffee. The waiter nodded assent, and then, as he turned away, Tomaso said, 'And a glass of whisky, please.'

It was something he had drunk only once in his life before; for an experiment which had proved distasteful.

The man was a long time returning with the order. Tomaso sat watching a crowd collect round the news-stand, a crowd that was agitated and yet hushed; they must know there could be nothing in the newspapers yet, but they continued to stand there, as though the proximity to the source of news gave them something they lacked. The waiter at last laid the cup and glass on the table before him.

'They have killed him,' he said, 'they have just discovered the body.'

Tomaso couldn't reply.

'I knew they would,' said the waiter. 'Bastards. Shot he was, and crammed into the boot of a car. Bastards.'

Tomaso picked up the whisky; even the smell was corrupt, associated with a style of life that had to go. He sipped it, and felt nausea.

The traffic moved as usual. It was as if a shiver had passed over a forest, disturbing the leaves a moment, and then all was as if it had never been. A girl, resting against the plane tree, with one foot drawn up behind her, its sole pressed against the bark of the tree, in such a way that even from his side-on position he saw both her thighs, turned her face to him, and smiled. She wore a very short, white dress and the smile she gave him was inviting. Tomaso felt himself flush; it was a world that embarrassed him. A man—German perhaps?—came up, touched the girl on her bare arm and spoke to her. She nodded slowly, and they went off together. The German tried to take her hand as they turned the corner. Tomaso saw her disengage herself . . .

It was extraordinary to be drinking whisky, just like two linen-suited Americans who had settled at the next table. He heard one of them say, 'You know the wops have surprised me. I didn't reckon they had it in them to behave as well as they have over this. No panic, no softness. They've come out of it well.'

Tomaso ordered another whisky. Someone, speaking in a Milanese accent, said, 'But who are the PDP? In my opinion they don't know themselves. Look at the results of their actions. They will not be what they ostensibly hope for, not at all, my friend. Quite the contrary. In effect, they will contribute towards the re-establishment, the re-invigoration of the Christian Democracy. I tell you there are many good Christian Democrats who are also good patriots who do not in their hearts regret the disappearance of Corrado Dusa, though they

233

would prefer that it should have been another type of heart attack perhaps.'

Tomaso went into another *caffè* and got a *gettone* and telephoned Kim's hotel again. This time he was put through to her room, but it was Ruthie who answered. There was a note of triumph in her voice.

'She won't speak to you,' she said. 'You've no right to telephone, no right to involve Kim . . . we're leaving anyway, but what you've done to Kim was wrong. It was wicked. You see, we know, we fucking know. I don't know how you could think to call Kim again, after everything . . .'

There was nothing Tomaso could say. He hung up. Back at the table he ordered another whisky.

What else was there to do?

He didn't go home that night. For the first time he felt hunted. In the early evening he found a *pensione* and, using the identity card of a student from Puglia with which he had been provided, took a room. He slept for fourteen hours and woke, drained, not refreshed at all, aching in his limbs. He spoke to nobody but went to a movie, and came out in the dark, not knowing what he had seen. He went back to the *pensione*. He hadn't bought a newspaper.

Sleep wouldn't come. He lay for a long time, stretched out stiff, almost as a corpse, looking at the ceiling on which orange sodium lights from the street-lamps played. There were movements, creakings and voices throughout the cheap hotel. He turned over and over, changing position in search of a sleep that refused to come. Around six in the morning he rose, went downstairs, paid the heavy-eyed girl he had summoned by repeated ringing of the bell, and went out into the freshness of a morning that assailed him with a leper's guilt.

He took an early bus dotted with the tired faces of all-night workers, and an exhausted looking girl with long streaked-blonde hair hanging in rats' tails, who looked at him and offered a half-smile. Tomaso looked away, and then got off the bus near the yard where he kept his car. Nobody had moved it. He drove off into the hills.

His mother received him with silence also. He wanted to ask her if the police had been there, but found he couldn't. She served him with food as though waiting on him in an hotel. Whenever he came into the room where she was sitting she would find something urgent to do. The spaniel kept close to her skirts.

Tomaso sat in the courtyard in the evening watching the storm clouds climb high in the mountains to the East. Westward the golden sky was streaked with savage red and green. Pigeons cooed in the eaves. Over in the town, across the high wall, a dog barked. A donkey clip-clopped up the steps between the wall and the hillside scrub. After a little he went to the outhouse where the wine was kept and drew some into a litre flask. He sat there and sipped as the light turned to violet and then died. For a long time his eyes stayed fixed on the window that had been Bernardo's, an innocence ago. You could never imagine truly what you were ignorant of.

Once his mother came to the doorway, looked at him as if she would have spoken; but the moment passed. She turned away, leaving him to his night and to the thin wine that brought no comfort but a blurring of sensation.

The next morning he drove away without a further word. His mother, rolling out the *pasta* in the kitchen, saw him through the slit window open the wicket-gate set into the heavy double door, and walk out. In a few minutes, when she had completed her rolling and stretched the sheets of *pasta* out, she went into the courtyard and crossed it and looked out of the gate, down the steps towards the piazza. There was no sign of her son, and perhaps one of the cars she caught sight of intermittently as they descended the hairpin bends to the main road was his.

He made a telephone call from the town, from the *caffè* where, before experience, he had met the lawyer. The line was dead. He drove, still eastwards, till he arrived in a small town by the grey of the Adriatic, sullen under cloud. Somewhere, beyond the sea, was Bernardo; it no longer seemed to matter.

He went into a haberdasher's and bought a pair of braces.

He stopped at a *caffè* within sight of the sea on which a thin rain was now slanting, and asked for whisky and writing paper. They brought him a yellowing pad and three fingers of Long John.

He drank the whisky slowly, watching men in dark hats playing cards at the next table, and ordered another, an action which caused them to look at him with furtive, appraising and distrustful eyes.

He began to write:

There is no one I can really address this to, so perhaps I shall send it to a newspaper. After all, it is not a message to anyone in particular, but just something I feel I have to say.

What we have done was necessary. I don't feel guilty. It's not a matter of right and wrong, and in any case humanity has proceeded beyond empty ethical considerations of that sort.

So there is no guilt, but there is no feeling either, except a deep exhaustion. I am drained and futile.

I thought there was deep purpose and significance in our action, which, it seemed to me, must certainly change something. But now it is completed and everything is exactly the same; and I realize that things cannot be made different in this way, as I had expected they would be, and so it was all in vain. It hasn't changed even me, except to strip me of this illusion.

I believed in belief; now I believe in nothing.

There was a man I used to know—I shan't give his name because I have no wish to involve him in this affair (on the other hand I am absolutely indifferent as to whether I do or not), but he will recognize himself when he sees this letter. This man used to speak to me of the necessity of the liberating action, the act capable of freeing me from the constraints of bourgeois morality. Well, I have performed it and there is no difference; it was a lie like everything else.

He used to say we must crack the mould of our present society and start anew. But I no longer believe it can be done. The forces of inertia are indescribably strong. They have not even been made to shift an inch by what we have done.

In the circumstances I no longer believe that man can grow to a height where lightning might strike him, and he breaks. He is quite beneath lightning. Everything that might be

236

worth doing is beyond our capacity. Men prefer to live like slugs.

I thought that what I was doing would make room in my heart for every kind of understanding, comprehending and approving. I find none of this any more true than a denial of the seasons can be true. And if it is impossible to make Spring in November, can we possibly go on living from November in the hope that yet again Spring will return?

I am very tired. I am worn out by consciousness. I have had enough of seeing and feeling. Especially feeling.

But I thought what we were doing would make us Caesars and I find we are no more than Catiline.

It's enough.

He asked for an envelope, read over what he had written, folded the paper three times and put it in the envelope.

'What is the name of your local newspaper?' he asked the barman. 'Give me some more whisky,' he said. 'No, not like that, let me buy the rest of the bottle.'

Then with the neck of the bottle of Long John sticking out of one pocket and the brown paper parcel containing the new braces stuffed in the other, he left the *caffè*.

He had earlier taken a room in a hotel. It had pale, dirty yellow walls. The window gave on the white-flecked grey of the sea. It was not yet dark and he sat by the window sipping the whisky. Then the street-lamps came on. Someone, passing along the front, his neck twisted to keep the rain from being blown in his face by a new-rising wind, later remembered the boy at the window with a glass in his hand.

Sometime in the night he fixed the braces to the electrolier that hung, meagrely supplied with little bulbs, from the centre of the ceiling. They found him hanging there in the morning. The letter addressed to the *Gazetta* lay on the little table by the window. There was only a little whisky, perhaps one drink, left in the bottle. The bedclothes had been disturbed and the sheets were crushed, so perhaps he had rested or slept for a little. He was still wearing his dark suit though. One cuff stank of whisky.

RAIMUNDO

'Can you come over?' said Nico. 'It is finished. We've just been visited by a ridiculous person called Dr Nittri, who says he has had a message from them. We believe him. We'd like you to come.'

The city was in no way different. Even in the street leading to the Largo Argentina, within a few yards of where, at almost exactly that moment, Corrado's body was to be discovered, it might have been an ordinary Thursday. But then I remember that the day Mussolini was overthrown was dominated for me by a quarrel with my mistress. What had she accused me of? It had seemed urgent to disprove it then, and now I simply couldn't remember which sin or crime or perhaps even simply misdemeanour I was supposed to have committed.

Ettore and Bella had already arrived at the villa, both in tears. Sandro was weeping too, but not Nico and not Elena, who was already dressed in black.

'Bastards,' Ettore said, holding me tight and banging his palms on my back, 'bastards'.

We couldn't leave each other, and yet, after the first five minutes, there was really very little to say.

Nico had taken my arm as soon as I was free of Ettore, and led me aside. 'We must stop them making propaganda of it,' he said. 'My father made that quite clear, that he doesn't want the men of power present at his funeral. Since we all, especially Mamma, regard them as murderers equally guilty as the terrorists, there is no dispute about that. But there will be an attempt, won't there?'

'Oh yes,' I said, 'but if we obtain the body as soon as the autopsy is completed, then I don't see what they can do.'

'I agree. Tell me, Uncle, will you go to San Grigliano, and make arrangements there. I shall have to hold the fort here, but we thought, a simple country funeral. Mamma and I, we have had time to discuss it . . .'

'Of course,' I said.

San Grigliano is the small estate in the Sabine hills which

came to us from my mother's family. It is also where the Partisans tried to hang Enzo Fuscolo. I was glad to get away, to take a train out of Rome and hire a car, and drive in sunshine into hills scented with thyme and origano.

The peasants were cutting hay in the fields on the slopes of the mountain when I arrived, making a pattern that was antique and charming. Someone, seeing the car and recognizing me, made off for the priest, and in a little he arrived, from the field where he had been working himself. He was an old-fashioned priest, wearing a cassock; when he worked he hitched it up to his knees. He greeted me with that degree of reserve he kept for a Voltairean sceptic who was nevertheless a man of some distinction.

'I know of course why you have come, and of course it shall be done.'

'We can't fix a date,' I said. 'We don't know when the body will be released.'

'I understand.'

'But what we would like to do is to drive here, as soon as we get it. And we should like the funeral service and interment to take place as soon as we arrive. Is that possible? Otherwise, you understand, we will be swamped by outsiders, by the international press, by politicians who want to force themselves into the act. We don't want that. We want to do as Corrado said, to exclude the men of power, and have only those who . . . loved him present. We should like to have all the villagers, all your flock. And you will conduct the service.'

'Everything will be ready,' he said. 'You have my word for it, *dottore*.'

Looking at his brown face, a face that spoke of experience and innocence at the same time, I was tempted to question him, or rather, I suppose, for who knows what trick the conscious mind is victim of, to seek reassurance from him; that is, I almost asked him if I had been right or wrong not to have told the policeman that I had recognized that photograph of the young man. But I didn't; and later I was glad I had restrained myself. It would have been self-indulgence on my part.

What's more, having rejected the Church, I have no right to seek consolation from its priests.

The bell commenced to toll from its tower, sending slow, ringing strokes across the valley and up the hillside. Figures detached themselves from the fields, laying down their labour, becoming men and women with tanned and cracked faces as they shuffled, mostly in black, the men with studs at the necks of their shirts but no collars, into the piazza, where the priest stood waiting for them on the steps of the church.

I couldn't help thinking, this is the real, the enduring Italy, the one Virgil celebrated, one that has changed nothing in essentials since his day. When they looked at me it was levelly, with no cupidity and little calculation.

The priest began to speak to them using the dialect that these days sounded both strange and familiar in my ears. As he spoke they listened, most of them with heads bowed.

Some of the older men might have been among the Partisans who had hanged Enzo Fuscolo. Remembering the madness of his talk in the railway station—when he had spoken of Corrado's imminent death in apocalyptic terms—I couldn't help looking for sanity among these peasants. Yet, when I thought about it, the rough justice of the Partisans had done nothing to prepare Italians for civil life; if we continued to tear ourselves apart, wasn't it to some extent at least because of the honour we accorded to that violence we had decided to commemorate?

In the same way the great vulgar Monument of the Risorgimento in Rome was over-blatant; a man shouting that his deeds might be ignored.

We have too much history.

I thanked the priest, and told the peasants I was grateful to them for their sympathy.

'My brother always loved San Grigliano,' I said. 'It represented to him so much of what was best in this Italy of ours that we cannot afford to lose.'

I arranged with the priest that I would telephone him as soon as we knew when we would be able to move.

I had said to Enzo Fuscolo:

'I thought you stood for order. You used to speak, all your miserable Party spoke, of the need for discipline, of the dangers of a liberty that degenerated to licence; and so forth. It was always empty as the wind, but in a cruel and corrupt way, it made sense. You could grant it some sort of validity. But now . . .'

His eyes were crafty as well as mad. 'It's too late,' he said. 'Even your nephew, *dottore*, has realized it's too late. Now it must all be eradicated . . .'

'Why did you want to see me?' I said. 'Simply to crow? You implied that you had some information.'

'Information?' The word asserted its old magic on him. 'Everyone is playing a double game, and nobody understands the significance of his own actions. That is what I have learned. Gianni Schicchi thinks this will strengthen the Christian Democracy—their display of firmness of purpose will please their masters. But who can applaud a puppet? What we are seeing is the crumbling of the State. You and your parasite family will be destroyed with it, and then? Out of the rubble of decay, out of the fire, the phoenix of the order that is the true liberty, the liberty of devotion . . .'

Mad words, as mad as Ed Mangan, as mad as Mastagni, as mad as the terrorists themselves.

They fitted themselves to the rhythm of the train's wheels descending the mountain track.

But Bella had telephoned me, and said: 'Uncle, you didn't like seeing me with Christopher, I think.'

'No.'

'Well, it's over. That sort of thing, it doesn't answer. Unless we behave ourselves . . . I don't know but it's all part and parcel of demoralization, isn't it?'

Young Mario had called on me again, and said: 'This woman who cleans for you, she's not much good, is she? Let me do some of that.'

I had gone to see my brother, who had said, 'He did his duty.'

And Nico, meeting me as I left the old woman, stony-eyed and self-righteously facing her dead future, had taken me by the arm as if one of his own age, led me to a little room, normally hardly used at all, and poured each of us a glass of French brandy.

'Have you heard?' he said, 'Bernardo is going to be on American television. I have arranged for a video to be flown to me. RAI refuse to carry it, even as a news flash.'

A terrorist camp somewhere in the Middle East. The reporter, nobly honouring the promise of secrecy that he had been obliged to give in order to obtain the interview, could not be specific as to the exact whereabouts. Bernardo looked plump in the face; I couldn't detect fear or guilt.

He was profuse: 'I loved my father, but I love Italy and humanity. I shall never have to make such a decision again. There was no choice. My father was himself, I shall always believe, a victim; how else could a man of such humanity have become the associate of those inhuman wolves who would not lift a finger to redeem him? We asked for very little, for recognition of our position, for the release of some comrades, themselves victims of the fraud and violence of this State, dominated by the multi-nationals and the CIA. Eventually we asked for the exchange of simply one prisoner: a woman. But the chiefs of the so-called Christian Democracy were adamant. Recognition of us would have involved admission of the justice of our principles. Accordingly, it is they, not my brother and sister partisans, on whom my father's blood rests. It is their names that are stained. Yes, I shall continue to struggle for the liberation of the Italian people . . .'

Nico switched off the set. He poured more brandy in my glass (we were back again alone in the little sitting-room). He stood with his back to me, elegant in a dark suit, looking out on a garden on which the first drops of rain were falling.

'I think we shall get the body tomorrow,' he said.

We didn't talk of Bernardo.

Ed Mangan said: 'You wonder who intervened. You really do.

Mastagni was just going to swing it, wasn't he, Ray, and they blew it. It makes you think. You know, you can't help wondering if in the last resort, at the very last moment, the plot wasn't switched. It looks like it was directed against Mastagni. After all, if he'd taken over, and I reckon if they'd admitted him to the Government, he would have—he's that calibre, isn't he?—well it would have given a new sense of direction. So was it aimed at keeping him out? Did that skunk Schicchi tip the word? I said at the beginning, if you recall, Schicchi's a motherfucker in the Nixon class . . .

'You know something,' he said, 'your brother nearly pulled it off. Another week and he'd have done the Richard II stunt. Well, Italy's in for a rough time now. That narrow, anal-fixated clique around Schicchi have really dug their claws in the nation now.'

He could be right.

Even Ed Mangan could be right.

International opinion—a phrase that has as much meaning as a cream puff—is highly impressed however. Not for a long time—not perhaps since the fall of Fascism—has Italy had such a good press. Who would have thought the Italians would have had so much steel in them? Gianni is featured on the cover of *Time* magazine. 'He stood firm,' they say. *The Times* observes that 'In this frightful ordeal the nerve, good sense and resilience of the oft-maligned Italian political class has been exemplary. Both the Christian Democrats and the Communist Party have shown courage and judgement in refusing to allow this tragedy to damage the structure of the State. These are dark days, and days of mourning, for Italy; but they should be days of pride also.' *Le Figaro* speaks likewise; and there is almost envy in the *Frankfurter Allgemeine*.

I can imagine Gianni preening himself, his hand closing on the mercury of power.

Carlo Poggi telephoned, desolate of course.

Five minutes of desolation; they proved the prelude to the request that the family should cease its obduracy, and co-operate with the State in celebrating Corrado.

'You cannot take his letters seriously. The autopsy will

reveal how he was drugged. Raimundo, no one has worked more closely with Corrado than I, I owe everything to him, I love him as a father. Can you deny me the right to participate in the mourning? Can you deny Italy?'

Gianni, wisely ignoring me, has spoken three times to Nico and has tried to bully him into allowing him to speak to Elena. He even presented himself at the villa seeking an interview. When he was refused he told the Press that 'The wholly natural desolation of the Dusa family, a desolation shared by the whole nation and in particular by the Christian Democracy, has blinded them to the realities of the situation, that Corrado Dusa was the martyr for the cause of Christian Democracy and the Italian nation. We lament him as brother, colleague and hero.'

Ah yes.

Nico arranged all admirably, and we escaped them. At the very last moment they had made their final appeal—His Holiness had consented to celebrate the Requiem Mass at San Giovanni. They understood that we might prefer a family funeral, but in the circumstances, could a devout daughter of the Church like Signora Dusa flout His Holiness?

Four cars, secretly hired in another name, followed the hearse out of the city. A grey heavy day, *scirocco* blowing dust and bad temper about the streets. We hardly talked on the journey.

Once Elena said, 'You are quite sure, Raimundo, all will be ready?'

'Father Martino assures me it will.'

'And we have evaded the journalists?'

'It looks like it,' said Nico. 'In any case we have certainly evaded the politicians. A few journalists . . . will they really matter?'

It started to rain as we turned up into the hills, the tops of which were swathed in mist. The hearse was being driven quickly now, the traffic jam at the edge of the city had delayed us by twenty anxious minutes.

Father Martino had been as good as his word. The little church had been swept clean. Someone had put roses, Corrado's only flowers, on the altar. The peasants, all in black

244

and almost all past middle-age, had gathered in the dripping piazza before the church, the men standing bare-headed. A small band of school-children—there were not many in the village these days—waited in their blue school tunics, the broad white collars of which were crumpling in the rain.

We all went into what had been my father's house for a few minutes. Someone had put a wreath of laurel over the lintel from which the Partisans had tried to hang Enzo Fuscolo. Nico and I spoke to the priest. I can't remember what we said.

The service was simple and brief. You don't need many words to see off a man.

Father Martino said: 'Corrado Dusa was a friend of the people of this village. We knew him as a humble man, an honourable man, a good man. He loved his family. He did his duty. He lived as a Christian towards his enemies. He did not, even in extremity, give way to despair. That was the final sin with which he was tempted; he withstood that temptation also. And, despair, my children, is the greatest temptation of all; for despair denies all virtue. Let us pray . . .'

We lifted the coffin on our shoulders, two sons, two brothers (one of each absent) and four villagers. The grey heavy clay of the churchyard gave an uncertain footing in the rain, which was now coming down steadily, blotting out the flank of the mountain across the valley. The grave had been dug near the wall of the churchyard, where the old chapel had been, at the top of the hill between two yew trees. We slithered as we climbed the slope, the coffin lurching. Someone coughed raspingly. Otherwise, the only sound came from the damp moving of feet.

Words were pronounced, words of an old ritual, an old dispensation, the Latin linking Corrado to our fathers. The women dropped flowers on the coffin as we lowered it to the soil. A little puddle had already formed where it would lie. The heavy clay fell to the wood. Elena raised her widow's veil a moment, looked dry-eyed down, nodded her head, and let the veil descend. Some of the village women were sobbing; Bella, Sandro and Ettore also.

Nico and I moved round the assembly shaking hands and speaking in low voices.

The grave-digger emerged from the shed at the back of the church, carrying a spade.

We all turned away, Ettore opening an umbrella above Elena.

I found Mario sitting on my doorstep.

He said, 'My friend's shot himself. He's talked of doing it so often I never thought he would, then I went there this afternoon and found him. It was horrible.'

'You'd better come in,' I said.

He was trembling.

'I've been burying my brother. Brandy?'

As I handed him the glass, I saw that his left eye was bruised, the skin broken and the pupil dilated and bloody.

'How did you come by that eye?'

'Oh that was the police. They wanted to be convinced I had just found Max like that. It's nothing; not important . . .'

He asked me about Corrado's funeral . . .

June 21 Ten days since it happened. Since they did it. And today, in a grand orgy of hypocrisy, Italy remembers the man they did nothing to save. But he is also, as I cannot help but recall, the man I did nothing to save, because of my error of judgement; but was it an error? If I could only be sure—but there is nothing of which I am certain. I can hardly contemplate the possibility. Nico said to me the other night, 'You know, Uncle, two things I must tell you. First, that I have committed myself utterly to the Bank, not because I believe the work at the Bank is noble, necessary or anything like that, though I suppose it is actually necessary, but because a man must have something; and anyway there are no ideals in banking. I am going to live with facts, not ideals or ideas. Second, and this is a fact too, one that I regard as central to my being, when a decent interval has passed, for we are formal, Mamma and I, we intend to observe traditional periods of mourning; after that though, I shall marry Bella. A dispensation will be necessary of course; there will be no difficulty there. I love Bella certainly, and I respect her; those aren't my

246

reasons alone however. If you forgive me, I have learned of the
necessity of marriage from you. We are very alike, Uncle. I, too,
am a natural sceptic. But it comes back to what the priest said,
a priest whose beliefs I don't need to tell you I cannot share.
You remember about despair. I think for those of our
temperament despair is never far distant. Bella can protect me
against it. Was it St Paul who said it was better to marry than
to burn? Well, marriage is certainly preferable to the con-
suming numbness that I can recognize in myself, that I see you
hold at bay with such fortitude, and that I suppose overcame
Uncle Guido. Isn't that so?'

Isn't that so? It was by far the longest speech Nico has ever
made to me—or is likely to make—certainly the most
intimate. But fortitude? He may have identified the malaise,
but fortitude? That is mere rhetoric.

They will assemble at San Giovanni. The Piazza will be full.
The newspapers, the radio, the television have seen to that.
His Holiness will speak, with his dying sincerity, of Corrado.
Smug heads will nod. Of course others beside the Pope will be
sincere. I cannot deny that many may have opposed negotiations for what seemed the best of reasons. For many the choice
posed was painful indeed. But they took the easy way.

I shan't go. None of the family will. Instead I shall make my
own pilgrimage, my own act of piety. More rhetoric.

I shall go to see Guido.

And I shall ask Mario to send his sister Renata to me this
evening. Is that my response to Nico? He picks a wife; I call a
whore. Well, it is a matter of generations and tastes.

19.00 Guido was better today, ambulant as they say.

The Fascist warder greeted me with that air of complicity
that I find so displeasing and embarrassing. He said, 'It'll be a
proper farce at San Giovanni, won't it? What a set of
hypocrites. You'll see, they'll make no real effort to catch those
bastards who did it. Whereas a man like me, he's watched all
the time. There's no justice, I tell you. But you've found out
that, haven't you?'

And he winked obscenely.

247

He led me to the courtyard round which a number of blanketed figures were shuffling.

'It's a great thing of the new Director's,' he said, 'this exercise.'

Guido moved with great concentration, making sure he kept always the same distance behind the man in front. He found it more difficult to keep in step, and it clearly displeased him when he had to change feet to regain a lost rhythm. Once his eyes flickered in my direction. For a moment—oh, shorter than the life-span of the most wretched insect—I thought I detected recognition there. At once however his gaze returned to the back before him.

After perhaps twenty minutes, one of the guards blew a whistle, and the movement stopped. The more self-aware of the lunatics began to shuffle off towards their cells. One of the guards took Guido by the arm and led him in my direction.

'Do you want to spend some time with him, *dottore*? There's no need to.'

'Yes,' I said.

'We'll take him to his cell then. He's more relaxed there. Familiar surroundings. But there's no real point, you understand. He's been very detached the last weeks, not taking in anything if you ask me.'

I sat with him in his cell. I told him—why not?—all about poor Corrado, from the beginning, in detail, admitting even, what I had admitted to no one else, my own failure. I have never been sure whether Guido doesn't sometimes, in certain states, understand everything that happens around him, everything you care to say; whether he doesn't understand and simply declines to respond; perhaps it is all there, stored-up, material for his dreams.

I don't know; it's possible; at that moment I believed that was how it is.

And speaking to Guido was a form of confession, the only one allowed to me, but one where one could not delude oneself with the luxury of absolution.

All the time I spoke, his fingers were busy, picking at threads in the blanket which covered him.

'That's it then,' I said, 'you know the whole story, my dear.'

I leant over and kissed his cheek as I had kissed Corrado's in his coffin.

Outside it was evening sunshine. The leafy suburban streets were filling with Saturday girls, laughing and lazy.

I walked for a bit, then took a taxi.

From its window, as we stopped at a traffic light, I saw the mad face of Enzo Fuscolo. He was sitting at a *caffè* table, with a copy of *Paese Sera* open before him. He was very pale and the tic in his face was working fast. I could see—or did I perhaps imagine?—the huge headline of the paper, and a photograph of the crowd at San Giovanni. And I thought of the waste land in which he must live.

A little later I paid off my taxi and walked through the streets to a wine-shop, not my usual one, but one just off the Corso where, for a reason I have never understood or troubled to inquire, the walls are covered with tiled reproductions of Beardsley drawings. I sat in that harmless adolescent decadence and drank a *quartino* of the house wine which comes from Marino. It was very still in the wine-shop, the only noise coming from the dripping of a tap and the buzz of two bluebottles. I sipped my wine and thought of Renata.

I can hear her light confident step on the stairway, but when I try to picture her face, Corrado's, then Guido's gets in the way.